The Traitor and The Chalice

What Reviewers Say About Bold Strokes Authors

Kim Baldwin

"'A riveting novel of suspense' seems to be a very overworked phrase. However, it is extremely apt when discussing Kim Baldwin's [*Hunter's Pursuit*]. An exciting page turner [features] Katarzyna Demetrious, a bounty hunter…with a million dollar price on her head. Look for this excellent novel of suspense…" – **R. Lynne Watson**, *MegaScene*

Ronica Black

"Black juggles the assorted elements of her first book with assured pacing and estimable panache…[including]…the relative depth—for genre fiction—of the central characters: Erin, the married-but-separated detective who comes to her lesbian senses; loner Patricia, the policewoman-mentor who finds herself falling for Erin; and sultry club owner Elizabeth, the sexually predatory suspect who discards women like Kleenex…until she meets Erin."– **Richard Labonte**, *Book Marks, Q Syndicate, 2005*

Rose Beecham

"…her characters seem fully capable of walking away from the particulars of whodunit and engaging the reader in other aspects of their lives." – *Lambda Book Report*

Gun Brooke

"*Course of Action* is a romance…populated with a host of captivating and amiable characters. The glimpses into the lifestyles of the rich and beautiful people are rather like guilty pleasures….[A] most satisfying and entertaining reading experience." – **Arlene Germain**, reviewer for the *Lambda Book Report* and the *Midwest Book Review*

Jane Fletcher

"*The Walls of Westernfort* is not only a highly engaging and fast-paced adventure novel, it provides the reader with an interesting framework for examining the same questions of loyalty, faith, family and love that [the characters] must face." – **M. J. Lowe**, *Midwest Book Review*

Radcly*f*e

"…well-honed storytelling skills…solid prose and sure-handedness of the narrative…" – **Elizabeth Flynn**, *Lambda Book Report*

"…well-plotted…lovely romance...I couldn't turn the pages fast enough!" – **Ann Bannon**, author of *The Beebo Brinker Chronicles*

The Traitor and The Chalice

Lyremouth Chronicles Book Two

by

Jane Fletcher

2006

THE TRAITOR AND THE CHALICE

ISBN 1-933110-43-0
This Trade Paperback Is Published By
Bold Strokes Books, Inc.,
Philadelphia, Pa, USA

New Revised Edition, June 2006

Originally published as Part Three and Part Four of *Lorimal's Chalice,* by fortitude press, 2002

Credits
Editors: Cindy Cresap and Stacia Seaman
Production Design: J. Barre Greystone
Cover Image: Tobias Brenner (http://www.tobiasbrenner.de/)
Cover Design: Julia Greystone

By the Author

THE CELAENO SERIES

The Walls of Westernfort

Rangers at Roadsend

The Temple at Landfall

THE LYREMOUTH CHRONICLES

The Exile and the Sorcerer

Acknowledgments

Thanks go to everyone at Bold Strokes Books, especially Rad, Stacia and Cindy, for their support, professionalism and for being great people to work with. I would also like to thank Pam and Ads for helping with earlier drafts of this novel.

DEDICATION

For Lizzy—

the book you browbeat me into writing

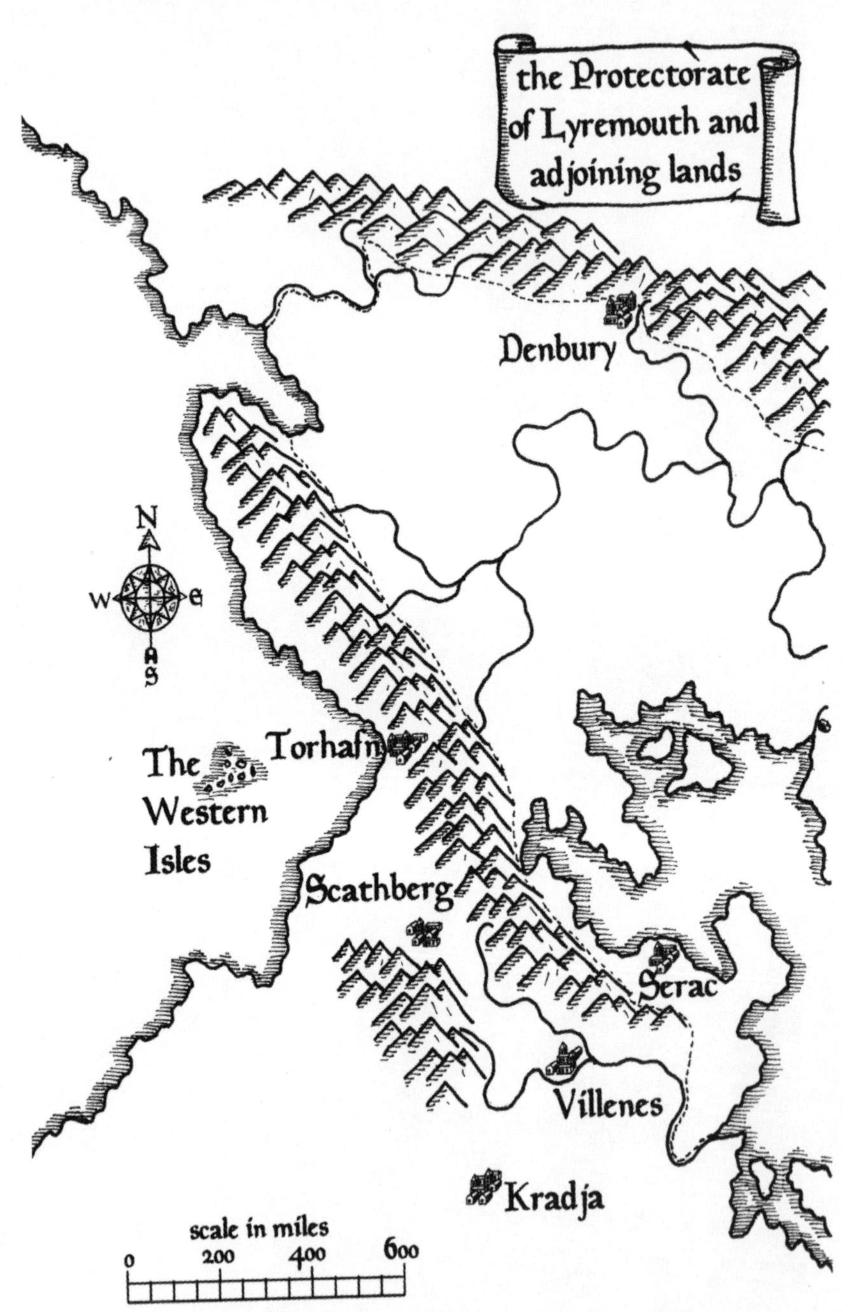

the dotted line markes the border of the Protectorate

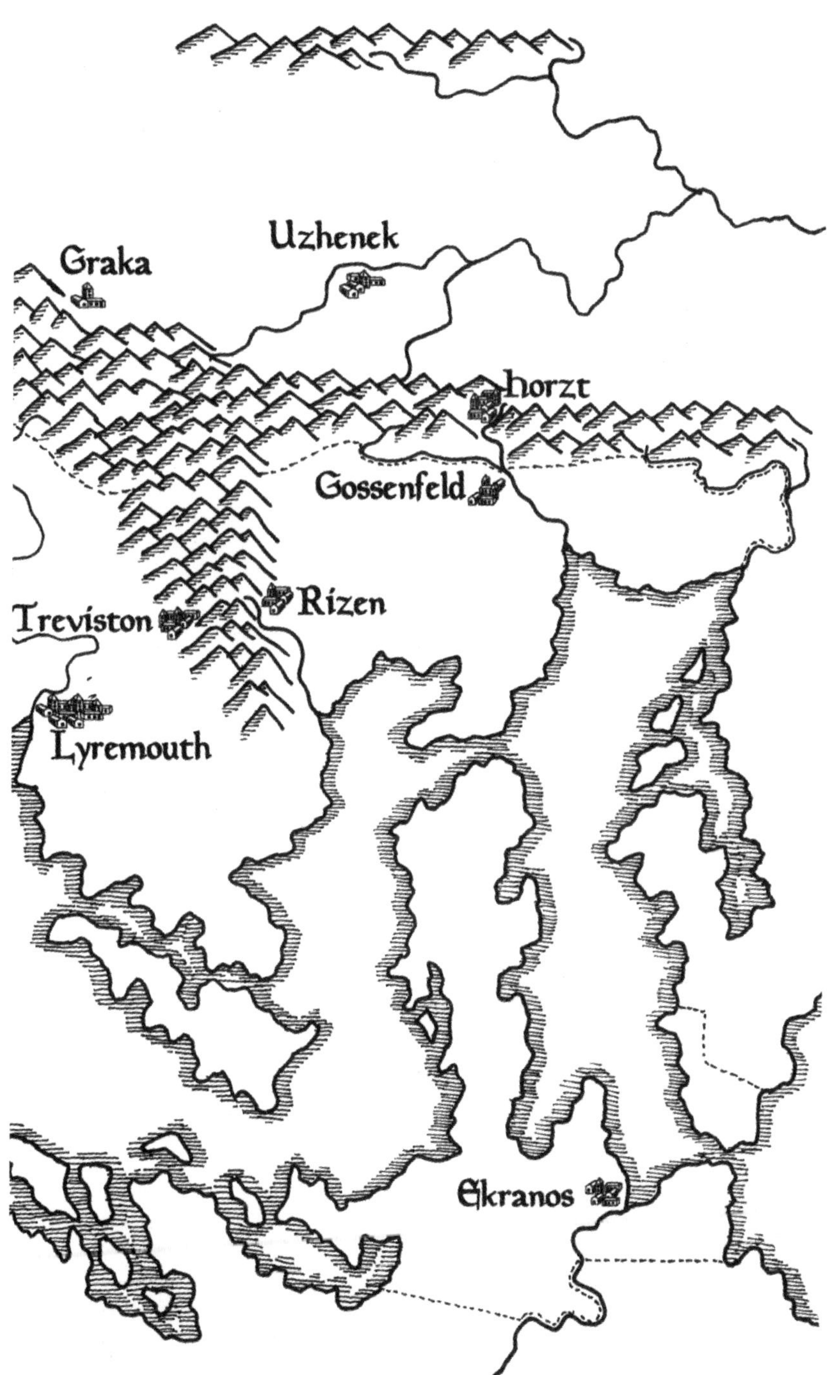

Uzhenek
Graka
Horzt
Gossenfeld
Rizen
Treviston
Lyremouth
Ekranos

FOREWORD—THE COVEN AT LYREMOUTH

Magic changes everything

The rare individuals who could directly access the higher dimensions had dictated the history of the world. These workers of magic perceived more than the four normal dimensions of time and space known by the ungifted majority, and thus could manipulate their surroundings in ways that seemed as mystical and unstoppable to the rest of the population as a sighted archer might seem in the world of the blind.

A witch was someone who was aware of just one or two paranormal dimensions. Maybe one person in every hundred might claim this title. A sorcerer was far more uncommon. They could perceive all three, including the paradoxical second aspect of time—the realm of soothsayers and oracles.

Nobody knew why some were born with these gifts. Whatever the cause, it did not lie in heredity. Children of the most powerful sorcerer were no more likely to be gifted with magic than those of a common shepherd. And therein lay the source of the chaos that sorcerers had inflicted on the world.

Their powers were vast. One sorcerer acting alone could carve out an empire, sweeping aside whatever small culture the ungifted had painstakingly built. Cities and civilisations were created by their paranormal abilities, and all fell back to anarchy on their deaths. Only another sorcerer could hope to seize such an empire, and countless conscripted soldiers had died in the resulting wars.

The acolytes of the great philosopher sorcerer Keovan of Lyremouth were the ones who broke the cycle of short-lived empires. Keovan's teachings had espoused knowledge as the greatest virtue. On his death, his magic-wielding acolytes joined together to form the Coven, with an elected leader—the Guardian. To the ungifted villagers of Lyremouth they offered protection in return for a modest tithe of their goods, thus freeing the acolytes for a life of meditation.

In the following years, the Protectorate expanded rapidly, by consent rather than invasion. Surrounding villages were eager for the security the Coven offered. More sorcerers and witches joined, attracted by the chance to study with others who saw the world in all its multi-dimensional complexity.

In time, Lyremouth grew from a village to a great city. Stability allowed the advancement of commerce and industry. The ungifted tradesmen formed guilds, modelled on the Coven, with elected leaders.

This growth made for changes in the nature of the Protectorate. The old tithe system was transformed into taxes. The guild masters came to swear allegiance to the Guardian on behalf of their members. Rather than remain remote with their esoteric studies, the sorcerers took their place at the head of the social ladder—unquestioned rulers of the Protectorate.

Yet the spirit of Keovan lived on. The Protectorate was still generally benign and just. The guilds could manage their own affairs. Ungifted citizens had rights under the law. Folk might grumble at the taxes and distrust the autocratic sorcerers, yet—uniquely in the history of the world—they lived their lives in peace and prosperity, with the hope that their children and grandchildren might do the same.

Nearly four hundred and fifty years after Keovan's death, the Protectorate had expanded to cover all the lands around the Middle Seas, dwarfing the overnight empires of lone sorcerers.

It was a society where the circumstances of one's birth counted for nothing, compared to one's abilities. What did it matter who someone's parents were, or where they came from, if that person was a sorcerer? Rich or poor, male or female, north or south—nothing counted in relation to the ability to work magic. Even the ungifted might advance through guilds and find wealth and status, unhampered by preconceived notions of their worth.

These possibilities drew many from the surrounding barbarian lands. Some came seeking riches, some fled from danger, and some arrived by chance, displaced from their homeland and washed up like flotsam in a strange new world—or so Tevi viewed her own arrival in the Protectorate.

Part One

The Traitor

Chapter One—Undercover in Ekranos

The man might have been six inches taller than the woman had he not been lying curled on the ground. Blood stained the back of his head red—a result of the blow that had floored him. The woman pulled back her foot, about to kick him in the kidneys.

"You keep your hands off Zak." Her voice was a shrill howl. Judging by her clothes and build, she was one of the dock porters.

Tevi hurdled over a row of barrels and cannoned into the woman, shoving her away before her foot made contact with her opponent. Tevi continued to press the angry woman backwards until she was pinned against a wall of crates. The woman struggled, but Tevi was able to restrain her without making too obvious a display of unexpected strength.

"Let me at him!" the woman screamed in Tevi's face.

Tevi thumped her against the crates, hard enough to jolt, but not to cause injury. On the third blow, the woman's eyes left her victim and focused on Tevi. From her change in demeanour, she finally registered the sword in red and gold, tattooed on the backs of Tevi's hands—the sign of the Guild of Mercenary Warriors, and also the badge of the port authorities on Tevi's leather jerkin—her current employer.

"He was after Zak." A pleading edge entered the woman's voice.

"Who's Zak?"

"He's mine."

"Did he threaten to hurt Zak?"

"Zak don't want nothing to do with him."

The answers were not helping. Tevi looked over her shoulder. Now it was safe, a couple of onlookers had gone to aid the injured man. They had him in a sitting position, clearly dazed, but not seriously hurt.

To Tevi's relief, at that moment, two more people arrived. Both were mercenaries and one had a second crossed sword on his tattoos, marking him as a senior guild member, and therefore someone to take charge and work out what was going on. The senior mercenary strode up to Tevi and her captive.

"What is it this time, Chel?"

"Tell him to keep away from Zak." The woman, presumably called Chel, sounded aggrieved.

"She's a frigging nutter, that's what it is." Chel's victim had recovered enough to give his own version.

"Keep your filthy hands off Zak."

The senior mercenary cut in before the argument went further. "Right. I get the picture." He looked at the group around the injured man. "Get him to a healer and check his skull ain't cracked. And you, Chel"—he turned back to the woman—"are coming with me for a little visit to the lockup."

"Zak loves me. I'll kill that pig if he tries to paw him again." Despite her defiant words, Chel let herself be led away.

With the excitement over, the onlookers dispersed, leaving Tevi alone with the other mercenary. Tevi had been working on the docks since her arrival in Ekranos, nine days before, but did not yet know all her colleagues by name, although she recognised this one's face from meals at the guild house.

"Have you been warned about Chel?" he asked.

"No. Does she do this a lot?"

"Every other month."

"And Zak—is that her partner?"

He gave a yelp of laughter. "Zak's a two-bit whore. He's anyone's for a copper shilling. But Chel thinks they are the great love story. Zak was probably trying to make a little money on the side and got caught out."

"Right."

Shaking her head, Tevi walked away. Even after a year on the mainland, she was still sometimes left dumbfounded by the ways of the Protectorate. Everything was so different from her childhood on the Western Isles. She stopped on the quayside and looked out over the water, still trying to adjust her thoughts.

Taking money in return for sex was the least of it. Even on the islands, a woman might try to win a man's favours with gifts. More unsettling was that nobody had been shocked by a woman assaulting a man. Admittedly, Chel had enjoyed no unfair physical advantage. In fact, had she not caught her victim by surprise, she might not have come out on top. Yet Tevi could not easily ignore the moral voice of her upbringing.

The situation would have been so different back on the island of Storenseg. Thanks to the legacy of a shipwrecked sorcerer, the women of the Western Isles enjoyed magically enhanced strength—something Tevi had to disguise on her current mission if she wanted to avoid attracting undue attention. On the islands, men were so weak by comparison that any woman striking one would be seen as a bully and coward, and in the warrior culture of the islands, cowardice was the gravest failing.

Tevi sighed at the thought. Actually, there were worse traits a woman could possess—such as wanting another woman as a lover—which was something else that nobody in the Protectorate would think twice about. Any more than the onlookers had been surprised that Zak might be an object of desire for both men and women.

Her preference in lovers was the reason that Tevi had been unofficially exiled. Her grandmother, the Queen of Storenseg, had seen to it, with the fake quest to retrieve the stolen chalice. Nobody knew where the chalice was. Nobody expected her to return. It was just an excuse to get her out of the way. Only Tevi's close family knew the true reason for her going.

Tevi continued walking along the quay, thinking about the irony of it all. Swapping Storenseg for the Protectorate had been the best move for her. She had found a place in the Guild of Mercenaries, and she had found a lover, the sorcerer Jemeryl. Even more ironic, the fake quest had turned out to be important—important enough to concern the Guardian.

Tevi stopped again and raised her eyes to the cliffs west of Ekranos. Perched atop was the School of Herbalism. Jemeryl was at the school, hunting the rogue sorcerer who had stolen the chalice. The artefact still meant nothing to Tevi. She would happily have forgotten all about it. But the Guardian had sent Jemeryl to investigate, and Tevi would not leave her to face danger alone. She only wished she could be closer at hand.

The work as a customs officer involved checking payment of port taxes and curtailing the smuggling of contraband. It meant long hours in an erratic shift rota, following the tides. Jemeryl's work at the school was more regular, but no more flexible. However, their free time coincided that afternoon—their first chance to meet since reaching Ekranos. Tevi took a deep breath and tried to let the thought wash away her anxiety.

❖

The sound of waves beating against the rocks below came softly through the thick glass. Jemeryl stared through the window, scrunching her eyes against the brilliant sunshine. As far as the horizon, the sea was dotted with boats: small fishing craft, trailing nets; and larger cargo ships, laden with merchandise, slicing through the waves. A seagull, rising on the updrafts created by the cliffs, steadied for a moment and then soared away.

Another headland rose across the bay several miles distant. The rocks around its base formed a jagged fringe in the surf. Its top was crowned with a lighthouse—a thin dark finger pointing at the cloudless morning sky. On the coast between school and lighthouse lay the wide estuary of the river Dhaliki. The nearer bank was lined with the red-tiled roofs and whitewashed walls of Ekranos. A soft smile lifted the corner of Jemeryl's lips. Tevi was down there.

"Hey. Stop gawking and give me a hand...or is something happening outside?"

The voice recalled Jemeryl to her surroundings. She turned and smiled apologetically at the speaker while her eyes adjusted to the subdued light of the hospital ward. Jemeryl's study partner, Vine, was sitting beside a patient. Her expression of eager curiosity raised a flicker of amusement. Vine was renowned for a love of gossip, in both the gathering and spreading of rumours. Her superiors could only wish she would devote a fraction as much enthusiasm to her work as junior sorcerer.

"No, you're not missing anything. My mind was just wandering."

Vine's face fell. She shrugged and held out a bloody bandage. "Oh, well. Throw this away and get some clean water. We need to wash the bite."

Somewhat gingerly, Jemeryl took the soiled linen. She dropped it in a bin at the end of the ward, trying to avoid seeing or smelling the other unsavoury contents. The combined aura was definitely best ignored. She rinsed her hands in a stone sink before filling a shallow bowl and returning. A few drops of antiseptic turned the water purple, then Vine dipped a cloth in the solution and began washing the patient's wound.

The man moaned in a semiconscious stupor. He was a docker who had been bitten by a rat hiding between sacks of grain on the quay. The wound had become infected, and the docker was carried to the school running a high fever and delirious. Jemeryl's stomach heaved at the sight of an ugly ring of black scabs, stark against the swollen, bloodless skin. She busied herself by taking another cloth and wiping the patient's face. Lank hair clung to the sweat on his forehead. His eyes were glassy and unfocused.

"The bite is clean. No sign of pus," Vine noted cheerfully.

Jemeryl clenched her teeth. She hated working in the hospital. Sunshine flooded through the windows, but for Jemeryl, the rooms held a murkiness the light could not pierce. Herbalism and medicine had always been her least favourite magical disciplines, and the addition of genuine patients had not improved her liking. It was unbelievable that any sorcerer willingly chose this work when there were so many other fields to explore, yet many did.

With hindsight, Jemeryl could see that she had been unwise to take her previous post in the valley, where her main responsibility had been caring for ungifted villagers. She had not meant the common people any harm, but she had confused and frightened them and had been relieved when they stopped pestering her with requests for aid.

A twinge of guilt hit Jemeryl. Maybe she had gone some way to deserving the reprimand when she was removed from the post and ordered to accompany Tevi. Yet equally, she knew the Coven leaders had been working on a secret agenda, rather than expressing any real anger on behalf of the villagers. And now she was back, caring for unwell citizens, more a servant than a sorcerer.

Jemeryl tried to take comfort that she had not been sent to the school before, as part of her general training—a fate that had befallen several of her fellow apprentices. At least her present stay in Ekranos need not be a long one. If only she could identify the traitorous sorcerer quickly.

The docker gave another rasping moan. He seemed to be attempting to swallow. Jemeryl stared into the man's face.

"Something's not right. His aura is more distorted than you'd expect."

Vine chewed her lip thoughtfully. "Maybe."

"Should we ask Neame to look at him?"

"It might be an idea."

"I'll find her." Jemeryl hurried off.

The hospital was a large collection of buildings laid out between trees and gardens. Searching it all would take a long time. Fortunately Neame was not far away. Jemeryl found her in an adjacent ward, deep in conversation with an elderly witch.

While waiting politely, Jemeryl studied the senior sorcerer, who was both head of the hospital wing and deputy to the principal. In Jemeryl's mind, the only good thing about the school was the chance to watch Neame at work. In the days since she had arrived, Jemeryl had acquired a great respect for the woman—even though Neame was one of the main suspects.

She was listening to her assistant, her forehead puckered in a distracted frown. Neame was a plump woman in her mid-fifties, with peppered grey hair twisted in an untidy braid. Much of it had escaped, and the wispy strands were tucked carelessly behind her ears. Her clothes gave the impression that they were following her around purely out of habit. Her face would have been ordinary were it not marked by intelligence and determination. Her manner would have been brusque were it not underlain by compassion. Jemeryl could not help hoping that Neame was innocent.

Eventually, the witch nodded and disappeared through a side door.

Neame pushed the hair back from her eyes "What is it?" she asked, noticing Jemeryl for the first time.

"Please, ma'am. I wonder if you could take a look at a patient."

"Of course."

At Neame's arrival, Vine vacated the stool, allowing the senior sorcerer to take her place. The patient's condition had not changed. Neame studied him intently, her fingertips just touching his forehead.

"The rat was diseased. Not surprising. A healthy rat would have run away when it heard the dock workers." Neame made her diagnosis. She picked up a slate and chalked a note before passing it to Jemeryl.

"We need different medication. Go to the dispensary and ask Orrago for this." She hesitated. "Have you met Orrago yet?"

"No, ma'am."

Neame looked at Vine. "You'd better go and introduce them. I'll take care of things here."

"Yes, ma'am."

The air outside smelt clean. The bushes lining the path were alive with the chirps of insects and the rustle of leaves. Jemeryl took a deep breath and ran both hands through her hair as if to brush away the aura of sickness. She glanced at the other young sorcerer.

Vine's expression was untroubled. She was shorter than Jemeryl by half a head, with a mat of straight black hair and a round, good-natured face. A guttural burr of an accent betrayed her origins far outside the Protectorate. Jemeryl had learnt that Vine was a nickname, short for "The Grapevine." Her real name was never used, mainly because it was both long and impossibly short on vowels.

"I don't know how you can be so cheerful in the hospital." Jemeryl's tone held more emotion than she had intended.

"You get used to it. You've only been here nine days. I've had fourteen years."

"You must have been young when you arrived."

"I was. I'm from a tiny tribe way down south in the rain forest. I don't think they'd ever had a sorcerer born there before. My family didn't know how to deal with me, but they'd heard of the Coven. They got river traders to bring me here. I was dumped in Ekranos, not knowing a word of the language. I caused a bit of commotion on the docks. You know what a seven-year-old sorcerer can be like. Fortunately, no one got seriously hurt. They coaxed me up to the school, and I've been here ever since."

"You weren't sent on to Lyremouth?"

"I went there to take my oath and stayed a few months, but I came back as soon as I could."

Jemeryl shook her head in bemusement. "You like it here?"

"Mostly. Some bits aren't so good. I've got to help Tapley with his precious ravens this afternoon."

"It can't be worse than working in the hospital."

"It is. Believe me, it is." Vine groaned for effect. "You're free this afternoon. Why don't you take my place and find out?"

"Thanks for the offer, but I've arranged to meet someone in town." The words drew an immediate reaction. Too late, Jemeryl realised she had been careless. Anything told to Vine would be circulating the entire school by sunset.

"Known them long?"

"We met on the boat from Lyremouth." Jemeryl lied. She certainly could not let Vine know they had been sent together by the Guardian's orders.

"A, er...good friend?"

Jemeryl shrugged, not wanting to answer. Vine was on the trail of gossip. Fortunately, the dispensary was at hand, curtailing the conversation.

As they reached the door, Vine stopped abruptly. "You've not met Orrago yet?"

"No."

"She's not..." Vine hesitated. "She's old. She used to be principal, but her wits are going and she had to resign. She looks after the dispensary now. Sort of. She's not really up to the job. You'll see what I mean."

Vine knocked softly. "I wouldn't want to wake her if she's asleep," she explained, but an elderly voice called out indistinctly.

An obstacle prevented the door opening fully, and Vine had to slip in sideways. Jemeryl followed dubiously. She came to a halt just inside the room and stared around.

A sweet, acrid smell pervaded everywhere. Mounds of dried vegetable matter littered every horizontal surface, stacked between precariously balanced bottles. Several crates stood in the centre of the room. It had been one of these blocking the door.

Vine was making her way towards a high-backed armchair positioned in the sunlight beside a tall window. She beckoned Jemeryl to follow. Great care was required not to dislodge anything, but Jemeryl managed to squeeze safely past the overflowing ledges.

The chair's occupant was an old woman wrapped in a thick woollen blanket. Wispy strands of hair made a halo in the sunlight. Her face was deeply lined, as was the sunken skin between her knuckles.

Vine spoke slowly. "Excuse me, ma'am. I've come to collect some things and want to introduce you to Jemeryl. She's been sent here to study herbalism."

The watery eyes examined them uncertainly. Yet Jemeryl could sense the remnants of great power. In her day, Orrago had been one of the Coven's foremost sorcerers. "You're like...what's her name...young Iralin." A frown crossed the lined face. "I haven't seen her for a while. Ask her to pop in and see me."

Jemeryl opened her mouth and then closed it again. Finally, she said, "I think you're confused, ma'am. Iralin is a senior sorcerer at Lyremouth. She was my mentor."

"Oh, no. She's a young thing, here to brush up her herbalism."

Vine spoke softly. "No, ma'am. Jemeryl is right. It's a long time since Iralin was here."

Orrago's gaze drifted away, and a pained expression crossed her face. Her hand tightened on the arm of the chair. "Maybe, maybe. People are getting to be like that."

Vine stepped into the silence. "Neame has given us a list of drugs she needs." She held out the slate, but Orrago brushed it aside.

"Let Frog see to it." Orrago's voice rose to a high-pitched waver. "Frog, come and be useful."

A large speckled toad hopped down from where it had been basking, unnoticed, in the sun. It crossed the floor in a waddling walk and then leapt onto the elderly sorcerer's lap to examine the slate.

"Frog will sort it out. I want to rest." Orrago's eyes closed, and she snuggled into her chair.

With obvious affection, Vine tucked the blanket around the ancient sorcerer. Orrago's features relaxed. Her hand reached out and squeezed Vine's before returning to her lap.

The two young sorcerers manoeuvred to the other end of the dispensary, where Frog was buried under a pile of papers. Only its webbed feet were visible, splaying out behind. A period of scrabbling followed before it re-emerged, dragging a vial of yellow liquid. Jemeryl watched as it then lurched across the desk and disappeared again into a half-open drawer.

"Why does Orrago call him Frog? Surely she knows it's a toad?"

Vine glanced down the dispensary. From Orrago's chair came soft, rasping snores. "It's a joke of hers. She's aware she gets people confused. She'll probably call you Iralin next time you meet. She named him Frog because she didn't see why a small amphibian should be the only one in the school she addresses correctly."

A succession of bumps and a forlorn croak came from the drawer. Frog crawled onto the bench with a small bag, which it laid beside the vial, before heading off again. While awaiting its return, Vine demonstrated how to enter items in the dispensary record. Before long, Frog's task was complete. It regarded them with moist, bulging eyes, croaked a mournful goodbye, and then waddled back to its spot in the sun.

Once they were outside again, Jemeryl asked, "How long has Orrago been like that?"

"She retired as principal six years ago, but her mind had been going for some time. Most of us hoped Neame would take over as principal. She was deputy to Orrago, but Bramell got the post."

"Why not Neame?"

Vine merely shrugged in answer.

Back in the ward, Neame had been busy. Already, the patient was more alert. His eyes followed her every move. In fact, all the conscious patients were watching from their cots. Jemeryl knew Neame was admired by everyone who worked in the hospital. In the patients, she inspired a devotion that could only be called love. Jemeryl understood the reaction. Neame was able, by her mere presence, to lighten the oppressive atmosphere of the wards.

Jemeryl and Vine supported the patient while he drank the contents of a tumbler. Once he was back on the cot, Neame turned to the two younger sorcerers. She picked up the vial and embarked on a lesson.

"You see how the effervescence fades off through the shadow axis." She indicated a strand of the fifth dimension.

"Yes, ma'am." Vine nodded quickly.

Jemeryl was less certain.

"This is what we need to de-skew the synthesis. Watch how the auras combine..."

❖

Tevi stood with the noisy squad of mercenaries awaiting assignment outside the customs office. Half her mind was listening to the chatter, the rest was watching seagulls fighting over a fish head. In a world that could seem so alien, the seagulls were reassuringly the same as those of her childhood. A shout recalled her to the present.

"Hey, Tevi. You're with us. We've got the holds."

The speaker was Faren, one of the older customs officers. Tevi joined the other mercenaries in his small group. "How many ships?"

"Three set to go on the tide. We're going to be busy."

Tevi grinned. There were worse jobs. They set off for the moorings, but before they had gone twenty yards a burst of muffled laughter made her glance back. An overweight young man was talking to the remaining mercenaries. One of them pointed in her direction. Tevi waited as the man approached.

"What is it, Zak?" Faren got his question in first.

Zak looked confused, but then his attention returned to Tevi. "Chel...I heard she...I'm...Do you...?"

At the rate he was going, Zak would not have completed a question by the time the tide turned. Tevi decided to give what was presumably the information he was after. "She attacked a man. She's been taken to the harbour lockup. You need to go there if you want to see her."

"What will happen?"

"That's up to the judge."

"About me?"

Tevi frowned, confused in more ways than one. She did not have a clue what Zak was after—she wondered if he did either. He was clearly not very bright, nor was he good looking. In fact, it was hard to imagine that anyone would think him worth fighting over.

"You can find someone else," Faren answered, clearly more in tune with Zak's thinking.

Zak smiled coyly at him. "Would you—"

"No. Piss off."

"I was just—"

"We're on duty. You know better than to start pulling tricks."

"When you're off duty, I'll be at the Navie." Zak's smirk took in all four mercenaries before fixing again on Tevi. "Chel, you know she's—"

"I told you to shove it." Faren broke in again.

Zak took a step back. He looked as if he was trying to think of something to say, but then gave another weak smile, turned, and trotted away.

The customs officers continued towards their destination. One of them nudged Tevi. "I'd say you're in with a chance with Zak."

"She's still breathing and she has two copper shillings to tap together. Of course she's in with a chance," Faren said. "But he ain't worth the bother."

"Is that experience talking?"

Faren's shoulder's twitched, as if at an unpleasant memory. "I was desperate. But he's just as pathetic in bed as he is out of it. He wants someone to play Mummy and wipe his nose clean."

The mercenaries laughed. Tevi joined in, although on Storenseg, men were expected to be simpering weaklings, needing women to take care of them. *That's what men are like,* the voice of her childhood said, but Tevi did not say it aloud, and she no longer believed it anyway.

It was Lorimal's fault. The shipwrecked sorcerer had been washed ashore on islands that had never seen a magic user. In their absence, physical strength counted for everything, and the islands were dominated by violent, patriarchal warrior clans—until Lorimal created the strength potion that resulted in the islands becoming dominated by violent, matriarchal warrior clans.

Tevi could not help thinking it would have been much better if Lorimal had found some way to create an equal society, more like the mainland. Although being imprisoned, tortured, and killed by the men who captured her may have given Lorimal an understandable desire for revenge.

"Are you going to meet Zak in the Navie?" One of her colleague interrupted Tevi's thoughts.

She shook her head. "Not my type."

"Why not?"

Tevi's grimace raised a laugh. Luckily no other answer was required. *He's male*, she could have said, but that would not be understood on the mainland, where the only significant difference between people was the ability to work magic. An exclusive sexual preference for one gender would be as strange as having an exclusive sexual preference for people whose favourite colour was green.

Tevi did not wish to get into explanations of the island culture, where men and women were believed to be, in some way, opposite. People would think it bizarre. Tevi was starting to agree, though this reappraisal of her upbringing had not made any impact on her deeper emotions.

Faren patted her shoulder. "Good call. He likes playing games of being helpless."

As they reached the ship's gangplank, Tevi glanced back. Zak was still visible, hanging around the customs office. For a moment she was tempted to run over to him and tell him to head west, across the Protectorate, over the Aldrak mountains and out across the Western Ocean. There he could find islands where the women would treat him like an infant for the rest of his life. Acting helpless would be a desirable trait. Perhaps he might be happy there. Or perhaps the attraction of the game would pall once he had no options.

❖

Midday was approaching by the time the treatment was finished. While Neame worked, the squares of light falling through the window had edged across the floor. They now lay as thin bars of dazzling silver on the windowsill. Someone had opened the door at the end of the ward to allow a breeze to circulate. Sounds of waves and birds drifted down the room. The docker was sleeping peacefully. The skin around the bite was still swollen, but the bloodless sheen was gone, and his breathing was soft and even.

"Did you follow the final stages?" Neame asked.

Vine nodded enthusiastically.

Jemeryl frowned. "I saw how you bound the auras together, but I'm not sure I'd be able to do it myself."

"I wouldn't expect you to. It needs practice. But you saw why I was doing it?"

"Perhaps if I read up on it..." Jemeryl trailed off optimistically.

"You must make sure you understand. Someday, people's lives will depend on you, and books are no substitute for experience."

"Yes, ma'am." Jemeryl sighed. Whatever else, experience was not in short supply at the hospital.

Neame patted her arm. "Don't worry. We've done enough for now. If you tidy things away"—she indicated Vine—"you, Jemeryl, can take a message to Bramell. Tell him I'll have to miss the meeting this afternoon. I'd like to stay with this patient." Neame nodded in dismissal but then added, "Oh, and can you have the cook send my lunch over?"

"Yes, ma'am."

At the exit, Jemeryl paused and looked back. Neame stood by the bed making ineffectual attempts to poke stray wisps of hair into place. At the same time, her astral projection was soothing the tangled strands in the docker's aura like a parent wiping the forehead of a sleeping child. The morning's work had been long and complex. Jemeryl was tired from just watching. It was amazing if Neame could still see straight, yet her attention was fixed on the sick man. This was what the patients sensed: the depth of her commitment.

If Neame's compassion is felt so keenly, is it surprising the villagers spotted my own disinterest? The thought was an uncomfortable jab to Jemeryl's conscience. She left quickly and set off to deliver Neame's messages. The sun was warm and the breeze carried the scent of fragrant plants, but her mood took longer than usual to pick up.

The path terminated at a small courtyard just inside the main gates. Straight ahead was the imposing archway to the central square, where all of the most important buildings were situated. Jemeryl paused in the shadow of the arch and considered the open grassy quad, colonnaded by stumpy trees. On the far side rose the white walls of the library, three stories high. To the north, a long, low building housed the senior sorcerers' residence. The other two sides were filled with academic and administration facilities, including her destination, the principal's chambers.

When Jemeryl arrived, a solitary witch was on duty in the scriptorium outside Bramell's office, supervising the work of three animated pens.

"Is Bramell in his office?"

"Of course." The witch glanced over his shoulder. "You didn't think he'd be off looking at potions or something, did you?"

"I admit I didn't bother searching the hospital for him."

"Wise. The only thing he'll happily doctor are the accounts. That's why they're so healthy."

The joke was a variant on one Jemeryl had already heard. Much of the junior washroom graffiti was concerned with Bramell's lack of interest in herbalism. Whatever his talents as a sorcerer, the man had the heart of a bureaucrat.

The principal looked up from the neatly arranged papers on his desk when Jemeryl entered. He regarded her with steady blue eyes. The first impression he gave was of confidence and efficiency. Middle age added authority to his natural good looks. The second impression was of inflexibility and aloofness. Even sitting, he seemed to be looking down his nose. Jemeryl tried not to fidget; something in Bramell's manner always made her feel like a misplaced child.

"What is it?" Bramell's voice matched his appearance, firm and well balanced.

"Excuse me, sir. I have a message from Neame. She won't be able to attend the meeting after lunch. She sends her apologies."

The news clearly annoyed Bramell. His lips tightened in a line, but he said nothing. Criticising a senior sorcerer in Jemeryl's presence would be inappropriate.

"Would you like me to take a reply, sir?"

"No. You may go." The blunt dismissal left no doubt of her junior status.

Once outside again, Jemeryl weighed up the idea of Bramell as the renegade sorcerer. She knew the principal was respected but not admired. He ran the school with scrupulous attention to the rules, but he lacked vision. Despite appearances, Jemeryl suspected that he possessed no inner strength. Jemeryl could not picture Bramell as the culprit; he lacked both the courage and the imagination.

An onslaught of noise shattered Jemeryl's deliberation as a group of apprentices burst from a doorway. Shouting and laughing, the young witches and sorcerers streamed past, jostling among themselves in a reasonably good-natured way. Jemeryl followed more sedately, as befitting one wearing a sorcerer's black amulet. Training healers was one of the school's most important functions. Jemeryl just wished it could be accomplished at a lower volume. She was certain that her classmates in Lyremouth had not been so loud.

The apprentices were soon out of sight, heading towards their dormitories. School accommodation was granted according to rank. Apprentices and servants lived in barracklike blocks on the edge of the site, whereas witches were two or three to a room. As a junior sorcerer, Jemeryl had her own bedroom, although she shared a study with Vine. The seniors got whole suites to themselves—plenty of space to carry out forbidden research. Jemeryl frowned. Her mission would be far easier if she could simply search the seniors' quarters.

Jemeryl arrived at the refectory. Through the open doors, she could see servants preparing for the midday meal, laying out baskets of bread on the long tables. The adjacent kitchen doors were also open, allowing cool air to enter and sound and smells to leave. From twenty yards away, Jemeryl caught the aroma of roasting meat and heard the cook bellow.

"You, girl! Stop playing with the onions, or I'll take the meat clever to you!"

The threats continued non-stop until the moment the cook caught sight of Jemeryl. Mid-sentence, his manner switched to self-abasement, complete with cringing posture and sickly smile.

"Good morning, ma'am. Is there anything I can do for you?"

"Neame would like her dinner sent over to the hospital."

"Of course, ma'am. It would be a pleasure. Was there anything specific she wanted?"

"I think she'll be happy with whatever's going."

"Thank you, ma'am. That's very, very kind of you."

The cook's transformation was startling. Jemeryl wondered if he had once yelled at a sorcerer and was keen never to repeat the mistake. She would ask Vine. In the meantime, the grovelling performance had her struggling to keep a straight face, particularly since, over his shoulder, she could see a teenage girl juggling four large onions, to the admiration of her friends.

Whatever the cause, the cook's personality change did not last long after Jemeryl left. Before she had gone a dozen steps, his voice rose to its customary roar. "Don't do that to the soup. Use a spoon!"

The junior sorcerers' quarters occupied a two-story building, built in the Ekranos style of whitewashed plaster and red roof tiles. Access to the upper floor, including her shared study, was via a wooden veranda that ran the length of the building, with a stairway at the end.

The study itself was not large, although the polished floor and white walls made it seem light and airy. A door on either side led to the adjoining bedrooms. Two desks beneath the window completely filled one wall. The only other furniture was a bookcase and a battered reading chair. A fair amount of rubbish was strewn about—all of it belonging to Vine.

Jemeryl stared vacantly through the window. She was now free for the rest of the day. Tevi's watch finished in the early afternoon, and she was not back on the docks until dawn. In a few hours, the two of them would be together. There would be plenty of time for talk—and other things.

For the first time since she had left the ward, a broad smile spread across Jemeryl's face.

Chapter Two—The List of Suspects

Sunlight fell through the open hatch. It formed a bright patch in the middle of the ship's hold but did not penetrate the distant corners. The four customs officers needed some time to be sure nothing was hidden among the barrels, crates, and sacks. In fact, it would have taken all day to search the hold properly, but there were quicker methods.

While her colleagues made a show of prodding the cargo, Tevi surreptitiously kept her eyes on the ship's mate, noting where he looked and where he avoided looking. It was a truism that while a captain might be unaware of illicit activity on the ship, the mate always knew. Even if they were not directly involved, they would have suspicions. Nine times out of ten, their demeanour betrayed them—if you knew what to look for. Her colleagues had already discovered that Tevi had a talent for it—a *nose*, as one old hand put it.

"Is your side clear, Tevi?" Faren called.

"Yep, I'm happy." Tevi answered the question meant rather than the one asked. In her opinion, the ship's mate was feeling guilty about something, but not contraband. An indiscretion in town was more probable. Everyone knew that sailors could be very indiscreet.

Sunlight was dazzling after the gloom of the hold. The sounds of the dock were no longer muted through the heavy wooden hull. Everywhere, sailors were busy making the ship ready for departure. They found the chief customs officer in a patch of calm by the gangplank, talking politely with the ship's captain.

"Fore and aft holds both clear, ma'am," Faren reported.

"Good. Wait on the dock."

"Yes, ma'am."

The mercenaries sauntered down the gangplank and joined the rest of the group assembling on the quay. Shouts greeted them. "What kept you? We've been waiting ages."

"Some of us like to do a job properly."

"True, some do, but that doesn't explain why *you* took so long."

The jokes were the standard banter Tevi remembered from the guildhall at Lyremouth, masking a strong team spirit—a consequence of their work. Mercenaries lived together, fought together, risked their lives for one another, and then maybe buried someone and moved on to the next job. They had to be close, but detached.

The friendly insults continued until the chief customs officer joined them and raised her voice.

"Right, that's it for today. You've got the afternoon off, but I expect to see you here at first light tomorrow. Hangovers or other self-inflicted injuries will get no sympathy. If you can't work, you won't get paid."

The officer was also in good humour and smiled at the ritual jeers. Her threat had no effect on the high spirits as the mercenaries strolled back to the guild house, making plans for the evening.

"What do you say we all go to Dano's tonight?" was one suggestion.

"Nah. The Navie has more"—the speaker paused for effect—"accommodating clientele. And I feel lucky tonight."

"That's more than I can say for whoever you pick up," someone threw back.

"I've never had any complaints."

"Probably because they all fall asleep from boredom."

Amid general laughter, one person embarked on a bawdy pantomime. "Who's rocking the boat? (yawn) Tell the captain I feel seasick (snore)."

Another turned to Tevi. "What about you? Have you been to the Navie yet?"

"No, and I can't go tonight. I've arranged to see a friend." Her words raised a chorus of whoops.

"That's quick work. Hasn't been in town five minutes."

"Will you be seeing a lot of your *friend*?"

"Or will you be too horizontal to get a good view?"

Tevi laughed, though she could feel a blush rising. "It's someone I met on the journey here."

"So you're not denying that it's a lover?"

Taking Tevi's expression as a yes, one man put his arm around her shoulder. "You know, I don't understand it. This person could have someone handsome, charming, and witty, like me, but instead, they've picked you. Why?"

"Perhaps Tevi's friend values critical self-awareness," someone answered for her.

The wisecracks continued without letup as the group left the wharves and warehouses behind and entered the district catering to the needs of sailors ashore, full of cheap brothels and rowdy taverns. These included the infamous Navie, which could fairly be described as either.

Ekranos was a sprawling affair of low buildings and tree-lined squares, designed for the hot summers—a lazy town with the air of an overgrown village. The houses were characterised by whitewashed walls, deep windows, and brightly coloured awnings. Only the main roads were paved; the rest were hard-packed earth. The people were friendly, noisy, and relaxed.

The avenue from the port ended at the old market square. It had become a slow backwater, even by Ekranos standards, since the creation of the new market on the east side of town many years before. Cobbles were missing, creating potholes. The buildings looked the worse for age. The central fountain was dry and, judging by the weeds in its basin, had been so for some time. However, Ekranos was a wealthy town. The neglect almost felt deliberate. The square seemed comfortable rather than derelict, like a well-worn but favourite pair of boots.

On one side stood the mercenary guild house. Its red and gold standard hung motionless in the baking afternoon air. Doors and shutters were open. The young mercenaries dawdled in the lofty entrance hall, finalising arrangements for the evening. Their laughter echoed in the cool interior. It reached a crescendo when Tevi took her leave.

The barrage of ironic cheers and ribald remarks followed her up the stairway, making her laugh despite doubts about what Jemeryl might think if she could hear. She also suspected that her colleagues would be less free with their innuendoes if they realised who they were unwittingly referring to.

The deference and distrust that most people gave to sorcerers was something Tevi found hard to understand. Jemeryl was exactly the same as everyone else, but Tevi knew her guild colleagues would not be able to see her as such. At the thought, a smile touched Tevi's face—well, maybe not exactly the same.

Tevi reached the room she shared with two other young mercenaries. It had a polished wooden floor and three narrow bunks, each with a shelf above the pillow and a large chest at the foot. Everything was clean and wholly functional. A window overlooked a dusty side street. The dull green paint on its shutters was crazed and flaking from the sun.

Few personal items were on show: a comb on one of the chests, a scabbard propped in a corner, a damp shirt hung by the open window. There was also Klara, asleep on the shelf above Tevi's bed. The magpie was Jemeryl's familiar, bound closely to the sorcerer. At the sound of the door, Klara awoke, but in accordance with the pretence of being merely a tame pet, she made no comment as Tevi opened her footlocker.

Lying at the bottom of the chest was something that looked like a polishing cloth, innocuous and commonplace. Tevi had been assured that any sorcerer would see through the magic and recognise it for what it was—the Guardian's warrant. Tevi had it for safekeeping. The risk that somebody at the school might see through the disguise was too great.

Tevi pushed the warrant to one side and pulled out a towel. She left the room again, heading for the bathhouse.

❖

Before long, Tevi returned. The dirt and tar of the docks were gone. Wet hair was plastered to her head. She was rubbing it vigorously with the driest corner of her towel when the door opened and one of her roommates entered.

"I've got a present for Klara." He opened a square of tarpaulin to reveal a handful of live worms.

Acting more like an overjoyed child than a hardened warrior, the young man enticed Klara onto his arm and then fed his offerings to the grateful magpie.

"You know, the way she looks at you, you'd almost think she could talk," he said as the last worm disappeared.

Tevi restrained her grin. If he but knew it, getting Klara to shut up was more normally the problem. Tevi finished buttoning her shirt and reclaimed the magpie. Her roommate studied her spruced-up appearance for the first time.

"You meeting someone?"

Tevi nodded.

"Don't suppose we'll see you again tonight, then."

"I'm certainly hoping you won't."

A scattering of people were dotted around the square when Tevi emerged from the guild house: several sailors sprawled in the shade, a noisy band of children with a ball, a pair of mercenaries arriving. Tevi waited until all were out of earshot before speaking to Klara.

"Can you give directions?"

"Sure thing, sweetheart. Head for the southern approach, and take the third road on your left."

In fifteen minutes, Tevi reached her destination: the Inn of Singing Birds. It was a modest establishment located on a square in the quiet part of town. The unremarkable facade blended with the other buildings. Jemeryl had evidently chosen their rendezvous to reduce the risk of meeting anyone they knew. The inn was neither prestigious enough for sorcerers nor lively enough for mercenaries.

The shutters downstairs were closed, but the double door was propped open by an old stick on one side and a large stone on the other. Tevi stepped into a long, thin room. A row of tables and benches ran up either side. The floor was red and white mosaic tiles, and the walls were covered in uneven, cream-coloured plaster. In one corner was a wooden counter with barrels stacked behind. From what Tevi could judge, the bar was not yet open for business but would be soon. Tankards were lined up, and a waiter was sweeping the floor.

As soon as he saw Tevi, the waiter put his broom aside. "Excuse me. You are the mercenary who has come to meet Madam Jemeryl?"

The words were said routinely in the lilting local accent, but Tevi could sense the disapproval. She was getting used to it. Ordinary people resented the Coven, disliked sorcerers, and regarded Tevi as a traitor to her own kind. *I must be predestined to have folk disapprove of my choice of lover*, she thought, *but it's an improvement on the islands. They aren't likely to stone me to death over it.*

"Yes. Is she about?" was all Tevi said aloud.

"Please follow me."

The waiter set off at a brisk pace. A narrow doorway at the rear led to a inner courtyard. From there, a flight of stairs took them to the upper floor.

"Will you be staying tonight?"

"Yes."

"You won't require a separate room?"

"No, thank you." Tevi bit back a less polite reply. She was sure the waiter already knew the answer. He just wanted to make sure Tevi knew that he knew.

They stopped outside a door. "Madam Jemeryl is expecting you." The waiter gave a curt nod and trotted away.

Irritated by his manner, Tevi pushed open the door without knocking. She had a brief impression of polished floorboards, solid furniture, and faded yellow walls before Jemeryl launched herself from a nearby chair and threw her arms around Tevi, threatening to knock them both over.

Prompted initially by the need to stop herself falling, Tevi clung to Jemeryl's shoulders. As her balance improved, the embrace became more tender. Laughing, Tevi gently pushed her lover away and looked into her eyes.

Jemeryl smiled back. "You found your way here all right? I asked the staff to show you up when you arrived."

"I gathered. But I don't think the waiter approves of us."

"In what way?"

"As in someone ungifted, like me, forsaking ordinary citizens and becoming a sorcerer's lover."

"Some people have overactive imaginations. He probably thinks I've bewitched you and turned you into a mindless sex slave who must obey my every whim, no matter how debauched or degrading."

"Watch out, Tevi. I think Jemeryl's getting ideas." Klara offered a warning.

Closing her eyes, Jemeryl snuggled back into Tevi's arms. "I've got the ideas already. Come on. Let me show you how much I've missed you."

Tevi did not feel her feet touch the floor—which might have been the case. She was pressed back until her legs hit the bed and she collapsed onto the mattress. Jemeryl all but dived on top of her. Tevi had no objections. Her mouth moulded hard against Jemeryl's, matching passion with passion. Her hands burrowed under Jemeryl's shirt, pulling it free of her belt and then rolling it up and exposing more of her lover's skin to her touch.

Abruptly, Jemeryl pulled back and brought her knees up, so that she was sitting astride Tevi's hips. She completed the task Tevi had started, pulling her shirt over her head and leaving herself naked from the waist up.

Tevi reached out to cup Jemeryl's breasts. The soft, warm weight filling her hands seemed to fill her soul as well. For this alone, her life would have been forfeit on the islands. Would she have ever dared take the risk? Her grandmother had exiled Tevi just on the suspicion that it was something she might want to do. Tevi smiled. Her grandmother had been right. She wanted to do it very much.

Tevi moved her grip to Jemeryl's shoulders and pulled gently, guiding a breast down towards her lips. She took as much of Jemeryl into her mouth as she could, feeling the nipple swell and harden under her tongue.

Tevi's whole body was thrumming with desire. Her senses seemed to overflow the normal bounds of her skin. Was Jemeryl spell-casting? Tevi did not care. Jemeryl's lovemaking was something worth dying for. Although she was very happy that she would not need to.

❖

With nightfall, the air became chill, sending folk indoors. The bar room at the Inn of Singing Birds was half full of middle-aged merchants and similar guild folk, busy but not crowded. It was conspicuous how everyone ignored Jemeryl and Tevi. All eyes skipped over the spot where they sat, as if their rear corner of the room did not exist. Nobody claimed the spare seats at their table. Although Jemeryl had concealed her black amulet, obviously the staff had informed everyone of her status. Tevi wondered what they had been told about herself and how they judged her.

Candles were set in wall holders; gnats swarmed around the flames. A wicker cage over the bar held two canaries, presumably to authenticate the inn's name. Their high chirps shrilled over the hum of conversation.

Klara eyed them disdainfully. "Call that a singing bird? Why don't I give you a chorus of 'The Good Ship'—"

"Hush. You're supposed to be an ordinary bird." Tevi smothered Klara's head with her hand while sending an exasperated glance at Jemeryl. The magic might be a mystery to her, but Tevi was well aware that Klara was little more than the sorcerer's alter ego. Jemeryl had explained the bond as being so close that she was, effectively, doing some of her own thinking in the bird's head. "Nobody at the guild house seems surprised by me having a pet magpie on my shoulder, but they would if she started talking."

"She won't. I can hardly feel her through the school shields. It's all I can do to keep her docile. Speech is out of the question."

Tevi frowned. "I thought the whole point of me having her was so that she could pass on messages."

"The extra-dimensional shields around the school are too strong, but I only need to step outside the school gates to talk to you, which will be much quicker than coming down to town."

"And supposing you're not able to step outside?"

"That would imply that something serious had happened."

"Serious is what I'm worried about."

"Don't." Jemeryl reached across and squeezed Tevi's hand. "As long as Klara doesn't start acting like a wild magpie, you know I'm all right. It means I'm still bound to her."

"And if she does start acting like a wild magpie?"

"Grab the warrant and rush to the school as fast as you can."

Jemeryl's words were not very comforting. Tevi stared at her tankard. Its pewter colour reminded her of the chalice that she had seen so often during her childhood. Back then, the chalice had been a reminder of the bygone sorcerer, but it had not been seen as valuable in itself. Who could have guessed that it would be the cause of so much trouble?

On the day that the big black bird had swooped in and taken it, the loss had been symbolic. Clearly, some mainland sorcerer had wanted the chalice, and that would have been the end of the matter—until her grandmother seized on it as a way to get rid of a potential embarrassment.

Not until she met Jemeryl had Tevi understood that the chalice was far more than a vessel to hold liquids. Within its structure, the chalice held the formula for every compound that had ever been made in it. In particular, this chalice held the results of some forbidden research, performed by the sorcerer Lorimal two hundred years before. Somebody had sent the bird for the chalice. The clear implication was that this person was now copying Lorimal's banned experiments. Hence their current mission in Ekranos, but they had not been given much information to work with.

Tevi frowned. "I wish we knew what this forbidden magic did."

"So do I, but I wasn't told."

"We don't even know how dangerous it is."

"Well, the Guardian said that Lorimal had been naïve rather than malicious. You don't create people-eating monsters through naïveté."

"So the same might be true for the person who took the chalice. Maybe they are just being curious."

Jemeryl shook her head. "If they found out about Lorimal, then they must have found out that she was stopped from completing her work. They can't claim ignorance. It is an act of deliberate treachery."

"That's a serious word to use."

"It's justified. Our oath of obedience to the Guardian is what holds the Coven together. It's what has kept the Protectorate going for centuries. Other sorcerers must have tried collaborating in the past, but whatever they did, it didn't last long enough to leave any trace. Once any sorcerer starts thinking that they can re-write the rulebook, before you know it, the Coven will be torn apart and the Protectorate will be destroyed. It doesn't matter so much what the rule is. Somebody has broken their oath and betrayed us all."

Tevi slumped down in her chair as familiar doubts resurfaced. "It doesn't make sense. On one level, your leaders in the Coven are saying that the future of the Protectorate is at stake. And then they send just you and me to sort it out on our own. Why didn't they send a dozen senior sorcerers?"

Jemeryl shrugged. "There's a lot they aren't telling us."

"Such as?"

"They were playing around with oracles before we met. Not just trying to read the future, they were trying to manipulate it. That was why they ordered me to go with you on your quest, even though, at the time, they didn't know you were looking for Lorimal's chalice."

"And I wasn't really looking for it."

"The important thing is that you are now—which was a result of their mucking about."

"So we know it is going to be all right? Their oracle told them that we'd catch the traitor without any other help?"

"I wish. Oracles don't work like that. And we're not even certain that the traitor is here."

"What happens if they're somewhere else?"

"The Guardian and the other seniors in Lyremouth said they'd take care of it."

"Supposing the person isn't even a member of the Coven?"

"Lorimal died over one hundred and fifty years ago. Only the Coven has records going back that far. Nobody outside the Coven could know that she had ever existed. Except..." Jemeryl's voice died.

"Except?"

"Even people in the Coven shouldn't be able to find out about her. All information about her work was deleted. And not long after she'd stopped working on whatever it was, she took her ill-conceived plant potion, which left her thinking like a daffodil. Everyone assumed she was then harmless and ignored her. No one paid any notice when she went missing off the coast of Walderim, until it was realised that her chalice had been lost with her. Then someone realised the formula was still in the memory chalice. So even more information about her was removed from the records. There shouldn't be anything left to set someone off on the trail of the chalice."

"Something must have been overlooked."

"Most likely yes. And Ekranos is the place to look, since Lorimal was a herbalist. All the Coven's leading authorities are here, and whatever record there is of Lorimal will be in the library."

"You said, 'most likely.' How else would someone find out about her?"

"Some people have always been told about Lorimal—such as the three most senior sorcerers at Lyremouth. The principal of the school here is another."

"Why?"

"On the off chance that the chalice turned up some day. The authorities thought it vital to keep watch against anyone trying to repeat Lorimal's work. That's why Iralin understood at once when I told her about your quest. Lorimal's name had meant nothing to me beforehand."

"So either the principal here is the traitor, or he's not doing his job very well."

Jemeryl smiled "My gut feeling is for the second option. Bramell is...well, let's say that it wouldn't be hard to pull the wool over his eyes. He lacks imagination. He clings to the rulebook like a limpet to a rock. It saves him having to make decisions. I don't think he trusts his own judgement, which is why I don't think he'd take Lorimal's chalice. He lacks the initiative and the nerve."

"I get this odd feeling you don't like him."

"No. I don't. He couldn't have got where he is without the ability to be a great sorcerer, but he wants to be a booking clerk. He's a waste of talent."

"Maybe taking the chalice is his bid to show what he can do."

"You haven't met the man." Jemeryl grimaced.

"Who, apart from him, is a suspect?"

"Surprisingly few." Jemeryl leaned forward and rested her head at an angle against her hand. "Our traitor had to find out about Lorimal, recover the chalice, and then work on it in secret. That last point means it has to be a senior sorcerer. A junior could manage the odd hour when no one was around, but it would be risky. They couldn't hide in a room all day without having to explain what they were doing."

"How many seniors are there?"

"Seven—including Bramell."

"Who are the others?"

"The second-most-senior sorcerer is the deputy, Neame. She's also free to do whatever she wants. Bramell leaves everything to do with herbalism to her. She's in charge of the hospital. In fact, if Bramell ever got his nose out of his ledgers, he'd realise that she's running the school, not him. It's ridiculous that Bramell was promoted over her."

"How did Bramell get chosen?"

"It would have been a ballot of the senior sorcerers in the Coven. Most would never have met either Bramell or Neame in person. Perhaps that had something to do with it. Bramell looks much more impressive from a distance."

"Might Neame be bitter and out for revenge?"

"I don't think so. It's purely personal, but I like Neame. I admire her for all the reasons that I don't admire Bramell. And she cares about people—the ordinary ungifted citizens. She really does. Her life is devoted to healing. I can't see her wanting to destroy the Protectorate."

"Could she have found out about Lorimal?"

"Possibly. All the books should have been removed from the main library, but there's a special section containing restricted information. Something about Lorimal is probably kept there just so Bramell can check up on what people shouldn't be doing."

"Neame has access to this area?"

"Yes. As do Bramell and Moragar, the librarian."

"Moragar's our third suspect?"

Jemeryl nodded. "He doesn't have the same degree of freedom as Bramell and Neame, but he's superbly placed to study anything that catches his attention. And if he wants to spend time alone in the library, after it has closed at night..." Jemeryl shrugged to emphasise the point. "Who's going to question it? Against him as a suspect is that he became chief librarian less than three years ago, a few months after the chalice was taken. Before that, he was deputy to the previous librarian and shouldn't have had access to restricted books, but—"

"The mate often knows more about what's going on than the captain," Tevi finished the sentence.

"True, although what I'd been going to say was that rules get broken."

Laughter erupted nearby. The sound dropped to an embarrassed murmur as soon as Jemeryl twisted to look, and the group of five merchants fixed their eyes on the tabletop. Jemeryl's face held a bemused frown when she turned back.

"Why do ungifted people assume sorcerers are offended by good humour?"

"Perhaps they're frightened you'll think they're laughing at you."

"I'm not paranoid. What is there to laugh at?"

Klara's beak opened a fraction. Tevi forestalled any comments with an admonishing finger, but a grin spread across her face and her mood lightened. It took little to imagine what Klara would have done with a gift like that.

Tevi reverted to the suspects. "Who else is on the list?"

"Levannue. She's in charge of non-medicinal herbalism and psychic studies. She has her own building where she can research whatever she fancies. Actually, her work is so specialised, most sorcerers wouldn't understand what she's doing even if she tried explaining it. I haven't had any contact with her, but I know she's been Bramell's partner for years. They have children and grandchildren in Ekranos. Which makes me think it's not her. I can't imagine anyone with the faintest tendency towards rebellion putting up with Bramell for longer than a one-night stand."

"Maybe his nitpicking has made her snap."

Jemeryl laughed. "Anyway, I don't see how she'd have found out about Lorimal. She doesn't have access to the restricted books, and Bramell would never break the rules by telling her."

"He might talk in his sleep."

"I think that if Bramell talks in his sleep, he'd be reciting the regulations concerning the maintenance of school property."

"Really? Do all sorcerers do that? I'd thought it was just a strange quirk of yours."

"Don't be silly. I'm sure I have far more interesting things to say."

"Well, maybe." Tevi grinned. "Who's next?"

"Orrago, I guess. She used to be principal, so she'll know about Lorimal, but she's not a serious suspect. Sorcerers don't generally retire. We usually patch ourselves together and die on our feet. However, Orrago developed a bad case of dementia. That's why she had to resign. It also means she's no longer capable of anything as complex as retrieving information from a memory chalice."

"Unless her mental state is due to taking some of Lorimal's plant potion."

"Nobody's mentioned her talking to the geraniums, and she was losing her grip long before the chalice was taken."

"Right, so there are just two more to go. Who are they?"

"One is master of apprentices, Uwien. But I don't think he's a candidate, as he's held the post for less than a year. Before that, he ran the apprentice school at Denbury—it's unlikely that any information about Lorimal is there. And even if Uwien got the chalice, he'd have no time to work on it. Keeping on top of the apprentices is a full-time job. I think he only sits down at mealtimes."

"We can't reject him. Maybe Denbury was overlooked too readily in the past and something was missed."

"A good point. But the last senior is definitely not a suspect. Roddis is head of admin, and she's a senior in name only. Administration used to be Bramell's post, and he's never let go. It would take a crowbar to separate him from his records. He double-checks everything Roddis does. She couldn't get away with an overdue library book, let alone researching into forbidden magic."

"That completes the list?"

"That completes the list," Jemeryl confirmed.

"You seem to be discounting all of them."

Jemeryl groaned. "No. It has to be one, and it's all just gut feelings. Hopefully I can find some real evidence."

Tevi leaned back and looked around the bar. While they had been talking, the number of customers present had dwindled. Candles had burned low; some had flickered out. Even the canaries were quiet. Klara had fallen asleep on the table, balanced on one leg. Tevi finished her drink and put the tankard down. She nudged it with her forefingers until the base lined up with two knots on the wooden surface. She had only to catch the eye of the bar staff to have the tankard refilled, free of charge, but she had drunk enough and would rather have paid anyway.

"How do we narrow down the suspects?"

"A good place to start is with the theft of the chalice. There are trained ravens at the school—for general use, not bound to any individual. I'll bet one of them took the chalice."

"Why does the school keep them?"

"Collecting samples. They can pick plants if a fresh herb is required urgently. They're big birds and can lift quite a weight. In the wild, they'll manage a rabbit without any trouble. Plus the whole crow family is particularly suited to magic." Jemeryl smiled affectionately at Klara. "A sorcerer can take over the bird and control where it goes and what it does. It's called mind-riding. However, with the shields, a sorcerer inside the school can't control a bird outside. I'll need to find out if anyone took a raven off for a few days during early summer, three years back." Jemeryl's expression shifted to a frown.

"What is it?"

"I'm wondering if I should add the raven keeper to the list of suspects. He could have sent a raven for the chalice without anyone else knowing."

"Is he a senior sorcerer?"

"Not technically. The way people talk about him, he doesn't seem to fit into the school hierarchy at all. He's a bit reclusive. I don't know how he could have learnt about Lorimal, but I guess information about her might have been overlooked in an unexpected place, such as a book of lunch menus for ravens."

"You're going to have to find out more about him—and everyone else."

"True." Jemeryl drained her drink. "I've had one stroke of luck, though I'm not sure if it's good or bad. I'm sharing a study with a sorcerer called Vine. She's the biggest gossip in the school. I might even add her to the list of suspects. If she's not found out about Lorimal's spell, it must be the only secret that's ever been successfully hidden from her."

"Why don't you ask her who's taken the chalice?"

Jemeryl laughed. "If I get desperate, I just might. She could be a useful source of information. The downside is that she may spread rumours about me. I daren't let her begin to suspect why I'm really in Ekranos. And I could tell she was dying to know who I was meeting today. I avoided her questions, but it can only be for a short time."

"Will it cause problems if she finds out?"

"I shouldn't think Vine personally will be bothered, but it won't go down well with Bramell. The authorities aren't keen on sorcerers getting emotionally involved with the ungifted. But he'll learn about us sooner or later. If I'm secretive, it will seem as if I'm trying to hide something. Anyway, he can't stop me. It counts as a private matter."

"Just as long as they can't stop us meeting." Tevi spoke softly. "I've missed you."

Jemeryl squeezed Tevi's hand. "I know. Come on. You've got to get up early. Let's go to our room."

The squeak as their chairs were pushed back woke Klara, who ruffled her feathers, then hopped onto Tevi's proffered wrist. Quietly, the two young women slipped out through the doorway at the rear of the bar.

Chapter Three—The Hunt Begins

Jemeryl rolled over, awakened by movement. The moon had long since set, but the outline of the window was visible. Dawn was not far off. She summoned a faint light globe, barely sufficient to reveal the room.

Tevi was sitting on the side of the bed, feeling for her discarded clothing. At the soft light, she glanced over her shoulder apologetically. "Sorry. I didn't mean to wake you. I'm due at the docks in an hour, but there's no need for you to get up."

"Yes, there is. I can sleep in tomorrow. This is our last chance to talk for days." Jemeryl scrambled out of bed and began pulling on her clothes.

"I don't know what there'll be for breakfast."

"Whatever it is will be all the better for eating it with you."

Tevi laughed. "Now you're trying to sweet-talk me."

"Just keeping in practice."

Nobody was about when they left their room, but a succession of loud snores issued from the common dormitory. The rasping bass followed them along the corridor and down the staircase. Jemeryl winced at the sound. Yet one more reason to be glad that her status meant she always got private accommodation at inns. Most folk had to share a room, and even a bed, with strangers.

The predawn air was chill in the open courtyard, and the stars were undimmed. However, a soft tinge stained the eastern skyline. The bar was dark and deserted when they entered. Shutters were closed, and chairs were stacked on tables. A band of light shone under the door to the kitchen. Jemeryl push it open and poked her head around.

In the light of an oil lamp, a boy was scrubbing the floor. Suds overflowed a large wooden pail. His clothes were as wet as the fistful of rags he was using and in only marginally better condition. At the squeak of the hinges, he sprung to his feet, futilely trying to dry his hands on his soaking apron. He backed away, wide-eyed.

His mouth opened and closed a few times before he managed to ask, "You're one of the ladies wanting early breakfast?"

"Yes, please."

"Cook's left the things out."

No further information was forthcoming. In the end, Jemeryl gently prompted, "Where?"

"Oh, no. Sit down. I'll bring it to you...ma'am."

The boy's eyes kept flicking to Jemeryl's wrist. She judged that fear of sorcerers had scared him witless, and there was little point trying to reassure him.

She let the door swing shut and joined Tevi, who had cleared one of the tables. Jemeryl floated the globe above them. Its light glinted off the row of clean tankards hanging over the counter and cast shadows in the far corners.

She pulled back a chair and sat down. "I think breakfast is on the way."

"You sound as if you have doubts."

"I wouldn't want to stake much on the abilities of our waiter for this morning."

Despite Jemeryl's misgivings, the door to the kitchen opened shortly, and the boy came out carrying a well-laden tray. With the general demeanour of a frightened rabbit, he sidled to their table and deposited a basket piled with rolls, bowls of honey and butter, an irregularly shaped lump of blue-veined cheese, two empty beakers, and a jug of warm milk. Then he turned and fled.

"What's up with him?" Tevi asked, stifling a yawn.

"He's frightened of me."

Klara landed on the table. "It's true that you don't look your best in the morning, but that's a bit excessive."

Tevi laughed and poured the milk. "So what's our plan of action?"

Jemeryl broke open a roll before answering and, after a critical appraisal of the cheese, rejected it in favour of honey. "I want to search the library. As I said last night, perhaps a reference to Lorimal was overlooked, and I could check if anyone's shown an interest in your islands. I'll also see if a record is kept of who takes ravens off-site. If not, it will be down to Vine's memory to work out who could have sent the raven to Storenseg."

Tevi had been less suspicious of the cheese and had squashed a wedge into one of the rolls. She swallowed before speaking. "Is there anything for me to do?"

"It's a long shot, but we must remember we're not sure the culprit is in Ekranos. One thing Iralin suggested is a rare component the spell requires, made from the nectar of the bucket orchid. The drug is narcotic and open to misuse, so it's strictly monitored. If someone is working on Lorimal's spell, they couldn't openly withdraw it from the dispensary. I'd like to see if any has gone missing. Unfortunately, I don't think we can trust Orrago's books, and not just because she's a suspect." Jemeryl looked at Tevi. "Could you get access to the customs records? The nectar requires a special import licence, so it will be logged. If you can note how much has entered the school over the last three years, I'll see if it can be accounted for."

"The records are kept in an office not far from our guardroom. It shouldn't be too hard to get a look at the books."

"Great."

"There's one problem."

"What?"

"I can't read."

Jemeryl caught her breath, surprised more by her own oversight than Tevi's admission. "No, I suppose not. I guess a lot of people can't." Literacy was widespread in the Protectorate but far from universal. Maybe a third of the population could do little more than sign their own names. "It doesn't matter. If you let Klara see the books, she can memorise them. I'll retrieve the information when we meet."

Jemeryl picked up Klara. For a few seconds, the two of them locked eyes. Then Jemeryl carefully returned the somewhat dazed bird to the tabletop.

"She knows what to do. Hold the page open in front of her; say the words, 'Read, Klara' and she'll store the image."

"Actually, I've just realised there's another problem with Klara. I haven't time to drop her off at the guild house."

"Don't worry. I'll see she gets back."

"People will wonder if she flies in on her own."

"Tell them she's a homing magpie."

"Even mercenaries aren't that gullible."

"Then say a friend dropped her off. I can't imagine anyone checking."

Tevi licked the traces of honey from her fingers before pulling back the shutters of the nearest window. The roofs on the far side of the square stood out against the lightening sky. The stars were fading. She shrugged. "Oh, well. Maybe no one will notice. I've got to rush."

A wave of cold air rippled into the room when Tevi pulled the door open. The town was emerging from darkness. A lone set of footsteps echoed from a nearby street. Somewhere, a shutter was flung back with a crash. Jemeryl stood at the doorway to claim one last kiss and then watched as Tevi strode across the square. She stayed until the mercenary disappeared into an alley, then she closed the door and looked around the tavern. Her eyes fixed on the remains of breakfast littering the table.

There was plenty of time before she was due back at the school. Dawn starts were not the rule for sorcerers. However, she would rather avoid the other customers and inn staff. The creak of floorboards overhead announced that people were stirring. The sound sent her hurrying back to the room she had shared with Tevi.

She had intended to pack and be gone as soon as possible, but a pensive lethargy washed over her once she was alone in the room. She wandered about restlessly, half-heartedly picking things up. It seemed so quiet and very empty now that Tevi had gone.

A pair of tall windows led onto a narrow balcony overlooking the square. Jemeryl abandoned the packing and leant her shoulder against the glass, feeling it cold and hard through her clothing. She stood for a long time, staring across the roofs of Ekranos while the growing light picked out the School of Herbalism, perched high on the distant cliffs.

❖

Tevi marched through the deserted town. The beat of her feet echoed between dark houses. At a fountain, she paused to splash ice-cold water over her face, watched by a pair of cats huddled in a baker's doorway. Two sets of unblinking eyes followed her as she set off again.

Cold air pinched the wet skin on her face. Tevi pulled her jacket around her and buried her hands in the pockets. The freezing water had swept away the last traces of sleep.

Soon, she emerged onto the quay. Dawn was breaking, pink on the horizon. Tevi walked along the salt-encrusted flagstones. The light was brighter in the open. The sea was a flat grey plain. Already, the dark figures of sailors were climbing in the rigging of the moored ships, readying their craft for departure on the tide.

A group of her colleagues was assembling by the customs house. Tevi slipped into their ranks while attempting to hide a yawn behind her hand, but it did not pass unnoticed. A string of predictable comments flew in her direction. Tevi laughed, taking the ribald teasing in good part. The senior officer arrived seconds later to instil order. After a few last jibes, the mercenaries settled down to receive their orders for the day.

❖

The sun was just past its zenith when Jemeryl entered the library, leaving the warmth outside for the cool interior. The sudden change in temperature made her shiver. She stood in the cavernous main hall and stared around. Bookshelves stretched away on all sides like the ranks of a sculptured army. The central hall rose through all three floors of the building. Jemeryl tipped her head back to view the windows high in the domed roof. Shafts of light streamed past the balconies marking the upper levels.

She strolled forward between the rows of books, manuscripts, and scrolls. The air felt chill. Jemeryl imagined that the building gained in popularity during the scorching Ekranos summer, but in late spring, the temperature outside was pleasant and the aisles were virtually deserted.

The bookshelves themselves were a jumble of styles and woods, some plain and functional, some intricately carved. An ornate end panel caught Jemeryl's attention. Through the branches of a tree, a tribe of monkeys played with books, squabbling and chasing among the leaves. One ape squatting near the bottom was experimentally chewing pages. Predictably, someone's name was scratched against the dim-witted animal. Jemeryl considered the scene. Was the carving supposed to show the abuse of the tree of knowledge, or had the carpenter's intent been more whimsical?

The shelves held dog-eared pamphlets, yellowing with age, although the protective spells of the library kept them intact. Jemeryl started to pull one out but stopped. She had not come for entertainment.

This was her first free afternoon since the meeting at the Inn of Singing Birds, four days before. She had been tempted to go down to Ekranos. However, Tevi was on duty until long after midnight. Catching a snatched meeting during a meal break was not worth drawing attention to themselves. Jemeryl pushed the pamphlet back into place and walked on. If she could not see Tevi, she could at least do something useful.

The library catalogue was in a small ground-floor room leading off the main hall. Jemeryl stood at the doorway. A shelf ran along one wall. On it, leather-bound index books were neatly arranged, each with a handwritten label. At the far end was a desk with a heavy wooden bench in front; both were pitted and stained with age, although their characters were incongruous. The bench was simple square-cut timber; the desk was decorative, with legs carved like an overweight griffin.

After selecting an index, Jemeryl slid between table and bench, and winced as she cracked her knee against the desk. Its style was definitely ornate rather than practical. She sat, rubbing the bruise with one hand while flipping open the book with the other.

To the eyes of the ungifted, each page was simply a list of library contents, with notes on location, usable by anyone who could read. But to a sorcerer, it marked the end of an incantation web, where the essence of the library was mapped into normal space.

It was an impressive feat of magic. Once done, it required only minimal maintenance. The core spells were old, the achievement of bygone librarians, but there were fresh patches, neat and efficient, by the new chief librarian. Jemeryl examined Moragar's handiwork, trying to gauge the abilities of her third main suspect.

He's wasted as a herbalist. No wonder he opted to work in the library. Jemeryl smiled wryly at herself. She was sure Moragar would be flattered by her commendation.

At the back of the desk, a well-chewed quill lay beside an inkwell. Jemeryl found a scrap of paper and began noting down references. While she worked, an older witch wandered in and began flicking through another index. The rustle of paper competed with the scratching of Jemeryl's pen to disturb the heavy silence of the library.

❖

The following four hours did not produce anything apart from one dead end after another. Whoever had deleted evidence of Lorimal's banned work had done a thorough job. Even her prior knowledge did not help Jemeryl discover anything prohibited. It was hard enough just to spot the holes where information had been withdrawn.

The afternoon was drawing to a close. Jemeryl wandered into the last section she intended to investigate that day, a long, thin room on the second floor. The walls on both sides were lined with rows of handwritten manuscripts, representing generations of sorcerers pursuing their own arcane interests.

According to the index, there was one junior thesis by Lorimal herself: "The prevention of cancerous growths and associated tumours." It predated her illegal work by several years and was undoubtedly harmless. The item was too obvious to have been overlooked before. Jemeryl's main reason for seeking out the handwritten thesis was a desire to touch something Lorimal had owned—a link with the woman.

The manuscripts were arranged, unhelpfully, by year rather than author or subject. Fortunately, Jemeryl could follow the web of the index, flowing down the room and along the shelves—to a blank.

She stopped short, staring at the spot where the manuscript should be. A second, meticulous search, taking in the shelves above and below, confirmed that it had not been misfiled.

Jemeryl tried to curb her excitement. There were legitimate reasons why the manuscript might be missing. First, she should make sure that the report had not simply been borrowed. Jemeryl pressed her hands against her face, trying to smooth her features into an expression of studious academic contemplation, and returned to the central hall.

If Lorimal's manuscript had been stolen, it would point to the traitor, whereas if the manuscript had been taken for lawful purposes, the borrower would have openly declared it. The place to start was the register of library withdrawals, on the lectern by the main door.

The thick book lay open on a page half-covered in assorted handwriting. Sorcerers were allowed to sign out books, although apprentices needed authorisation. It took seconds to check that none of the entries on the first page related to Lorimal's report, and then Jemeryl began working her way back.

Page after page turned. Jemeryl's finger traced up the column of titles. By the time she was two-thirds of the way back through the register, the issue dates were a year old, and there were no longer any blank spaces in the column for date of return.

Jemeryl flipped to the preceding page. Her attention was totally given to her search, blocking out all else, until a voice made her jump.

"Can I help you?"

Jemeryl turned around to find herself face to face with the chief librarian. "Er...I was after a book, but um...someone seems to have borrowed it."

"Which book was it? Perhaps I can remember." Moragar raised a hand to his forehead as if hoping to push the memory into place.

Seen at close quarters, Moragar was both younger and shorter than expected, a squat, energetic man of about thirty. He possessed a bouncy enthusiasm seeming out of place in the solemn library. He also had a strong Walderim accent that caught Jemeryl's ear even as she tried to extricate herself.

"Oh, it's not important. I can probably find another book that will do."

Jemeryl's words were dismissed with an upheld hand. Moragar stepped to the lectern and looked at the open page. He shook his head vigorously. "Nothing is outstanding from that far back. Have you looked in the permanent loan record?" Without waiting for a reply, Moragar marched to a shelf and pulled down another volume. "What's the name of the author?"

"Please, there's no need to trouble yourself, sir." If Moragar was guilty, she dare not alert his suspicions by showing interest in Lorimal.

"It's no bother, and there's no need to call me 'sir.' I'm not old enough to carry it off." Moragar smiled in a friendly fashion and leafed through the book. He looked up, waiting.

Further evasion could only make things worse. In her most nonchalant tone, Jemeryl said, "It was a manuscript by a sorcerer called Lorimal."

"Well, *that's* not in here." Moragar slammed the book shut and rammed it onto its shelf. The anger left Jemeryl off balance, but the librarian calmed just as quickly and patted her arm. "Don't worry; it's not you I'm annoyed at. I hate it when books go missing, especially originals. But we have a copy. Come on; follow me."

Moragar bounded away down an aisle, leaving Jemeryl trailing in his wake, dazed by the librarian's lightning mood shifts. He halted by a bookcase at the back of the hall. A thick volume removed itself from the top shelf and gently drifted down to land in Jemeryl's hands.

"There's a transcript in there. I think it's Chapter Three."

"Thank you."

Jemeryl stared at the green leather binding while her suspicion grew. Why was Moragar so familiar with Lorimal's work? Carefully shifting her expression to one of innocence, Jemeryl raised her eyes and smiled. "I'm impressed. Do you know the location of every article in the library?"

"Hardly. But that one is etched on my memory. Orrago borrowed it years ago, although she can't remember. Poor thing. Druse was furious. He was chief librarian at the time. He didn't make much fuss. He didn't want to upset Orrago. She'd only just resigned, but he had me turn the entire school upside down looking for it. Strictly speaking, the manuscript isn't lost. I was able to dowse it to the dispensary. But you could lose half the library in there. I should delete it from the catalogue, but I keep hoping it will turn up."

Moragar led the way back to the withdrawal register, where Jemeryl entered her name and the book's title.

"Thank you again."

"Oh, don't mention it." Moragar's voice was casual to the point of being dismissive.

Something about the tone jarred. As Jemeryl left the building, an instinct prompted her to look back. Moragar was still by the register, staring at her intently. His forehead was knotted, and a hand was pressed firmly against his lips. When he saw her looking, Moragar turned around sharply and disappeared into the depths of the library. Jemeryl knew there was something important that the librarian was not saying.

❖

Rapid footsteps clattered on the veranda overhead as Jemeryl reached the juniors' quarters. Rather than pass on the narrow stairway, she waited at the bottom. Feet came into view around the corner, followed by legs and a body belonging to her study partner.

Vine grinned and took the last two steps with a hop. “Have you been in the library?”

“Yes. But you don’t get points for soothsaying, since I’m holding a book.”

“I wasn’t expecting any. Merely demonstrating my uncanny powers of observation. Anything exciting happening?”

“In the library? Do you mean apart from the massed barbarian drummers and the usual wild orgy in the index room?”

“How inconsiderate. All that banging when you’re trying to read. The drumming can be distracting as well.”

Matching Vine’s cheerful smile, Jemeryl leaned against the wall and let out a deep sigh. “Actually, it’s been incredibly tedious. I’ve spent all afternoon searching for some information that’s not there.”

“Did you ask Moragar? He’s usually helpful.”

“We had a brief meeting.”

“What did you think of him?”

“Like you say, he was helpful and friendly. For a senior. He seems young, though.”

Vine nodded. “He is. It wasn’t expected he would be promoted so soon, but Druse died unexpectedly three years back. He was the previous librarian. We had plague in Ekranos, you know. Someone came for treatment and passed it on to most of the school.”

“That’s awful. How many people died?” All amusement left Jemeryl’s voice.

“Druse was the only sorcerer. Surprising, as he wasn’t old, while people like Orrago survived. I suppose you can’t tell with these things. Moragar was devastated. He’d been close to Druse, and I suspect he’d been a good bit closer than was generally realised, if you get my drift.”

“According to you, most people in the school have been a good bit closer at one time or another.”

“They have. Believe me, they have. It gets very incestuous,” Vine said emphatically. “But I’ve got to dash. Catch you later.”

Vine trotted away, leaving Jemeryl to climb the stairs. Sitting in the study, she examined the book’s cover before leafing to the right page. The area of magic was not one that interested her. It was too reminiscent of the hospital wards. However, if the original was worth stealing, the copy must contain some clues. Jemeryl pursed her lips. If she could only spot them.

❖

The dim alley was not so much a thoroughfare as a space between two warehouses, too narrow for the sun's rays to penetrate. In the enclosed space, the salty tang of the sea was laced with fragrant scents—leather and spice and grain—seeping through the wooden slats on either side.

The sweet smells teased Tevi's nose as she strode along. She emerged into sunshine at the far end, on the main road leading from the port into the centre of Ekranos. A barrage of noise assailed her. Laden carts rolled by, wheels clattering along the worn cobbles. Porters, sailors, and merchants called to one another. Tevi paused before launching herself into the melee, dodging the carts and the people for the few dozen yards it took her to reach her destination: the record offices belonging to the port authorities.

Even before the door shut behind her, blocking out the clamour, Tevi was aware of an atmosphere of calm, at odds with the chaos outside. Orderly rows of books lined the walls, dampening any sounds. The tiled floor was swept clean. Pens, inks, and sealing wax sat in their holders. The desk filling the middle of the room was large enough for a dozen people to work at comfortably, although the office was deserted apart from a middle-aged woman with a hard face and ink-stained hands—a single priest in this shrine of bureaucracy.

The clerk looked up. "Can I help you?"

"The *Ruby Wand* is about to depart, bound for Lyremouth. The captain needs these stamped." Tevi held out the papers.

"You'll have to wait. The administrator has been called out. He should be back shortly. Take a seat, if you want." The clerk gestured at a stool and turned back to her work.

Tevi ignored the offer and instead slowly paced the length of the room, considering the bookshelves. This was the third time she had been inside the office. The information Jemeryl wanted was there, but how to find it? Tevi glanced at the grey head bent over the desk. The clerk must know exactly where to look. Asking her directly was not prudent, but there might be other ways.

"It must be wonderful, being able to read and write."

"It's a valuable skill," the clerk conceded without looking up.

"Not needing to rely on memory. You just write something down and then go back years later and see what it was. The very words. I mean, you can do that, can't you?" The display of naïve innocence was not hard. The idea of writing had Tevi in awe.

The clerk was clearly torn between irritation and amusement. In the end, the latter won out, and she lay down her pen. "That's the general idea."

"Is it hard to learn?"

"It takes perseverance and aptitude."

"Then you can write down anything at all?"

"If you can say it, you can write it."

Tevi shaped her lips into a soundless whistle. "You record all the shipments and taxes here?"

"That's our job."

"So if someone wanted to know...oh, for example"—Tevi stared at the ceiling and snapped her fingers, as if picking an item at random—"how much nectar of the bucket orchid had arrived in the last three years. Could you tell them?"

"That would be an easy one. The nectar requires a special licence. Only the sorcerers at the school are allowed to import it." The clerk pointed to a thin book. "It will all be logged in there."

Tevi extracted it from the shelf, while trying to disguise her delight. Memorising one thin book was surely a feasible task for Klara, but more was to come.

The clerk beckoned Tevi over and took the book. She flipped it open with deft fingers. "There. That's the page you'd want. All you'd have to do is tally up the numbers in this column. Of course, you'd need to be able to add as well as read."

The patronising tone might have stung, had Tevi not been feeling more than a touch smug herself. Anyway, she was sure the clerk was trying to be friendly.

Tevi lifted the open book from the desk and strolled back while counting the pages. There would be no problem finding the records again. The clerk returned to her work, her face making it plain that she felt she had been generous enough with her time.

Tevi did not have long to wait. The book was scarcely back on the shelf when there was a rattle of the door latch, and the administrator stepped into the office.

"Sir. The *Ruby Wand* is about to sail for Lyremouth. The captain needs these stamped." Tevi scooped the papers from the desk and presented them.

The administrator studied the sheets while walking to one end of the desk. With a nod, he picked up the wax. The seal itself hung on a chain from his belt. In short order, the papers received their imprint and Tevi was out in the sunshine, heading back to the docks. A broad smile lit her face. She had been more successful than she had dared hope. All that now remained was to return with Klara when the office was empty.

❖

Heavy thunderclouds hung low in the sky. The sixth dimension was rippling and snapping, energised by the impending storm. Jemeryl slumped back and held out a hand. Charged ions leapt between her fingertips. The sparks dropped to the desktop in a dazzling snow. Fun, but it made concentrating on the text very difficult.

After more wasted minutes, Jemeryl abandoned the attempt to read. She closed the book and sat with her fingers drumming on the cover. This was the third time she had gone through Lorimal's thesis, and she still could find nothing to explain why someone had stolen the original. The theory was innocent, although unorthodox. Lorimal had been an unconventional thinker of the first order.

"But nothing like as unconventional as she was after taking the plant potion," Jemeryl addressed the empty room.

She stretched back and frowned at the book. Perhaps when the storm broke, she would be able to think more clearly. A distant boom rumbled over the cliff tops. In the following silence, she heard footsteps. The study door opened with a squeak, and then there was nothing. Jemeryl twisted in her seat. Vine was holding the door slightly ajar and peering out through the crack.

"You know, I think I'm right. There *is* something going on between those two." Vine pushed the door shut. She plonked herself down in the free chair and propped her feet on her desk. "I wonder what Beck will say when he finds out. We could be in for fireworks."

A flash of sheet lightning interrupted Vine's musing. The sky lit up from deep within the clouds. Thunder crashed over the school, and the first belt of rain splattered against the window. The staccato rhythm combined with the shrieks of a group of apprentices caught in the open.

Vine rolled her head to look at Jemeryl. "You know, this is bad timing from your point of view. If the storm had hit tomorrow morning, you'd miss your session with Tapley."

"I don't mind. I'm looking forward to it."

"You're what?"

"It has to be more fun than the hospital."

"Now, there we hear the voice of inexperience. Working with Tapley is as much fun as trapping your fingers in the door and far less exciting."

"It can't be that bad."

"It is. Oh, it is. I can guarantee that by lunchtime, you'll have discovered whole new meanings for the word 'boredom.'"

Jemeryl grinned. "At least I've got the afternoon free. Hopefully that will keep me going."

"Especially if you're going into town to meet your young mercenary," Vine said with feigned nonchalance.

Jemeryl's smile faded. Their extended perceptions meant a community of sorcerers could not maintain the same standards of privacy as the ungifted, but deliberate prying was a breach of etiquette.

"Go on, then. Ask me how I found out." Vine was clearly delighted with herself.

"I assume you've been indulging in unofficial scrying."

Vine shook her head vigorously. "One of the kitchen staff at the Inn of Singing Birds has a sister who works in the fish market. She told our cook's son that a junior sorcerer spent a night with a mercenary. He told me. I worked out who was free that night and came up with your name."

Jemeryl sighed in resignation. Vine was incorrigible, but it was impossible to stay angry with her, especially as no worse intrusion was involved. "All right, I confess."

"So what's she like?"

"You mean your sources haven't given a graphic description?"

"Well, yes. But I'd still like some of the details confirmed." Vine's expression became more serious. "Actually, you're wise to play it quiet.

Bramell won't approve. Not that he can do anything, but you'll be in for the lecture entitled 'Suitable relationships with the ungifted.' I know; I had it myself last year."

"Someone nice?"

"A relative of one of the patients. It wasn't a big thing, but Bramell stuck his nose in. It's all right for him; he's been hitched to Levannue for years. The rest of us appreciate the occasional change of scenery."

"What's Levannue like? I've only seen her from a distance."

"She's all right, I suppose." Vine did not sound convinced. "Competent. Takes herself too seriously."

"Most seniors do."

"She's turned it into an art form. She can also rub people the wrong way." Vine glanced at the closed door and swung her feet down. She leaned forward and pitched her voice just loud enough to be heard over the pounding rain. "There are rumours about her as head of psychology. Levannue was treating Orrago's dementia even before she retired. It's been suggested that she used undue influence, prompting Orrago to endorse Bramell for principal rather than Neame. Not only is she Bramell's partner, but she and Neame hate each other and have for years."

"Orrago would have guarded herself."

"Orrago was already going senile, and you have to drop your defences when you become a psychiatric patient."

It was a valid point. However, Jemeryl's interest had been caught by something else Vine had said. "Why do Levannue and Neame hate each other? "

"It's an old argument, going back to when they were students," Vine said uneasily.

"What about? Does anyone know?"

"It wasn't really...I guess they were both partly in the wrong..." Vine ground to a halt.

Jemeryl was astonished. There was a topic that the school gossip did not want to discuss! And although it was probably of no relevance to the search for the traitor, it might give an insight into the two senior sorcerers. She was trying to think of a way of probing tactfully when the door was flung open. One rather damp witch burst in.

"Hey, Vine! Have you heard about what's just happened between Beck and Jona?"

Vine spun to face the excited speaker. "No, what?"

Despite irritation at the interruption, Jemeryl could not help grinning. Vine's network of sources was so very efficient. It was a pity she could not recruit them in the search for the traitor.

Chapter Four—Trouble from the Past

Jemeryl crossed the yard inside the school gates. A small globe lit her way. The ground was drying, but numerous puddles still dotted the paving. Only ragged bands of cloud remained, scraps of toned grey against the black sky. Stars shone bright and hard, as if scrubbed clean by the storm. A breeze stirred the clammy air.

"Excuse me, ma'am. Please, can you help us?" The speaker was a young man, tall and fair-haired. His face showed pale in the light of the globe. Behind him, two others were supporting another, who hung motionless in their grasp.

"What do you want?"

"It's Gewyn. We've just come back across the Eastern Ocean. We docked this afternoon. Gewyn's picked up something nasty. Please, ma'am. We're worried about her."

It did not take a close inspection for Jemeryl to know their fears were justified. The woman was almost unconscious in her friends' arms. Her breath came in strained gasps. Her skin had a blotched yellow sheen that matched her aura. The gatekeeper, who should have been there to direct visitors, would probably return shortly, but the sick woman was in no state to, literally, hang around.

"Follow me." Jemeryl led the way to the hospital.

This was definitely one for Neame. However, Jemeryl did not wish to go traipsing through the wards with her sorry retinue. She halted in the lobby of the main building and was looking around, wondering what was best, when a door opened.

To Jemeryl's relief, it was Erlam who appeared. He was a skilled healer with a reputation for calmness and competence, although his caring nature was sometimes undermined by a cynical sense of humour. He was not yet thirty but was already tipped as Neame's successor.

"Erlam. This woman's just arrived. I think Neame should see her."

Erlam grasped the situation immediately. "How long has she been like this?" he asked the friends.

"She's been complaining about aches for two days. It was only last night she really got bad."

"I'll get Neame. I was talking to her only a few minutes ago."

Before going, Erlam beckoned Jemeryl aside. "Take her straight to the quarantine quarters, and keep her friends with her. Try not to worry them, but don't let anyone wander off. The fewer people they meet, the better."

"What's wrong with the woman?"

"I'm fairly sure it's marsh plague."

"It's serious?"

"Of course. Neame needs to be here." Erlam hurried away.

The quarantine section was on the upper floor in an adjacent block. The room was austere, empty apart from two beds, a table, and a wooden chair. Jemeryl was grateful that the bars on the window were less conspicuous than in daylight. There was also a lock on the door, more to keep out the unwary than to confine the patient, although that option was available.

The cell-like room depressed the spirits of the small group even further, if that was possible. After laying the sick woman down, two slumped despondently on the other bed, holding hands. The third friend, the tall man who had first hailed Jemeryl, came to stand beside her.

"Will Gewyn be all right?" His strained tone made it clear he feared the worst.

Fortunately, Jemeryl was spared the need to answer by footsteps in the corridor outside. She rushed to the door, hoping to see Neame. However, Erlam was alone, and if he had looked concerned before, his expression now was positively grim.

Jemeryl stepped forward to meet him and pulled the door closed behind her. "What's wrong? Couldn't you find Neame?"

"I found Neame. She won't be long. But I've just met Levannue, who's also looking for her. She's lying in wait downstairs. I think she wants to have part two of an argument they started earlier today."

"Are you sure it isn't part four hundred of an argument they started a couple of decades ago?"

Erlam glanced at Jemeryl. "Of course. You share a study with the Grapevine, don't you?"

"Just something she mentioned in passing."

"What hasn't she mentioned in passing?"

Jemeryl shrugged in place of an answer. The uneasy silence did not last long. Almost immediately, they heard the door below open.

"Neame. I want to talk to you." It was Levannue's officious voice.

"Tough. It will have to wait," Neame snapped back.

"It's important."

"You might think so."

Jemeryl realised that she was about to be caught in the middle of a quarrel between two senior sorcerers. Despite the chance that the suspects might, in anger, slip their guard and drop a clue, Jemeryl would still far rather have been somewhere else. Giving any impression of taking sides would be extremely unwise.

"I'd expected better manners from you."

"You can expect what you like."

"This will only take five minutes—"

"I don't have five minutes to waste swapping insults with you."

Neame reached the top of the stairs. Her lips were compressed in a tight line, and her eyes glinted. Jemeryl had never seen the deputy look so unapproachable. Wordlessly, Erlam pointed to the room containing the patient. Just as Neame was opening the door, Levannue appeared in the stairwell.

The head of psychic studies was obviously furious, although her appearance was as neat as ever. Levannue's short iron-grey hair was moulded to her head like a helmet. Her tendency to appear hawk-like was not improved by her temper. Her frame was light, with finely formed bones. Jemeryl could imagine them rattling with anger.

The sight of two junior sorcerers listening to the argument brought Levannue to a halt and left her clearly wondering how best to maintain the dignity of her status.

"Neame. What is so important that it can't wait?" Levannue made a last bid for attention.

The deputy acted as if she had not heard and entered the quarantine room. Levannue, after a moment of hesitation, made as if to follow.

Erlam managed to interpose himself. "Excuse me, ma'am. There's a patient who's just arrived with some friends. Neame will be examining them."

His tone was pitched somewhere between explanation and entreaty, but his point was not lost. Bad enough that junior sorcerers had overheard the quarrel. Levannue would certainly not continue bickering in front of the ungifted.

"Neame should have said."

"I'm sure if she hadn't been so concerned—"

"And I'm sure she enjoyed the chance to be unpleasant." After a last furious glare at the door, Levannue marched off, leaving the two younger sorcerers alone.

Jemeryl had been holding her breath. She let it out in a rush. To her surprise, she felt sympathy for Levannue. It was as if Neame had been deliberately provoking her adversary by refusing to provide any explanation. Yet the behaviour was so untypical that Jemeryl was sure there had to be more to it.

"Squabbling like children." Erlam's voice carried surprising vehemence.

"Neame wasn't helpful."

"She never is where Levannue is involved."

"Vine didn't tell me what the original argument was."

"Didn't she?" Erlam sounded surprised but then shrugged. "Anyway, it's irrelevant by now; there's too much history in between. And to be honest, they aren't usually this bad. I think Neame was genuinely worried by news of marsh plague."

Jemeryl noticed Erlam also had avoided telling her of the root of the argument. She was going to have to pump Vine for details. The school gossip would be an easier target than Erlam. She contented herself with asking, "Is the disease serious enough to upset Neame that much?"

"Yes."

"How far could it spread?"

"It could cause trouble in Ekranos, but it won't infect the rest of the Protectorate. It's linked to the breeding cycle of a type of gnat, so it's restricted to spring in hot climates. It also requires still water to breed. Unfortunately, there are several spots around the Dhaliki that suit it perfectly."

"You sound very certain. Have you seen it before?"

"I think so. It was a month or so later when it arrived last time, but there was a late spring that year."

"Was that three years back? When your sorcerer died?"

Erlam flinched. "Vine told you about that as well?" His tone was icy.

The severity of his reaction surprised Jemeryl. Vine had said nothing to predict it. "Druse, your librarian. Vine said he died of plague."

Erlam's shoulders sagged. "Oh, yes. Him."

"Did another sorcerer at the school die as well?"

"No."

"Oh." Jemeryl was confused. "Do you think we'll be all right now?"

"The main risk is to other patients who are already sick and vulnerable. But Neame developed a cure. And I'd better see if she wants my help. You can go." It was a curt dismissal. Then Erlam rubbed a hand across his face as if sweeping a bad memory away. His expression softened, and he gave Jemeryl a sad smile. "Go on. You've done your work for today. If you hang around, someone will only give you more."

It was good advice. As Jemeryl walked back to her room, she considered what she had learned. Erlam's reaction to Druse's death was unexpected, as was Neame's behaviour with Levannue. In all likelihood, neither was relevant to the search for the traitor, but one fact had registered firmly: Plague had been raging in Ekranos at exactly the same time as the theft of the chalice. Exactly how it tied in was unclear, but Jemeryl had the sure sense, born of her sorcerer's training, that it was no coincidence.

❖

At the rear of the school was an open field. The turf rolled away, dotted with white flowers, until it abruptly cut short at the cliff's edge. The early morning sun warmed the air, although the ground was still squelchy underfoot from the previous day's rain. The risk of slipping forced Jemeryl to go cautiously. Fortunately, her destination was not far, and she reached the shack where the ravens were kept without mishap.

The roost was built from rough timber, open along one side, with a low thatch roof. Jemeryl ducked under the eaves. The ground inside was covered in loose straw, mud-soaked in places. Running along the back was a shoulder-height rail.

Four ravens were perched there, huddled at one end as if engaged in a private debate. They were bigger than she expected, stocky, boxlike shapes easily three times the length of Klara. They fixed her with beady eyes. Not a feather was out of place, yet they gave the impression of being untidy. There was no sign of the keeper. A sound made Jemeryl look down. Two more ravens hopped over the straw towards her, bounding in an ungainly, sideways fashion.

It was hard to tell if the ravens were friendly and unwise to use magic until she knew what other spells controlled them. Jemeryl was considering a strategic retreat when she heard someone coming, muttering cheerfully. The ravens clearly recognised the voice and replied with throaty chirps that rose to full-volume caws as Tapley arrived, carrying a large wooden bucket.

The raven keeper was roughly Jemeryl's height, but his build could only be described as scrawny. Deeply lined skin was drawn tight to the outline of his skull. His pale hair was cropped short. He moved with jerky, exaggerated gestures, as if imitating the ravens, although his looks were more reminiscent of a newly hatched, featherless chick. His age could have been anywhere between forty and seventy.

At the sight of his visitor, Tapley came to a standstill.

"If you please, sir, I have been detailed to work with you. My name's Jemeryl." She was uncertain of Tapley's status. The keeper was too old to count as a junior sorcerer, but nobody spoke of him with the respect a senior position usually received.

"You're new here."

It could have been a statement or a question. Jemeryl gave a nod that would meet either case.

"And you've got to learn about the ravens."

"Yes, sir."

Tapley's face lit up. "Yes. We can start with food—*because we loves our din-dins."* His last words were spoken in sibilant baby talk to the ravens.

Tapley reached into the bucket and scattered a fistful of chopped meat on the ground. The ravens descended in an explosion of black feathers, squabbling unnecessarily; there was plenty of food for all. The racket almost drowned out Tapley's broken monologue.

"We get leftovers from the kitchen. The cook's all right, but you have to watch the rest. They'd give the ravens any old muck, carrot tops and stale bread—*and we don't like that.* They aren't finicky, except Sniper, who won't eat pork—*you're an old fuss-pot.* Sniper sleeps on the post by the door. He's Pollo's youngest son. His sister, Spludge, is on your right. She's seven years old. Toggle and Dork are her babies—*you're big babies now.* Whomper is the oldest, Pollo's father. He keeps the rest in order, but you must make sure Toggle doesn't take anyone else's share of the food— *who's a greedy guts?"*

The keeper rambled away, losing Jemeryl within seconds. She looked at the six identical birds and abandoned all attempt to identify them by name. Unaware of Jemeryl's lapse in concentration, Tapley had jumped onto the eating habits of birds from years gone by. His remarks then lurched on through a random sequence of topics.

Once the food was gone, the ravens dispersed around the roost. They directed unblinking stares at the two sorcerers, their small black eyes similar to Klara's but seeming both more critical and less intelligent. Under their gaze, Jemeryl felt tremors running through the higher dimensions, carrying the taste of magic. She had the growing suspicion that the object of the morning's work was for the ravens to learn about her, rather than the other way around. Just as well, since she was unlikely to gain much from Tapley's babbling. However, it would be better to act as if she were paying attention. She composed her expression into one of polite interest.

❖

Three hours later, Jemeryl had reached the end of her endurance and given up any pretence of listening. Fortunately, Tapley was too obsessed with his ravens to notice. Vine's warnings had fallen pitifully short of the truth. Jemeryl spent ten minutes staring at her feet, scuffing dry straw into a patch of mud and watching the pattern as the wet soaked through.

In her growing cerebral numbness, Jemeryl's attention to her surroundings was minimal. The trance-like state broke suddenly when she realised that Tapley had stopped speaking and had left the shed with a raven on his wrist.

In vain, Jemeryl tried to recall his last words. Was she supposed to follow? Bring something? Wait behind? The keeper was out in the sunshine, walking across the grass. Making a quick decision, Jemeryl hurried after.

By the time she caught up, Tapley had stopped in the open field, well beyond the perimeter of the school's guarding shields. His face was lifted upwards and showed no awareness of Jemeryl's presence. Then he asked abruptly, "Have you done this before?"

"Er...maybe not exactly," Jemeryl hedged.

"When you're a raven, flying is so easy."

"Oh, mind-riding a bird? Yes, sir."

"Don't be heavy-handed. Ravens aren't machines—*yes my precious; we don't care what Neame thinks, do we?*" Tapley's conversation degenerated into mumbled half-sentences while he stroked the raven.

"Is there anything in particular you want me to do, sir?" Jemeryl reminded him of her presence.

"Fly with Whomper. Fly...up, up over everything, on the wind." His voice was a dreamy singsong. "I've done that."

"Yes, sir," Jemeryl said, adding silently, *It's obvious you have.*

Tapley showed the classic symptoms of having spent far too much time outside his own skull. Many sorcerers had fallen into the same trap and become victim to the accumulated effects that turned the brain to mush. Consequently, the dangers of prolonged mind-riding were so well known that it was surprising no one had intervened before Tapley had reached his current pitiful state. Someone must have seen the risks he was taking.

"Whomper will know what he's doing even if you don't." Tapley thrust the raven in her direction, with obvious misgivings. "Now take the raven. Look into his eyes, and—"

Jemeryl braced her arm to take the weight. "I know how to do it, sir. What's the core binding spell?"

At first, it seemed that Tapley would ignore Jemeryl's question and carry on rambling, but then something in the keeper seemed to mesh. His eyes focused on Jemeryl.

"It's the Three Calling Circles."

"Three Calling Circles?" Jemeryl was surprised. The spell was not one she had expected.

Tapley backed away and was waiting for her to begin. Jemeryl did not have the time to think the implications through. Delaying might make him think she needed instructions after all.

Jemeryl lifted the raven so that its shrewd eyes bored into hers. Latching onto the core spell, she started interlinking the circles of calling. All unnecessary thoughts were swept away, leaving awareness only of herself and the raven. Jemeryl sank deeper into the lacework of thoughts. As always, childhood memories of playing cat's cradle wove themselves into her spell as she caught the links that spun through their joint minds. Then, with the gentlest of shifts, she made the transition.

The sky was wide and tempting; Jemeryl launched herself towards it. The buildings of the school fell away. Earth and sky hung around her. The wind was moulded by the beat of her wings. Jemeryl climbed through the sky. The body was strange, like ill-fitting clothing, but wonderful in its power. She played with the air currents, looping and dancing on the wind. The tedium of the morning was forgotten in the joy of flight.

"Enough. You can come back now." Tapley's cry drifted on the wind.

Jemeryl circled, looking down at two small figures on the grass below, earthbound. One was her, strange and unlikely though it seemed. Again, she heard the call, and tempting as it was to disobey, she knew her time was up. A last sweep through the heavens, feeling the wind rippling over her feathers, and then she glided down, breaking through the confusion of sensation as an arm under her claws matched the claws clasping her arm. The links snapped, and she was back, standing on the ground with a raven on her wrist.

Tapley trotted to her side and reclaimed the raven. A huge beam spread across his face. "You love the ravens."

"I enjoy the work."

"No. You need to love the ravens to work with them. Aris loved the ravens—*and you loved her, too; we miss her, don't we?* Neame doesn't like the ravens—*no, she doesn't, nasty woman.* She wanted to get rid of the ravens and replace them with her pretend bird. Real ravens are best. Neame thought she could make a better one, except she couldn't. She hoped a third-rate witch could use it—*she'd like that, wouldn't she?* A good job Bramell stopped her. She's no sorcerer."

Jemeryl's attention was immediately hooked by what Tapley was saying, or by what she thought he was saying. "A pretend bird? You mean a golem?"

"Nasty thing."

"What happened to this bird?"

"Whomper's here."

Jemeryl sighed. Tapley was lost again. "Neame's pretend bird. What happened to it?"

"You can't have a pretend bird; it won't work. I told you that." Tapley scowled. "You need to love the ravens, like Aris did—*even though she lost your sister; she didn't mean it.*"

It was hopeless. Was the pretend bird a golem or just something that wasn't a raven? The only thing Jemeryl could be certain of was Tapley's outrage directed at Neame. Who was Aris, anyway? Jemeryl was certain that she was no longer at the school.

"What happened to Aris? Where is she now?"

"Poor Aris."

"Why 'poor'?"

"Aris died."

Jemeryl's sorcerer senses prickled. "When?"

"At the time of the plague, and we didn't know. We lost Whomper's sister as well." Tapley's face twisted in grief, though whether it was for the death of the raven or the sorcerer was hard to say.

Jemeryl was confused. Vine had said that only Druse died of the plague, but Erlam's reaction the night before had implied otherwise, and now Tapley had given a name.

"She caught the marsh plague?"

"Ravens don't get plague."

Before Jemeryl could rephrase her question, the refectory bell rang out.

Tapley nodded. "We're finished. You can go. It's lunchtime."

Jemeryl was about to leave when a fresh question struck her. "Why do you use the Three Calling Circles? Surely Treascal's Binding would be better."

"Treascal's Binding?" Tapley nodded. "It's a good spell, but the sixth dimension...some people"—a sweep of his arm took in the school—"can't manage it. We used to use the Long Ties of Anima, but Orrago forbade it."

"I'm not surprised." It was an extremely risky spell, used only as a last resort.

"Orrago said we couldn't after...after what happened to me. I was flying and...the tie broke." Tapley turned watery eyes on Jemeryl. "I've not been very well since."

"No, sir. I guess you haven't."

Tapley walked away, muttering to himself.

Jemeryl wanted more details about Aris, the ravens, and Neame's artificial bird, but there were better sources of information, sources such as Vine. Jemeryl headed for the refectory, her mind whirling as she considered the implications of the binding spell. She had a lot to discuss with Tevi.

❖

Shouts and laughter rang out in the warm spring evening. To the west, the last touches of pink and purple smudged the undersides of wispy clouds. The square outside the Inn of Singing Birds was busy. Activity centred on the tables outside taverns, where lanterns marked the traditional boundaries to what the innkeepers considered their own territory.

The clientele outside the Inn of Singing Birds were noticeably older and quieter than the others, although there was little to choose in the flow of wine and beer. Tevi and Jemeryl sat at the back, beneath one of the trees lining the square. No one paid them any attention or showed any inclination to sit at their table, but Tevi noticed that there was always a discreet waiter circulating like a guard dog, ready to head off the unwary. She found it irritating, but it guaranteed them the privacy to discuss what they had learnt.

Jemeryl was musing aloud. "I wasn't expecting Three Calling Circles. It's got me rethinking my assumptions about the ravens. It's such a limiting spell. But from what I think Tapley said, some sorcerers can't handle the sixth dimension."

"How does that affect it?"

"For mind-riding, you bond with the aura on the fifth dimension via the tensors of the sixth. Various binding spells use different methods to achieve this. By definition, a sorcerer can work in all three paranormal dimensions, but usually, you're better in one than the others. The sorcerers here are primarily herbalists, so you'd expect the fifth to be their strength. The Three Calling Circles is notable for being very undemanding on sixth-dimensional ability. The Long Ties of Anima is another easy spell in the sixth, except it's risky. Tapley implied that

Orrago made them stop using it after he'd had an accident. It explains the state he's in."

Tevi held up her hands. "I'll take your word on it. What does it mean to our hunt?"

"For starters, Tapley is off the list of suspects. But also, I'd assumed that the culprit had taken a raven away for a week or two, saying they were going for samples. The raven was then dispatched to Storenseg, and the culprit collected the plants in a conventional manner while it was gone. A spell like Treascal's Binding would allow this. However, the Three Calling Circles is a close binding spell. You have to physically touch the bird to make the initial bond, and all the time you're linked to it, you're in a trance. You can't eat or drink or even sleep properly."

Tevi's face cleared. She could see where Jemeryl was going. "You mean a sorcerer can only link to the raven for"—she paused, thinking—"two...three days at most. Which limits how far you can send it."

"Exactly. And having been a raven, I know they aren't—"

"When were you a raven?"

"This morning."

"You..." Tevi banged the side of her head with her open palm. "Right, forget the rest. What would be the limit to send a raven to collect something?"

"Four hundred miles, maybe five hundred if you were lucky with the winds."

"So a sorcerer on the mainland could have got the chalice?"

"Only if they were in southern Walderim."

"Could someone have taken a raven and changed the spell to treacle binding?"

Jemeryl laughed. "It's Treascal's Binding, and they couldn't change the spell without killing the raven."

Klara joined in. "Which would have a negative impact on its flying ability. Speaking as the expert on this."

"You're supposed to be a simple pet." Tevi tapped the magpie's beak, but with a sorcerer present, nobody would be surprised even if the table started talking.

"So you're saying that either the traitor was in Walderim, or it wasn't one of the school ravens?"

"That sums it up."

Tevi chewed her lip. "People who saw the chalice taken described it as a huge black bird."

"That sounds like a raven."

"Could the culprit have got another raven from somewhere else?"

"It's not that easy. Animals need a couple of months to prepare for binding spells, and the work is rather conspicuous. It would be noticed if somebody did it inside the school, so the enchanting would have to be done after leaving Ekranos. Whichever way you look at it, the traitor had to be away on a very lengthy trip. It certainly ought to narrow down the suspects."

Tevi leaned back and stared up at the trees. A breeze rustled overhead, producing a flickering effect as the pale undersides of leaves caught the lamplight.

"How about this artificial bird you said Tapley was so upset about? Could that have been used instead, without the traitor leaving Ekranos?"

"It's a possibility. I've got to find out more. How much work was done on it and what its capabilities were."

"It would point to Neame, since she initiated the thing."

"Yes." Jemeryl drummed her fingers on the table. "Assuming that I understood Tapley correctly."

"You're not happy with Neame being the guilty one, are you?"

"No."

"Because you think she's a good person?"

"I respect her."

"Both Levannue and Tapley dislike her. Perhaps they're right. Perhaps there's a less-than-pleasant side to Neame that she keeps hidden."

"Perhaps." Jemeryl sighed. "There are too many questions and loose ends. Things don't tie up. And there's something odd going on. Both Moragar and Erlam were keeping secrets. Even Vine has clammed up once or twice. To call that out of character is like saying the sea is a bit damp on occasion."

The analogy made Tevi laugh. She took a sip of her beer. Not far away, the innkeeper was passing on her rounds. The stout woman smiled deferentially in their direction. Tevi acknowledged the smile and then put her tankard down as another idea occurred.

"Could one of the seniors have persuaded a younger sorcerer to get the chalice?" Magic might be outside Tevi's understanding, but the abuse of power was not.

"It would mean letting someone else in on the crime. You know the saying—two can keep a secret if one of them is dead. It's hard enough to keep anything private from other sorcerers, even without Vine's help. I'd have thought involving another person was an unacceptable risk."

"Couldn't the culprit use magic to make a weaker sorcerer get the chalice and then forget what they'd done?"

"Not a sorcerer. There'd be no trouble enslaving the ungifted or a low-grade witch, but someone like that wouldn't be able to control the ravens."

"You're sure?"

"Yes. Snaring someone's mind is like tying their hands with cotton thread." Jemeryl held her wrists together to illustrate. "It's easy if the person holds their hands like this for five minutes so you can make several dozen loops, but if they see what you're doing and move..." She pulled her hands apart. "Equally, it's easy to ensorcel someone who can't see what you're doing. But anyone who is aware of the fifth dimension would have to do the magical equivalent of standing still."

An unrelated problem struck Tevi. "If it's so hard to overpower a sorcerer, supposing we find our traitor, how do we take them back to Lyremouth as a prisoner?"

"We use an enslaving ward. Levannue probably has one we could borrow. It's a device that exploits the elemental powers of the sixth dimension to bind someone's mind. And before you ask, I'm quite sure nobody at the school is trapped by one. Enslaving wards are very crude in their effect. The victim would be expressionless, sluggish, and probably unable to speak."

"I suppose that would be noticed."

"It wouldn't take Vine to spot it. Mind you, I could probably muster a fair number of votes for having one snapped on her."

"Supposing that Levannue doesn't have one of these wards?"

"We could revert to a simple iron collar. Iron is funny stuff; it distorts magical forces even more than water. For a sorcerer, wearing an iron collar is like having fireworks continuously going off in your face. Iralin had me wear one briefly as a demonstration." Jemeryl shuddered at the memory. "The combined forces of the school would be enough to restrain the culprit while the collar was put on. After that, I think we can leave it to you to take care of them."

"That simple?"

"Providing we don't take too long getting back to Lyremouth."

"How long before the collar stops working?"

"It doesn't exactly stop, but given time, you can get used to the effects. There's a story of a group of bandits who took a sorcerer prisoner by using one and treated him rather badly. After a year, he was able to overcome the iron sufficiently to teleport the key into his hand one night."

"That must have surprised the bandits the next day."

"I don't think many of them got to see dawn."

"If iron is so distracting, why do you have iron caps on the end of your staff?"

"The caps reflect energy waves, forming a resonating cavity as an amplifier. The wooden staff in the middle is irrelevant. It's simply to hold the iron reflectors a precise distance apart. We use oak since it has the right thermal coefficients."

Tevi frowned. What was a thermal coefficient or a resonating cavity? While she was trying to frame the question, noise from the square caught her attention. Several young people were splashing water from a drinking trough at each other. The horseplay was comprehensibly human. Magic left Tevi uneasy. So much she could not understand, yet she did not want her lover's abilities to be a barrier between them. *I just need to simply accept it,* she told herself. *As long as it makes sense to Jem, I won't worry.*

Tevi focused on another part of Jemeryl's report. "You think the person who took the chalice also stole Lorimal's manuscript from the library?"

"It's a bit of a coincidence otherwise."

"Does this mean we can be sure the traitor is here?"

"I've been certain from the start. Call it a sorcerer's hunch." Jemeryl gave a lopsided grin. "Not that it means much. Like most people's hunches, they work better with hindsight."

"I've found out where the customs record for the nectar is. Do you still want Klara to read it?"

"If you can. There may be some useful information, not least the dates. I'd like to know if the traitor is still working on the chalice—"

"Or if they've perfected the spell and are ready to wage war on the Protectorate, starting tomorrow," Klara interjected.

"There's a cheering thought."

Tevi was less amused. She hunched forward. "I won't be happy until we have the traitor. I worry about you up there alone. Promise me you won't take risks." As she spoke, Tevi felt Jemeryl shiver. "Are you cold?"

"No, it was..."

"Was what?"

"Nothing."

"It wasn't a premonition or anything like that?"

The night air was growing cooler. Jemeryl slid along the bench and put her arm around Tevi. "No. Don't be silly"

Tevi did not push the issue, but neither could she dismiss it from her mind. Her eyes fixed, over the rooftops, on the cliff-top school. The sooner the traitor was identified and captured, the better.

Chapter Five—Unplanned Conversations

The pale liquid began to simmer. Bubbles frothed around the sides of the pot. They hissed when Jemeryl dislodged them with a wooden spatula before pushing the pot to a cooler spot at the rear of the stove. Vine knelt to open the fire hatch. Her face looked demonic in the red light, scowling at the heat as she fed in more logs.

Neame bustled over. "How's everything going?" She carried on without waiting for an answer. "I've got to go upstairs. I won't be long. I've left a list of the compounds we need. Could you get them ready? And be careful; some are dangerous if mishandled."

"Bet she just wants a break from the heat," Vine said, once the sound of Neame's footsteps had faded away along the corridor outside and up the stairs at the end.

Jemeryl glared balefully at the stove. Its cast-iron frame was a magic-disrupting epicentre that prevented them from alleviating the heat it generated. The room was a bakehouse. Being in the low vaulted cellar under the dispensary did not help. The windows were little more than slits at ceiling level. The stove was built into an open chimney. Shelves lined the walls. Apart from this, furniture in the room consisted of a large wooden bench against one wall, a small round table by the stove, and two stools.

The claustrophobic chamber, generally known as *Neame's Kitchen*, was the place where potions were prepared. Neame was in charge of this work, so the cellar was the only part of the dispensary where order prevailed. The ingredients were arranged on the shelves by strict classification. Nothing except for items in use were laid out on the bench.

Vine picked up Neame's list and got as far from the stove as possible—not that it did much good. The heat was inescapable. Jemeryl could feel sweat trickling through her hair as she peered over Vine's shoulder.

"It's pretty straightforward. Won't take long." Vine nodded.

"If you say so." Many of the names on the list were unfamiliar to Jemeryl. She leaned against the bench and watched Vine work her way along the shelves, picking out jars. After a short while, Jemeryl asked, "You remember telling me Druse was the only sorcerer killed by the plague?"

"Yes."

"Tapley mentioned someone called Aris. Was it me getting confused, or did she die at the same time?"

"She died, but it wasn't the plague." Vine deposited the jars on the bench. "Here, hand me that flask."

Jemeryl did as asked. She waited until Vine had finished measuring out an oily green fluid before continuing. "So what did she die of?"

"Suicide."

"She killed herself?"

"That's what 'suicide' usually means. She was unstable—putting it mildly. I suppose it shouldn't have been unexpected, but it was hard on Erlam. I don't think he's over her. They were partners, you see."

"Oh, that would explain..."

"What?"

"Erlam got prickly when I was talking to him. It would make sense if he thought you'd been gossiping about him and Aris."

"Would I do a thing like that?" Vine's tone was all hurt innocence.

"Yes."

"Charming! Anyway, you're not just here to be ornamental. If you took those over to the stove, it would help."

"How close in time did the two deaths take place?" Jemeryl asked while transferring the indicated bottles to a tray.

"Pretty much the same day, as far as we could tell."

"Were they linked?"

"Must have been a coincidence. They happened over two thousand miles apart. Druse was here, and Aris was out travelling in Walderim."

"Walderim!"

"It's the strip of land between the Aldrak Mountains and the Western Ocean."

"I know where it is." Carelessly, Jemeryl dumped the tray on the small table by the stove and turned back, almost tripping over one of the stools. "Whereabouts in Walderim?"

Even as the words left her mouth, Jemeryl knew she was sounding far too eager. Vine's curiosity was easy to attract and very, very hard to evade, but before either could say more, they heard Neame's footsteps on the stairs. In a flurry of activity, they assembled the remaining items. By the time Neame opened the door, Vine was wiping the bench with a damp rag and Jemeryl was at the stove, spatula in hand.

"How's the list going?" Neame asked.

"Just finished, ma'am." Vine gave a last sweep with the cloth and went to assist Jemeryl.

From the calculating expression on Vine's face, Jemeryl could tell that the school gossip was puzzling over her interest in Walderim. Vine's lower lip was caught in her teeth. Her eyes were fixed on the distance. She certainly was not paying attention to where she was walking.

Jemeryl realised the danger a split second too late. Vine's knee cracked hard against the stool in the middle of the floor. She staggered sideways, with her toe caught in the rungs and her hand thrown out for support. Her fingers snagged the tray that Jemeryl had left precariously overhanging the edge of the table. The table tipped over and the tray flipped up, catapulting its contents into the air. Vine's balance was completely lost. She stumbled forward, straight towards the hot stove.

There was no time to think. If Vine landed on the stove, she would be badly burnt. The mass of iron was a deep vortex in the paranormal planes. Yet somehow, responding by reflex and making up with force what she lacked in subtlety, Jemeryl summoned the powers of the sixth dimension. Vine flew back across the room and crashed into the bench on the opposite wall. She would be bruised but not seriously injured.

Bottles from the tray landed with loud cracks and the tinkle of breaking glass. One smashed on the stovetop; the contents hissed over the hot plate and ran down the sides, giving off wisps of yellow smoke. Still shaken, Jemeryl stood in the middle of the debris—liquids, powder, and shards of glass. Cleaning up would not be fun.

"Jemeryl, move!" Neame shouted.

Jemeryl stopped considering the mess around her and looked back. Neame was in the doorway at the rear. Vine was scrambling painfully to her feet. Suddenly, Jemeryl became aware of the creeping smoke.

What was it burning? Without thinking, she reached for a cloth before the emphasis of Neame's words registered.

She began to step backwards, but too late. The pungent smell of fumes reached her. Acid vapour rasped Jemeryl's throat. A muscle inside her chest contracted convulsively while the floor lurched under her feet. She gasped, breathing in more poisoned air.

"Jemeryl!"

Grey darkness flowed before Jemeryl's eyes. Her left knee buckled. Jemeryl knew she was about to pass out. She was drowning in the yellow air. Then a hand grabbed her shoulder and yanked her away from the stove.

Jemeryl was dragged stumbling backwards from the room and into the corridor. Feeling strangely detached, she watched Vine slam the door shut and realised that Neame was the one who had hauled her out. Together, they half carried her up the stairway.

In the fresh air of the ground floor lobby, Jemeryl's head started to clear, but a feeling of nausea grew. Uncontrollable shaking overwhelmed her. Neame's face wavered too close for Jemeryl to focus on.

"I guess you'll survive." The forced lightness in Neame's voice did not hide her relief. "You can sit in Orrago's study. I'm sure she won't mind, under the circumstances."

Jemeryl surrendered to being led a short distance and guided into a chair. Despite the careful treatment, her stomach spasmed. The bucket placed near at hand was reassuring. She stared miserably at her knees, trying to ignore everything else. She heard talking; then the door closed, and Vine knelt by her side.

"Neame's gone to sort out the mess downstairs. I'm going to look after you. Don't worry. You'll be fine. I've got instructions." She squeezed Jemeryl's shoulder. "And I must say you've gone a really unusual shade of green."

Jemeryl closed her eyes, trying to relax. An inner cold gnawed into her bones, but after a while, the convulsive shuddering subsided. She raised her head carefully.

She was in a small, cosy study. A lifetime's accumulation of clutter swamped any academic aspect of the room. A few feet away, dozing in a second chair, was Orrago, with Frog perched like a carved ornament on the armrest. Jemeryl shivered and shifted back in her seat. Even that slight movement increased her nausea. She pressed her hand against her mouth.

Vine returned with three steaming mugs. "Thought I'd have one myself. I even made a cup for Orrago, if she wakes up. Yours has got extra honey, plus a few more bits."

"Thanks." Jemeryl was surprised at how raw her voice sounded. She wrapped her hands around the cup, sucking the warmth into her fingers, and took a cautious sip.

Vine plonked herself down on a footstool. "You know, I was just as keen as you to get away from the heat, but I think your escape plan was a little overdramatic."

"I admit it didn't work out quite the way I intended."

Orrago coughed and opened her eyes. The elderly woman peered around the room. "Where's my hat? Has anyone seen my hat? It was here just now. I need my hat. I've got to go to the library...got to see..."

Vine went to her side. "It's all right, ma'am. You don't need to bother. I've made you some tea."

"Oh, that is good of you, Kally." The ancient sorcerer calmed at the sight of the mug. "It's nice of you and Iralin to visit me."

"It's Vine and Jemeryl, ma'am."

"Where? Who are they?"

"They're us, ma'am. Vine and Jemeryl. We had a small accident, and Neame has sent us here to recover," Vine explained slowly.

"Oh, young Neame...yes." Becoming more animated, Orrago leaned forward. "You must ask Druse to see me this afternoon. I have to talk to him about some books he's repairing. He's not supposed to touch—" Orrago broke off and pointed at a shadow on the wall. "Oh, there's my hat. What's happened to the brim?"

The sweet tea was calming Jemeryl's nausea and thawing her inner chill. She exchanged a sad smile with Vine. Orrago's grasp of reality was more tenuous than usual.

For a while, the elderly sorcerer rambled on. She tapped Vine's arm. "Kally, can you go and find Druse for me?"

"Ma'am, don't you remember? Druse is dead."

"Don't be silly. Of course he's not dead. I talked to him only this morning." However, a puzzled frown grew on Orrago's face, undermining the conviction of her words. Frog gave a forlorn croak.

Abruptly, Orrago put down her mug and stood up. She scooped Frog from the armrest and dropped him in a pocket. "I've got to go now."

It was anyone's guess what was happening with Orrago's jumbled wits, but at the very second she pulled the door open, Levannue appeared outside. The door opening in her face clearly startled Levannue. She stared through the doorway, her expression of surprise quickly changing to one of censure as she saw the two junior sorcerers.

"You know you're not supposed to be in here. Who gave you permission?" Levannue stepped past Orrago into the room.

"Neame sent us here, ma'am," Vine replied.

"Why?"

"I'm keeping an eye on Jemeryl. There was an accident in the cellar."

"Was someone being careless? What happened?"

"I think, ma'am, it might be better if you ask Neame for the details."

"I'm asking you." The senior sorcerer locked eyes with Vine, blatantly trying to intimidate.

"Neame was in charge, and she knows more about what happened than me. She's the one you should ask, ma'am."

The silence dragged out uncomfortably. "Hmmp. Well, as long as the situation is under control." Levannue's tone was too sharp to count as backing down, but she was apparently ready to let it drop. Her manner softened, and she linked her arm with Orrago. "Would you like to come with me?"

The door closed, and Vine gave a sigh of relief. "And there you have a object lesson in school politics. Levannue will stick her nose into things that don't concern her, and if you're not careful, you can end up on the wrong side of Neame."

"I know. I got caught in the middle when the two of them had a squabble before."

"When was that?"

"In the hospital a few days ago."

"Was that when the woman with marsh plague was brought in?"

"You heard about it?"

"Of course." Vine sounded indignant.

Jemeryl's laughter turned to coughing. The tea had relieved her nausea, but her throat felt as if she had been gargling with broken glass.

Vine stood anxiously by Jemeryl's shoulder until the coughing subsided. "You're sounding like a candidate for the hospital yourself."

"If the plague gets out of hand again, we could all end up there," Jemeryl said between gasps.

"It won't. We know how to deal with it now." Vine dropped into Orrago's vacated chair. "I don't think I could face going through it again."

"It must have been chaos here."

"It was. I was one of the first to get sick. By the time I was better, half the school was down. I was nursing three whole wards on my own, though there were fewer patients left each day. The weaker ones didn't stand a chance. Moragar was the most senior sorcerer left standing. He was running the place. Part of the reason they made him head librarian was that he did such a good job. He went to pieces when Druse died, but by then, Levannue had recovered." Vine adopted a confidential manner—always a sign that she was hunting gossip. "We had just about settled down when the news came about Aris."

"It happened out in Walderim, you said." Jemeryl did her best to act like someone pretending to be indifferent.

"Yes."

Jemeryl left a significant pause. "I don't suppose it was near Oshen, in the north?"

"No. It was just outside Scathberg."

"Oh."

"You've been there?"

"No."

"You know someone there?"

"Er...not quite." Jemeryl made her voice drop. "An ex-lover of mine, another apprentice at Lyremouth, he came from Oshen. He used to talk about the town....promised he'd take me there. We're not together anymore, but—"

"You're still keen on him?"

Jemeryl shrugged, as if avoiding an answer.

"What's he like?"

Jemeryl averted her face and whispered, "I'd rather not talk about him."

"Oh, right. Still feeling sore?"

Jemeryl gave another miserable shrug. Strictly speaking, she had not lied. However, it was a safe bet that the inferences Vine drew from her words would be complete fiction. Failed love affairs were Vine's favourite topic for gossip. Jemeryl could almost see the cogs going around in her head as she added up two and two. By now, Vine was probably past the conjecture that the affair with the mercenary was started on the rebound and on to more elaborate hypotheses, safely diverted from the truth. Just as long as Jemeryl said nothing else.

Unfortunately, Jemeryl desperately wanted more answers. Who was with Aris? Where were they? And who came back with what? To ask would only set Vine off on the hunt again. It was frustrating. Vine was the best source of information in the school, but Jemeryl dared not let rumours spread that she had an interest in the events in Walderim three years earlier.

They were draining the last of their tea when Neame returned. Vine stood up. Jemeryl made to do likewise, but her knees gave way.

Neame put a restraining hand on her shoulder. "Stay still. I guess I don't need to ask how you're feeling."

"I'll be all right in a minute."

"It'll take a bit longer than that. But your aura's recovering nicely. I think you should lie down in your room. Vine will get some porters and a stretcher." Neame's tone allowed no argument.

Jemeryl felt conspicuous being carried to the juniors sorcerers' quarters, with Vine in attendance, but it was a relief to be laid on her own bed with the shutters closed.

Once the porters had gone, Jemeryl gave an apologetic smile. "I'm sorry about the accident. It was my fault. I should have been more careful how I put the tray down."

"And I should have been looking where I was going," Vine replied. "Don't worry. Neame wasn't angry. Just as well. It takes a vast amount of provocation to get in Neame's bad books, but if ever you do, you're stuck there for life."

Vine shut the door, leaving Jemeryl alone to ponder that final thought.

❖

Tevi's slow footsteps rang hollow on the flagstones. There was no point rushing her solitary patrol. Dusk was gathering. The horizon was shrouded in misty purple. Across the bay, a lone fishing craft was returning with its catch, while high above, the first faint stars dotted the darkening sky. The moon, well past its full, hung above the water. It had a translucent sheen in the last remnants of daylight.

On reaching the end of the quay, Tevi balanced on the edge and looked down. The tide was out. Water slopped against the pockmarked stones twenty feet below. Farther along the shoreline, away from the deepwater harbour, banks of sand and shingle broke the waves, hissing as the surf sucked over them.

Tevi turned and strolled back, passing the dark hulks of moored ships. There was little to do. All the vessels currently docked had been checked, and with low tide, nothing could move for a couple of hours. The customs officers on duty were responsible solely for ensuring that nothing was smuggled aboard and limiting the havoc caused by gangs of drunken sailors.

One such group was assembling on the foredeck of the nearest ship. The sailors laughed among themselves. They were currently well-behaved. The night had not yet started, and most were reasonably sober, although a visit onshore to sample the pleasures of Ekranos would undoubtedly change that.

As Tevi passed by, one sailor leant over the railing. "Hey, officer. I've got some really unusual merchandise here you might like to inspect personally." Grasping the rigging, the sailor leapt onto the rail and posed provocatively, the innuendo clear.

Tevi looked up and smiled. She was already accustomed to the good-natured verbal sparring of the docks. "If it's what I think, then it's readily available in town and doesn't require customs inspection. Unless it's malfunctioning and might create a public nuisance."

"Would you like to come below decks and help me test it out?"

"You don't need me. I'm sure you've had plenty of practise testing it out on your own."

Unperturbed at being beaten in the battle of gibes, the sailor joined in the general laughter before jumping back onto the deck to join her companions.

Tevi's patrol reached a gap between the moored ships. She paused and looked back along the dock. The group from the ship was heading into town in search of an evening's entertainment and maybe someone to test the sailor's merchandise—at a price. Tevi shook her head in bemusement, but it set her thoughts drifting to Jemeryl.

From where she stood, Tevi had a clear view of the school. The jumble of silhouettes crowded the cliff tops. Their next meeting was two days away. In the meantime, she had no way of knowing how the search for the renegade sorcerer was going. It left her desperately uneasy. Her eyes fixed onto the distant buildings as if trying to drill through the walls.

"Dominates the town, doesn't it?" An elderly sailor had noticed the focus of her attention.

Tevi recalled herself. "Pardon?"

"The school up there. Dominates all of Ekranos."

"I suppose the town has grown up in its shadow."

The sailor was dressed in the local style—a loose-yoked smock with embroidered patterns, barely visible beneath an assortment of stains. Despite his clothes, the sailor spoke with the wide rolling vowels of the lands north of Lyremouth. His face was deeply etched. Calluses on his hands showed the effect of a lifetime's work on the seas.

The sailor folded his arms and leaned against a mooring post, clearly readying himself for a long chat. "No. Ekranos was here long before the school came. It used to be an independent port. Pretty rich, too, as long as whichever sorcerer ruled here was strong enough. It could control trade on the river and through the straits."

"What made it join the Protectorate?"

"About three hundred years back, the ghost riders appeared out in the Eastern Ocean. They killed the sorcerer prince, so Ekranos swore allegiance to the Coven. It was a case of urgently needing the protection of the Protectorate. The school was originally built to secure the Straits of Perithia against anything that might want to sail in."

"I thought they were herbalists up there."

"They are now. But they're a later arrival. For the first one hundred years, it was purely a defensive outpost. Then new castles were built farther up the straits, and the healers moved into the old buildings. They said they could get better supplies here. But I reckon what they really wanted was a bit of independence from the rest of the Coven. There's always been friction. If it went to a vote of the ordinary citizens, the healers would run the Coven. In practice, it don't work out like that. But it's true the supplies are better here than at Lyremouth. Down south are the rain forests. I've been told more plants grow there than in all the rest of the world put together. Mind you, I've seen some strange things in other places—flowers that eat birds and the like. I've sailed way beyond Cape Tallis in my time. You wouldn't credit some of the things I've seen."

After a month on the harbour, Tevi recognised the introduction to a sailor's tall yarn. It was not something she was in the mood for.

"It's good the herbalists can get everything they need. I can see they wouldn't want to go trotting around the world, picking things themselves," she cut in quickly, then smiled and started to walk on.

The sailor did not take the hint. "Oh, the sorcerers still go travelling now and again, trying to find new specimens. Though I admit most aren't keen on it. The deputy, Neame—she's the one who travels the most, and I reckon that's down to a dislike of the company in the school. I hear she's planning a trip out east next year, and she had a long trek up and down Walderim three years back. Was gone for the best part of a year. Then she had that shorter trip down the Dhaliki."

Tevi stopped in her tracks. If what the sailor said was true, it could be very important. However, she should not seem too eager. She switched the action of her aborted departure into a stretch, then matched the sailor's causal stance and let her gaze drift across the roofs.

"Do all the rest of the sorcerers stick in Ekranos, then?" Tevi tried to sound as if merely making polite conversation.

"Well, some juniors are forever going off in the hope of finding something new and making a name for themselves. There's a couple on the *Sea Witch* right now. But by the time they get older, they tend to stay put. Bramell has been to Lyremouth twice since he took the headship, but it wasn't to do with herbs. Just as well. He couldn't tell a cabbage from a carnation, even if he ate it. Orrago was quite a traveller in her time. Of course, she's not up to it now. Levannue is the only other senior who's set foot outside Ekranos recently, and that was just a quick visit to see her family the year before last, which was odd, because I didn't think she got on with them. But I've heard she's going off again—heading up north in a month or so." He held up a finger. "No, wait. I tell a lie. Roddis also went off last spring, but she'd been gone weeks before anyone noticed. She's too quiet. Always gets overlooked."

"You know a lot about the sorcerers." Doubts concerning the information's accuracy grew in Tevi's mind. The sailor's claimed knowledge of school matters was far more intimate than seemed likely, even allowing for the dockside grapevine.

The sailor smiled, clearly taking her words as a compliment. "Up until last autumn, I was first mate on the *Sea Witch*. That's the school's own ship. But I'm getting too old, so I chucked it in for a shore job. I've known all the senior sorcerers since they were youngsters, except for Uwien, the newcomer. I still see Neame from time to time, and we have a little chat. She's decent, as sorcerers go. The only one you can really trust. Don't get me wrong, I respect sorcerers, but they don't think like us. You never know where you are with them. Take Bramell, for instance. I used—"

The peace of the dock was shattered abruptly. Voices rose, becoming more aggressive by the second. If it was not a fight, it would be soon. All across the dock, heads turned towards the source of the commotion: an animated group clustered around a ship's gangplank. Already, a ring of onlookers was forming. More people appeared on deck, hanging over the rails to see what was happening.

"I'd better go and sort it out." Tevi was moving even before she spoke.

"Take care. It sounds like trouble."

"It's probably just some drunk. I'll see you around."

Tevi jogged down the quay, noting with relief that another of her mercenaries colleagues was also converging on the rumpus, making an exaggerated show of the heavy baton they carried. Tevi sighed. It was going to be another busy night on the Ekranos docks.

❖

The section devoted to nonmedicinal herbalism and psychic studies was situated behind the hospital. A dark corridor ran the length of its main building. Jemeryl stood at one end and considered the eight doorways. There was nothing to identify which one she wanted. *I guess mind reading would come under psychic studies*, she thought wryly, *but nameplates wouldn't hurt*.

Both junior sorcerers who normally worked in this section were busy elsewhere, and Levannue had urgent need of assistance. Jemeryl had been lent from the hospital, but her instructions had only gone as far as telling her to report to this building. She tried three doors before meeting with success. At the sound of it opening, Levannue looked up from the instruments on the desk.

"Excuse me, ma'am. Neame has sent me. You asked for help?"

After subjecting Jemeryl to a critical appraisal, Levannue twisted several sixth-dimensional power tensors into an elemental knot. "Can you dissipate that?"

Jemeryl took a sharp breath. Levannue's tone was not aggressive, but it was definitely confrontational. However, the test was simple. Jemeryl slipped the knot free and allowed the trapped forces to flow away.

"Well, that's a pleasant surprise." Levannue sounded satisfied. "Though it must be pure luck that Neame sent someone competent in the sixth dimension."

Jemeryl thought it wiser not to reply. True, many sorcerers in Ekranos were weak with sixth-dimensional forces; their skills generally lay with the life auras of the fifth, but the situation was not quite as bad as implied. Maybe Levannue was assuming that Neame would not put much effort into meeting her rival's request. Yet surely Levannue must know that the deputy principal would not risk the school's safety over personal animosity. Neame had even taken advice from Erlam about who to send.

"Take these and come with me." Levannue's tone was brisk.

Jemeryl grabbed the items indicated and followed with haste. She had the feeling Levannue would not tolerate laziness or negligence.

Two witches were already making preparations at the node point. A section of the school shields had become unbalanced and needed realignment. The witches were clearly both adept in the sixth but blind to other paranormal dimensions. They would be responsible for balancing the elemental forces while Levannue made the delicate repairs. Jemeryl's role was as an intermediary. With Levannue so close to the node, it was essential that the final link be controlled by someone who could separate her life aura from the flux. Jemeryl tried not to grin, but she was looking forward to the challenge.

The job lived up to her expectations. It was easily her most enjoyable project since she arrived at the school. Sixth-dimensional magic had always been her favourite. Levannue worked quickly and deftly. Within the hour, the realignment was complete. Jemeryl stepped back, feeling both exhausted and faintly surprised. She had been so engrossed that only now did she realise how draining it had been.

She was even more surprised when Levannue looked at her with approval. “You did well.”

This time, Jemeryl did not hide her smile. Levannue was not someone who would give out praise indiscriminately. It was not in her nature to either flatter or spare her subordinates’ feelings—definitely not where work was involved.

The witches were dismissed, and the two sorcerers returned to Levannue’s room, where a record book for the shields required both their signatures. Jemeryl quickly scanned the page. As she suspected, the two-name rule had been enforced only since Bramell became principal. Her smile faded when she saw that until three years ago, the sorcerer’s name beside Levannue’s had invariably been Aris.

“What is it?” Levannue must have noticed the change in her expression.

Jemeryl hesitated, but there was no reason not to tell the truth. “It’s just...Aris. Vine told me about her unfortunate...er, death.”

“Yes. She was a sad loss. Her abilities have been greatly missed.” Levannue seemed about to say something else but then stopped, in a rare show of indecisiveness. She averted her face. “You may put the book away and go.”

Levannue hurried off, as if running away. Jemeryl pursed her lips. Apparently, the head of psychic studies was not quite as unfeeling as she made out. Aris’s death clearly upset her.

Jemeryl ducked down to return the record book to its cupboard. She heard the door of the room opening, although in her crouching position, she was hidden from its view.

“Hello, Snuggums. Did it all go all right, my poppet?”

Jemeryl nearly choked. The voice was Bramell’s, but the sugary tones were unlike anything she had heard from him before. He obviously had no idea that she was there. If only Levannue were similarly unaware, Jemeryl might have kept out of sight until they had gone. However, she did not have that option. Unwillingly, she stood up.

At the sight of her, the principal’s face went through a range of expressions—all of them hard to name, whereas Levannue definitely looked embarrassed. Without a word being said, Jemeryl sidled out of the room, past Bramell, who had not moved from the doorway.

Only when she was outside the building could Jemeryl give way to giggling. Unfortunately, she dared not share the story with Vine. If the name "Snuggums" started circulating the school, both Bramell and Levannue would know who to blame. Jemeryl shook her head. She had realised that Bramell's authoritarian manner was a facade, but she never guessed that it covered a soppy, sentimental interior.

❖

The tide was ebbing. Wading birds probed the wet sand with long, thin beaks. They scattered at Tevi's approach in a flurry of white wings and wailing cries. Only Tevi's footprints defaced the featureless surface of freshly exposed sand—a single track leading back to Ekranos.

The high-tide point was marked by a thick line of dead seaweed, broken shells, and driftwood. Tevi stopped and looked up. Cliffs of pitted white chalk rose in broken tiers, dazzling in the morning sunshine. Irregular bands of stunted gorse and sea grass sprouted from cracks. The only break was where a wide seam of harder rock split the chalk in a diagonal line.

A narrow path picked its way down this route, hollowed by the passage of feet. Steps were cut into the chalk at the steeper points. The ledge faded into the cliffs at the top, where a wooden handrail edged the last precarious section. Higher still, the footpath disappeared over the cliff top through a small gateway set under a wooden arch—surely not to guard the rear entrance to the school of herbalism, but to mark the start of the path for those leaving.

Tevi walked farther up the beach, crossing from wet to dry sand. Sun-baked seaweed crackled under her feet, and sand flies rose in buzzing swarms. She selected a patch of clean, soft sand, then turned around and sat cross-legged, looking over the water. The familiar sour smell of seaweed and the hissing of waves evoked memories of Storenseg. Tevi rested her chin on her fists. The breeze off the sea gently lifted her hair, tickling her face and forehead.

"Tevi."

She twisted around. Jemeryl was a third of the way down the cliff path. Tevi scrambled to her feet and raced up the beach. Dry sand slipped under her feet so that each step took her only a few inches forward. By the time Tevi reached the foot of the path, Jemeryl had completed her descent. She threw her arms about Tevi and held her close while they kissed.

"I'm sorry I'm late. Have you been waiting long?"

"Only a few minutes."

With arms wrapped around each other's waists, they wandered along the shore until out of sight of the path. A spur of rock made a natural windbreak, sheltering a warm, sandy spot.

Tevi let go of Jemeryl and flopped down on the sand. She stretched out her legs and leaned back with her arms as props. Her eyes were closed, and she smiled, enjoying the sun on her face. Jemeryl knelt beside her and knocked a supporting arm away, pushing Tevi flat on her back.

"How long before you have to return?" Jemeryl's smile made her intention clear. Her fingers moved to unfasten Tevi's shirt.

Tevi struggled to sit up. "No, wait, Jem. We've got to talk. I've learnt something. Neame was in Walderim when the chalice was taken. A sailor on the docks told me. Neame must be the traitor."

The smile left Jemeryl's face. She sat back on her heels, braced her hands on her knees and listened to Tevi's report of the conversation, staring silently into the distance.

"That was all he had to say?" Jemeryl asked when the account was finished.

"Yes, and I can't be sure he was telling the truth. But in my experience, when sailors make up stories, they're much more dramatic."

"He's obviously familiar with the school. And he's getting correct information from somewhere. Levannue is taking a trip north later this year. I've heard about it from Vine."

"So Neame is the one we're after?" Tevi prompted, seeking agreement.

"It's still only a guess. There's no proof."

"You can't let your liking for people influence your judgement."

"I know that." Jemeryl bit her lip.

"There's more to it. I can see it in your face." Tevi felt a sudden certainty.

"Yes, there is. The sailor was right about a party of sorcerers being in Walderim at the time the chalice was stolen. I'm not sure who, but Neame may well have been leading it. I could ask Vine; she's bound to know. The problem is that I don't want to set her off wondering why I'm interested." Jemeryl sighed and shifted around, pulling her knees up. "One member of the group I do know about was a sorcerer called Aris. But she never came back to Ekranos, with or without the chalice. She died in Walderim. The story is that she killed herself."

A long silence followed. When Tevi spoke, her voice was soft but very serious. "That leaves us with two possibilities. Either her death is a coincidence, or she found out about the chalice, and Neame killed her and made it look like suicide. Jem, you've got to be careful. I know that you like Neame, but we aren't just talking about someone playing games. We're talking about murder. I'm worried about you. You mustn't take risks."

"I admit it looks bad for Neame, but we need proof."

Despite her own conviction, Tevi could sense her lover's unhappiness. Jemeryl had to be alert to risks for her own safety, yet a rift between them would be unbearable. She took hold of Jemeryl's hand, trying to think of some conciliatory words. "Well, yes, I suppose we need to eliminate other people, to be totally certain. Like Levannue. She made that trip to her family. Perhaps the sailor got the dates wrong, and maybe she comes from Walderim."

Jemeryl shook her head. "From her accent, Levannue comes from around Serac."

"Perhaps her family has emigrated recently."

"It's all right, my love. You don't have to strain conjecture too far." Jemeryl put her arm around Tevi's waist. "If Neame's guilty, then we'll get her. But it will mean that I've been totally duped, and I'll never trust my own judgement again."

Jemeryl rested her head on Tevi's shoulder. The sun was beating upon the sand and cast a dazzling glitter over the waves. The sea was deep turquoise. Birds scurried at the water's edge, darting back and forth between the waves.

"Will you be really upset if it's Neame?" Tevi asked eventually.

"Yes. But if Neame is guilty, then her caring manner is a sham, and the woman I admire doesn't exist. Whatever the truth is, it can be sorted out later. For the moment, I've got some time with you, and it's too precious a commodity to waste brooding." The grin returned to Jemeryl's face. "And you didn't answer my original question. How long before you have to go back?"

"I've got to be on the docks two hours before noon."

"Plenty of time."

The hand around Tevi's waist started to tug her shirt free of her belt.

"Jem! Supposing someone comes strolling along the beach?" Yet Tevi knew there was no real protest in her voice.

"I'll set a shimmer screen for the eyes of the ungifted, and sorcerers ought to have better manners than to pry. Even Vine has her standards." Jemeryl paused and then shrugged. "I think."

Tevi laughed. She wrapped her arms around Jemeryl's shoulders and fell back, pulling Jemeryl on top of her. For a while, they lay, kissing, while their actions increased in passion. Tevi's hands burrowed into Jemeryl's clothing until they reached the soft, warm skin. She felt Jemeryl's mouth and teeth on her throat. Tevi knew a barrage of jokes awaited her if she returned to the docks with marks showing, but she was not worried enough to ask Jemeryl to stop.

The sounds and smells of the sea and the hot sand beneath her carried Tevi back to Storenseg. It could have been one of her adolescent fantasies made real, but the woman in her arms exceeded anything she had imagined. She was amazed at how much she wanted Jemeryl. The physical ache was the least of it. Her desire to touch Jemeryl and be touched, although rooted in her body, went far beyond. It was a passion that engulfed her soul.

Jemeryl's hand was kneading Tevi's breast through her shirt, taking her swiftly to a state of advanced arousal. Tevi pulled away and began loosening her clothing. It was wisest to get undressed while she could still muster some self-control. She drew the line at returning to work with torn clothes.

Chapter Six—A Sorcerer's Pride

Jemeryl shouldered the door shut and deposited the tray containing potions and other equipment on the table. The whitewashed walls of the quarantine room were oppressively cheerless. The patient, Gewyn, lay deep in a coma, as she had since the night she arrived. Her skin was dry, hot to the touch and covered with livid blotchy marks. Scabs encrusted her lips and eyes. Jemeryl bent to pull the covers straight, gently tucking one trailing arm back under the blanket.

"She's not getting any better, is she?"

Jemeryl glanced over her shoulder. The speaker was the fair-haired man who had scarcely left Gewyn's side all the time she had been there. His mournful face had become a familiar sight around the hospital. He wandered listlessly across the room, pausing to look at the sky outside yellowing to evening.

"We're doing everything we can." Jemeryl used her most reassuring tones.

"Oh, I know. I'm very grateful, ma'am." He left the window and joined Jemeryl at the bedside. His lips worked against each other. At last, he said, "I'm so frightened for her."

Sympathetic noises were all Jemeryl could offer.

The young man carried on in a despairing monotone that lurched through unfinished sentences. "What will I say...her parents won't...if I go back without her...Gewyn was so..."

"It may not come to that."

"We've known each other two years. We met at the midsummer festival. She was with friends...drunk. They were falling over and singing. The first thing I noticed was her voice. She's the worst singer you've ever heard. Raucous and tone-deaf and..." His rambling ground to a halt.

Jemeryl looked at him. The man's head was bowed. The heels of his hands were pressed hard against his eyes. Her gaze shifted to the hapless patient. Gewyn was an ordinary, ungifted citizen, someone who would usually go unnoticed. Suddenly, Jemeryl was hit by the image of Tevi, also ungifted, lying near to death. She pushed the vision away, but the image stuck, so strongly that Jemeryl felt certain it was a foretelling. In panic, she clawed at the seventh dimension, and the vision dispersed, striking no resonance in the web of fate. Relief washed over Jemeryl. Not a true oracle, just normal human anxiety.

The room settled back into its standard time phase. Jemeryl looked again at the young man. Tears of sympathy stung her eyes. Almost without intending it, she put her arms around him. At her touch, his self-control broke, and he clung to her like a child, shaking with sobs. When the tremors finally subsided, Jemeryl sat him on the free bunk, filled a cup with water, and placed it in his hands. The cup chattered against his teeth as he sipped.

"I'm sorry, ma'am. I'm just—"

"Don't apologise. I understand."

"I've made your shoulder wet." He forced a feeble smile.

"It'll dry."

The door opened. Neame said nothing when she entered, but she clearly absorbed the message in the man's red eyes. Parts of her face softened in compassion, while other parts hardened in resolve. It was a strange composite expression that left no doubt of her commitment to Gewyn's health. Neame was not magically casting a glamour. Jemeryl was certain of that. Either the response was genuine, or it was a superb piece of acting. *And if she's acting, then I'm a pink tree frog.* The thought shot through Jemeryl's mind.

The folded back covers revealed Gewyn's plague-wracked body. Sweat marks stained the sheet, streaked with blood. Neame perched on the bed and examined the patient. Her hands moved deftly: taking the pulse, pressing the swelling at neck and groin, and probing the sticky thinness of her aura.

From the other side of the room, the young man watched with an expression of tormented misery; yet a desperate hope lay there also. Neame could probably inspire hope in the dead. Again, Jemeryl felt her eyes fill with tears.

Neame had recently platted her braid, and for once, there were no wisps of escaping hair. It would not last. Neame never bothered about her appearance while working. Her current task was a typical example. Heedless of the blood and pus, Neame had an arm around the patient's shoulders to hold her in position while inducing her to swallow an elixir. Achieving the same thing by telekinesis would require slightly more effort, but Jemeryl knew which option she would take.

Once Gewyn was lying back on the bed, the two sorcerers daubed lotion on the raw sores. The patient showed no sign of stirring. Her breathing was shallow, but the elixir had eased the dry rasping in her throat.

"Right; nearly finished." Neame glanced at Jemeryl. "We must change the bottom sheet. Can you lift her on your own, or shall I call another sorcerer to help?"

Jemeryl spotted a suitable sixth-dimensional current. "I should be able to manage."

Even with the current, Jemeryl needed immense concentration to float Gewyn two feet clear of the mattress. At least Neame wasted no time in yanking the old sheet away and replacing it. In less than a minute, Jemeryl was able to lower the patient, ready to be tucked up.

While Neame exchanged a few comforting words with Gewyn's companion, Jemeryl tidied up, aware of feeling irked. She supposed it was flattering that Neame trusted her to lift the patient on her own, but it would have been far easier if the senior sorcerer had played her part. Then Jemeryl froze, registering that Neame had offered to call someone else. Why call a third sorcerer when two were already present?

Jemeryl realised she had never seen Neame make use of the sixth dimension. At the time of the accident in the dispensary, she had been in no condition to think, but Neame had physically pulled her from the room, risking her own life with the poisonous fumes. Admittedly, the iron stove made telekinesis difficult. *But it didn't stop me throwing Vine back.*

The demarcation between superior witch and sorcerer was blurred; the Coven never bound itself with inflexible rules. An awareness of all seven dimensions was the customary minimum criteria for sorcerer, yet Neame's abilities seemed suspect.

Jemeryl picked up the tray and went to wait by the door. For the first time, she considered Neame's persona, using the full range of her senses. Now that she was alerted, it was impossible to miss the unbalanced stance and the way Neame followed rather than flowed with the currents—two classic traits of those blind to the sixth dimension.

Jemeryl jerked a small power tensor, making it seem an involuntary twitch. To a sorcerer, the effect was like a loud cough. Neame did not react. Again, Jemeryl disturbed the sixth dimension, a blatant upheaval that should have earned her a disapproving frown. However, Neame appeared no more aware than the young man she was speaking to.

Jemeryl's eyes fixed unseeing on the washed yellow sky outside while her thoughts raced. The hunt for the renegade sorcerer was turned on its head. Neame was off the list of suspects.

❖

Night had fallen by the time Jemeryl returned to her quarters. Darkness lay thick between the school buildings. Her thoughts were absorbed with Neame as she climbed the stairway and walked along the veranda, past the rooms belonging to other junior sorcerers. She pushed open the door to her shared study.

Vine was sitting at a desk overloaded with academic clutter. Encroaching piles had been elbowed aside to clear a workspace. At the edge, several books were threatening to topple off. Another book was propped open a few inches from Vine's nose. She sighed loudly, scrunched up the paper she had been writing on and tossed it over her shoulder. It joined several others on the floor with a soft rustle. Vine was not the tidiest of workers.

Jemeryl dropped into the other chair and rested her elbows on her desk. Her reflection in the window looked back at her, with chin resting on cupped hand and forehead knotted in thought. She considered the rubbish from Vine that had spilled onto her space. It was a long-running but minor source of irritation. Normally, she would have said something, but her mind was elsewhere.

Vine stopped scribbling. "What's up?"

"Neame's blind to the sixth dimension, isn't she?"

There was a long silence. "And the seventh," Vine conceded eventually.

"But she ranks as a sorcerer rather than a witch." Jemeryl merely spoke her thoughts aloud. She was unprepared for the violence of Vine's response.

"Of course she does. Only a bigoted idiot would think otherwise. You've seen her work. No one's ever been able to manipulate the fifth dimension the way she does. She's the most inspired healer there's ever been in Ekranos. Anyone who says Neame doesn't—"

Jemeryl held up her hands. "It's all right. I'm not—"

Vine showed no sign of hearing. She stormed on. "They had no doubts in declaring Neame a sorcerer. None at all. From the day she came here, people knew she was the sort of talent you tear up the rule book for."

"I wasn't trying—"

"Of course some blockheads find it hard to cope with. It's why she was passed over for principal, though it leaves her free to do what she does better than anyone else—saving people's lives. Thousands of people are walking around out there who'd be dead without Neame."

"I don't—"

"She's as much right to her rank as any—"

"I'M NOT DISPUTING IT!" Jemeryl was getting heated herself.

"Oh." Vine sagged back, deflated once her flow of rhetoric had been disrupted.

Jemeryl took her chance. "You know I respect Neame. I've learned more from her in these past weeks than I did from some of the fully gifted teachers after years at Lyremouth. You don't need to argue the point. I was surprised; that's all."

Vine's mouth twitched in a faintly apologetic grimace. "I got a bit steamed up."

"Yes. You did."

"Sorry. All of us in the hospital are devoted to Neame. And when some pigheaded fool who hasn't been here five minutes thinks they're better than—"

Jemeryl cut in. "I wasn't—"

"I know. I wasn't referring to you. There have been others."

"I shouldn't think it was possible to work in the hospital and not admire her."

"Some have managed it."

"That would say more about their lack of ability than Neame's."

"True," Vine agreed. "It also shows a lack of wisdom. It's not a clever stand to take. Making an issue about her rank is just about the only thing, other than deliberate cruelty, that'll get Neame screaming for blood."

"I suppose she feels vulnerable."

"Maybe. It's caused real trouble in the past."

"It was the start of her feud with Levannue?" Jemeryl was struck by the insight.

"Yes. With a couple of added ingredients."

"Such as?"

Vine hesitated, but discretion never stood a chance. She leaned forward and lowered her voice, although no one was around to hear. "What I've heard is, Levannue came here when Neame was finishing her apprenticeship. They were lovers for a while. Very intense and steamy, by all accounts. Then Neame chucked her for someone else. Levannue was heartbroken. Went around crying for weeks. I know it's hard to imagine when you look at her now. Anyway, when she realised she wasn't getting Neame back, she embarked on the spiteful stage of a breakup. She started saying loudly, to anyone who'd listen, that Neame was too handicapped to be ranked as a sorcerer, and *kaboom!*" Vine made an explosive gesture, throwing her hands up into the air.

"They're still arguing about it?"

"Oh, things have moved on. I mean, Levannue's been with Bramell for decades. Presumably, she's over the broken heart. But Neame...she doesn't develop a grudge easily, but once she has, she'll nurse it. I never said she was perfect. And there's been enough sniping down the years to keep things boiling nicely."

Jemeryl tried unsuccessfully to imagine Levannue as a heartbroken teenager. Perhaps the prickly aloofness had been cultivated as a defence. It must be a strain sharing the same site with an ex-lover who would not drop a grudge.

"It sounds as if they could have done with putting space between themselves."

"Maybe, except they couldn't leave Ekranos without sacrificing their careers. Neame had to stay at the hospital, and Levannue was training under old Thirese. He was the Protectorate's leading authority on charms."

"I guess it's one reason to avoid having affairs with other sorcerers."

"Maybe, but I wouldn't recommend using them as an example when Bramell calls you in for a talk about your mercenary."

The reminder of the predicted confrontation made Jemeryl groan. "Do you think anyone's told him about it yet?"

"Probably not. He's usually the last person to hear things. You should be all right for at least another ten days."

"It's none of his business."

"True, but I wouldn't recommend telling him that, either."

"I was intending to phrase it a bit more tactfully."

Vine laughed, her normal good humour restored, until her eyes fixed on her overloaded desk. She glared at the mess as if considering hurling a small fireball. "I don't suppose you fancy finishing this report for me so I can go to bed?"

Jemeryl smiled as she got to her feet. "No. Because that's where I'm headed."

Vine sighed. "You know, just once in a while, do you ever ask yourself what we're doing here in the Coven, writing poxy reports? We could be ruling mighty empires, with thousands of slaves obeying our every whim."

Jemeryl stopped in the doorway and looked back. "I can't see you in the role."

"Why not?"

"Imagine the scene. You, an all-powerful empress, stride into your imperial audience chamber. Ranks of black-clad warriors fall silent. You summon your most trusted warlord to your side and say," Jemeryl switched to an eager undertone, "Hey, have you heard the latest about—" She got no further. Laughing, she dodged the missile Vine tossed in her direction, and dived into her own tidy bedroom.

With the door closed, Jemeryl peeled off her outer layer of clothing and slipped into bed. She lay on her back, hands clasped behind her head, and considered the implications of the evening's disclosures. It was all information, but it did not seem to get anywhere much, except that Neame, blind to the sixth dimension, could neither mind-ride a raven nor read a chalice.

Jemeryl rolled over and pulled the blanket up. As she drifted off, Vine's comment about empires echoed in her head. It had been said in jest, but the question it raised was serious. So far, her attention had been fixed on the who, not the why. Speculating about the traitor's motives was not comforting. Iralin had known the purpose of the spell, and Iralin had been frightened.

❖

The small cellar tavern was crowded and noisy. The air smelt thick from lantern smoke mixed with sweat and spilt beer. The atmosphere was friendly—extremely friendly, since whores and their customers formed a large section of the clientele.

In one of the rowdier corners, Tevi sat with Klara perched on her shoulder among a group of mercenaries. A member of the bar staff appeared between the press of bodies with three tankards of beer in either hand. He deposited them on the table, the contents miraculously unspilt.

"I'll pay for these." Tevi's offer was greeted by loud cheers.

She stood up, fumbling with the purse at her belt. As she shook out the coins, a brass key slipped through her fingers and clattered to the table. One of the others picked it up.

"What's this?" he asked once the waiter had gone.

Someone else suggested, "Back door of a...ahem...friend's house, for use when their partner is away?"

"No. It's the key to the customs office. I was supposed to hand it in at the harbour master's. I must have dropped it into my purse instead." The words themselves were not untrue, although implying an oversight was misleading. Tevi reclaimed the key and twirled it thoughtfully between thumb and finger. "I'd better take it back."

"You can drop it in first thing tomorrow."

"It's not far, and I don't want to get into trouble."

"I doubt anyone will notice it's missing."

"Hopefully not, but I'll do it anyway. Look after my beer. I expect to see a full tankard when I return."

"There's an optimist for you." The speaker was teasing. There was no doubt that Tevi's drink would be safe and untouched on her return. Stealing from your comrades, no matter how trivial, was unthinkable.

Tevi squeezed her way to the door, edging between the drinkers. Once outside, she leapt up the flight of steps to street level and expelled the thick air from her lungs. The tavern was in the run-down section of town backing on to the docks. Given the late hour, a surprising number of people were about. The hubbub from the tavern followed her down the street.

A brisk pace took her through the maze of alleys to the customs office. Before opening the door, she hesitated and looked up and down the street. Three drunken sailors were staggering back to the harbour. They were attempting to have a repetitive conversation, although they did not all seem to be discussing the same thing. In the other direction, two merchants were talking far more purposefully in a warehouse doorway. No one paid any attention as Tevi inserted the key in the lock.

A lamp and flint stood on a shelf just inside the door. It was the work of seconds to find the right book and carefully count out the pages. Tevi propped the import records open on the desk and lifted Klara down from her shoulder.

"Read, Klara. Go on. Read for Jem."

The magpie's beady eyes glittered. Her head bobbed twice; then she stepped close, her beak almost touching the paper. Tevi hoped it would not take her long to memorise the page.

Tevi wandered to the front of the office and peered through a window. Sneaking Klara in during the day had been impossible. Pets were not allowed on duty, and the office was rarely left unoccupied. She had eagerly seized the chance to take the key. The scene in the tavern had been staged to provide witnesses to her "accidental" discovery of her mistake. When she handed it in, she would also say that she had popped into the office to check that nothing else had been left undone—just in case signs of her visit were discovered in the morning.

A soft squawk from Klara announced that she had finished. Quickly, Tevi replaced the book and blew out the lamp. Only a couple of minutes after entering, she was again outside, locking the door and fighting hard to keep a self-satisfied smile from her face.

The two merchants were still in the doorway. If asked, they could confirm that she had been alone. But surely nobody would suspect her of deliberately taking the key to a room containing nothing but books she could not read.

❖

The school bell was just striking noon as Jemeryl swung the bag over her shoulder and closed the study door behind her. She hurried along the veranda and leapt down the staircase, eager to be gone. She was missing Tevi even more than she had expected. At the stables, a horse was already saddled and waiting. Within minutes, she was outside the school and trotting along the dusty road into town.

The midday sun bleached the colour from the landscape. Spring was turning to summer, and the transient green was fading to parched brown. The horse's hooves sent gravel bouncing through the dry dust. A sprinkling of traffic was also on the road, mainly farm carts.

Before Jemeryl had covered a quarter of the distance, sweat was flecking the horse's flanks. Despite her impatience, she would have to slow her pace. She was just about to rein back when she overtook Erlam, who was travelling on official business, judging by his formal clothing.

Jemeryl hailed him and brought her horse to a walk. "You heading into Ekranos?"

"Yes. A meeting with the town council."

"Anything exciting?"

"Have you met the town council?" The ironic edge answered the question.

"Nearly as much fun as working with Tapley?"

"Exactly. Though I hear you made quite an impression on him."

"I did?" Jemeryl was surprised the raven keeper could even remember her.

"Vine hasn't told you?"

"No."

"Apparently you've got real talent for mind-riding, which is rare in the school, apart from those in Levannue's section."

"So why do all sorcerers train with them? Why not just one or two who have the talent? I can't see that they're used very often."

"Sorcerers' pride. You know what we're like. None of us wants to lose face in front of the witches by having to ask another sorcerer to do something for us."

"I'm sure that..." Jemeryl stopped. Erlam was not so far from the truth. It made her think of Neame's sensitivity about her limitations. "I suppose that's why Neame wanted to make an artificial bird?"

"You've heard about it?"

"Tapley told me. He was outraged."

"I can imagine."

"He didn't think it could work."

"It should have. In theory."

"But not so easy in practice?" Jemeryl suggested.

"Exactly."

"Were you one of the people working on it?" It seemed a likely bet for Neame's assistant.

"I helped."

"Was it a true golem, with a pseudolife of its own?"

"That was the intention."

"So as long as you told it what to get, it could have gone to the ends of the earth and back?"

"Again, in theory."

"How far had the project got?"

"Hard to say. It seemed as if it was almost done. Then there were a couple of minor accidents. They might have been teething problems, or they might have been serious design flaws. We never got the chance to find out." Erlam sounded annoyed. "Bramell took fright and ordered Neame to stop. It was unpleasant. He marched in, confiscated everything, and locked it up in his office. Neame was furious."

"So she took herself off to Walderim for a while to calm down?"

"That was about it." Erlam's voice tightened noticeably.

Too late, Jemeryl remembered that mentioning the expedition to Walderim was not diplomatic. Understandably, his partner's death was a painful subject for Erlam. By mutual consent, the subject was dropped. For a while, they discussed general school matters until, at the outskirts of Ekranos, Erlam changed topic.

"I hear you've got yourself a lover in town."

"I guess there was no chance keeping it secret when I share a study with Vine."

"None whatsoever."

"I've been warned I'll be in for a lecture when the news gets to Bramell. I know they prefer for us to stick to Coven members, but it's not as if affairs between sorcerers haven't caused problems in the past." Jemeryl was thinking of Neame and Levannue; however, Erlam took her statement more personally.

"You've heard about me and Aris." His voice was strained.

Again, Jemeryl cursed her own tactlessness. "Um...yes."

"It's all right. I can talk about her. It's supposed to be good for me."

"Oh." Jemeryl was at a loss. The grief in his voice was overwhelming. She could not bring herself to probe at the raw wound, but Erlam seemed suddenly eager to talk.

"The relationship was trouble from the start, but if I had my time again, I'd—" He broke off. "She used to say she needed me, but often, it seemed like I only made her worse. Anything could send her into a depression, crying. And then other times...I never knew how she'd be from one day to the next. She was impossible to live with, but I miss her."

"Could nothing be done?"

"Not without going back in time and blasting her parents to ashes. It was their fault. I know our families have a hard time, but my parents still loved me, even when they realised I was a sorcerer. Hers were vicious. They were frightened of her. From when she was a baby, they used every cruel, spiteful trick to keep her under their thumb. They made her hate herself." His voice dropped so that it was barely audible. "That's why she did it. Climbed to the top of a tower and jumped off. I keep telling myself it wasn't my fault, but she needed me, and I wasn't there."

"Couldn't Neame..." Jemeryl began, although she was not sure what anyone could have done.

"Aris was alone at the time. The expedition to Walderim was just her, Neame, and two witches. The others went off for a few days to get samples. They left Aris behind to do the processing. When they got back, she was..." Erlam did not finish the sentence. "I know Neame curses herself for leaving Aris alone. But she had been getting so much calmer, and they thought a break from the school would help."

By now, they were riding through the streets of Ekranos, but Erlam seemed unaware of the bustle around them. His eyes were fixed on the distance. "I was sitting here waiting for her to come back, counting the days and watching the boats sail into harbour, and all the time she was already dead and gone."

Jemeryl searched desperately for something to say that was neither trite nor hopelessly inadequate. Nothing felt right, yet silence was the worst response of all. "I'm sorry. I didn't mean to dredge this up for you."

"It's all right. I'm starting to come to terms with losing her. Maybe another few years..." Erlam's bitter smile looked more like a grimace. "Perhaps the talking will help."

The junction where their paths separated was close. After a few parting words, Jemeryl turned onto the side street. She was ashamed of her relief. Erlam's misery was infectious, but the feeling did not last. With rising spirits, she headed for her rendezvous with Tevi at the Inn of Singing Birds.

❖

The windows of the upstairs room were flung wide open. Tevi sat on the deep wooden sill with her feet up, enjoying the sun on her face and the gentle breeze carrying the sounds and smells of the city. In the square below, people moved about their business, but the pace was slow and lazy in the late afternoon heat.

It was easy to fall into the unhurried rhythm of Ekranos, to sit and watch the world go by. Tevi yawned and looked back into the dimness of the room. The solid furniture had seen better days; time had left the surfaces pitted and stained. A fresh coat of paint would have improved the walls, and the green window glass was poor quality. However, the room was clean and comfortable.

Just inside the window, Jemeryl sat writing at a small table. Her face was serious in concentration as her hand flew across the page. The sun caught on the sharp lines of her cheekbone and jaw, emphasising the texture of her skin and making a soft shadow where her shirt hung open at the neck. Tevi sat studying her lover. Her life had changed so much since leaving Storenseg. It was barely over a year but seemed a lifetime. She felt as if some other woman had been entrapped, betrayed, and exiled that evening in the hay barn.

Tevi slipped down from the windowsill and stood behind Jemeryl. She leaned against the back of the chair and watched the lines of writing appear under the pen. Four columns were forming, one wide and three narrow, marching steadily down the page. The numbers were familiar, thanks to lessons with Marith. The letters were a complete mystery.

At the back of the table, Klara was frozen in a trance. Only the ruffling of her feathers in the breeze showed that she was not a painted statue. Where bright sunlight fell across her plumage, it shimmered metallic blue-black, set against crisp white. Abruptly, Klara stirred. A twitch of the head and neck spread down her back, growing into several full beats of her wings.

Jemeryl sighed and put down the pen. She leaned back and rested her head against Tevi. "Well, that's the information I needed."

"I got the right page?"

"Spot on." Jemeryl pulled Tevi's head down for a quick kiss. "All I have to do now is find out how much nectar can be accounted for in the school records."

"Anything else you want me to do?"

"See if you can pick up any more gossip in town."

"There's not much chance of that. Most ordinary people don't concern themselves with the doings of sorcerers."

"I suppose I should be pleased you're not ordinary."

"Even I'm not very interested in sorcerers in general. Just two in particular."

"Two?" Jemeryl raised her eyebrows.

"You and our traitor."

"Oh."

Tevi returned to the windowsill. "You're sure Neame is in the clear?"

"Yes." Jemeryl swivelled to face Tevi, resting her arms on the back of her chair. "The fifth dimension holds the spirits of life; they're called auras. Neame is able to manipulate them like no one else in the Coven. But to mind-ride, you have to control both auras and power tensors, and that needs access to the sixth dimension. She couldn't have sent the raven to your island."

"Maybe she tricked Aris into doing it for her."

"Even if she had, Neame would be incapable of reading the information from the chalice." Jemeryl stared through the window, frowning. "Nobody outside Walderim could have got the raven to the island. Aris was the only person in Walderim capable of mind-riding, but she's obviously not a suspect now."

"You seem to be saying that the party in Walderim wasn't able to take the chalice, and nobody else could either."

"Yes, if they used the ravens, but there's another possibility. Neame's golem bird. Erlam claims that it was functional, but Bramell had it under lock and key."

"Why?"

"Safety, so he claimed. He was very keen to get his hands on it." There was no need for Jemeryl to spell out the implications.

"Could anyone else have got to the...what did you call it—golem bird?"

"Unfortunately, yes. At the time the chalice was taken, the entire school was in chaos due to plague. Moragar was in charge and free to do anything he wanted. Levannue also recovered quickly, and since she shares Bramell's quarters, she'd have no trouble helping herself to his property. However, given the state of anarchy, virtually anyone capable of standing could have done the same. The only two we can eliminate are Neame, who was out in Walderim; and Uwien, the master of apprentices, who was still in Denbury. He was never a strong candidate anyway."

"So you think it was Bramell, Levannue, or Moragar?"

"I suppose there are a few weaker bets."

"Such as?"

"Erlam. He's not a senior sorcerer, but since Neame's blind to the sixth dimension, she can't supervise him as tightly as I'd assumed. He might have used the golem bird to get the chalice himself, or he might have been working with Aris...or not." Jemeryl corrected herself. "She couldn't have returned it to him."

Tevi's head shot up. "Perhaps Aris did take the chalice. The only thing we know for certain is that it went from Storenseg. There's no evidence it ever got to Ekranos. It might be buried with Aris, for all we know."

"It's possible. But I've got this gut feeling it's here. We need proof, which is where cross-referencing the import list will be useful."

Voices and laughter from the square were getting louder as the sun dropped. A breeze stirred the warm air. Jemeryl left her chair and put her arm around Tevi's waist. Early evening sunlight dusted the city with yellow. The first groups were congregating on the benches in front of the tavern. Distant flocks of seagulls circled above the harbour.

Jemeryl rested her head against Tevi's. "It's going to be difficult getting access to the dispensary. The trouble is I'm not senior enough. I wish Iralin had been sent to investigate here."

"She couldn't be allowed to."

"Why not?"

"She must be under suspicion herself."

"Don't be silly."

"I'm not. Surely you realised that since Iralin knew all about Lorimal to start with, she's right up with the rest of the suspects. The Guardian said the three seniors were going to investigate in Lyremouth. I bet they started by investigating one another. The last thing any two would allow is letting the third one out of their sight."

"You may be right. Except I can't imagine Iralin breaking the rules."

"But we don't know just how much of a temptation this spell is."

"True."

"Have you really no idea what it does?"

Jemeryl shook her head with a sigh.

"What sort of things aren't you allowed to try doing?"

"Reversing death is a big one—like creating zombies. All experiments have failed, but some very nasty things have happened along the way. Searching for immortality is also banned since it involves trying to steal someone's life essence or playing horrendous games with time."

"What else?"

"We aren't allowed to enslave the ungifted, and anything which might undermine the Protectorate's economy or cause wide-scale destruction is out. I'd say the most tempting violation is changing the past, which is theoretically possible, but insanely dangerous."

"Do sorcerers outside the Coven ever try to do it?"

"Some have. The spots where they made the attempt are usually marked by rather large craters." Jemeryl's normal grin returned. "After that you get to esoteric experiments, like infinite loops impinging on physical space, but you'd have to be a bit unbalanced to even want to try those."

"You're a young ambitious sorcerer, like Lorimal. What would tempt you to break the rules and poke into things you shouldn't?"

Jemeryl scowled in mock outrage. "Would I do a thing like that?"

"I know a hundred villagers who'd say yes."

"I thought we'd agreed they misunderstood me?"

"Maybe."

"Anyway, it's not the same. Lorimal was an herbalist, which is my weakest discipline. It's certainly not straining my acting, playing the part of someone who needs to improve her skill."

"So where does this leave us?"

Jemeryl chewed her lip. "If I had to make a guess, I'd go for Lorimal's spell being a method of mind control. There are several drugs that make people more malleable, and her speciality was formulas producing permanent physical or mental effects. She may have produced a potion that would turn people into willing slaves."

"Is that likely? I thought the Guardian said she wasn't malicious, just naïve."

"I'm afraid some sorcerers are convinced the world would be a happier place if everyone obeyed the Coven without question." Jemeryl shrugged and pulled Tevi from the window ledge. "But it's all just guesswork on my part. Come on; it's cooling down. Let's go for a walk before dinner."

Arm in arm, they left the room.

❖

Jemeryl awoke in the middle of the night. In deference to the heat, the shutters and windows were open, but the weather had changed. She could hear the rustle of light rain hitting the leaves outside—a rare occurrence in the Ekranos summer. The soft sound was carried on a current of fresh, sweet air.

The light was just sufficient for Jemeryl to see the woman lying beside her. Tevi's face was relaxed and artless in sleep. Strands of dark hair fell across her cheek. One arm was flung over the covers. Her soft breathing made an undertone to the rainfall. At the sight of her lover, Jemeryl felt her insides melt into a soft gooey mess with a small hot fire at the core.

Jemeryl resisted the temptation to wake Tevi. Instead, she rolled onto her back, listening to the patter of water. Restless thoughts pushed sleep away. Tevi's comment about the seniors in Lyremouth not trusting each other was an obvious point that had not occurred to her before. In Jemeryl's mind, Iralin personified the integrity of the Coven, but of course, Tevi was right. The world was out of kilter. Jemeryl shook her head at her own naïveté; maybe if she were more cynical, she might make better progress.

Despite all she had learned, she had no evidence implicating anyone. Jemeryl knew she was pinning a lot on the dispensary records. Not that she thought the renegade sorcerer would have boldly signed out large quantities of the drug. An unaccountable shortfall was all she hoped for, but it would confirm her belief that the traitor was in Ekranos and working on the forbidden spell.

It was not going to be easy. Jemeryl stared into the darkness, contemplating her chances. Even if the dispensary records had been in immaculate order, she had no hope of being allowed to peruse them at her leisure. Sneaking in after dark to study Orrago's data seemed hardly worth the risk.

A harder belt of rain hit the window. The rhythm of Tevi's breathing faltered and then resumed with a sound halfway between a cough and a snore. Jemeryl sighed and adjusted her pillow. She was about to attempt a return to sleep when a flash of inspiration struck her, the beginnings of a plan—one that would take a degree of luck but might just work.

A grin crossed Jemeryl's face. Her scheme contained no serious risk and even a degree of entertainment. She was sure that Bramell's face would be a picture. Jemeryl rolled onto her side and snuggled against Tevi, pulling her lover's arm around her. The fine detail could wait until morning. She had the basic plan.

Chapter Seven—A Discovery in the Dispensary

The time for the library to close was getting near. Jemeryl wandered aimlessly, trailing a hand along the book spines. She was supposedly there to find a work recommended by Neame but was expending more effort in brooding on her lack of progress. From the start, she had known her plan to gain access to the dispensary records would require a combination of luck and timing. Over the previous six days, she had put a lot of ingenuity into manipulating events and got nowhere.

The drifting took Jemeryl to a balcony overlooking the main hall. Nearly everyone had departed the upper floors. Only two apprentices were visible, gossiping in the room opposite, and a lone set of footsteps echoed from above.

Jemeryl rested her arms on the rail and gazed down on the central body of the hall. Rows of bookshelves stretched across the black and white mosaic floor. The number of people visible between the shelves could be counted on the fingers of one hand. Abruptly, Jemeryl froze, arrested by the sight of the very situation she had been trying to contrive.

Bramell was seated at a side table, running his finger down a ledger, engaged in his favourite pastime of checking records. Slightly behind him stood Moragar, looking peeved and obviously unappreciative of the principal's interest in library affairs. Not twenty feet away, in an aisle between two bookshelves, Vine was flipping through a volume. She was obscured from the sight of the other two but not out of earshot.

There was no time to waste. Jemeryl scuttled to the stairway as quickly as possible without attracting attention. On the ground floor, she stole around the edge of the hall so as to approach Vine without encountering Bramell.

One by one, the deserted aisles slipped by. She reached the final row. Vine had not moved. The plan required that Bramell also still be in place, but she dared not peer around the corner or disturb the ether by scrying. Jemeryl slowed her steps to a sullen prowl and entered the aisle. A few nagging doubts were summarily dismissed. Now was not the time to worry about the chances of success.

The first part of the plan required adopting a demeanour of angry irritation.

Vine glanced up. Her smile of greeting faded as she registered Jemeryl's expression. "What's wrong? Is something bothering you?"

"Orrago," Jemeryl snapped at the maximum volume acceptable in the library. "The dispensary is a pigsty."

"It's not that bad."

"No, it's worse. Pigs would be more organised."

"But it's not your problem." Vine's voice dropped to a warning hiss.

Jemeryl ignored the hint. "It is my problem when I've wasted an hour learning we're out of the thing I want. Of course, I feel sorry for Orrago, but the dispensary is beyond a joke. Which idiot had the idea of putting her in charge? I hope if ever I turn senile, they'll have the discretion to hide me somewhere where I won't be an embarrassment."

Vine made a damping-down gesture and said pointedly, "You don't really mean that about Orrago."

"You're right. It's not Orrago's fault. Bramell's the one who needs a good kicking. I don't understand him; he's usually so keen to stick his nose into other people's business. Surely he could get off his arse and get someone to sort it out. He's supposed to be good at ensuring that things are organised into neat little rows. Nobody can be useless at everything."

Vine was now frantically trying to point through the bookcase and mouthing Bramell's name.

Jemeryl acted as if she did not understand the gesture. If anything, she raised her voice. "I suppose you can't expect someone of Bramell's ability to understand the importance of having the dispensary in order. But maybe it's deliberate. Perhaps he hopes if nobody else can get the things they want, it won't be so obvious that he needs three attempts to guess the name of a buttercup."

Vine opened her mouth, although all that came out was a faint squeak.

"I've always thought Bramell was a waste of space. And it's not as if it requires any ability or initiative on his part. He just needs to delegate someone to help Orrago. The dispensary is a total disgrace."

"And that is a disgraceful way to refer to senior members of this school." Bramell's voice rang out from the end of the aisle.

Jemeryl had to make a conscious effort to hide her relief. She had been starting to fear that Bramell had left the library. Her eyes dropped while she composed her expression into one of shocked dismay. She almost lost her self-control again when she caught sight of Vine's pitying look.

"Jemeryl," Bramell snapped.

Slowly, Jemeryl turned to face the furious principal. "Er... yes, sir?"

"What were you saying?"

"Nothing, sir."

"*Nothing*?" Bramell's voice cracked like a whip. He was shaking with outrage.

"No, sir."

"Well, I heard quite a bit of your *nothing*. And I think we should go to my office and discuss this *nothing* in more detail."

Jemeryl was unceremoniously marched across the main quad. Bramell's manner was such that Jemeryl half expected him to take hold of her by the ear. She felt a rising indignation. After all, she was an amulet-wearing sorcerer, not an unruly apprentice. Nothing in the Coven rules forbade her having, or expressing, critical views about the seniors.

Bramell strode into his office. Jemeryl stopped on the rug in the middle of the floor and looked at her feet. She was quite literally on the carpet. The door shut with a firm, deliberate clunk, and Bramell stalked around the desk to his chair. His eyes fixed her with a frosty stare; his lips were firm in righteous condemnation. Even his nostrils were flaring.

The silence stretched out, and even though things were going to plan, Jemeryl felt her stomach knot. Eventually, Bramell took a deep breath. "Now. Perhaps you would like to explain exactly what you meant?"

❖

It was an hour before Jemeryl left the office with a very clear understanding of Bramell's opinion concerning her. He had also used the opportunity to include the anticipated lecture on relationships with the ungifted. On his words of dismissal, Jemeryl fled across site to her room.

Since Vine had witnessed the incident, it was certain that half the school would already know what had happened. Those who saw her running from Bramell's office might well interpret it as distress and assume that she was seeking somewhere private to cry. Jemeryl was not about to correct the misconception.

She leapt up the stairs of the junior's quarters, burst into the study, and dived into her bedroom. With her shoulder, she slammed the door shut and then leant her weight against it. At last, she could give vent to her elation. Both fists punched the air. Bramell was so predictable, once you got the measure of the man. She had been sentenced to spend all her free time tidying the dispensary.

❖

The dull beat of waves vied with the trill of grasshoppers in the darkness. Moths fluttered on soft wings through the warm air. Jemeryl and Vine walked away from the hospital side by side, comparing notes on the day's gossip—who had said what about whom, and why. It could be fun. Vine had been right about the incestuous nature of life in the school.

Jemeryl halted where the path to the dispensary split off. "I'm going to put in a bit more work on tidying."

"Didn't you hear Jan say he's perfected his recipe for mulled wine? Aren't you coming to help test it?"

"It's a shame to miss the wine, but I really want to push on."

"You know, no matter how much enthusiasm you show, it's going to be a while before you'll be a candidate for the post of Bramell's favourite junior."

"It's not to impress Bramell."

"Then why are you so keen?"

"I'm hoping another hour will see the thing finished."

"It's taken you long enough."

"Best part of a month." The work had exceeded Jemeryl's most pessimistic prediction.

"And you haven't seen much of your young mercenary. She might have forgotten you..." Vine stopped. "Oh, of course! You've got a free afternoon tomorrow. That's why you're so keen to finish the job tonight. Well, I won't keep you."

Jemeryl let her grin confirm the speculation. She had gone a few yards when Vine hailed her again. "Oh, and Jem?"

"Yes?"

"If ever you want to do something like that again, let me know in advance. I could have sold tickets."

Jemeryl walked on alone, smiling at the irony. Vine had been joking and clearly had no idea just how deliberate the whole scene had been. This was very comforting. If Vine did not suspect that she had ulterior motives, it was a safe bet no one else did either. However, Vine had been quite right about her reason for wanting to finish the job that night. Jemeryl was missing Tevi with a painful intensity. She did not think she could bear another day without seeing her. It was not just about making love. She wanted to see Tevi's face, hold her hand, hear her voice—although making love as well would be pretty good.

Jemeryl's polite call announcing her arrival was met with silence. Luckily, Orrago was not in the dispensary. The work would go quicker without interruptions. In the light of a conjured globe, Jemeryl looked around, feeling considerable satisfaction. The packing cases were gone. Jars stood in orderly rows, arranged alphabetically by section, each clearly marked with a new label. Neat bunches of herbs hung from racks. The surfaces were clear. Of the previous disorder, only a pile of wooden boxes remained, balanced on the top of one tall cupboard.

Jemeryl flipped open the pages of the inventory. In the course of tidying and organising, she had performed a full audit. A significant quantity of the nectar was outstanding. *But it's too soon to be certain.* Jemeryl cast a critical eye at the last few boxes. *There could be several gallons of the stuff up there.*

The first box dislodged itself from its perch and floated across to Jemeryl. Dust arose in a cloud when she lifted the top off. Inside was a jumble of half-empty bags and grimy bottles. Grimacing slightly, Jemeryl pulled out the first of the contents and set to work.

❖

Time passed quickly. Each box was emptied in turn. Anything rendered useless by age was discarded and the rest was added to the appropriate stock. Jemeryl tried to contain her growing excitement at the absence of the nectar. Not until the final item was checked could she be sure.

At last, only one large bottle remained. A film of dirt and fluff coated the outside. Its contents were translucent yellow. Jemeryl lifted it up, squinting to read the faded label. Faintly legible were the words "garlic oil." She grinned. Her nose could have told her as much.

She wrote a new label, wiped the bottle, and placed it in the correct spot on the shelves. Then Jemeryl made one last circuit of the dispensary, looking under benches and behind doors, and checking that no drawer had been overlooked. Now she was certain. The inventory was complete.

Jemeryl leaned against a counter, triumphant. During the past two years, someone had pilfered over half the school's supply of the nectar. Her hunch was confirmed. The renegade sorcerer was in Ekranos and working on the forbidden spell. And as a final bonus, she would be free to meet with Tevi tomorrow afternoon. Surely, the dispensary was now tidy enough to meet the terms of Bramell's sentence. Or was it?

Rubbish littered the floor: leaves and scraps of paper, even a half-chewed worm, undoubtedly a contribution from Frog. It might be as well to put the finishing touch on the job. She did not want to give Bramell an excuse to confine her within school grounds for a day longer.

Jemeryl found a broom. The task of sweeping was half complete when the door opened and Orrago hobbled in. The elderly sorcerer looked about at the neatly stacked shelves with a delighted but vacant smile.

"You've done a good job, Iralin. Or is it Jelimar?"

"It's Jemeryl, ma'am."

"Oh, yes, yes, of course." Orrago dug Frog out of her pocket and deposited him on a bench. The toad's bulging eyes blinked wetly in the mage light. "Anyway, as I was saying, you've done well. It was kind of you to volunteer. I needed a little help."

Honesty forced Jemeryl to admit, "Er...I didn't quite volunteer."

She was uncertain how fully the reason for her working in the dispensary had been explained. Not that Orrago would remember anyway.

"Oh, dear. Who was it, then?"

"Who was what, ma'am?"

"The one who said...who was...oh, you know." Orrago shook her head and wandered off to her chair. "They can tell me in the morning. You can carry on."

Jemeryl returned to sweeping. She worked her way around the room until she reached a small bookcase. It stood an inch or two clear of the wall, which had allowed a good assortment of litter to slip down the back and form a thick wedge at the bottom. Jemeryl grabbed one end of the bookcase and pulled hard, hoping to swing it out enough to get the broom in. Even as she did so, it occurred to her that removing the rubbish by telekinesis might be easier, especially since the bookcase was heavier than expected and only shuddered forward a few inches. The feet screeched on the floorboards but not loudly enough to mask the sound of something dropping.

A second, stronger tug shifted the bookcase farther from the wall. Jemeryl peered over the top. Lying on the floor amid the general debris was a handwritten pamphlet. Jemeryl retrieved it and walked over to examine her find in the light of the globe. Neatly printed on the cover were the words "The prevention of cancerous growths and associated tumours, by Lorimal of the Coven."

"What is it?" Orrago asked from her chair.

"It's a manuscript." Jemeryl had forgotten that Moragar claimed the pamphlet was lost in the dispensary.

"Oh, that's good."

"It's the one that's went missing some time ago." Jemeryl walked over to the ancient sorcerer and held out the pamphlet. "Do you remember this, ma'am?"

"What is it?"

"A manuscript."

"Yes. Can you give it to Druse for me?"

Jemeryl abandoned the pointless questions and returned to the bookcase. A horizontal strut ran across its back about eighteen inches below the top. A disturbance in the dust midway along marked the spot where the pamphlet had lodged. There was also a slip of paper trapped between the strut and the backboard by a corner, crumpled where the pamphlet had pressed down on it. Jemeryl plucked the paper free and smoothed it flat. It was a receipt from a supplier in town.

The date caught her attention immediately—just under four years old. According to Moragar, it was six years since Lorimal's thesis had been lost. Anyone might have assumed that the manuscript had slipped down behind the bookcase and lain undisturbed for all that time were it not for the receipt. The manuscript had been on top of it and therefore must have been put behind the bookcase some years after Moragar had dowsed it to the dispensary.

Jemeryl studied the marks in the dust more carefully. It looked as if the manuscript had been taken and replaced several times. Presumably, on one occasion, the receipt had been accidentally pushed down as well and become trapped.

Jemeryl completed sweeping, then bid Orrago good night and walked back to her room, holding the manuscript firmly. Cleaning the dispensary had been a long job, but it had furnished the wanted evidence. The traitor was in Ekranos, and she had found the stolen manuscript. All in all, it had been most worthwhile.

❖

The distance was lost to a shimmering haze. The sun blazed down on the school without a wisp of cloud to weaken its force. On the upper balcony, the door to the study shared by Jemeryl and Vine was wedged open for the breeze. Light bounced off the floorboards and gleamed yellow on the ceiling.

Jemeryl sat hunched over her desk, rocked forward on the chair's front legs. She was alone, making use of the break before the midday meal. In front of her, the two copies of Lorimal's report lay open at the beginning. Once again, she thumbed her way through the pages, trying to spot differences between the original and later transcript.

Lorimal's manuscript was scribbled in a childlike, block-letter hand. The lines rose and fell across the page. The paper was yellowing, worn from handling, with occasional dog-eared corners. By comparison, the transcript was neatly set on crisp white pages, in the classic unvarying letters of magical graphology. That was the only difference: Not a single letter was missing from the copy.

Jemeryl frowned in confusion. She had been sure she would find notes in the margin or a missing appendix. Else why bother to steal the original?

She reached the final page. In the transcribed book, the next chapter moved on to an associated report by another sorcerer. The remaining few pages in the original were blank except for a collection of circular stains. Every test Jemeryl could think of showed the paper to be free of concealed writing. The only thing she could learn from the pages was that Lorimal had used the rear of her manuscript as a table mat.

She leaned back, glaring at the ceiling and wondering if she was missing the obvious. Perhaps a different viewpoint was needed. Jemeryl's expression softened. In a few hours, she was meeting Tevi. Talking it over with someone else might help. Jemeryl's gaze drifted back to the sprawled handwritten lines. She imagined a young woman much like herself who had written the words, and then the old woman who had died on Storenseg and the life in between.

Her musings were interrupted by the sound of rapid footsteps coming to a halt outside. Jemeryl swivelled, hooking an arm over the back of her chair. A young apprentice rested a hand on either side of the door frame and leaned into the room.

"Bramell wants to see you in his office immediately." The boy gave the message with a breezy lilt to his voice. "And he says to bring the book you found in the dispensary with you."

"What did..."

The messenger was not available for further questioning. Already, his footsteps were fading. Jemeryl grabbed the book and followed. Surely Bramell was not planning fresh ways to keep her and Tevi apart, but whatever the problem, things would not be improved by making him wait. Yet despite the need for haste, she hesitated at the door to his office, daunted by memories of her last visit. Through the solid wood came the rise and fall of voices, although too muffled for her to distinguish words.

Her cautious knock was answered by Bramell's autocratic tones. Jemeryl pushed the door open. The principal sat behind his desk, a flush of anger darkening his features. Moragar was also present, standing by the window with arms crossed and a stubborn frown. A disagreement was obviously in progress. Jemeryl's entrance put a halt to it. Bramell looked at her as if she were something unsavoury that had just crawled into his office.

"You wanted to see me, sir?"

"Moragar informs me you're in possession of a book that was improperly removed from the library. Is this true?"

"Not by me, sir. I found it in the dispensary while cleaning."

"Why didn't you return it immediately?"

"I only found it last night, sir."

"You should have informed me at once"—Moragar joined the attack—"rather than leaving me to find out at second hand."

"I'm sorry, sir. I hadn't realised you'd be concerned."

"It's my job to be concerned over books that belong in the library."

Jemeryl bowed her head while directing silent curses at her study partner. She had no need to guess who the second hand belonged to. Why couldn't Vine mind her own business for once?

Bramell spoke again. "This book can be left here with me."

"Er...I had intended to borrow it formally next time I went to the library, sir."

"I've been told that you already have a perfectly adequate copy."

"It's nice to have the original."

Bramell's eyes bored into Jemeryl. "I don't understand why you want the book at all. Surely it falls outside the scope of your work at the hospital."

"It's just something that caught my attention, sir."

"It would be better if you focused on things that are relevant to your studies." There was a long, painful silence. "It might also be better if we made more effective use of your talents. Medicine is not your strength. I'll arrange for you to transfer to Levannue's section. She needs assistance with work on charms. Return anything you have out at the moment. You can start by leaving the manuscript with me."

"Yes, sir." Jemeryl put the pamphlet on the table and stood with her eyes fixed on the floor.

"Report to Levannue first thing tomorrow." Bramell leaned back, steepling his fingers. "That is all. You may go."

Jemeryl stormed back to her study, furious to have lost the manuscript. She threw herself down in her chair and glared through the window. She was certain she had just had an important clue snatched from her. If only she could have identified it.

❖

"It's so frustrating. I had the manuscript in my hands, and I lost it."

Tevi rolled onto her side. Jemeryl was lying on her back with her hands behind her head, staring at the ceiling. Soft, early evening sunlight streamed in through the open widow of their room. They had spent the past few hours alternating between making love, talking, and dozing. This was obviously going to be a time for talking.

"There was nothing you could have done," Tevi said reasonably.

"I know. Bramell made certain of that."

Tevi snuggled closer in the bed and wrapped an arm around her waist. "Come on, Jem. Cheer up. Think of what you've achieved. We know the traitor is here."

"True." Jemeryl did not sound mollified.

Tevi rubbed the side of Jemeryl's breast with her thumb, in a gesture intended to be comforting rather than arousing. For a moment, her thoughts diverted, struck by a recognition of how much her attitudes had changed since leaving the islands. There, to have another women as a lover would have been so very dangerous. Any liaison would need to be confined to furtive minutes, a secret severed from any other daily activity. Here, Jemeryl and she could lie together naked and talk as casually as if they were dressed and seated in the bar. Being lovers was integrated into the pattern of her life in a way that would be inconceivable on Storenseg.

Her mind returned to the manuscript. "Could you tell anything from Bramell's attitude?"

"Such as?"

"If he's the culprit, he'd be very sensitive about Lorimal. Did he give anything away?"

Jemeryl pondered the question. "I think it points to him being innocent. Otherwise, he'd have been keener to know why I was interested in Lorimal's work. All he did was divert me away from it. To be fair, it's what he's supposed to do. But it's going to make things harder. Bramell will be making sure I stay clear of Lorimal."

"You said he was overzealous."

"That's Bramell for you. It's what the man does best."

"How about Moragar?"

"I was too angry to pay much attention to him. But..." Jemeryl paused.

"Yes?"

"I think he and Bramell were arguing when I arrived."

"Over the manuscript?"

"That's the most likely topic. I know Bramell has kept hold of it. Perhaps Moragar wanted the original back." Jemeryl looked thoughtful. "Now that I think about it, he got very heated once before when talking about it. If he went as far as arguing with Bramell, he must be very keen to get his hands on Lorimal's handiwork."

"But that's only guesswork?"

"Yes. And the thing is, I'd have thought Moragar and Bramell were the two people least likely to have hidden the manuscript in the dispensary to start with. Moragar can do whatever he likes with the books in the library, and Bramell has access to much better hiding places."

"It might depend on the reason why the book was put there."

"It can't have been simply to keep it from others; else why not destroy it completely?"

A light breeze gusted in through the window. Evening was drawing close and the air was noticeably cooler on Tevi's skin. She reached down and pulled up a light sheet to cover them. When Tevi lay back down, Jemeryl twisted to burrow into the circle of her arms, although the matter of the manuscript still clearly preoccupied her thoughts.

"From the receipt, we know the book was removed and replaced behind the shelves at least once. I'd guess someone hid it so they could consult it whenever they liked without drawing attention by continually borrowing it from the library. The book was out of sight but would have been easy to reach, even without telekinesis."

"Wouldn't Orrago notice someone taking it and putting it back?"

"Doubtful, and even if she saw, she wouldn't remember long enough to tell anyone, and they wouldn't pay much attention if she did."

"Why would someone need to keep looking at the manuscript?"

"A good question. It's a short work. Whoever it was could have made a copy."

"So there must be something special about the original."

Jemeryl shifted away slightly so that she could meet Tevi's eyes with an expression of frustration. "Obviously, but I haven't a clue what. I've read the entire report six times. and there's not a word that offers the merest hint."

"Perhaps the words weren't the important bit. What else was in the original?"

"An assortment of stains."

"You can't learn anything from them?"

"Lorimal didn't own a proper table mat."

Tevi smiled and pulled Jemeryl back into a tight embrace. "That wasn't what I meant. You don't need writing to leave a message, like the tracks of an animal. You can tell where it came from, what it was, where it went."

The feeling of Jemeryl going rigid in her arms alerted Tevi that some new idea had struck.

"Oh, of course." Jemeryl mouthed the words into Tevi's neck.

After a minute had passed in silence, Tevi said wryly, "I suppose you will explain eventually."

"Sorry. I was thinking it through."

"And...?"

Jemeryl pulled free of Tevi's arms and raised herself on an elbow. Her manner became noticeably more businesslike. "It's to do with finding the chalice. Remember, the elders of the day couldn't locate it after Lorimal's death."

"The stains help?"

"They could. When a person or an object makes a mark, such as a footprint, they leave a resonance in the astral domain."

"A resonance? Like an echo?"

"A bit, though it's more like a thread linking the maker to the mark. In most cases, the bond isn't strong and fades quickly. However, crystalline silver leaves a permanent resonance, which is why it can be used for recording. Lorimal had used the last two pages of the manuscript as a mat. There were several circular marks, which I bet were made when she put her chalice down."

"You could follow the thread to the chalice?"

"Not quite that simple. It'd be exhausting, given the distance between here and Storenseg. A sorcerer couldn't track for more than a few minutes without getting a splitting headache. The elemental forces of the ocean would make it like chasing a spider thread in a gale. The search must have taken months, possibly years."

"Which is why they had to keep going back to the manuscript."

"Quite."

Jemeryl shifted round and sat up. The sheet rumpled around her waist. Tevi rubbed a hand down her back and over the swell of her hips, but Jemeryl's expression remained detached. Clearly she was too busy mulling over the evidence to be interested in anything else.

Tevi grinned and also sat up. A change of location and something to eat and drink would not be such a bad idea. "Shall we get dressed and go down to the tables?"

Jemeryl nodded. "Fine." She slipped out of the bed. While reaching for her clothes, she continued hypothesising. "Our traitor hid the manuscript where they could get to it easily, yet somewhere that wouldn't raise suspicion if it was discovered. It would be assumed that the book had accidentally slipped behind the bookcase. Orrago's dementia provided a cover. No one would blame her or inquire too closely. Except..."

"What?"

"Orrago must be involved. She was the one who borrowed the manuscript from the library in the first place."

"Could someone have forced her?"

"I don't think so. Even in her present state, she still has full awareness of the upper dimensions, and six years ago, when the manuscript went missing, she had only been retired as principal for a few months. Presumably, she was far more lucid back then. And I can't see her being involved in a conspiracy. Certainly not now. Her rambling would have given the game away."

Tevi was having trouble finding her clothes. She had obviously discarded them with more abandon than she had realised, although tidiness had not been high in her priorities at the time. One of her socks was lying on the table, but there was no sign of the other. She was wondering if she should give up and go barefooted, when she saw it draped over the door handle.

Jemeryl continued talking. "I suppose Orrago might have borrowed the book and left it lying in the dispensary. Someone else saw it, realised its potential, and hid it in the nearest spot." She paused, thinking. "But it's not likely. Orrago's main interest was always contagious diseases. This manuscript was about cancer. Why would she have borrowed it?"

"There may have been nothing rational about it. Her wits were wandering. Perhaps she picked up the book at random." Tevi finally located her britches, scrunched between her backpack and the wall.

"It's too big a coincidence that of all the books in the library, she took this one. And it was seen by someone who knew about Lorimal. I think someone deliberately went looking for the manuscript."

"So what options are there?"

"Someone forged Orrago's name in the register, knowing she wouldn't be able to swear she hadn't taken the manuscript."

"Can you check?"

Tevi's jerkin lay in the middle of the floor, but her shirt was lost—until she spotted one sleeve sticking out from under the bed. She was reaching down when she was startled by Jemeryl's shout. "Yes, there is!"

"Pardon?" Tevi was confused by the tone rather than the words.

"Remember what I said about the resonance linking a mark to the thing that made it?"

"You can trace the signature?"

"Not quite. The resonance would have faded years ago, but all the writing in the library is caught in an information web. Since the loan register is in the library, the person's identity will still be there. It's probably deeply stratified, but it should be quite gettable. I'd just need a suitable astral filter to separate the name from aura synopsis."

"I think you've lost me."

"It's hard to explain. But it should work."

Jemeryl was always less coherent when excited. Tevi smiled in resignation as she pulled her shirt over her head. "I'll take your word on it."

"The only problem is reconstructing the signer's name."

"Is it difficult?"

"Not really. It's just a bit tricky, and I haven't tried anything like it since I was a junior apprentice. I'll need to practice. Come here."

Jemeryl's arms wrapped around Tevi's waist and propelled her towards the table. She was still struggling to get her hands through her shirt sleeves when a pen was thrust in her face.

"But I can't write."

"It doesn't matter. Just make a mark. If I can remember the spell, I'll be able to work out your name."

"You already know it."

"So I can tell if I've got it right."

It was logical. Tevi cautiously took the pen and rolled it experimentally in her fingers, trying to remember how Jemeryl had held the implement. A scrap torn from a larger sheet and a pot of ink also arrived. Klara had been woken by the activity and now landed on the table to watch. Tevi dipped the nib in the ink and made a bold cross on the blank side.

"Will that do? I could add a couple of squiggles."

"That should be fine."

Jemeryl displaced Tevi from the chair and sat down with the paper. Her eyes bored into the tabletop while her fingers wove complex patterns in the air above her head.

Tevi looked on, waiting for something spectacular to happen. She thought she could detect a sour-sweet smell and soft bass rumble, almost too low to be heard. In the end, the result was anticlimactic. Jemeryl's expression become steadily more confused. Eventually, she swore softly and shoved the paper away.

"Didn't it work?" Tevi was disappointed at the failure of her first attempt at literacy.

"Oh, something happened. But it wasn't your name. All I got was 'Strikes-like-lightning.' What is *that* supposed to mean?"

"Oh, well...um, it's...my real name. Tevi's just a nickname, but I prefer it. I've never liked Strikes-like-lightning, but it's traditional."

Klara strutted across the table, shaking her beak from side to side. "Isn't it always the same? Just when you think you're getting to know someone, you find out they're not who you thought."

"Even on the islands, no one ever called me Strikes-like-lightning."

"Except your mother," Jemeryl suggested.

"I think she only did it the once. At my naming ceremony."

"I'll call you it, if you want."

"Oh, please don't." Tevi could hear the horror in her own voice

Jemeryl laughed. "Where does the name Tevi come from?"

"It's short for Tevirik. In my people's stories, she's blacksmith and armourer for Rangir, goddess of the sea."

"They named you after her?"

"At second hand. It's the crabs that got named after her. Because of the armour."

"Crabs?"

"We call them tevies. I got the name when I was three...at my first sword lesson. I was knocked to my knees. I had one hand on the ground, and I was waving the wooden sword above my head with the other. Blaze just stepped back, crossed her arms and said, 'I don't know if anyone will mistake you for a warrior, but you can do a great impression of a tevi.' Before then, I think people used to call me Flash—because of the lightning—but Tevi was what stuck."

"It's all right, my love." Jemeryl's teasing tone was replaced with gentle affection. "I think Tevi suits you. And it's just as well you hadn't mentioned it before. It proved my spell worked. All I have to do now is break into the library."

"You're going to break in?" Tevi said in alarm.

"I don't want anyone around. Otherwise, I'll attract attention if I start casting spells in the main hall."

"Isn't it risky?"

"Less risky than my other option of breaking into Bramell's rooms to get the manuscript and then tracing the resonance myself to find out who's got the chalice now."

Tevi was not comforted. "I worry about you."

Jemeryl stood and wrapped her arms around Tevi, hugging her tightly. "Don't."

"I can't help it."

Tevi rested her head against Jemeryl's and closed her eyes.

Jemeryl broke the silence. "Come on. I'm thirsty. Are you ready? Let's go and get something to drink."

"Um...I can't find my boots."

With Jemeryl and Klara's help, the boots were found. Once seated outside, by mutual consent they let the subject drop. Jemeryl returned to the confrontation with Bramell. "I know he didn't mean to do me a favour, but I'm pleased he's moved me into Levannue's section. Wards and charms are much more my sort of thing, and Levannue's the leading authority in the Protectorate."

"What are charms and wards?"

"Combinations of things to attract or repel people and animals."

"And you find that interesting?"

"Oh, it's fascinating. For example, you've probably heard that rowan keeps sorcerers away."

"Yes, but isn't it just a superstition? I mean, rowan is harmless."

"Not if you can perceive it on a psychic plane. It's horrendous stuff." Jemeryl squirmed. "It's hard to describe, but if rowan's aura was a smell, it'd be rotten eggs, and if it was a sound, it'd be a tin fork scraped on glass. And the overall effect is worse than either."

"Really?"

"Yes. It won't force a sorcerer to go away. I could put up with it, if I had to."

"But you'd rather not?"

"Definitely."

"Someone told me that people in the Barrodens make door lintels out of rowan. Are they trying to stop sorcerers visiting?"

"More likely for ghouls. If anything, they like rowan even less than we do. But it won't work with werewolves. For some perverse reason, they seem to like the stuff. Nobody knows why. That's what makes the whole area of wards and charms so much more interesting than healing colds."

"Perhaps not to ordinary folk."

"No point being healthy if you've got a ghoul sitting beside you."

CHAPTER EIGHT—A VISIT TO THE LIBRARY

The lock on the library side entrance yielded to a simple spell. The door opened with a squeal that caused Jemeryl to stop and glance over her shoulder. Behind her, the school buildings huddled in darkness. The moon had long since set, and the twitter of insects was muted in the chill before dawn. Nothing moved. No lights or voices pierced the night. Jemeryl gave a nod of satisfaction and slipped through the doorway.

Once inside the building, she risked a light globe. The walls of a long room sprang up around her—a store for furniture needing repair, by the look of it. Jemeryl hurried through a series of rooms. Wild shadows leapt around her, jumping between the bookshelves. Darkness receded ahead, to flow back and swallow the aisles she left.

The cavernous central hall felt menacing in its dark silence—or would have, had Jemeryl wanted to waste time indulging her imagination. She had located the relevant loan entry on the previous day. It took her only a few seconds to find the correct expired ledger and carry it to a desk. At first, the writing danced in front of her eyes, taunting her, until Orrago's signature slipped into focus.

All other thoughts were swept aside as Jemeryl concentrated on her spell, weaving the lines of knowledge and time with the essence of paper and ink. The projections of her fingers plucked the nets of the higher dimensions. Before her eyes, the image of a name formed, the name she least expected: Orrago.

Confusion and frustration swept away Jemeryl's previous excitement. She sat scowling at the page, shoulders slumped. Her only remaining option involved breaking into Bramell's office. But would it be any more successful? She scraped her chair back, heedless of the loud screech, and reached out to shut the register, treating the page to one last resentful glare.

"What do you think you're doing?" A voice rang out.

Jemeryl froze at the sound of footsteps. Moragar strode into the light. He stopped at her shoulder and looked down at the register. For a while, neither moved. Then he stepped around the desk, pulled out a second chair, and threw himself down. Moragar's eyes drilled into her. Finally, he leaned forward.

"I should take you straight to Bramell, but I doubt he'll be much help. So I'm going to give you the chance to explain it to me first. I want you to tell me about Lorimal."

"I was just curious about the manuscript I found, sir."

"I think not." Moragar tapped the entry beside Orrago's signature. "Any other book, and I might just have believed you. But not this one."

"I don't know what you mean." Jemeryl's mouth was dry.

"You're sure about that?"

"Yes, sir."

"Perhaps you might have more to say if I tell you why I'm interested."

It sounded like a challenge. Moragar's expression was of constrained anger. Although, Jemeryl thought, not aimed directly at her. She nodded cautiously.

"It's not something I've discussed with anyone, but I think you might have some answers."

"I'm not..." Jemeryl's voice trailed away, uncertain.

"It goes back to Druse and his death. He called for me when he was very ill, bedridden, but I could tell something else was wrong. There's a restricted section of the library. You need Bramell's permission to enter. I'm sure you can guess what sort of books are kept there. Druse had detected someone taking advantage of the chaos to break in. The chief librarian has a watch ward on the room, but it was set on the assumption that Druse could investigate the second the alarm was triggered. Incidentally, that's how I knew you were here. There are wards on all doors. You should have been more careful."

"Yes, sir." Jemeryl felt foolish.

"Druse was too ill to go himself, so he sent me to find out what had been taken. It was just one book: a history of a sorcerer called Lorimal. Druse thought the person would try to sneak it back. He gave me a more sensitive ward, one that would let him detect the culprit's identity. As you can imagine, what with plague rampant, I didn't give it much attention. I assumed one of the apprentices was playing childish games. Very stupid, but hardly a priority at the time. I set the watch ward and thought no more of it. Then, two days later, Druse died. When I checked, the book was back in place. And ever since then, I've been wondering. Perhaps Druse confronted whoever it was, to let them explain, and perhaps his death wasn't due to the plague."

"You think he was murdered?"

"He wasn't old or infirm, yet he was the only one to die." Moragar looked steadily at Jemeryl. "You don't seem surprised."

"Of course...it would be appalling, if it were true."

"Yet you have no trouble accepting the idea," Moragar said pointedly. "Bramell did. He dismissed my suspicions. He said Druse was very ill and imagined things. However, he took the book out of the library." Moragar tapped the register. "Then I remembered this lost manuscript had been written by Lorimal. It seemed too much coincidence. Two missing books linked to the same person. So I tried finding out more about her. I was astonished. There's hardly a word in the whole library, just neat little patches where things have been removed. Now you come here from Lyremouth and start digging up information about her." Moragar fixed Jemeryl with a piercing stare. "I want to know what's going on. I want to know who Lorimal was. But most of all, I want to know if someone murdered Druse."

Moragar had said his bit. He sat back, waiting. Jemeryl stared at the tabletop, considering her options. Everything Moragar had said could be a lie—a ploy to make her reveal her hand. Equally, he might be innocent. Either way, she had to tell him something, else Bramell would be called in, with disastrous complications.

"I'm afraid I'm not allowed to tell you much," Jemeryl said slowly.

"A handy excuse."

"No. Lorimal performed some forbidden research nearly two hundred years ago. Her work was so dangerous that all record of it was destroyed. However, someone in Ekranos has found out and has been trying to repeat her experiments. We were sent to find out who." That much could be told with safety. If Moragar were the traitor, he already knew about Lorimal, and if not, the information was only what the innocent seniors would be told anyway, when the time came to call on their help.

"*We*?"

"I can't reveal my colleagues' identities." Letting Moragar know she was not alone seemed a good idea, as did implying that her backup was more substantial than it really was.

"What were you doing in the library?"

"Checking whether it was really Orrago who borrowed the manuscript. I thought her signature might have been forged. I was wrong. My colleagues are following other trails. Hopefully, they'll have more luck." Jemeryl looked straight at Moragar. "Once we've identified the culprit, I promise we'll find out how Druse died. A sorcerer has broken the oath of loyalty to the Coven. We're after a traitor, and murder is not too unlikely. You must realise how serious this is and that I can't say much. You're a suspect yourself. Every sorcerer in Ekranos is."

There was a long pause. "Yes, I can see that."

"I have to ask you to trust me."

"That's a bit too much to ask." Moragar smiled grimly. "However, you weren't in Ekranos when Druse died, so you weren't his murderer. And what you've said about Lorimal fits in with my guesswork."

"What are you going to do?"

"Nothing, for now. I'll be watching you, and I'll make sure that if anything happens to me, Bramell and Neame will find out all about this conversation."

"Thank you." In the circumstances, it was the best Jemeryl could have hoped for.

"I know I should go to Bramell, but he couldn't cope with this. He'd refuse to believe you or insist on doing something inappropriate. I don't want the guilty to escape. I think someone murdered Druse, and I want their head on a platter. I'm not accepting everything you've said without question. I'm not that naïve. But I think leaving you with a free hand is the best chance to flush the bastard out." The ferocity in Moragar's voice was plain. Jemeryl did not envy the renegade sorcerer if they fell into the librarian's hands.

He stood and pushed the chair under the table, clearly intending to escort Jemeryl from the building; however, she remained seated. With the need for secrecy gone, there was no harm in asking a few direct questions.

"Rather than me digging the information out, perhaps you could help with a few more things."

"Such as?"

"Has anyone else shown an interest in Lorimal over the past eight years or so?"

Moragar rested his hip on the table. "No. You're the first."

"Or information about Walderim?"

"Neame did, when she was organising her expedition. Apart from that, a few people have got out books on the flora. If you like, I'll scan the records tomorrow."

"Thank you."

"Anything else?"

Jemeryl thought for a moment. "Well...do you know anything about the artificial bird Neame was making? How close it was to completion? Where is it now? Who had access?"

"Why?"

"A raven was spotted somewhere a raven couldn't have been. I wondered if it was this device instead."

Moragar shook his head. "Not if it was mistaken for a raven. It was called a bird because it flew, but it looked more like a green octopus with wings. I haven't a clue where it is now. Probably sludge in the bottom of a bucket. It never worked. They couldn't sort out the problems with holding shape when airborne."

Jemeryl covered her eyes with her hand. The bird's appearance was an obvious point she had not considered.

"Anything else you want to know?"

"No. Thank you." Despondently, Jemeryl followed the librarian out.

It was still dark, but dawn was not far away. The air was charged with the possibilities of the coming day.

Moragar turned for a last word. "In future, if you want something from the library, ask me. Don't try breaking in."

"Yes, sir."

❖

Jemeryl sat at her desk a long time after returning to her study, trying to order her thoughts. The sky through the window lightened to washed azure. Birdsong filled the deserted paths and courtyards with discordant cascades of crystal-clean notes.

The dawn chorus was fading when Jemeryl stood up, stretching her arms above her head. The joints in her shoulders cracked. On her desk, several sheets of paper were covered in notes and untidy diagrams—an attempt to order everything into a coherent framework. She shook her head with a bewildered frown. It appeared to prove that no one could be guilty.

The nearest thing to an easy solution was that Moragar was lying about Druse's death and the golem bird's appearance, that he had used the confusion due to the plague to send the golem to Storenseg, and that his story was solely to buy time while he escaped, taking both chalice and spell with him.

However, this only raised more questions. Why would Moragar hide the manuscript in the dispensary? Even as assistant librarian, he could have left the manuscript in place and consulted it whenever he wanted, after hours. It also meant that Aris's death in Walderim was simply a coincidence. Jemeryl was unhappy with the idea. Neither could she forget Moragar's face when he had called for the murderer's head. She would have staked anything that he was telling the truth. Yet it was impossible to come up with any other vaguely plausible scenario.

If Moragar's statement was true, it put Bramell in the clear. Why would the principal break into a library area that he was allowed to visit whenever he wanted? And if the golem did not work, he had no way to obtain the chalice. Neither did anyone else in Ekranos.

Starting logically from the beginning did not help. Orrago had borrowed the manuscript. Since it must have been taken to locate the chalice, it implied she had done that as well, which meant her dementia was a trick. This, in turn, meant that Levannue, as her doctor, was either spectacularly inept or involved in a conspiracy.

With the golem bird discounted, only Aris could have taken the chalice. She had committed suicide through remorse or been murdered. In the meantime, Orrago had either left her sickbed or persuaded Levannue to break into the library and murder Druse. Neame must have bought the chalice back to Ekranos, although it was useless to her, and merrily handed it over to the other conspirators.

Somehow, it all seemed less than likely.

Jemeryl rolled her head back and stared at the ceiling. It was too late to return to bed. Soon, she would be off for an early morning rendezvous with Tevi. The library break-in had been timed in the hope of getting definite evidence. Then she could have collected the warrant from Tevi and returned to the school, ready to present Bramell with her findings, or if the principal was the culprit, to muster the other seniors against him. It was another plan down the drain.

Jemeryl shuffled the papers together and slipped them into the bag that was already packed and waiting by the door. After tightening the drawstring, she propped it against the wall and stepped out onto the veranda. The air was clean and sharp. The dawn breeze felt chill through her thin cotton shirt, but the sky held the promise of another hot day. Dust hazed the horizon.

The crunch of footsteps on gravel cut through the peace. Leaning on the wooden balustrade, Jemeryl watched two of the kitchen staff stroll across the courtyard below, deep in murmured conversation. Jemeryl's gaze returned to the building opposite. The sun's first rays struck the roof, dusting it with gold. Gulls' raucous cries rose above the fading chorus of songbirds. From the distance, the hollow clanking of a dropped bucket echoed in the stillness.

A door opened, and a neighbour emerged, blinking blearily in the daylight. Jemeryl acknowledged the wave of greeting and turned to the open door of her own study. Sounds of movement were coming from Vine's bedroom. Hastily, Jemeryl hoisted her bag over her shoulder and scuttled along the veranda to the stairs. She had no wish to be questioned by Vine.

The kitchen doors were open as Jemeryl passed. The warm smell of fresh baking halted her. She had intended to take breakfast with Tevi, but a second waft, seasoned with cinnamon, changed her mind. On a table inside the door, a wicker basket was piled with small cakes. Jemeryl dropped two into her bag to eat on the way and took a mouthful from a third. One of the kitchen staff grinned and indicated a pitcher of milk. With a dusty ride ahead, Jemeryl gratefully poured herself a mug and drank while looking around the kitchen.

At the far end, the cook was at the ovens, dividing his time between examining the bread and yelling abuse at his underlings. He had not noticed Jemeryl, which was how she preferred it. Swallowing might be difficult if confronted by one of his lightning personality changes.

One of the smaller boys was the current target of the cook's rage. "Stop flapping the thing in my face. Put it down over there, and I'll pick it up later."

The woman who had pointed out the milk exchanged a smile with Jemeryl. No one was afraid of the cook's blustering temper. Then the expression on Jemeryl's face froze as the cook's words registered. *Put it down over there, and I'll pick it up later.* The sentence was not a clue in itself, but it was the missing bit from her calculations. The kitchen faded around her as Jemeryl stood, transfixed. Everything tied together. It was almost too easy.

She knew who had Lorimal's chalice.

❖

A scattering of customers was at the tables outside the Inn of Singing Birds. Some were guests taking their morning meal; others were locals stopping off on their way to work. Tevi was among them. Her head rested on her folded arms as she dozed in the early morning sun, having come straight from a night shift at the docks. The remains of her breakfast littered the table.

Jemeryl's shadow fell across her. "Good morning. How are you?"

Tevi jerked awake and sat up, stifling a yawn. "Er...morning. I'm fine."

"Been waiting long?" Jemeryl ducked her head to plant a soft kiss on Tevi's lips.

"I don't think so." Tevi looked at the crumbs apologetically. "I've eaten most of the food. I'm sure the waiter will get more for you."

"Doesn't matter. I ate on the way down."

Something in the tone alerted Tevi. She shaded her eyes from the sun and examined Jemeryl's face. "What's up?"

"I know who did it."

"The spell worked?"

"No."

"It didn't...but you've found out..." Tevi shook her head, hoping to clear it. "Who was it?"

Jemeryl held up a hand. "In good time. First, I want to tell you about last night."

"Oh, come on!"

Tevi's protest was ignored. Jemeryl slid onto the opposite bench and launched into an account of the events at the library. Her obvious excitement drew curious but discreet looks from surrounding tables. A waiter came to take the breakfast order but was waved away. Pages of notes were dragged from Jemeryl's bag and supplemented by invisible diagrams in the air. None of it was the least bit enlightening for Tevi. In the end, she cut off Jemeryl's stream of words.

"Look, I don't see where this is going. You're saying no one could have done it."

"I want you to understand the bewilderment I felt."

"All right. I'm bewildered. Now will you tell me who did it?"

"Well, as you can see, it was impossible. Then I overheard a chance remark, and everything fell into place."

"And?"

"Don't you want to know what the remark was?"

"No."

"But it—"

Tevi caught hold of Jemeryl's hand. "Please, just tell me who."

Their eyes met. Jemeryl took a deep breath. "Levannue."

"But she was in Lyremouth when the chalice was taken." Tevi released Jemeryl's hand. "How?"

"I've been guilty of one big oversight. I was right when I said Levannue couldn't control another sorcerer without their consent, but I missed Vine's point about dropping defences when you receive psychiatric treatment."

"Didn't you say others would spot the effect of entrapment?"

"Yes, they would. There would be a noticeable personality shift. However, when someone receives treatment, a change in behaviour is exactly what people hope for. In addition, Orrago is so erratic that no one questions her moods. Even so, Levannue can't have her in complete thrall, or she'd be acting like a listless dummy."

"You think she has just enough control to make Orrago take the manuscript and hide it?"

Jemeryl nodded. "Something like that."

"It doesn't explain how she got the chalice."

"I'm guessing, but remember, Aris had problems. It's very likely that she'd have gone to Levannue for help. And there's evidence for a personality shift just before she left for Walderim. Erlam told me Aris was improving, but it could have been the effect of Levannue clamping down on her mind. Levannue couldn't have controlled Aris directly when she was so far away, but she could have imprinted a set of instructions to be followed when the chance arose."

"And you think Levannue also made Neame bring the chalice back?"

"No. In fact, I'm quite certain she didn't," Jemeryl said emphatically. "Neame would never let Levannue tinker around with her head. And all the sorcerers in the Coven combined couldn't trap Neame's aura without her consent."

"But I suppose you've worked out how she got the chalice back."

"Of course. That was the chance remark I mentioned. And once I'd tied it in, everything else was easy. I'll start at the beginning. I think things went something like this." Jemeryl leaned forward. "Levannue was treating Orrago for dementia. In the course of probing, Levannue found out about Lorimal, or maybe Bramell had already given a clue and she dug out more information. However it was, Levannue started to investigate Lorimal. She realised that the stains on the manuscript could be used to find the chalice and so made Orrago hide it within easy reach. Levannue is always popping in to see Orrago. Once she'd traced the chalice to your island, she had the problem of recovering it. I'll bet she talked Bramell into confiscating the golem bird. She'd have had precious little joy asking Neame if she could borrow it. It must have been a blow when she found out the golem wouldn't stay in one piece. Then Neame started planning her trip to Walderim. Erlam said that someone suggested the expedition would be good for Aris. To me, it sounds like Levannue used her position as doctor to get Aris within range of the chalice."

Jemeryl found a blank sheet of paper and hastily sketched a rough map of Walderim and the Western Isles, marking a spot above Scathberg. "This was were Aris was. In two days, she could have ridden a raven to your islands and back. She then needed a break to catch up on food and rest and things like that."

After a long night with no sleep, Tevi was struggling. "We've already worked that out."

Jemeryl expanded her map, drawing in the Middle Sea. "Aris then sent the raven off again, but going east this time—to around here." Jemeryl pointed to the map. "I told you Levannue has a Serac accent. The chalice was hidden in a suitable spot. I'm sure Levannue could think of somewhere. She let the chalice lie there for a year, waiting to see if there was any reaction. Once she was happy the alarm hadn't been raised, she went on a short visit to her parents, picked it up, and brought it back with her."

"Levannue made Aris commit suicide to hide her tracks?"

Jemeryl's smile faded. "I don't think so. At least, I'd like not to think so. Mind-riding a raven for that length of time would be unsettling for anyone. It must have been the last straw for Aris. I don't think it was deliberate on Levannue's part. There was no need. She could have scrubbed Aris's memory once she returned. And I don't believe she'd callously murder one of her patients—someone who trusted her. Erlam said Aris jumped off the top of a tower. Perhaps it wasn't intentional suicide; maybe she still thought she was a raven."

"The suicide was still quite convenient for Levannue." Tevi did not share Jemeryl's faith. "And how about Druse? Remember, he died only after Levannue was back on her feet."

"I suppose so," Jemeryl conceded after a pause.

"One death might be bad luck; two look deliberate. My hypothesis, to add to yours, is that once Levannue recovered from the plague, with Bramell ill and Moragar busy, she decided to investigate to see if she could find out anything that might make her work with the chalice easier. When Druse discovered it was Levannue who had broken into the section, he probably assumed that she was merely running errands for Bramell. Rather than raise the alarm, he had a private word with her first. But Levannue didn't want Bramell to find out, so she killed Druse and passed it off as the plague."

"Maybe. It would tie in. The problem is we don't have a scrap of evidence."

"Since Bramell and Levannue have been partners for years, it's going to take more than guesswork to convince him."

"True. And it all rests on the presumption that Levannue has been entrapping other sorcerers."

"Don't you have any evidence?"

"It's not conclusive, but there is one incident. It happened when Levannue came to collect Orrago from her private study. Vine and I were there, due to circumstances Levannue couldn't have expected. Without warning, Orrago jumped up and trotted over to open the door. At that second, Levannue arrived. There was no way Orrago should have known Levannue was outside."

"It might have been coincidence."

"Levannue was shocked. At the time, I assumed it was surprise at the door opening in her face. Plus I was unwell and didn't pay much attention."

"I can't see it persuading Bramell."

"I know, and we don't have much time. Levannue is due to leave Ekranos at the end of this month. She's supposed to be going north to test a new ward, but I'll bet she's planning on not coming back. If I can't get any definite evidence before then, I'll have to persuade Bramell to use the manuscript to trace the chalice to its current location, which won't be either easy or fun. Hopefully Levannue is hanging on to the chalice and didn't destroy it once she'd finished probing its memory."

"Do you think you should keep the Guardian's warrant up at the school, in case you need it in a hurry?"

"It will be safer with you. If Levannue gets suspicious, the first thing she'll do is search my room. If anything happens, I'll get a message through to Klara, and you can come running. And it might be best to go to Neame first rather than Bramell. She'll be much more receptive to the idea of Levannue as a traitor to the Coven. But it shouldn't get to a last-minute rush. I'm going to start collecting proof. Now that I'm working on charms, I've got plenty of chances to watch Levannue."

"Be very careful. Remember it's likely she's murdered two people already. If anything should happen to you—"

"Nothing will."

The two women sat in silence for a while. The sun was now clear of the rooftops. The euphoria of solving the mystery was fading, melting in the rising heat. Each time Tevi blinked she found it harder to open her eyelids again. She realised that she had started to drift off when Jemeryl shook her gently awake.

"Come on. I think I should take you to bed and make sure you get some sleep."

Klara's beak opened a fraction.

Jemeryl anticipated the magpie, placing a forefinger on her beak. "And you can keep that remark to yourself."

❖

The nauseating stench of rowan permeated the upper dimensions. Jemeryl tried to ignore it while she placed a set of talismans in a circle on the bench. The carved bone tingled under her fingers in a way that was nearly as disagreeable as the rowan. Once the arrangement was complete, Jemeryl lit a red wax candle under the small tripod at the centre and stepped back, futilely trying to wipe the rowan aura from her hands.

"I think it's ready, ma'am."

"I'll be over in a minute."

At the other end of the bench, Levannue was deftly cutting open berries and removing their black seeds. Long fingers moved with practised skill. Old hands, yet graceful, unmarred by redness or blotches. They matched Levannue's fine-boned features, sharp eyes, and pale lips. Each short grey hair lay as straight as if it had been drawn on her head with a rule. The tracery of lines on her skin added texture without sagging. Everything about Levannue suggested elegance and dispassionate precision.

Jemeryl studied her quarry. Was this a woman who had murdered Aris and Druse? A woman who planned to overthrow the Protectorate? It was something Jemeryl had wondered repeatedly during the previous nine days. Her eyes returned to the candle and talismans. How could she get the evidence she needed? One thing was certain: she dared not let Levannue leave Ekranos. Yet, the proposed departure date was getting close. Only another eleven days were left. If she learnt nothing more before then, she would have to present her suspicions to Bramell and rely on the Guardian's warrant to demand further investigations.

"Now we can begin." Levannue took her place on the other side of the table.

The elderly sorcerer adjusted the axis of two talismans. Jemeryl nodded, seeing how it improved the balance of forces. Levannue placed a crucible containing the seeds on the tripod. Light from the candle reflected in the polished underside, magnified by the curvature of the bowl.

Soon, the bitter scent of roasting seeds wafted in Jemeryl's direction. A pinch of horsehair was added, along with shavings of rowan bark and a few grains of sea salt. Levannue seemed oblivious to the rowan, although Jemeryl knew she was, if anything, even more sensitive than Jemeryl herself. The horsehair crackled and writhed in the bottom of the crucible. Wisps of grey smoke spiralled up and were trapped in mid-air by forces radiating from the talismans, turning the fumes back on themselves. The smoke thickened into an opaque form, dancing above the crucible.

Levannue replaced the candle and tripod with a small glass flask. Then the two sorcerers moved the talismans in unison, adjusting the play of forces. The smoke shape spiralled down like a vortex into the flask. Quickly, Levannue pressed a cork stopper in place.

"That went smoothly," Levannue said in satisfaction. "We're finished for today. Could you tidy up?"

It was an order, not a request, and Jemeryl hastened to obey. Levannue sat at her desk and began writing. For a while, the two worked in silence.

"Excuse me, ma'am. Where do these go?"

Levannue looked at the bone talismans in Jemeryl's palm. She picked a leather pouch from her desk. "Put them in here. They then go in my storage chest. You'll need this." She snapped a long brass key free from a ring at her belt.

The chest stood at the back of the room. It was three feet long, made of solid oak and mounted with iron bands. In it were kept items deemed too dangerous to be left lying around. The key rarely left Levannue's belt.

Jemeryl raised the lid and glanced inside cautiously, well able to imagine the sort of items Levannue might need to keep secure. Her face twisted in a grimace. The contents seemed unexceptional to her sight and so very deadly to her extended sorcerer senses. She dropped the talismans into the chest and reached for the lid, about to pull it shut, when she froze. Lying at the back, half hidden by a pale blue cloth, was a memory chalice.

Jemeryl glanced over her shoulder. Levannue was engrossed in her work but would certainly notice any attempt to probe the chalice. Jemeryl turned back to the chest. The lock was protected by magic, impossible to pick, but there was another option.

She flicked the cord of the pouch forward so that it fouled the lock mechanism. Something that could be passed off as an accident, if discovered. Holding the lid to stop it slamming, Jemeryl let the lock's tang press down on the cord, squashing it double into the catch. No click sounded, and the catch did not engage. She stood and stepped away. Only close inspection would detect the narrow gap between lid and base.

Levannue accepted the return of the key without looking up.

"Is there anything else, ma'am?"

"No. If you've finished, you may go."

"Yes, ma'am."

Jemeryl walked down the hallway and out into a small paved courtyard. It was stifling in the late afternoon as the flagstones released the heat they had absorbed from the scorching midday sun. Two other doorways opened onto the courtyard. One was the route Levannue would take when she left. The other had a large enclosed porch that would be an ideal hiding place. A stone bench was carved on the inner wall, with gargoyles peering through the armrests. Jemeryl sat and swung her legs up so they would not be visible from the courtyard.

The wait was not long. Soon, brisk footsteps tapped across the flagstones, and a thin shadow flitted past. Jemeryl tried to look relaxed, as if merely waiting in the shade for a friend. The subterfuge was unnecessary. The footsteps continued without interruption. Jemeryl peered around the corner just in time to see Levannue disappear into the doorway opposite. The last echo of her footsteps faded into silence.

Back in the room, Levannue's notes were in a neat pile, and her chair had been pushed under the desk. Otherwise, nothing was changed. Levannue had not noticed the cord fouling the lock.

Jemeryl opened the chest. The chalice inside had twin S-shaped handles—a style typical of two centuries before. Jemeryl sat back, holding the chalice in her cupped hands. It was scratched, stained, and dented, just as if it had been pulled from the sea with a half-drowned sorcerer. To the ungifted eye, it was unremarkable, but beneath its casting, the chalice was a tight ball of memories.

Gently, Jemeryl teased apart the strands of information. The shadow of a name hung loose, stamped with the original owner's claim to possession. A few deft moves brought it into view: Lorimal of the Coven.

Jemeryl's fist pumped the air in triumph. At last, she had evidence that even Bramell could not deny and time in hand. With the chalice in the crook of her arm, Jemeryl peered into the chest, wondering what else she might find. Trying to see through the jumble of forces taxed her concentration and meant she did not hear the sound of the door opening quietly behind her.

"How dare you?" Levannue's voice crackled with outrage.

Jemeryl twisted about, nearly loosing her balance in surprise. Levannue stood in the doorway, arms folded. Two assistant witches peered over her shoulder, enraptured horror on their faces. Levannue's expression was far harder to read.

Jemeryl rose from her awkward crouch and waited as the trio advanced from the doorway. Levannue strode confidently; the other two bustled after. The witches were clearly taking a huge amount of enjoyment from being scandalised. If they were involved in a conspiracy, it was a wonderful piece of acting on their part. Far more likely that their ill-timed arrival was unconnected with her discovery of the chalice. Having got over her surprise, Jemeryl was not worried. The witches' testimony could be useful.

Levannue took the chalice from Jemeryl's hands and examined it before speaking again. "Are you going to explain this to me, or shall we go straight to Bramell?" Her voice held no trace of fear.

Levannue's display of composure made Jemeryl hesitate, but the chalice reassured her. Whatever the plan, Levannue had miscalculated. Once the evidence was before Bramell, the charade would be over. Until then, silence was best. Even with the witches as witnesses, it would be dangerous to mention the Guardian's warrant and run the risk of Levannue getting to Tevi first.

Levannue spoke again. "I wonder if you realise how much trouble you're in. You've been very stupid."

The malicious edge stung Jemeryl. "I was going to say the same to you."

"Bravado isn't going to help your case."

"*My* case!" Jemeryl was incredulous. "Oh, come on. It's too late to play games."

"What do you mean?"

"You know what I mean."

"You're talking as if I'm the one in trouble." Levannue sounded offended.

"And you are."

"You have the nerve to threaten me!"

"Why did she say that?" one witch asked, puzzled.

"She thinks she has something up her sleeve."

"Oooh." Both witches were thrilled. They clearly possessed the maturity level of five-year-olds.

Levannue carried on. "I'm not about to be intimidated by a young fool. I've got an old iron collar around here somewhere."

"Yes, that would be sensible, ma'am."

"She might try to run away." The witches spoke in unison.

"I won't," Jemeryl said, scornful of the pantomime.

"I'm not going to take chances."

Levannue got awkwardly to her knees and put the chalice in the chest. After turning over a few items, she dug out a collar. One witch helped her back to her feet. The other shut the lid, making a point of pushing down firmly with both hands and looking smugly at Jemeryl.

It was demeaning, but there was no point wasting time by protesting. The collar would not stop her speaking to Bramell and ending the charade. Jemeryl's face showed her contempt, but she did not resist. In her mind, she was already planning the forthcoming meeting and rehearsing her arguments. Only when the collar was about to close around her neck was she hit by alarm. Something was terribly wrong. The true nature of the collar was disguised. It certainly was not iron.

Jemeryl opened her mouth, but the words never came. The collar snapped shut, and a fog descended on her mind. She was caught in a daze. Her thoughts remained clear, but the world seemed lost. Reality slipped through her fingers, leaving Jemeryl's mind adrift, with only the bitter knowledge that after all her promises to Tevi, she had allowed herself to become ensnared.

Chapter Nine—Outmanœuvred

Bramell's study appeared around Jemeryl with no sense of transition. Voices boomed, muffled as if echoing down a long corridor. Jemeryl battled to force a firm contact with the world. The tendrils of fog shifted, and Levannue's voice became distinct.

"I've had suspicions for some time. Several things have gone missing since she joined my section."

"I'll send someone to search her room." Bramell's words were out of step with the blurred movement of his lips.

"It might be better if I do that. I'd know what to look for."

"Good idea." Bramell's face floated before Jemeryl. "Are you still refusing to explain yourself?"

Try as she might, Jemeryl could not make her throat and lips obey her.

"She wouldn't answer before, apart from making threats," one of the witches volunteered from somewhere out of sight.

"Yes, she did. She said Levannue was in big trouble," the other added.

Jemeryl mentally swore at the pair. Presumably, it was not a conspiracy, else the scene staged in Levannue's room would have been unnecessary. The three could simply have invented the whole story from beginning to end. However, Levannue had obviously taken great care, picking witnesses who were totally lacking in mental ability, magical or otherwise. Neither witch had noticed the use of power when Levannue activated the enslaving device, and neither was giving a second thought to the instantaneous change in behaviour it caused.

"Perhaps she'll be more forthcoming when she's had time to think." Bramell glared through the fog at Jemeryl. "I'll speak to you again tomorrow."

"It might be wise to lock her in the quarantine rooms," Levannue suggested.

"Yes. Then we'll be certain where she is."

Jemeryl raged at Bramell's incompetence. Neame would have noticed the lines of force binding her aura, and anyone with half a brain might suspect that something strange was happening. Only Bramell could mistake bewitchment for sullen defiance.

Jemeryl made one last attempt to give a sign, but the collar absorbed all her efforts. Someone took hold of her arm and towed her from the room. She was unable even to control her eyes. The blur of movement broke her links with the world, and once again, she was swallowed by fog.

❖

Jemeryl sat slumped on one of the narrow bunks in the quarantine room, in a position of enforced inactivity. She had overcome the clouding of her senses and could now see and hear clearly. However, this merely left her as a passive observer, trapped in her body. Absurdly, the thing that chafed the most was that she could not pace the room. The device bound her on all seven dimensions. Attempts to contact Tevi via Klara had failed. She was completely isolated. Not a trace of the bond with her familiar remained.

The outlook was bleak. So far, Jemeryl knew she had been outmanoeuvred at every point. What was Levannue planning? How was she going to deal with it when people started to question her victim's apathetic silence? What was the next step?

Footsteps sounded outside the room. A key rattled in the lock. Jemeryl could not raise her head, but out of the corner of her eye, she saw the door open and Levannue's feet enter. The door shut with a hollow clunk, and then a chair's legs scraped against the floorboards as it was pulled into position. Jemeryl could see no higher than Levannue's lap when the elderly sorcerer sat down. Abruptly, Jemeryl's back jerked straight, forcing her head up. Her eyes met Levannue's. The two of them were alone.

"I'm sure you aren't surprised to learn that I found several incriminating things in your room. Officially, I'm here to ask you about them." Levannue gave a humourless smile. "I've had doubts about you for some time. You've definitely had your eye on me for a few days, and I'm not conceited enough to think you've fallen in love. Letting you see the chalice was an easy way of getting confirmation. It would have meant nothing to you unless you'd known about Lorimal."

Jemeryl impotently cursed her own stupidity for not spotting the trap.

"What I don't understand is why the Guardian waited so long before sending you. I'd also like to know what sort of resources you have, since I hardly think she'd send you alone. When did you work out I was the one? Who have you told? What are your plans?" Levannue paused. "And you're going to tell me, aren't you?"

Hands burst into Jemeryl's mind, picking apart her thoughts and digging through the layers of memory. Her life dissolved into fragments. She felt lost, like a floating carcass shredded by scavengers. She almost surrendered herself to the invasion, but one anchor held firm—the knowledge that Tevi's life was at stake. Levannue had broken her oath to the Coven and had probably murdered two sorcerers. She would not hesitate to kill an ungifted mercenary and take the warrant if she learnt the truth.

The collar held Jemeryl's aura more surely than chains would have held her body. She could not fight back. Her only option was a shell-like defence, reclaiming her thoughts and pulling her mind shut. She wrapped her being tight within herself.

Levannue drew a sharp breath, either in frustration or anger. Jemeryl did not care. The mode of attack changed. The probing hands became white-hot claws. Pain exploded inside Jemeryl's head. She would have screamed if she could. Yet still she resisted, clinging to the knowledge of what defeat would mean. She could not retaliate or hide, only endure.

The onslaught continued. It shifted in intensity and focus, forcing Jemeryl to retreat further. She felt the shattering of bonds holding flesh and spirit together. Pain ceased to be important; life ceased to be important. Her heartbeat faltered, resumed erratically, and then stopped again. Her breathing became weak. The fight could not continue much longer. Jemeryl knew death would claim her soon, but even this would be a victory. The dead reveal no secrets.

Suddenly, the battle was over. Levannue conceded defeat and withdrew, leaving Jemeryl to catch the threads of life again. Blood pounded in her ears. Cold lightning flared through her arms and legs. Her lungs burned raw with each gasped breath.

Levannue's face was flushed from the effort. She scowled angrily. "So. You are not the raw novice you seem. I should have known the Guardian would send someone able to look after herself."

This was the highest praise she had ever heard from Levannue, although Jemeryl was in no condition to feel flattered. The elderly sorcerer left her seat and stalked around the room. Her hand slapped the tabletop in frustration—the first chink in Levannue's composure. Her nostrils were pinched. Her lips were compressed in a thin line. She stopped at the window and stared through the bars.

When eventually she turned back, her expression was again controlled. "You must be aware that I'm leaving Ekranos soon. My plans weren't secret. Of course, you'd have tried to stop me, which is why I had to pre-empt you. Unfortunately, you haven't told me what I really want to know. Do I flee tomorrow, or can I stick to my original schedule? You are no longer a threat. The trouble is, I don't know who else I have to contend with, or how much evidence they have."

Levannue sat down, tapping her fingertips together. She continued in the manner of someone voicing her thoughts aloud. "You've been meeting a mercenary in town on a regular basis. The pretence of being lovers was very good. It had me fooled for a while. In reality, she must be a go-between, passing your reports on. I could talk to this mercenary. I'm sure she'd be more cooperative than you, but I'm also sure she'll be guarded in some way. Would talking to her justify the risk?"

Levannue sighed and rubbed her forehead. "I can manipulate Bramell into keeping things quiet here. He won't want rumours about a sorcerer's disgrace spreading outside the school. But if I stir things up in town, your associates will hear about it. If they don't know I'm the one they're after, I don't want to enlighten them by abducting their messenger."

The pain in Jemeryl's head had eased, but she was still a powerless spectator. Her only comfort was that Levannue had wildly overestimated the party sent to catch her and had talked herself into leaving Tevi alone. It was one of Levannue's rare miscalculations, but not an unreasonable one. How much more sensible if the Guardian had assigned a dozen sorcerers as backup instead of one ungifted mercenary. Was there really such a drastic need of secrecy?

"You last met the mercenary nine days ago. I'd been suspicious ever since you showed so much interest in Lorimal's manuscript, so I took the opportunity to search your room—not that I found anything. But from your behaviour up until then, I hadn't got the feeling that you were mutually suspicious of me. Only after your return did you start watching me. Obviously your mercenary passed on some information." Levannue frowned. "I wonder what it was. However, it can't have been conclusive, or I'd already be under arrest. So they must be waiting for you to provide some extra proof. Which you're now unable to do."

Another mistake by Levannue—and again, not unreasonable. However, there seemed little benefit that Levannue was unaware of the sudden, cook-inspired insight on the way into Ekranos.

"Even without proof, your associates won't let me leave Ekranos. But if they're hoping for word from you, they'll leave it until the last moment before acting." Levannue's eyes fixed on the ceiling while she thought. "All of which means that it would be safest for me to bring my departure forward to tomorrow. I'll make arrangements with Bramell and manufacture a reason to keep it secret. You won't be able to pass on the news, so I'll be far away before your associates know I've gone." She looked at Jemeryl sadly. "However, you present a problem. The disguise on the collar won't stand scrutiny when people start wondering why you don't speak. Even if I fled tonight, you'd set the pursuit on my tail tomorrow, and I'd like a bit more head start. It's not personal, but I must have you out of the way."

Levannue stood and pushed the chair back under the table. A cold lump formed in Jemeryl's stomach. Levannue took a twist of paper from a pouch and emptied the contents into her palm: two dozen green berries. Levannue studied them for a moment and then pulled open a pocket on Jemeryl's shirt and poured them in.

"I'm going to leave you and make myself conspicuous elsewhere. In an hour, someone will bring dinner. You'll be too upset to eat. After they take the plates away, you'll feel compelled to eat the berries. I'm afraid it's a fatal dose. When I 'discover' your body tomorrow morning, I'll change your collar for an ordinary iron one. It will be assumed that you killed yourself rather than face the consequences of your actions. It won't take much prompting to ensure Bramell keeps the news of a sorcerer's suicide as quiet as possible." Levannue's voice faltered. "I'm really very sorry it has worked out like this. The Coven was wrong to ban Lorimal's work. Perhaps you can now appreciate what it means to me."

Levannue's hands shook as she opened the door. She gave a last sorrowful look back. Jemeryl heard the key turn in the lock.

❖

Time dragged by. The sun's rays climbed the wall and faded. Jemeryl struggled to gain enough control of her body to make a sign. Alerting the person who brought the food would be her last chance.

Her dinner arrived on schedule. The rotund, middle-aged witch spared one disapproving glance for Jemeryl as he dumped the tray on the table. He stomped out and slammed the door, as if trying to demonstrate his support for the school authorities by the volume of his actions. Jemeryl almost gave up, but there was nothing else to divert her thoughts. After a while, the door opened again, and the witch returned. This time, Vine squeezed in behind him. She scuttled to Jemeryl's side and dropped to a half crouch.

"Jem, what happened? What did you do? "

Had the situation been less desperate, Jemeryl would have been amused. As it was, Vine's curiosity was the one thing that might save her life. If only Vine would act like a sorcerer and use her senses, rather than focus exclusively on the pursuit of gossip.

Using all her knowledge of magic, Jemeryl flung herself at the cage around her aura. She fought for the right to control her own voice and her own body. Seldom had she put so much effort into anything—never with so little result. The rhythm of her breathing faltered. Her lower lip twitched, but there was no sound, no recognisable gesture.

Vine's expression softened, obviously mistaking Jemeryl's response for mute distress. "Jem. Aren't you going to tell me anything?"

The witch spoke. "Don't waste your time. I told you she wasn't talking to anyone. We'll take the plates and go."

Vine's excitement waned. She stood and walked to the table. The puzzlement on her face intensified. "She's not eaten anything."

"Not surprising. I wouldn't have much appetite in her shoes, either."

"You'd think she'd eat for consolation."

Even the sour-faced witch laughed. "*You* would. Anyway, you've seen her. That's the favour I owed. Now leave her to sulk." He picked up the untouched tray.

Vine was clearly unhappy. She stared at Jemeryl with confused intensity, as if trying to form a new question. Then her expression changed to one of pique. "I do think, if you're going to do something outrageous, you could at least give me the inside story." Vine flounced out of the room.

The door shut with a final hollow thud.

The room was as bleak as the first time Jemeryl had seen it, on the night Gewyn had been carried in. Gewyn had walked out, weak but smiling. Jemeryl held no such hopes for herself. Although she had control of her mind, Levannue held her body in complete subjugation.

From her work in the dispensary, Jemeryl recognised the seeds Levannue had put in her pocket. They would act quickly, with little pain. It would be an easy death. Was Levannue's choice of poison prompted by practicality or compassion? Not that it mattered. Already, Jemeryl's hand was moving like a marionette on the end of a string. Her forefinger slipped into the pocket, digging out the seeds. Her hand continued in its slow advance, ending cupped over her mouth. The seeds had a sweet, scented taste; her jaws moved, grinding them to pulp in a mechanical, cowlike action. Jemeryl swallowed.

For a long time, nothing happened, except for details fading in the advancing dusk. Then Jemeryl became aware of numbness in her fingers and toes. The sensation spread, while a range of emotions contended for primacy: anger at her own stupidity; bitterness at defeat by Levannue; guilt that she would not say goodbye to Tevi; and a growing, helpless panic.

The numbness reached her waist. Spikes leapt up her spine and coiled about her heart. Her chest contracted, squeezing the air from her lungs. A black well opened behind her head, sending tendrils of darkness streaming past her eyes.

Jemeryl's last sensation was of tumbling backwards into a pit.

❖

The band of young mercenaries bundled through the door of the guild house and gathered inside, loudly discussing plans. The dim interior echoed with voices arguing the merits of various taverns. Tevi listened with half an ear. Her next meeting with Jemeryl was not for several days, and she was willing to go along with anything the others agreed.

A guild master strode through the lobby. Spotting Tevi, he stopped and tapped her shoulder. "If you keep pets in your room, you must have them under control. In future, your magpie must be in a cage."

"But she's perfectly tame. She just sleeps when I'm not here."

"Honest, Klara's never any trouble," one of Tevi's roommates backed her up.

"She's been trouble today. She frightened the life out of the orderly who went to your room an hour ago—flapping and squawking. Anyway, it's not a request; it's an order. Restrain your pet, or we'll review your permission to keep her." The guild master stalked off.

Tevi shared a bewildered look with the others before heading to her room, convinced that there was a mistake. Her two roommates followed. However, as soon as she opened the door, Tevi knew the orderly had not been exaggerating. Feathers littered the floor—mainly from pecked pillows. Items had been knocked over and broken. The damage was everything that might reasonably be expected from one small magpie. Tevi stepped cautiously into the room.

A black and white blur exploded from a corner and threw itself at the window, beating against the thick blue-green glass. Tevi advanced slowly, trying to make reassuring noises. Klara stopped flapping and backed into a corner, cheeping pathetically. At first, it seemed as if she would allow herself to be stroked. The attack came without warning. As Tevi reached out, Klara lunged forward.

Tevi jumped back, staring in astonishment at the blood on her thumb.

One roommate peered over her shoulder, mirroring Tevi's expression of confusion. "What's wrong with her?"

"I don't know. Maybe she's ill."

"Are you sure it's Klara?"

"Who else could it be?"

"This might be a wild magpie that's scared Klara away. It's acting like one."

Realisation hit Tevi like a kick to her stomach. Without pausing to answer, she dived to the bottom of her bed and wrenched open her footlocker. The magically disguised warrant was still in place. After snatching it up, Tevi launched herself through the door, hurtling past her surprised colleagues.

"Tevi. What's wrong?"

"I've got to go."

"Why?"

"Haven't time to explain." Already, Tevi was off, running.

The man followed Tevi into the corridor. "Do you need help? Is it trouble?"

For a second, Tevi stopped. "I hope not. By the gods, I hope not." Then she leapt down the stairs.

The young man looked back at the other mercenary. "Well, what are you waiting for?"

The pair chased after Tevi.

❖

The library was almost deserted. A few globes floated in the dim, cavernous space, lighting the rows of books. Levannue and Moragar stood in an alcove off the main hall, conferring in low voices.

"But I'm keeping you."

"Oh, no. It's been a pleasure."

The trite pleasantries terminated the conversation. Levannue smiled and walked to the exit, clasping a book. They had been talking for half an hour, and she could not remember a word they had said.

She paused at the door and stared across the school's main square. The last traces of pink had left the eastern sky. Overhead, the deep blue was speckled with stars. By now, Jemeryl would be unconscious. The end could not be far away.

Satisfaction at her success had worn off, leaving only the stale taste of guilt constricting her throat. The corners of Levannue's lips turned down. How had it come to this? At the outset, it had seemed a game. Somewhere, over the years, things had become serious. But it had never been her intention to cause harm, to break her oath of loyalty to the Coven so completely. It had crept up, step by bitter step.

Levannue paced along the path, brooding on the turn of events. There was no way back. It was far too late to change her mind. But what if she had her time again? Levannue shook her head irritably. "What if?" was always a fruitless question. She tried to focus on happier thoughts: her plans for that evening, although even this had a raw edge. It was the last she would spend with Bramell.

The sounds of a disturbance by the school gates distracted her. A young apprentice appeared, running towards the seniors' quarters.

Levannue put out a hand. "What's happening?"

The apprentice was out of breath. She gasped, "Ma'am, there's a group of mercenaries. They want to see Neame or Bramell. It's about Jemeryl. They've got a warrant from the Guardian."

A lifetime of self-control helped Levannue hide her shock. The first thing was to buy time. She pointed to the library. "Neame was entering as I came out. You should look there first."

The apprentice rushed off with a word of thanks. Levannue wasted no time. It would not take long to discover that Neame was not there. At the doorway to the seniors' quarters, Levannue spared a quick glance towards the gates. Three figures were discernible standing in the forecourt. Levannue hastened inside before she was seen.

Somehow, Jemeryl's associates had been able to penetrate the school defences and learn what had happened. Levannue's mind seethed in turmoil. She would have staked her life that no message had got in or out. Levannue shuddered—her life was, quite literally, at stake. She had strengthened the school shields to block everything. She could not guess what skills and powers her enemies had used. The unknown subtlety was the frightening thing, or more basically, the unknown.

The three mercenaries at the gate could only be messengers. Other, more formidable forces would be mustering. Her hope for escape rested solely with speed and the chance they had not thought to guard the rear exit.

Levannue arrived in her quarters. Two bags were stashed at the rear of a cupboard. One was a conventional backpack containing everything she would need on her travels. The other was a dimensional gate for use when she was re-established elsewhere. Levannue congratulated herself on the forethought to have them ready.

She hoisted the bags over her shoulder, grabbed a cloak, and was ready to depart. At the doorway, she stopped for one last look back at the rooms she had shared with Bramell. Abruptly, tears threatened her composure, spurred by dozens of barbed memories: their children crawling on the mat, a long midwinter's night by the fire, the reflected light on the ceiling when she woke on a sunny day. Although leaving had always been inherent in her plans, she was going now because she had no other option. She could not stop herself wondering if she had lost far more than she would ever gain. She would never see Bramell again, not even to say goodbye.

But there was no time to waste on regrets. Levannue shut the door and fled. Her route slipped behind the junior washrooms and outhouses, sticking to the shadows and ripples in a sorcerer's multidimensional space. The small gate above the cliff path was unbarred. Levannue halted, studying the trail intently. She noted each shift in light and balance, but there was no guard she could detect, nothing to block her way.

On the field behind her, the school building blended into the night. The scene was so very familiar from the long years since she had come to Ekranos as a young woman. Again, her lips quivered. This was not the way she had wanted to leave, although perhaps it was for the best. A formal farewell would have been too painful.

Levannue stepped onto the path. The moon was rising over the bay, high tide no more than an hour away. She had to be gone before the pursuit reached the harbour. Speed was of the essence. Her face hardened. Once she was safe, she could indulge in self-pity, if she wished.

Levannue hurried down the path, a dark shadow in the descending night.

❖

Tevi stood impatiently in the forecourt. Behind her, the other two mercenaries shifted from foot to foot anxiously. One of them whispered, "What have you got mixed up in, Tevi? "

Tevi did not reply. She walked to the archway onto the main square, scouring the darkening pathways for sight of the returning apprentice. Her hand thumped in frustration on the brickwork. At last, a figure emerged from a distant doorway and hurried towards them.

As the girl approached, her voice lifted to a shout. "I can't find Neame anywhere! Are you sure you can't come back tomorrow?"

"No, I can't. I want to see Neame or Bramell. And most of all, I want to see Jemeryl, and I want to see her now!" Tevi answered angrily as the apprentice came to a halt.

"Well, that's just not—"

Tevi's patience snapped. She strode forward, intending to search the school herself if need be.

The apprentice's hand shot out to block Tevi's way. "We don't allow—"

The sentence was never finished. Tevi shoved the apprentice aside, catching her so much by surprise that she tripped. The other mercenaries shrunk into the shadows, vainly trying to make themselves invisible. It was madness to treat any member of the Coven like that, even an apprentice. However, the fallen youngster was too shocked to retaliate.

Tevi marched to the entrance to the main square. She stopped, fists on hips, and bellowed, "*I want to talk to somebody in authority!*"

"Will I do." The voice came from a darkened alleyway. The firm tone made clear that despite the words, it was not a question.

Tevi spun around. A stocky figure emerged into the forecourt—a woman in late middle age, with untidy grey hair tacked up in a bun. The new arrival considered the scene, taking in Tevi's defiant scowl, the fallen apprentice, and the cowering mercenaries by the gatehouse.

"What exactly is going on?"

The apprentice scrambled to her feet, relief evident on her face. "Oh, Neame, ma'am. These mercenaries want to see you. They've got a warrant from Lyremouth." She cast a dubious look at Tevi. "But they're a bit overexcited. Perhaps they should explain what it's about for themselves."

❖

"These accusations are preposterous. You cannot expect me to take them seriously." Bramell's well-modulated tones did nothing to mask his anger.

Tevi was unimpressed. "I'm simply telling you what we've learned."

"What you *believe* you've learned from this childish subterfuge. What right did you have to act like that?"

"We were obeying the Guardian's orders." Tevi was politely stubborn.

"Preposterous or not, we've got to look into it. You can't ignore the warrant." Neame added her support.

Tevi looked at her with gratitude. They three were the only ones in the principal's study.

Bramell carried on. "Why didn't Jemeryl tell me this herself?"

"I don't know. Why don't you bring her here and ask her?" Tevi was mastering her impatience with difficulty.

"I will. We can also hear what Levannue has to say." Bramell made his decision. He opened the door and called to an assistant. "I want to see Jemeryl at once. And could you also find Levannue and ask her to step in here?"

The room was quiet while they waited. Tevi looked at the bare walls. Bramell's study was smaller and plainer than she had expected. Sun-bleached outlines on the walls indicated that previous occupants had preferred a little more ornamentation. The man himself matched Jemeryl's description perfectly. Neame also was true to the portrait Jemeryl had painted, although Tevi sensed a mind at once both subtler and more straightforward than she had anticipated.

The delay dragged on. Bramell grew increasingly irritable. He paced to the window, although nothing was visible in the darkness outside. Turning his back on the night, he resumed his attack on Tevi. "Do you realise how serious your allegations are? Levannue is a senior sorcerer. If this is a joke, you're in for some nasty shocks."

Tevi bit her tongue; she had other concerns. She had the impression that Jemeryl was being held nearby, but it was taking considerable time for her to arrive. The assurance that Jemeryl was safe, even if incarcerated, had gone part way to easing Tevi's anxiety, but she would only be happy once she had seen her lover in person.

"Is it possible Jemeryl has duped this mercenary in some way?" Bramell addressed Neame.

"I don't see how. The warrant is undoubtedly genuine."

Bramell opened his mouth to speak but was forestalled by the sound of running feet.

The door to the study flew open, and a young witch burst in. "Please, sir. Jemeryl's ill. She's taken something. We couldn't wake her."

❖

The quarantine rooms lay along a narrow corridor, leading from a central upstairs lobby. Despite the late hour, the hallways were busy. Huddled groups exchanged whispers that hissed like waves on a beach. Distant doors slammed.

Tevi sat at the top of the stairs on the lobby floor, trying to ignore the inquisitive looks sent in her direction. Her back was against the wall, and her eyes were fixed on the door to the room where Jemeryl lay. Nearby stood a group of apprentices. Their juvenile excitement jarred on Tevi's nerves. Another young woman, with a sorcerer's black amulet, was going from group to group, desperately questioning anyone willing to talk. Most were only too eager. From the description, Tevi guessed that she was Vine.

The school gossip was eyeing Tevi and obviously preparing to accost her when the door down the hallway opened and Bramell emerged. He strode to the intersection.

Tevi scrambled to her feet. "How is Jemeryl?"

Bramell did not answer. He glared at the other occupants of the lobby. "Will everyone who has no business here leave immediately."

Everyone made haste to comply, until only one small apprentice remained. "Please, sir."

"What is it?"

"We couldn't find Levannue. Do you still want to talk to her?"

Bramell's expression barely changed, but Tevi sensed that something inside the man crumpled.

The apprentice carried on speaking timidly. "If you wish, sir, I could go to your rooms and see if she has returned."

"That is not necessary." Bramell's voice was devoid of its usual confidence.

The apprentice made her escape, running down the now-vacant stairway.

Bramell stood, looking around without appearing to see anything, but then he lurched towards the stairs. No trace remained of the arrogance and self-assurance he had shown in his office. Tevi could have pitied him, except she had her own worries.

As he walked past, she caught his arm. "How is Jemeryl?"

"Neame is attending to her. Everything is being done." Bramell spoke the bland phrases in a daze.

"Can I see her now?"

"No. You would disturb Neame's work." Bramell looked at Tevi as if trying to remember who she was. "I want you to take a message to the mayor in Ekranos. I've already sent sorcerers to aid the harbourmaster. But she..." He stopped, gathering himself. "Levannue may attempt to escape by other routes. Have the mayor send messengers to all surrounding towns. Ordinary folk won't be able to stop her, but they might raise the alarm. The Coven will dispatch more resources as soon as possible."

"Two of my guild comrades are outside. They can take the message."

"There's nothing you can do here. We will take care of Jemeryl." Bramell's voice lacked authority, but he would have made no impression on Tevi regardless of how he had spoken.

"I'm staying with her."

Bramell did not have the spirit to argue. He turned and walked down the stairs with the bearing of a condemned criminal on the way to the gallows. His footsteps faded along the corridor below. A door banged shut, then there was silence.

Tevi paced the length of the corridor. She stared through the window at the end, haunted by her brief glimpse of Jemeryl's pale face and the cold touch of her skin.

After a long time, she moved away and stopped outside the room where Jemeryl lay. The night had grown chill, but Tevi could not leave. The door to another quarantine room stood ajar. It was unoccupied, but the two narrow bunks were made. Tevi pulled a blanket from one and returned to the corridor. She sank to the floor, hugging her knees and facing Jemeryl's room. It might be a long vigil. She wrapped the blanket around her shoulders and prepared to wait.

❖

The creak of the door roused Tevi from a doze. Neame's haggard face peered around the edge. Tevi leapt to her feet, disentangling herself from the blanket. Hours had passed. Faint grey light, preceding dawn, lay beyond the window. The wind off the sea rustled under the eaves of the roof.

Neame looked exhausted. Her drawn face revealed nothing.

"How is she?" Tevi forced herself to ask.

"She'll be fine." Neame lifted a hand and pushed back a stray wisp of grey hair. "Another quarter hour, and it would have been a different story." She beckoned Tevi into the room.

Tevi stumbled past, crying with relief, and collapsed beside the bed.

The covers rose and fell with Jemeryl's breathing. Her face was pale, but a faint flush coloured her cheeks. When Tevi caught hold of Jemeryl's hand, the skin felt cool, dry, and supple. Stifling a sob, Tevi pressed it against her face.

Neame shuffled to Tevi's side. "I need to sleep. Jemeryl should be all right, but someone should keep watch, and if she shows signs of distress summon"—Neame waved her hand, searching for a name—"the sorcerer on duty downstairs." She pointed vaguely through the floor.

The elderly sorcerer turned towards the door. On her way out, she collided with a small table bearing a collar, sawn open. She picked the device up and stared at it with contempt. "Levannue...damn her." The collar flew across the room and struck the far wall. It dropped clattering to the floor.

The door shut behind Neame. Tevi shifted onto the edge of the bed and brushed the auburn curls back from Jemeryl's face. The sleeping woman's lips moved slightly. Tevi thought she recognised her own name.

Tevi's legs were numb from sleeping on the floor. To ease the stiffness, she stood and wandered to the window. Dawn was breaking over the sea. Off to the east a pale smudge was cut on the horizon. One bright star hung low in the sky, vying with the growing light.

Tevi left the window and dragged a chair across. She sat and again took hold of Jemeryl's hand. At that moment, the simple contact was the most precious thing in Tevi's world. Her eyes fixed on her lover's face.

Nearly a year and a half had passed since she had left Storenseg. Much had happened. Tevi remembered the distress she had felt the first time she had killed someone—a young bandit. Her expression became grim. Now there was someone she wanted to kill. Tevi knew that when Levannue lay dead before her, there would be no regrets.

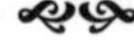

Part Two

The Chalice

Chapter Ten—Stinking Dog-Root

Tevi bounced down the steps of the guildhall. She hit a wall of heat. Ekranos was simmering at the height of summer. Sun beat down on her head, baking her into the pavement. Shade was at a premium. Tevi set off through the airless town, keeping to whatever shade she could find.

On a tree-lined avenue, a group of mercenaries was gathered outside a busy tavern. Tevi stopped for an exchange of stale jokes and gossip. Several asked her to stay, but the invitations were half-hearted. Tevi declined and pretended not to notice the relief. She concealed her own grimace until after she had turned away.

The noise of the tavern faded as Tevi joined the main road leading through the western gates. The midday heat reduced the usual crowds to a trickle. Beyond the town, there was little to offer protection from the sun, although a breeze blew off the sea, cleansing the air of dust. The road ahead climbed across the parched landscape. Tevi adopted an easy, mile-eating stride and, to the rhythm of her steps, mused on her current status.

She had divided the previous month between the school of herbalism and the mercenary guildhall, and had felt an outsider in both. At the school, she was neither a healer nor a patient, and many clearly thought she had no place there. At best, she was ignored; at worst, she was treated like Jemeryl's unwelcome toy.

When she was grudgingly offered a bed in the servant's dormitory, she had opted to remain in the guildhall. However, this was not without tension, as demonstrated by the group at the tavern. The other mercenaries now treated her with strained politeness. Gone were the horseplay and crude good humour, inhibited by her newly perceived role as a sorcerer's lover, or should the word be "partner"? Tevi was unsure if the term needed official ratification.

Tevi shook her head, partly to clear sweat from her eyes and partly to dismiss the troubling thoughts. She paused to catch her breath in the shade of a stunted tree. Branches fanned out close to the ground, covered with bark that peeled in ragged fibres. Dull olive leaves rattled in the breeze.

Ekranos was laid out below her, white walls and black shadows in a bleached landscape. Only the blue sea was unfaded until the sparkling ripples blended into a silver plain, meeting the sky. Tevi's eyes rested on the familiar horizon of her childhood, but the sight stirred no memories of Storenseg. Somewhere out there was a woman who had tried to murder Jemeryl. The thought overrode all others.

Tevi resumed her trek. The climb in the heat was draining. The guildhall would have loaned her a horse if she had been willing to trade on Jemeryl's name. Walking was a way of asserting her independence, although it was doubtful that it affected anyone's perception of her. Sweat trickled down her sides. Her shirt clung to her back. By the time the school walls appeared above the crest of the hill, she was cursing her own pride.

The main entrance was a wide stone arch, without gates or barrier. The school was guarded by nothing visible to the eyes of the ungifted; yet there were guards. Tevi shuddered, remembering the way she had charged in. She was wiser now. Jemeryl had made sure of it.

The school layout had become very familiar to Tevi, and no one challenged her as she crossed the site. She reached her destination to find the study door wedged open and Vine alone at her desk. A book lay open in front of her, although the young sorcerer was showing no sign of reading.

She greeted Tevi's arrival eagerly. "Hi. Jem's expecting you. She's outside. I'll show you where."

Vine was a rare exception at the school, willing to treat Tevi as a friend. In cynical moments, Tevi wondered if it was because you did not pick up gossip by offending your sources. Vine would undoubtedly pump her for information, but Tevi had already learnt that asking your own questions was the best way to deflect Vine's curiosity.

"Is there any news of Bramell or Levannue?" Tevi asked as they walked along the veranda.

"Bramell should have reached Lyremouth by now, but it'll be some time before we hear back. As for Levannue..." Vine shrugged. "I think she's slipped the net."

"I'd have thought the school could have traced her with magic."

"But that takes sixth-dimensional ability, and nobody here could match her skills. Lyremouth should be able to do better, which is why Bramell went there."

"It must all be awkward for him. Do you think he'll resign?"

"I don't know. When he returns, it..." Vine's voice faded. The idea obviously interested her.

They rounded the building. A couch was set in the shade of a faded blue canopy. Jemeryl lay sprawled amid piles of cushions with Klara asleep on the headrest.

"You found me, then." Jemeryl glanced between them. "Has Vine been quizzing you?"

"Actually, I've been the one asking questions."

"Tevi was asking for news of Levannue. I don't suppose Neame has told you anything?"

Vine's casual tone did not hide her eagerness, but for all her news-gathering skills, Tevi suspected that she missed the twitch of Jemeryl's eyebrows. And Tevi was not about to enlighten her. "No. Nobody tells me anything. They're worried about upsetting me."

Vine directed a frown at Jemeryl. "But you aren't saying much either. I wish I knew what it was all about. I don't even know what Levannue has done. Apart from trying to murder you, of course."

"It must be very trying for you." Jemeryl sounded more amused than sympathetic. "But you know we can't say anything."

"Come on...a clue, a hint? You could do a mime." Vine's plea was met by laughter.

"I thought you were supposed to be studying," Jemeryl said pointedly.

"All right, I'm going." Vine stalked away with her nose in the air, but the exchange was good-natured. Her pout consisted entirely of self-mockery.

Jemeryl watched her go. "Poor Vine. I think she feels physical pain knowing a secret is being withheld from her."

Tevi kissed Jemeryl gently and then sat on the grass. She stretched out her legs and rested her shoulders against the couch. Her head lay cushioned on Jemeryl's lap. Above her, a sea of ripples chased across the canopy in the breeze. Tevi shifted her focus to the upside-down face. Jemeryl's lips were pale and a yellow tinge stained her eyes, but health was returning. The skeletal gauntness had left Jemeryl's naturally sharp-boned features. The listless weakness had also gone, and today, there was an extra glint in her eyes.

"You've learnt something about Levannue." Tevi stated it as a fact.

"How do you know?"

"By your face when Vine mentioned her name."

Jemeryl sighed and brushed the hair from Tevi's forehead. "Just don't teach Vine the knack."

"So what is it? Has she been caught?"

"No. It's only some guesswork."

Tevi swivelled around to face Jemeryl. "And...?"

"I've been thinking. They've lost track of Levannue. The only thing we can do is try to work out where she's going. This would be difficult, except we know her claimed destination. It was probably the truth. She had no reason to hide it back when she first announced her plans, and she wouldn't have wanted to raise an alarm if she didn't arrive as expected."

"So we can eliminate that town and narrow our search down to the rest of the world?"

Jemeryl laughed. "It's actually a rather significant piece of information. Levannue was due to stop off on the way, but her final destination was a town called Corrisburn, near where Whitfell Spur joins the Barrodens. It's a plausible place to test out wards. A lot of nasty things live in the high mountains. But it is also only eighty miles from where Lorimal did her original research."

"There's something there. Something Lorimal left behind." Tevi guessed immediately.

"That's one possibility, and I'm sure the Guardian will spot it. I've come up with another idea. The name *Corrisburn* struck a chord with me. Yesterday, I remembered why. There's a plant that grows wild in the mountains that's used in various spells. There are several towns where it's harvested. Corrisburn is the source the school uses. I must have written the name a dozen times while I was tidying the dispensary. I suspect Levannue wants the plant and checked the school records to see where she could get it."

"Surely the closeness to where Lorimal did her work isn't a coincidence."

"It's not. This plant only grows on the southern slopes of the Barrodens. Elsewhere, you have to get it dried. It's known by a number of local names. The least romantic is 'stinking dog-root.' I assume fragrance isn't its greatest charm. Several sorcerers claim that the fresh berries have unusual properties, but they're lost when the plant is dried, so they haven't been thoroughly investigated. To tell the truth, nobody is certain what potential these berries have. It's the sort of thing an ambitious young sorcerer would study, given the chance. Lorimal invented her spell while she had access to fresh berries. If they're used in the spell, it would explain why Levannue had to go to the same region to repeat the work."

"You say if. Do you have any firm evidence?"

"Two things." Jemeryl counted on her fingers. "One, Levannue's arrival in Corrisburn would have coincided with the fruiting season in early autumn. Two—and this is the clincher—while I was working with her, I noticed she was growing some potted plants. I checked this morning. It's the dog-root."

"Then why would she need to go to the Barrodens?"

"They were weak, stunted specimens. It isn't a tropical plant and wouldn't reach its full potency here. Probably no more than to confirm that the spell would work."

Tevi nodded slowly. "Can the Coven guard the entire area where this plant grows?"

"People may not realise they have to. I don't know if the Guardian will pick up on the dog-root. We can be certain Bramell won't. The only ingredient Iralin knew about was the orchid nectar, because Lorimal needed special requisitions for it while she was experimenting. If Lyremouth gets their supplies of dog-root from a different town, they might not even make the link. So we've got to catch Levannue ourselves."

"How can we cover the entire mountain range?"

"No need. Levannue won't dare visit any spot along the Barrodens that's under Coven control. Every witch and sorcerer is on the lookout for her. And since the northern border has been prone to attack, the Coven has it heavily guarded, even at quiet times. There's only one place outside the Protectorate where she can get the dog-root: Horzt. That's where we'll wait for her."

"It could be another trap."

"I don't think so. Levannue can make mistakes. Like when she fled, rather than overpowering you at the gates. She could have taken the warrant and lied to Bramell about it."

"Pretending to flee might be part of her plan."

"From what she'd said to me beforehand, I'm sure she assumed that you were the messenger for a powerful group of sorcerers. How else could you have known that something had happened to me? She can't have realised that she effectively sent the signal herself. My link to Klara had been weak through the school shields, and Levannue didn't know about her. So when she ensnared me, the bond was severed, and Klara was just an ordinary magpie again."

Tevi felt her throat tighten. "When she pecked me, I thought you were dead."

"Yes, well, killing me would have the same effect as far as Klara's concerned."

Jemeryl's light-hearted tone only intensified Tevi's fears. "We don't need to chase her ourselves. We should tell the Guardian where you think Levannue's going. It would be safer."

"There isn't time to get a message to Lyremouth. We'll have to move sharply ourselves to be sure of reaching Horzt before her."

"What will Neame say?"

"She'll say I'm not well enough. So we won't tell her."

"Might not Neame be right?"

"Levannue has to be stopped. I know I'm not fully recovered, but I'm still the strongest worker in the sixth dimension left here."

Tevi frowned but said nothing.

Jemeryl studied her expression. "Don't you want to go after Levannue?"

"Oh, yes." Tevi took a deep breath. "And it's not just the quest. I'll never forgive that she tried to murder you, but it's going to be dangerous tackling Levannue on our own. Especially if she's just acquired a new weapon."

"It'll come sooner or later. I'm sworn to die defending the Protectorate, if need be. A surprise attack before she's mastered the spell might be my best chance." There was no humour in Jemeryl's voice, but then her grin returned. "Anyway, it's vital that we leave Ekranos soon."

"Why?"

"Probably a sign that I'm getting better, but it's starting to get to me that they won't let you share my room."

❖

The road cut a diagonal slash up the side of the gorge. Tufts of grass sprouted on the central ridge between two deep ruts marking the passage of carts. Rain had scored fernlike patterns in the dust. On one side, pines overhung the trail and purple heather clung to exposed rocks. On the other, the slope dropped so steeply that the tops of tall trees were at eye level with the riders on the road.

Tevi stopped her horse by the edge and looked down. Far below, the river Danor thundered through the ravine. Her eyes scanned along the trail. Apart from songbirds, the only activity was the first wagon rounding the bend several hundred yards back. A second team came into view. Tevi spurred her horse on to catch up with the other two mercenaries in the caravan's vanguard.

After half a mile, the gradient eased. The roar of water grew close and then softened. They rounded another bend, and abruptly, the valley fell away. Ahead lay a wide basin, hollowed in the mountains. The rim was a circle of wooded slopes broken by scree, leading up to bare mountaintops.

Miles away, a tumulus erupted from the basin floor, covered with buildings and surrounded by a high stone wall. The mercenaries stopped their horses by a patch of meadow, and the eldest pointed to the distant town.

"That's Horzt. We'll be there by evening. Beyond is the high pass—if you've changed your mind."

"I haven't." Tevi's tone was polite but obstinate.

"I'm sure the caravan master will have no trouble replacing you," the older mercenary said sourly. He indicated the stretch of grass. "We'll stop for one last break."

Tevi swung a leg over her horse's rump and dropped to the ground. She climbed to the top of a bank to view the terrain. In the distance, Horzt was a confused mound of walls and towers. The river Danor threw a loop around its base before winding through swaths of farmland dotted with small hamlets. The water flowed over shingle as it eventually passed the slope where Tevi stood.

The Danor had carved the only wagon route through the Barrodens east of Whitfell Spur. Barges navigated the river as far as Gossenfeld, which was also the boundary of the Protectorate. From there, Tevi had taken a guard's contract on a caravan to Horzt. Part of her salary paid for Jemeryl's place on a wagon, since the sorcerer was disguised. Even Tevi was using a false name. She suspected that Jemeryl was enjoying the game, but personally, she thought it an unnecessary strain.

The wagons began to arrive. The creek of axles and shouts of drivers broke the peace. A few passengers emerged, yawning and stretching cramped muscles. Traders clambered over the loads, pulling on ropes. More wagons arrived, and suddenly, travellers sprang from everywhere.

Tevi trotted across to one of the covered wagons. She pulled back the awning. All the passengers had left except for a withered crone. Ancient eyes blinked in the light. Etched lips puckered on toothless gums. One knotted hand gripped a walking stick; the other hugged a wicker cage containing a sorry-looking magpie.

"Is that you, Laniss?" the ancient voice quavered.

"I've come to help you down, Gran." Tevi spoke loudly, as if addressing the deaf.

"Are we there yet?"

"Nearly. You can see Horzt."

Tevi assisted the old woman to a spot where they could view the town and, more important, not be overheard.

"Are you sure this disguise is worth it?" Tevi asked wearily.

"Yes, I am." Jemeryl spoke with her own voice. "Levannue may scry the town before showing her face. Even disguised like this, I'll need to keep a low profile, but all she'll have on you is a name."

"If it's so risky, won't she avoid the town altogether?"

"She has no choice. The dog-root doesn't grow profusely this far east, and it's usually in awkward places. Levannue isn't young. She's not up to rock climbing, and enthralling people won't help, as they'd be too clumsy to do much apart from fall down cliffs."

"Who normally harvests the dog-root?"

"It's too rare around here to do it commercially. Herdsmen gather the odd sprig if they spot it and trade to the alchemists in Horzt. Which is where Levannue will have to go to buy it in quantity."

The magpie gave a pathetic croak. Tevi held the cage at eye level.

"Klara's not enjoying this. I'd be happier without it as well. I'm no good at acting."

A bell sounded the signal for the midday meal. Tevi offered Jemeryl her arm for the walk to the food wagon. She tried to take comfort that the worst of the acting would be over when they reached Horzt and were no longer in close contact with fellow travellers.

"Think of this disguise as a rare opportunity." Jemeryl's voice reverted to the elderly quaver.

"For what?"

"It gives you the chance to work out if you'll still love me when I'm old and wrinkly."

Tevi snorted derisively, but the corners of her mouth twitched in a smile. "I'll let you know."

❖

A rolling blanket of grey hung above Horzt, hiding the mountaintops. Light rain blew in clouds of mist over the city walls and fell as a persistent drizzle in the narrow streets, running down walls and dripping off lintels. Everywhere smelt sour of damp stone

The road split just inside the city gates. The lanes fanned out through the packed mass of houses that clung to the sides of the tumulus. Wet cobbles glistened with an oily sheen. Small torrents cascaded over wedged dams of rubbish in the gutters. More water flowed from passageways where worn steps scaled the hillside between featureless walls.

Tevi stood in the shelter of one such alley, not that it offered much protection. She made another futile attempt to adjust her militia-issue cloak so that the water running off her militia-issue helmet did not drip down her neck, while again cursing the militia authorities for issuing the poorly designed uniform.

Tevi had joined the militia on her arrival in Horzt. Although the town was outside the Protectorate, well over half its militia bore red and gold tattoos of the mercenaries. There was even a guild house in the town. The disguise was good for watching every traveller who entered. Yet nearly a month had passed without sign of Levannue. Jemeryl still spoke confidently, but Tevi knew she was starting to worry.

From the alley, Tevi had a clear view of traffic through the gates. The people wisely did their utmost to avoid attracting her attention. She was off duty, but the passers-by were not to know. The Horzt militia were notorious for their ready use of fines, stocks, and the whipping post. It gave Tevi mixed feelings. She was in favour of lawful behaviour but did not enjoy playing the bully.

The clouds began to break up, although a moist wind still gusted under the gatehouse. The outline of the sun appeared briefly before dark tendrils obscured it again. A last burst of rain splattered the ground. Tevi dislodged a row of drips from her helmet's eye guard and then froze at the sound of an urgent metallic beat: three taps, a rest, one tap, and then two taps. The sequence repeated.

The helmet made it hard to locate the source of the drumming. Tevi looked all around. Then she looked up. Klara was perched on a rusted bar sticking from the wall a few feet above her head. Raindrops rolled like diamonds off her stark plumage. The magpie's head bobbed, again beating out the signal, but Tevi did not wait for confirmation. She spun around and leapt up the stairway. Puddles splattered explosively under the impact of her feet. She took the last flight three steps at a time.

Tevi burst onto the street above and raced past shops stacked with barrels, dried meat, and cheese. A thin band of grey sky snaked overhead between the roofs. Civilians melted from her path. A stout trader stumbled as he flattened himself against a wall. Running militia meant trouble.

The streets flew by. Tevi ducked into a crooked alley that twisted behind shops. Around a bend, she collided with a handcart. The porter mumbled a confused apology. Tevi squeezed by. Her cloak scratched on the stone wall, and her jerkin became drenched as it wiped along the cart. The material flapped cold against her stomach as she ran on.

Another bend hid the cart from view. Tevi slowed to the purposeful stride of a routine patrol while fighting to steady her breathing. She rounded the last corner and emerged into a small square.

Technically, the shape was more a bent triangle, formed where five roads met. A drinking fountain shaped like a lion's head spewed water into a basin at one end. Tevi halted by it and looked up at her destination: the steep road known as Abrak's Alley. Here charm sellers, alchemists, and healers plied their trades. The street seemed to revel in an arcane sleaziness. The gradient was so steep that steps were provided for pedestrians.

Tevi leaned against the wall by the fountain and folded her arms as if waiting for trouble, adopting a typical militia pose. A group of drunken barbarians quietened instantly. Tevi hardly noticed them. Klara was the one she wanted.

A dilapidated inn filled one side of the square. Its tottering facade bore witness to a history of modification. Tevi did not bother looking for Jemeryl at the window to their room, with an unobstructed view up Abrak's Alley. Levannue was about. Jemeryl would not be so stupid as to stand where she could be seen—on any plane of existence. Instead, she would use Klara's coded signals to identify the traitor.

A simple physical description was useless, as demonstrated by Jemeryl's own disguise. Levannue could be anyone: the gap-toothed street urchin darting past; the rich trader sauntering by, until the edge was taken off her swagger by Tevi's attention; the lounging whore whose clothing, or lack of it, left no doubt of his profession. He noticed Tevi watching and smiled coyly; the militia were good customers. Tevi's eyes swept on. Still, Klara did not arrive.

The minutes passed while Tevi's anxiety grew. People flowed in and out of the square. Already, Levannue might be leaving with her purchase complete. Jemeryl had been sure that Klara would go undetected, but something was wrong.

Tevi pushed away from the wall. Her first impulse was to rush into the inn. She forced herself to stop and think. In all honesty, if Levannue had discovered Jemeryl, there was nothing Tevi could do. It was better to be optimistic. Klara's signal meant that Jemeryl had spotted Levannue. The place to look was in the alchemists' shops. Maybe Klara was waiting farther up the street. Tevi turned her back on the inn and started to climb the uneven cobbles.

The first alchemist's shop was a cavelike opening lined with ramshackle wooden shelves stretching back into darkness. The ceiling was an upside-down forest of herbs hanging from the rafters. Tevi glanced in. The bandy-legged owner was smiling benignly at two potential customers who were examining a small bag. Tevi noted their hawkish features and dark, knotted hair. She recognised them as traders travelling with a mule train from the eastern reaches. *It's one useful thing to do*, she told herself. *Remember who's here. Then Jemeryl can describe Levannue's current appearance so I can identify her.*

Tevi continued the climb. People slid away from her belligerent gaze. A dozen yards farther on, she passed another alchemist's, identical to the first. Only one customer was lost in the gloom at the rear, and shrouded by a voluminous grey cloak.

The rhythm of Tevi's stride did not falter, but she could have laughed. The customer was Levannue; her posture said it all. The whole stance, from rigid neck to shuffling feet, shouted fear and guilt. If the customs officers of Ekranos had seen a captain stand like that, they would have torn the ship apart plank by plank.

At the top of the street, Tevi stopped and looked back. Rooftops fell away before her, stretching down to the city walls. On the fields beyond, over a hundred wagons were camped in a temporary city. Tents wove rivers of canvas along muddy trackways. Herds of lumbering carthorses filled the water meadows. Farther away still were farmlands and mountains.

Tevi's gaze returned to the street. The woman in grey scurried from the shop, clutching her purchase. Tevi caught a glimpse of the traitor's disguise. Levannue had chosen a face so lacking in distinctive features as to defy description. Once seen, instantly forgotten. But the way she moved! Short, desperate steps revealed tension in the knees. Tevi could have picked her out of a crowd at a hundred yards.

Tevi strode after the retreating figure but hesitated outside the inn, tormented by the urge to go and check that Jemeryl was all right. The shutters were half open on the window to their room, just as she had left them that morning. Surely there would be some sign if Jemeryl had been attacked.

Tevi bit her lip. She dare not waste time. After her month in the militia, she knew every alleyway and shortcut in Horzt. It would take all this knowledge to shadow Levannue without attracting suspicion, although the militia uniform would help. The militia were expected to be everywhere, asking questions. Tevi had lots of questions to ask. She threw one last pleading look at the window before setting off. The hunt was now on in earnest.

❖

Darkness had fallen by the time Tevi returned to the inn. No moonlight penetrated the unbroken sheet of cloud, yet few were deterred from venturing forth. Shouts and laughter echoed along the ill-lit streets.

They were high points over the continuous chaotic background hum of Horzt by night, the sound of eager people in search of pleasure. At times over the previous month, Tevi had been reminded of Torhaven. Horzt was also a frontier town outside the Protectorate. However, the differences were equally strong, and the nightlife was, if not completely harmless, at least mainly devoid of malice.

Horzt was the first taste of familiar civilisation for those returning from the wildlands. It was also the last that those heading north would get for months, maybe years, maybe forever. Danger was always present in the wildlands. Some would never return, and their bones would rest forever in a wayside grave.

Travellers indulged themselves in Horzt, aided by the sizeable proportion of the local population who made a living by catering for them. As long as the road beyond was passable, the nights in Horzt were one continuous party. The excesses had frequently shocked Tevi. Her month in the militia had finished off what little naiveté she had possessed on her arrival. There was small wonder that the Horzt militia had needed to acquire their reputation.

By now, Tevi was inured to the debauchery, and other worries claimed her attention. She reached a quieter street, lined with the shuttered shop fronts of tanners and cobblers. The smell of leather vied with stale beer on revellers. A group blocked the road and forced Tevi to squeeze through. One man, too drunk to register her uniform, shoved her and cursed. Tevi regained her balance and glared at the offender, but his companions were already hauling her assailant away, with a chorus of nervous apologies.

Tevi let them go. She wanted to get back to Jemeryl rather than waste time improving the manners of a drunkard. All afternoon, while trailing Levannue through city and camp, Tevi had refused to worry about Klara's non-appearance. Levannue certainly had not acted like someone who had just defeated a major adversary. However, each minute was eating away at that confidence. As the inn came into view, Tevi's tension solidified painfully in her stomach.

Light from the inn's open doorway glinted on water flowing from the lion's mouth. The gentle splashing was incongruous in the decadence of Horzt by night. Then rough voices erupted in the bar, drowning out everything else. The cacophony was singing but hardly inviting. Fighting her way through to the rear stairway would be a slow job, not least because the innkeeper clearly regarded Tevi as his personal police force.

There was another route to their room. A side alley gave access to the inner courtyard. In it would be empty beer barrels, broken furniture and, frequently, drunkards sleeping off their beer. It was quicker, but not Tevi's favourite passageway. The stench of urine lay thicker than the shadows. Tevi held her breath until she emerged into the marginally fresher air of the courtyard.

A rickety stairway climbed the walls. Decaying timbers revealed years of neglect. Tevi stood and listened. Horzt had its share of footpads, but nothing stirred, except maybe a rat.

As Tevi stepped into the open, a small shape leapt from between the mounds of trash. Too late, Tevi realised that it was not a rat.

"Laniss. Laniss. I've been waiting for you."

Tevi jumped even as she recognised the shrill voice of Rill, the innkeeper's young daughter. The child was awake, as usual, long past a sensible bedtime for someone her age. The girl grabbed Tevi's hand and swung back and forth. This did not unbalance Tevi, but it prevented her progress.

"Have you been in any fights? Have you killed anyone?"

"No. I've told you, the militia isn't like that. I just walk around and shout." Tevi's patience with the girl had been tested on many occasions.

"I wish I was grown up and could join the militia. I'm going to join as soon as I'm big enough."

Rill let go of Tevi's hand to practice wild swings with an imaginary sword. Tevi suspected that another twenty years would see Rill as an overweight and overcautious barkeeper.

"Is my grandmother all right?" Tevi skirted around the prancing child.

"Oh, she's been asking about you all afternoon."

Tevi's heart leapt at the reassurance. She reached the stairs, with Rill tagging after. The child's chubby legs made hard work of the uneven steps. Tevi wished there were some easy way to shake off the jarring hero worship. However, help was at hand. The kitchen door was flung open. Candlelight played among the courtyard shadows.

"Rill! Is that you? Get yourself in here. Haven't I told you..." the innkeeper's voice boomed.

Rill scrambled crablike down the stairs. She scuttled quickly past her father but was only partially successful in ducking the swipe aimed at her ear. The innkeeper scowled at Tevi, made a token effort at a nod of acknowledgement, and then slammed the door.

Darkness reclaimed the courtyard. Then Tevi was aware of a new light falling from above. She looked up. Jemeryl's disguised form was framed in a doorway at the top of the stairs.

"Tevi. You're safe. I've been..." Jemeryl was too agitated to use the false name. Fortunately, there was no one to hear.

Tevi did not answer. She leapt the remaining stairs and shepherded Jemeryl back along the corridor and into their room. Once the door was shut, she held Jemeryl tightly, unperturbed by her seventy-year-old appearance, and soaked in relief from the rhythm of Jemeryl's heart thudding against her own.

"What happened? I couldn't see Klara. Did something go wrong?" Tevi asked.

"Levannue had a watch ward on the sixth-dimensional channels. It must have taken her weeks to construct. Probably why she's so late getting here. I didn't dare let Klara get within one hundred yards of her. She'd have spotted the link at once. But what happened to you? I was expecting you to come back so I could give a description of how Levannue looked. I've been so frightened."

"And I've been worried about you. You are all right, aren't you?"

Jemeryl grabbed Tevi's hands and held them to her lips. "Yes, now I know you're safe." She raised her eyes to meet Tevi's. "What have you been doing? We've got to find Levannue. She was—"

"The nondescript middle-aged woman wearing the large grey cloak."

Jemeryl looked stunned. "How did you know?"

"By the way she stood. It's something I learned on the docks. How to read someone's posture. It had to be her. She looked so ineptly guilty. She was obviously doing something wrong but wasn't a professional criminal."

Jemeryl studied Tevi with surprised appreciation. "So I suppose you've found out where she's staying, when she's leaving, where she's going, and what colour underclothes she's wearing?"

"I didn't make any progress on the underclothes, but I got answers for the rest."

Tevi threw herself onto one of the two lumpy mattresses that took up most of the floor and were the only furniture in the room. The walls were greasy and damp-stained, the woodwork was rotten, and the bedding was filthy. Even these facts failed to diminish Tevi's self-satisfied grin.

Jemeryl joined her. "When does Levannue leave Horzt?"

"First light tomorrow, with a caravan bound for Uzhenek."

"That makes sense. She left the dog-root until the last moment. It leaves less time for alarms to be raised."

"But why is she going north? Why isn't she returning to the Protectorate?"

"Perhaps she wants more time to master the spell. Or perhaps, even with it, she doesn't think she can tackle the whole Coven. Maybe her ambitions lie with claiming an empire outside the Protectorate."

"So what's our next step?"

Jemeryl rested her shoulder against the wall. "I don't want to challenge her in Horzt. There are defences against magic built into the walls. Wards to counteract anyone tinkering with the higher dimensions. They attempt to nullify spells or turn them back on the caster."

"You mean magic can't be used here? I could have taken Levannue prisoner on my own?"

"No, you couldn't!" Fear made Jemeryl's voice sharp. "The wards wouldn't stop a sorcerer. I could blast through them, and so could Levannue."

Tevi swallowed, taken aback by the vehemence of the response. "Oh."

Jemeryl's expression softened. "I don't want you doing anything stupid. The wards are merely an inconvenience to sorcerers, and some passive types of magic aren't affected, like my bond with Klara and my disguise, although it only goes unnoticed as long as I don't alter it. If Levannue or I were to shape-shift, even by reverting to our true forms, the wards would react. They wouldn't stop us, but they would alert the mayor. And neither of us wants to attract attention."

"I thought you were just being overcautious in keeping disguised all the time."

Jemeryl laughed and scooped up Tevi's hand, interlocking their fingers. The back of Jemeryl's hand was uppermost. The swollen red knuckles and blotched skin contrasted with Tevi's smooth fingers. "I can't wait to change back."

Tevi looked sideways at her lover and grinned mischievously. "Don't be so hasty. Has nobody ever told you wrinkles add character to your face? And I'm not sure if teeth really suit you."

"Thank you!"

Tevi's face became more thoughtful. "If the mayor controls the wards, perhaps he would help you. I know Horzt is keen to assert its independence from the Protectorate, but I'd bet he'd rather keep in the Guardian's good books if he could."

"He might help if he were able, but the mayor has no control over the wards. They're purely reactive devices built into the foundations of Horzt. They were a gift from a sorcerer long ago. The mayor has artefacts that let him monitor the wards, but as for making them attack someone or even turning them off..." Jemeryl shook her head. "He can't do a thing. Not that you think it from the way he talks. By all accounts, he thinks he can defend Horzt against anything and doesn't need the Coven's assistance. The wards keep out minor threats, such as basilisks, but nothing more."

"Surely the rest of the population know they're at risk?"

"The rest of the population know the Coven won't allow a belligerent sorcerer to carve out an empire south of the Barrodens, whether they pay taxes to Lyremouth or not, and on the whole, they prefer not."

Shouts and whoops cut through the night. Tevi leaned against the wall and grimaced at the chill of damp plaster. She would not be sorry to leave. "I'm still not sure why you don't tackle Levannue here. Won't the wards affect her as much as you?"

"It would be dangerous. Wards are Levannue's speciality. Even if she can't control them, she'll know what to expect. I'd be more vulnerable to surprise, and in sorcerer's combat, any distraction can be fatal." Jemeryl shook her head. "No. We'll let Levannue get away from Horzt and wait until she starts to think she's safe and relaxes her guard."

"What about my contract with the militia?"

"You're going to have to desert."

"The guild masters won't like me breaking a contract."

"Your chief guild master personally assigned you to this quest, which will take priority over other tasks you've taken."

"I suppose so, but—"

"If you want, I'll command you to desert. As an ordinary Protectorate citizen, you're supposed to obey Coven sorcerers."

Tevi could not stop herself tensing. There was nothing condescending in Jemeryl's tone, but it raised uncomfortable issues for her.

Jemeryl must have seen the reaction. She leaned over and kissed Tevi tenderly on the lips. "Don't worry. I wouldn't dream of ordering you around."

"But you could if you wanted."

"Believe me, I never will."

CHAPTER ELEVEN—PRISONER AND ESCORT

The drumming of rain on canvas was loud inside the cramped wagon. The lack of space forced Tevi to adopt a half crouch. She peered around the jam-packed interior in the dull light of another wet dawn. The three passengers huddled in whatever niches they could find amidst the cargo. Two watched Tevi with anxious expressions; the third was in a state far beyond mere anxiety.

Tevi observed Levannue out of the corner of her eye. The renegade sorcerer looked as if her nerves were trying to crawl out of her skin. The pulse in her neck was racing visibly, and despite the chill, sweat glossed her forehead. It was lucky that no other militiaman was witnessing Levannue's blatant display of guilt. Tevi could almost have pitied her, were it not for the attempt on Jemeryl's life.

At that thought, Tevi touched the hilt of her sword. Levannue looked so helpless. It was tempting to think that a surprise attack might work. However, Jemeryl had made her promise repeatedly not to make any rash move, and Tevi knew it was not the militia uniform that was frightening Levannue, but the imagined approach of a dozen Coven sorcerers. Tevi's lips tightened. How much easier it would be if such a force were on hand.

For the sake of appearances, Tevi made a few militia-style grunts and prodded the baggage. She treated the passengers to a last suspicious glare before leaving. Once out on the tailboard, she straightened her legs with relief and viewed the scene.

The drizzle had returned with dawn. The wagons stood forlorn in the dismal light. Tracks through the encampment were ankle-deep in mud, and the pennants over traders' booths hung limp. Tevi tried to identify some firm ground before jumping down; even so, her feet skidded. Only a colleague's hand saved her from ending up in the mud. Tevi smiled her thanks as she regained her balance.

Some yards away, the caravan master was watching them hopefully. A nod from Tevi's companion was taken as permission to leave. With loud shouts and the creak of timber, the first team of horses surged forward. Motion rippled along the road. Tevi stepped onto the low embankment and watched the caravan pass. The fifteen wagons squelched by. Mud oozed in waves from under their wheels and clung to the horses' fetlocks. Outriders flanked the caravan, cloaks wrapped tightly, hoods pulled up.

The other militiaman stood by Tevi's shoulder. He studied the leaden sky and said in a deadpan tone, "They picked a nice day for travelling."

"Tell me, does it ever stop raining in Horzt?"

"It will in a couple of months." He wiped a dangling raindrop off his nose. "Then it starts snowing."

The caravan left the outskirts of the encampment. Tevi watched it ford a river and turn north through the sodden farmlands. The road headed straight for a break in the mountains. The high pass. She and Jemeryl would not be far behind the caravan. At that moment, Jemeryl was packing their belongings and paying the innkeeper in preparation for their departure.

"It's the mountains that do it," the militiaman observed.

Tevi took her eyes from the dwindling wagons. "Pardon?"

"The rain. In autumn and winter the wind comes from the southeast, carrying lots of water from the Eastern Ocean. The clouds rise to get over the mountains, so they drop all their rain. Right here. Twenty miles farther north, and you don't see rain from one week to the next. I reckon they built Horzt in the wrong place. It's a wonder we don't grow webbed toes and fingers. And how'd we put our gloves on then?"

Any further thoughts on the climate of Horzt were curtailed by a shout behind them.

"Hey! Laniss!"

Tevi turned to acknowledge the name. Two other militiamen were headed towards her.

"What is it?"

"The captain wants to see you in the gatehouse."

"Could it wait? I'm on my way to do something."

"She wants to see you now."

The tone left no room for debate, and Tevi could guess the reason. Her absence from her post on the previous evening must already have been reported. Although expected, the summons was unwelcome. Not that Tevi foresaw any problems. She had a plausible story prepared, and she would have left Horzt before it was disproved, but she hated lying.

Tevi shrugged and started to pick her way through the morass. The two messengers fell in beside her.

"It's all right. I'm going. I know the way," Tevi protested.

"We were told to accompany you."

No other words were spoken until they reached the doorway set just inside the massive arch of the gatehouse. Tevi was directed to the stairway leading to the office over the gate. The two militiamen took up positions at either side of the entrance.

Something about their actions sent a ripple of disquiet through Tevi. It seemed an excessive precaution for a minor misdemeanour. There was, however, no time to consider it further. Tevi tugged off her helmet and combed her fingers through her hair before knocking. A loud voice answered immediately.

Tevi marched in and came to a bewildered halt in the middle of the room. The militia captain was standing by a window. A scowl made her weather-beaten face look even more threatening than usual. Her eyes raked over Tevi. The captain's expression was worrying enough, but in addition, seated at the desk, was Mayor Gunather. His flabby bulk was held in a pose that was probably intended to look commanding but was more reminiscent of indigestion.

This summons was not about a missed duty. Without thinking, Tevi took a step backwards. She heard the door behind her slam before her foot had left the ground. Tevi spun around. Three unfamiliar mercenaries lined the rear wall.

The tallest was a mountain of a man with a ruddy complexion and hands that looked as if they were hacked from granite. The man beside him had the solid build of a professional warrior but seemed delicate by comparison. He was the oldest by a decade or more. A scar ran across one weathered cheek and disappeared beneath greying temples. The third was a woman with cropped blond hair and sharp hazel eyes. She stood balanced lightly with the deadly grace of an experienced scout. All their hands bore the double swords of vouchsafed guild mercenaries. Tevi was sure that none had been in Horzt before that day.

"Sit down, Tevi." Mayor Gunather reclaimed her attention. He gestured to a round stool. Only after she had complied did Tevi register the name he had used. She met the mayor's self-satisfied smile. "So Tevi is your real name."

"No, it's just a nickname. But I'll admit I've been known by it before," she said defiantly—and truthfully.

"Then you'll be the person we want. We're not bothered by what your parents called you," the oldest mercenary said cheerfully.

Mayor Gunather looked irritated at the interruption. He cleared his throat. "These comrades of yours have just arrived from the Protectorate. It seems a young mercenary matching your description has fallen in with bad company and has broken numerous guild rules. They have the guild master's warrant for your arrest. Do you have anything to say for yourself?"

Tevi lurched to her feet but froze at the sound of a sword half-drawn. There were footsteps, and a hand fell heavily on her shoulder. Tevi let herself be pushed back onto the stool despite her urge to resist. In both Ekranos and Horzt, she had concealed her true strength to avoid attracting attention. Her chances of escape would be better if these strangers remained unaware of her capabilities.

Tevi shrugged off the restraining hand. "I've done nothing wrong."

"Then you've got nothing to worry about. The guild master just wants to ask you a few questions," the eldest mercenary said calmly. By his actions and manner, he was the leader. Tevi felt him lift her leather sword belt from her shoulder over her head. The weapon was pulled free and tossed to one of the others.

"Honestly, there's been some mistake. I'm not going to put up a fight." Tevi hesitated, watching the mayor. "But I wasn't aware that the guild master's warrant was valid in Horzt."

"It isn't," the mayor snapped. His ego was an easy target. He rose and leaned over the desk, gesticulating with the warrant in his hand. "It goes without saying that this piece of paper has no authority here. Horzt is outside the jurisdiction of the guild master and the Coven."

The woman mercenary spoke. "We're not asking you to obey an order, merely to demonstrate goodwill to the guild. So many of our members work in Horzt; a friendly relationship is in everyone's best interest." Despite her conciliatory tone, there was no mistaking the threat in her words. Without the guild, the town militia would collapse.

The captain by the window shuffled her feet. Her eyes flitted anxiously around the room and ended up fixed on the man standing behind the desk. Mayor Gunather continued to wave the paper, but it was empty posturing, as everyone knew.

"I'm not going to interfere between the guild and its members," the mayor said at last, glowering at Tevi. "Permission is granted for these three to take you prisoner. You are relieved of your contract. Any outstanding salary is forfeit. " He sat down with the expression of a sulking child.

The captain claimed Tevi's helmet, cloak, and cotton surcoat. Tevi looked at her remaining clothing thoughtfully. The material was warm, and the leather jerkin was sturdy, but they were not sufficient for a long journey.

"Could someone collect my belongings from my lodgings?"

"And alert your friends? I think not," the mercenary leader said.

"I can't go all the way to Lyremouth like this," Tevi pointed out reasonably, although getting news to Jemeryl had indeed been her main intention.

"I'll see what I can find," the captain volunteered quickly, undoubtedly wanting the guild master's emissaries away from Horzt before the mayor did something silly.

While waiting for the captain's return, the mercenary leader ordered, "Hold out your hands."

Tevi froze in dread. Expelled mercenaries lost their hands, but surely only after due legal process. However, the man merely pulled a cord from his pouch. Tevi meekly allowed her wrists to be bound.

"We want to leave before any of your friends learn what's happened. We don't want you slipping out a message, do we?" he said in conversational tones as he tied the knots.

"You don't want to take these accomplices as well?" the mayor asked.

"I doubt we'd be able to. Apparently, they include a high-level magic user. We've been given a charm, so they can't trace us magically once we get a couple of miles away. But you'd better be on the lookout. They might cause trouble here."

"I doubt there'll be anything I can't cope with. Even a sorcerer might think twice about tackling Horzt." Mayor Gunather spoke breezily.

The man tying Tevi's hands had his back to the mayor. Judging by the look he shot at his colleagues, he thought the mayor was absurdly overconfident, although nothing was said.

The door opened for the captain's return, bringing a waterproof riding cloak and a couple of worn blankets. Tevi was hauled to her feet.

The mercenary leader shook out one blanket thoughtfully. "At least you won't freeze." He tossed it over Tevi's head, hiding her from view. "Can't do any harm, and it may slow down any gossip in town. Plus there's less temptation for you to do anything rash. We'll take it off once we're well away."

Tevi was propelled down the stairs and hoisted onto a waiting horse. She clung to the saddle horn with her bound hands. The congested mud tracks of the trader's encampment slowed the horses to a walk, but soon, the sounds faded and the pace increased. The blanket prevented Tevi from seeing where they were going, and she could learn nothing very useful from the sounds. The only thing she could do was hang onto her horse and hope.

❖

After an hour of hard riding, the group stopped, and the blanket was removed from Tevi. They had reached the western flank of the valley, where farmland gave way to rough pasture and pine forest. With each gust of wind, heavy droplets fell from the rain soaked trees towering over them. The road was a mosaic of puddles laced with ripples. Tevi almost asked for the blanket to be replaced. It had kept her dry.

The oldest of the mercenaries reined his horse around and faced her with an ironic smile. "I guess it would be polite to introduce ourselves. My name's Russ. I was born in Horzt, so I know the local roads. I will be our guide on this little expedition."

Tevi had surmised as much from his guttural, singsong accent.

Russ pointed to the woman mercenary. "Sharl is a tracker, in case we're careless enough to lose you. Flory is simply solid muscle, including the contents of his head. He'll be keeping an especially close eye on you, so with any luck, Sharl's talents won't be needed."

Flory was unperturbed by the jibe. "Mercenaries need a bit of muscle. Maybe not so much scouts, but warriors..." He treated Tevi to a critical look.

"Don't be so confident. Our instructions warned she's a lot stronger than she looks," Sharl said.

"It also said we'll be well rewarded. I wouldn't take it too much on trust," Flory threw back at her.

"The sooner we get back, the sooner we'll all find out." Russ pointed to a broken cliff above the trees. "The path we want leads off in about a mile, up the side of that escarpment."

Flory nodded and set off at a trot, pulling Tevi's horse by a tether. The others fell in behind. Around the next bend, they passed a farmer herding three placid brown cows. Her colourful string of curses did not falter as the riders passed. If she noticed Tevi's bound hands, she wisely gave no sign, but a young child tagging along stopped and stared until another turn took them from view.

The farmer's swearing had just faded when a shout from Russ halted the group. He pointed at a ragged break in the wall of pine branches lining the road. The gap was unrecognisable as the start of a path.

"Not the scenic route!" Flory groaned. "I don't want to spend the next month going in circles around a peat bog."

"And we don't want to be followed. It'll be fine. We don't all have as little sense of direction as you," Russ replied

Sharl smiled as she slipped from her saddle. "Go ahead with the prisoner. I'll disguise our tracks."

The trail was so narrow that they were forced to go single file. Russ led the way with Sharl's horse in tow. After a long look at the impenetrable forest on either side, Flory slipped the tether from Tevi's horse and slapped its rump. The horse trotted along the path a couple dozen yards to where Russ had stopped. Despite her bound hands, Tevi managed to scoop up her reins, although it put her no more in control. She felt utterly trapped. The weak daylight was reduced to heavy dusk under the trees. She twisted to peer back, but Flory's bulk blocked the view of the road they had left.

"It all went to plan. No hitches, which is better than I expected from the instructions," Russ addressed Flory.

"You can say that when we deliver the prisoner."

"You're such a pessimist. If we'd had longer in Horzt, I'm sure I could have put a smile on your face."

"I saw enough of the town. I'm quite content to be away in one piece."

"You don't know what you've missed."

"I'll try and live with the loss."

Russ laughed. "I know this bar on the south side where—"

Tevi could stand the trivialities no more. "Tell me, now that there are no witnesses, are you going to kill me here, or will you hand me over to Levannue?"

Confused silence greeted her words. Eventually, Russ answered. "Neither. Like we said, we're taking you to Lyremouth. I don't know who Levannue is."

Tevi stared at him. The eyes that met hers seemed free from deceit or coercion, but how could any ungifted human tell for certain?

Sharl pushed past Tevi's legs and swung onto her waiting horse. "It's all right, boys. I've finished the arty bits."

Tevi kept her eyes on Russ. "Whether you know it or not, Levannue is the one behind all this."

"Who's Levannue?" Sharl asked innocently.

Russ shrugged his ignorance and urged his horse forward. Behind her, Flory also moved, herding her horse through the tunnel of trees.

Tevi looked about, searching desperately for some way of escaping. On either side, the forest floor was thick with pine needles, but scant undergrowth grew. Low branches, knotted with fir cones, swept close to the ground. To leave the trail, she would have to crawl while being an easy target for arrows.

Tevi chewed her lip. She would have to bide her time, but how long did she have? How long before Levannue showed up?

❖

At midday, they rested in a fern-filled clearing atop a ridge. The rain had ceased temporarily, but the wind was damp. A ragged belt of blue broke between the clouds. Tevi stood, kicking her feet to aid the circulation to tired muscles. She rotated slowly as she did so, absorbing the view.

Folds of tree-clad mountains rolled away south. To the north, clouds swallowed the higher peaks. To the east, the air was streaked yellow with falling rain. Her captors also stretched cramped limbs. They acted in a relaxed fashion, yet Tevi was aware of their continual attention. Someone was always between her and the grazing horses.

Russ opened a bag and passed around hard cheese, dried fruit, and drier bread.

"The delights of the open road," Flory muttered. "Anything to wash this down with?"

"Water."

"Anything better?"

"Not unless you pop back to Horzt and get it."

"Do you think if we'd asked nicely, the mayor would have given us a few bottles from his cellar?" Sharl joined in.

"Empty ones, maybe."

The exchange was light-hearted. The same natural banter had been going on all morning. Tevi was increasingly convinced that her captors were not ensorcelled. They certainly did not match Jemeryl's description of listless puppets, and neither did they seem corrupt. Tevi was confused. It did not make sense.

"Who told you to come to Horzt to take me prisoner?" she asked in a lull.

"Our captain," Russ answered.

"The instruction came direct from Lyremouth?"

"Yes, via carrier pigeon. We're from the garrison in Gossenfeld. The order arrived two mornings ago. The captain picked us for the job."

"Oh, of course," Tevi said with sudden enlightenment.

Three confused faces turned towards her.

"You've got to believe me," Tevi said earnestly. "The order wasn't from Lyremouth. It must be a forgery by Levannue."

"What makes you think that?" Russ was clearly unmoved.

"Because I know I haven't done anything wrong."

"And this Levannue's got a grudge against you?" Flory was also sceptical.

"Maybe not me in particular. But she's a renegade, and I'm with a group trying to capture her."

"It's a pretty neat trick to kidnap one of the guild pigeons and forge the guild master's seal. This Levannue is obviously very resourceful."

"She could do it easily. She's a Coven sorcerer."

There was a long moment of startled silence.

"Oh, girl, what have you got yourself messed up in?" Sharl asked softly.

"If you credit the story," Flory said.

"It may be true," Russ said slowly. "I've heard rumours. The whole Coven is in uproar, and now I think of it, the name Levannue does sound familiar." He fixed Tevi with a level gaze. "Take my advice; you're well out of it. Let the sorcerers sort out their own problems. It doesn't concern the likes of you and me."

"But you've got to let me go. Levannue is probably lying in wait ahead. If she captures me, she'll read my mind, and..." The three faces watching Tevi were implacable. She sighed. "I know it sounds like I'm making things up so you'll let me go."

"It certainly does that," Russ agreed.

"What can I say to make you believe me?"

"It's irrelevant what you make me believe. I've been given orders, and I'm obeying them. It can all be sorted out in Lyremouth," Russ said firmly, clearly terminating the conversation as far as he was concerned.

A canteen of water was passed around. Tevi took a long swig, restraining any further pleas. It would be wisest to avoid conflict with her captors. She had to escape and knew she would get only one chance. In the meantime, she had no choice but to let herself be taken farther away from Horzt—and Jemeryl.

The route Russ picked kept to little-used forest trails and was clearly chosen for secrecy rather than speed. They saw no trace of human habitation until two days later, when their path descended the wooded side of a broad valley. At the bottom was a fast-flowing river with farmlands on the other side. The hills rising beyond were far lower than those they had been through. They were leaving the Barrodens. Somewhere downstream, the smoke from several chimneys drifted in the wind.

Russ grinned at Flory. "I told you we wouldn't get lost, and it should have thrown any pursuit. Now we can quicken the pace. Gossenfeld is sixty miles southeast of here, but we'll head straight for Rizen and take the Langhope Pass. We'll be at Lyremouth inside twenty days."

Flory merely grunted and looked at the raging waters, swollen by the recent rain. Fierce eddies sucked at the banks. Cascades were stained brown by mud and interspersed with strips of glassy black water. Leaves and other debris danced in frenzied swirls to the thunder of the river.

"How do we get across?"

"Can't you swim?" Tevi asked with mock innocence.

Flory's momentary look of horror brought amused chuckles from Russ and Sharl. An easy rapport had grown between Tevi and the others, despite their respective status as prisoner and escort. Tevi could admit to a genuine respect for her captors. They had acted with capable professionalism, allowing her not the slightest chance to escape, but never treating her vindictively or unfairly.

"Anyone who fancies the swim is welcome to try. However, there is a better way," Russ said as he steered his horse onto the mud-clogged path along the riverbank.

"If I volunteer to try swimming, would you untie my hands first?" Tevi asked, joking.

"No." Russ matched her tone and turned to look at her. "Hopefully someday, we'll travel together in happier circumstances. You can demonstrate your swimming ability then."

"You mean you think I might be innocent?"

"I think you've got involved in things out of your depth. But no, I don't think you're a wrong 'un. And I'll say as much for you at Lyremouth."

"Thanks, but there should be no need. I really have done nothing wrong."

Sharl leaned over and squeezed Tevi's shoulder. "I hope so, for your sake. You've got nice hands."

Even Flory managed a few words of comfort. "Look on the bright side. If you are innocent, you'll get to spend a free winter in Lyremouth, which will be more fun than freezing your arse off in the snow at Horzt."

Tevi sighed. Despite her liking for the three, she had no intention of going to Lyremouth, but it seemed that she might get no option. At least her fears of being ambushed by Levannue had diminished.

The river had burst its banks in places. The horses waded knee-deep between half-submerged bushes. It was slow progress, hampered by the fading light. Sunset was more than an hour away, but thick grey covered the sky. It grew steadily darker as storm clouds rolled over the mountains. Branches shook in the rising wind. Fumbling with bound hands, Tevi tugged her cloak around her shoulders.

Eventually, a hamlet came into view on the far bank, made up of a dozen squat cottages with adjacent barns and pigsties. Tevi peered down the river, hoping for a sight of a bridge. Just before they drew level with the first building, the path crossed a broader road that rolled down the hillside and disappeared into the water.

Russ stopped his horse. “There’s a ford here in summer.”

“There isn’t now.” Flory stated the obvious.

“So it’s just as well that there’s a ferry.” Russ grinned and led on.

A hundred yards below the hamlet, the river looped away from the side of the valley. The trees gave way to an uneven expanse of hummocks and tufts of waving long grass. The river broadened out, which took the edge off the torrent. A thick rope was strung across the river at the widest point. Beached half out of the water on the far side was a raft, attached to the line by running loops and a pulley arrangement.

“Ahoy!” Russ shouted, hands cupped around his mouth.

Before his voice had died away, a door to the nearest cottage swung open, and a thickset man strode down to the water’s edge.

“I’ll bet he was watching us ride along, but they do like to be called.”

“And paid,” Sharl added softly.

The ferryman shoved his craft into the water and leapt on.

Flory was not comforted. “You seriously expect me to cross the river on that?”

“You could swim, like Tevi suggested,” Russ said.

“Is it safe?”

“People don’t drown here often.”

“I know. They only do it once.”

The ferry was now halfway across. The force of the water tugged the raft downstream, making the strained rope creak alarmingly. However, the ferryman was unconcerned, judging by his tuneless whistling. On either bank, the line was tied around a stake the size of

Flory's forearm, driven obliquely into the ground. The one on their side was several yards back from the water's edge and presumably beyond the risk of flooding.

"It will be twelve copper pennies for you and your horses," were the ferryman's first words, even before he had stepped off his raft.

Sharl muffled a laugh.

Russ leaned forward. Tevi noted that he made sure his mercenary tattoos were showing. "And how much will it be after we've stood here in the cold for half an hour, haggling?"

The ferryman's eyes flitted between them. "Eight."

"I'd have guessed at six."

"All right," the ferryman said after a slight hesitation. "You'll have to go in two lots. I can only take two horses and two people."

"I don't suppose you'd stretch to two horses and three passengers?"

"Nah." The ferryman spat. "To tell the truth, it's overloaded with two."

"In that case, you can have your eight pennies, and we'll have three trips. I'll take the first two horses. Flory can follow with Tevi, and Sharl can bring the other two horses."

The ferryman's forehead knotted in confusion.

Tevi held up her bound hands for him to see. "What he means is they don't want to leave me on either bank with only one of them to guard me. Think it through."

Russ met Tevi's eyes with a nod of agreement for her reasoning. The ferryman looked startled but no more enlightened, although he was not about to argue at the prospect of extra coins.

The horses needed blindfolds before they could be persuaded onto the raft. Russ hugged their necks while the ferry was hauled back across the river. While waiting her turn, Tevi stood at the river's edge and watched the water swirl past. The river had not burst its bank but was clearly deeper than normal. The tops of submerged shapes loomed ghostlike below the surface.

Sharl joined Tevi and put an arm around her shoulder. "Of course, we all know that this is your best chance to escape. Do yourself a favour and don't try it."

Tevi glanced behind her. As ever, Flory was between her and the horses, watching. His great arms were folded across his chest. Tevi turned back to the river, adding up the chances. Both guards were alert. Even Sharl's friendly contact was intended partly to hold her secure. However, she still had one element of surprise. Despite their instructions, Tevi was sure that her captors were unaware of her true strength. It might prove decisive. If not, Tevi guessed, she would spend the rest of the journey trussed and bound over the saddle of her horse. Either way, she had to try.

The ferry with Russ had almost reached the far side. Sharl's attention was on watching it negotiate the last few yards. Tevi took a deep breath. Now was the time.

Tevi ducked and turned. Her shoulder slammed into Sharl's back. For a moment, the scout fought for balance. A second nudge completed the job. Sharl toppled into the water, and Tevi spun to face Flory.

The tall mercenary's expression changed from complacency to outrage. "Why, you little—"

Flory leapt forward, fists raised, not waiting to draw his sword. Tevi ducked under his arms and grasped his leather jerkin. His momentum kept him ploughing forward. Tevi used it against him, hoisting him into the air and hurling him out over the riverbank. Tumbling backwards, one leg trailing, Flory hit the river. A hole seemed to open under him as walls of water shot up; then the surging river rolled back over his head.

Shouts from the far bank announced that Russ had seen what was happening. With no time to waste, Tevi dived to the stake securing the ferry line. Her fingers locked around the rough wood. Knees bent, feet braced, she threw every ounce of her strength into the effort. For a heart-stopping moment, the stake remained firm, but then a faint shift trembled up Tevi's arms, followed by a larger movement. To the wet sucking of mud, the stake pulled free.

More shouts erupted across the river. Russ had disembarked and was pulling his bow from a saddle pack. On the near bank, Sharl was hauling herself out. Flory had surfaced mid-river. Somehow, the huge warrior had gained his feet but was unable to move against the current. A bow wave streamed around his thighs. One cautious attempt to move almost cost his balance, and he slid a few more feet downstream.

Sharl lay sprawled half out of the water. Tevi shoved the scout back, then knelt and held out the stake. "Why don't you take this and rescue Flory? Russ can pull you both to the far side."

Sharl gave her a venomous look. "Don't be a fool. The guild will get you."

"I swear I've done nothing wrong. You're the victims of a trick. I'm quest-bound at the moment, but I promise when it's over, I'll come to Lyremouth and answer for everything."

Tevi pressed the rope at the half-submerged woman. At that moment, a fresh vortex hit Flory, causing him to shout in alarm as stones slipped under his feet. Fear was starting to show on his face. Sharl looked over her shoulder and then, without a word, took the stake. She wrapped the rope once around her body and kicked off, letting current swing her in an arc across the river.

The horses were standing a few yards away. Tevi leapt onto the nearest and caught the dangling reins of the other. She headed for the trees and protection from arrows. Only once she had got there did she look back. There was no need to worry. Russ had abandoned his bow, and with the help of the ferryman, he was pulling his comrades to safety.

Tevi found a sharp knife in the saddlebags. Soon, her hands were free. Meanwhile, Sharl and Flory had been dragged ashore, aided by several other villagers who had been attracted by the commotion.

Tevi looked at the sky. Night was approaching rapidly. The storm clouds were hanging low and heavy. She doubted the others would be able to cross the river again before dark, but it was certainly advisable to get far away as quickly as possible.

Sharl, Flory, and Russ stood in a grim line on the far bank. Tevi raised her hand in a friendly salute that was not returned, then she urged her horse around and rode back down the trail.

Chapter Twelve—Victims of Magic

Ponderous clouds, black and purple, loomed over the farmlands, hastening the onset of night. Under the trees, it was even darker. A rising wind shook the branches in a hissing imitation of the river's roar. The weak light glinted off pools of black water that flooded dips in the riverside path.

At the point where the track reached the trees, a smaller trail branched up the side of the valley. Bare earth showed pale in the gloom, littered with pinecones and mud-smeared rocks. The path rose steeply before levelling out and disappearing between the trees. A line of hoofprints indicated that the track was passable on horseback. There was no way of knowing where it led, yet it had to be safer than the flooded riverbank.

Tevi looked back. Russ and the others were watching, but her route could not be kept secret. Sharl would have no problems tracking her across soft ground. The most important thing was to put as much distance as possible between herself and the pursuit. To that end, the track up the hillside was probably as good as any other.

After a few hundred yards, the path rounded a rock face where water dripped from clinging beards of moss. The track bent north, still climbing steadily, but the trees were closing in. Tree roots jutted clawlike from the eroded red soil. The sound of the river faded away below to be replaced by an oppressive silence in which the horses' hooves fell with dead thuds. Tevi had to duck repeatedly to avoid low branches and was eventually forced to lead the horses on foot.

Higher up, the wind blew fiercely but provided little relief from the heavy, charged air. Thunder boomed in the distance. Eventually, the track rolled over the brow of the hill and began a steep descent while degenerating into little more than a mud-filled gully. The horses' nostrils flared as they slipped and skidded. Tevi carried on doggedly, although she was increasingly aware that she might have to retrace her steps.

There was little now to distinguish the path. The light was so poor that Tevi had to guess the way. Before she could stop, the horses slithered down a vertical bank, and then the ground bottomed out in a grassy hollow. Tevi halted at the edge of the clearing to calm the animals. She prayed there was a way forward. Getting back up that last sheer section would be a challenge.

The first drops of rain splattered on Tevi's face. Within seconds, the downpour rose into a crescendo of drumming. Tall grass in the clearing was flattened by the force of the rain.

Tevi was looking up, cursing the storm, when the sky was torn apart by white-hot lightning, etching the treetops in silhouette. Thunder broke as a pounding onslaught of sound. The panicked horses wrenched Tevi off her feet, yet she managed to hang on and regain control. She dragged them under the shelter of a pine and tied their reins to the trunk. Progress would be impossible until after the storm had blown over. Maybe not even then.

Tevi returned to the open ground in defiance of the storm. The ground squelched underfoot, even more than could be attributed to the pelting rain. The clearing was not manmade, but a spring. On the downhill side, straggling bushes knotted in an unbroken hedge. Uphill, the steeply rising ground formed the sheer sides of an eroded basin. There was no exit. It would seem that she had reached the end of the trail.

Tevi sank back against a rough tree trunk. Continuing to wander aimlessly in this nightmare of mud and rain was completely insane, risking injury to herself and the horses. By morning, they would be exhausted and still no farther from the pursuit. There was also not the slightest risk of anyone's crossing the river that night. Making camp was easily the wisest course. Maybe daylight would reveal a missed turning in the trail.

The centre of the storm was moving away, although thunder still pounded over the mountains. It alarmed the horses and complicated the task of removing their saddles. Tevi discovered her confiscated sword wrapped in one pack. The emotion was totally irrational, but she felt less helpless with it in her hands.

She shared a couple of apples between the horses. It was insufficient for their needs, but the animals seemed to find it reassuring. Her own meal came from food rations she found in the saddle packs. A waterproof sheet made a tent.

By the time she had finished, the thunder was just the occasional rumble in the distance. However, rain still fell in sheets, lashing the forest. The horses had calmed. They nuzzled against her hands with only the softest whicker of complaint. There was little chance of their straying—not least because there was no obvious way out of the hollow. Tevi turned them loose to graze or find shelter as they chose and crawled into the damp blankets of her bed.

❖

Tevi awoke to the first uncertain trill of birdsong. The storm had blown itself out. Predawn light picked out details of the sodden vegetation. Across the hollow were the dark forms of two horses. Stars still twinkled brightly, but to the east, a pale tint was gaining strength. The air was bitterly cold. Tevi pulled herself from her tent and stood, stamping her frozen feet and slapping her arms. The horses ambled to her side.

Hazy blue-grey light filtered through the forest. The trees stood like ranks of ghostly soldiers, wreathed in tendrils of mist. Some twenty yards downhill, a brighter patch in the forest indicated another clearing. Tevi set off to investigate.

The wet grass drenched her feet and legs. Heavy splats of water dripped fitfully from branches. Somewhere, a bird warbled out its territorial claim. The song and the snap of twigs were the only sounds as Tevi broke through the thicket barrier and onto a well-trodden forest road.

The route was deserted. To the west, Tevi guessed it led to the spot that Russ had claimed was a ford in summer. In the other direction, it headed into the unknown, although surely it would eventually link with the Gossenfeld-to-Horzt road.

Tevi chewed her lip as she thought. This was clearly a well-used highway. Her experience of the previous night had proved that she could not match Russ's ability to navigate the wilderness. Her best hope lay in speed and taking advantage of the head start. Maybe, in the traffic, Sharl might lose her tracks.

A short way off, a lively stream washed across the road. Tevi walked to the spot and peered into the forest. The remnants of a path ran beside the brook. The summer's growth of bramble had obscured the track but proved no match for Tevi's sword. In a matter of minutes, she had hacked her way through to the marshy spring head.

The daylight was strengthening, putting green back into the foliage. The horses were swiping huge mouthfuls of the wet grass. They watched with disinterested eyes as Tevi packed. She saddled both horses. The chance to swap mounts might give her the decisive edge.

Tevi led the horses along the newly hacked path. The first bands of pink were touching the eastern sky as she swung into the saddle. The horses raised their heads to sniff the sweet dawn air. They needed no urging. Her mount sprung forward. The other, tethered to the saddle, matched it stride for stride. The pounding of their hooves resounded over the forest as they galloped towards the rising sun.

On the afternoon of the following day Tevi re-entered the Horzt valley. So far, everything had gone without incident. Nobody had paid attention to the young guild mercenary racing by like a courier on official business. The good roads had cut a day off her return journey—a healthy pace, even allowing that Russ's route had been chosen for stealth rather than speed.

Now things needed a bit more thought. Entering Horzt could be dangerous, but Tevi did not know how else to find Jemeryl. She stared at the distant walls. The mayor had been unenthusiastic at handing her over in the first place. Would he see it as purely the guild's problem that she had escaped? Or was he too dependent on the guild to risk a show of defiance?

Not that it matters, Tevi told herself. *If the other mercenaries believe I'm a renegade, they'll take me prisoner without needing his say-so.* She would have to slip in at dusk under cover of the general licentiousness. No one bothered with drunks as long as they did not cause trouble. It was not a great plan, but nothing better came to mind.

Tevi pressed the horses on in a steady canter until she came across a fork in the road. An impulse prompted her to take the smaller branch, which hugged the western flank of the valley. However, she had not gone far before she was questioning her hasty decision. The rutted cart track would have fewer witnesses than the main road, but those she did meet might wonder what a guild courier was doing out in the farming fringes. Yet now that she had made her choice, there seemed little point going back. Tevi shook her head, trying to clear her thoughts.

An hour later, the road began to look familiar. This puzzled Tevi until she recognised the spot where the foul-mouthed farmer had been driving the cows. She was now heading in the opposite direction and must already have passed the start of Russ's forest trail. Soon, she reached the place where the blanket had been removed from her head. A narrow track split off from the road she was on and headed through the fields straight for Horzt—the route by which the mercenaries had escorted her from town.

Although she was unclear about her own reasons, Tevi kept to the edge of the valley. She stopped only when a farm appeared, sprawled along the side of the road. Chickens and children ran between the buildings. In the fields were horses and farm workers. Tevi was not sure why she wanted to avoid the inhabitants, but she spotted a path running up the hillside. Without thinking, she left the level road.

For the first few hundred yards, the trail climbed across open sheep pasture. Thereafter, it entered dense woodland with no obvious destination, still rising steeply, although unlike the one in her previous experience, this path showed no sign of fading away.

For once, the clouds had dispersed, and autumn sunshine bathed the woods in a mellow afternoon light. The heavy warm silence was broken only by the clump of hooves, distant birdsong and the drone of insects. The peace soaked into Tevi, filling her with untroubled drowsiness. She was barely aware of it, and certainly not concerned, when her head began to nod.

❖

Tevi awoke to find herself high in the mountains. Rocky outcrops broke from the upland, their bases littered with cracked boulders and rubble. The trees were sparse and stunted amid the gorse and heather. From the sun's position, Tevi knew it was nearly evening. Hours had passed in her daze.

Tevi pinched the bridge of her nose hard, partly to drive away the cobwebs, partly to give expression to her anger with herself. Succumbing to sleep went against all her training. Not even the last two restless nights offered an excuse. Now it would take hard riding to reach Horzt by dusk, if she could work out where to go.

Neither signpost nor landmark were in sight. The path behind disappeared over a ridge, while ahead, it dipped down into a valley. Her first thought was to turn the horses around, but the idea left her uneasy. She had no idea how she had got where she was and no wish to spend the night criss-crossing the mountains. Perhaps the valley would contain a road or a hamlet where she could ask directions.

A prod set the horses off at a brisk pace, but ripples of lethargy begun to wash over Tevi again. The hillside was drifting into nothingness as she left a wooded hollow and the valley floor came into view. With an almost audible snap, the spell broke. Someone had made camp beside a leaping brook. Tevi dropped from the saddle and pulled the horses back under the cover of the trees.

From behind a dense bush, she surveyed the scene. A simple tent was strung between two trees. A horse was grazing upstream, and a trickle of smoke wafted into the air from a campfire. There was no other sign of life and nothing to explain Tevi's certainty that this camp was the centre of the summons that had ensnared her. She eased back, about to slip away, when a harsh voice spoke.

"You could just walk down to the camp."

Tevi spun about, half-drawing her sword even as she recognised the voice.

A magpie was perched on her horse's rump, head cocked to one side. Klara continued speaking. "You'll have to excuse Jem for not rushing out to greet you, but she's very tired. She's been calling you for days."

Ripples of flame chased over the logs. Tevi snapped another branch in half and fed it to the campfire. A light breeze fanned veins of red through the ash and wafted a rich aroma of stew that made Tevi's stomach growl. She gave the pot another unnecessary stir before settling back.

The dark mass of the hillside rose opposite. Its top was fringed with trees. Clouds were rolling in from the south, swallowing the stars, but for now, the moon floated clear, pure, and cold against the black sky.

The new wood crackled as sap exploded under the bark. Other sounds came from farther off—a snort from a horse and the undulating gurgle of the brook. Tevi felt at peace, especially since Klara was patrolling the treetops.

Tevi shifted so she could see inside the tent. Firelight rippled over Jemeryl's sleeping form in dull reds and warm shadows. The sight held Tevi a long time, watching.

It was obvious that the sorcerer had scarcely slept in all the time they had been apart. On Tevi's arrival, Jemeryl had staggered from the tent, clung to Tevi like she never meant to let go, sobbed, "I'm so pleased you're here," and fallen asleep on her feet. The food was ready, but despite her own hunger, Tevi was happy to wait until her lover woke.

Eventually, Jemeryl stirred. She rolled over, and her eyelids flickered. "What time is it?"

"Late."

"Is dinner cooked?"

"It was ready ages ago."

"Was?" Jemeryl levered herself up. "Have you scoffed the lot?"

"I was very tempted."

Jemeryl shuffled out of the tent, dragging a blanket behind her more by chance than design. She burrowed into Tevi's arms in an emotional, although clumsy, embrace. Her lips steered towards Tevi's as she mumbled, "I didn't say hello properly before."

The kiss that followed was also slightly uncoordinated, but Tevi was not complaining. Her stomach, however, was not so patient.

Tevi broke off at the rumbling. "I'd better serve up the food."

Jemeryl gave Tevi one last hug and then sat by the fire looking dazed. Her eyes stared blankly, and her hair was even more dishevelled than normal. Tevi smiled as she handed over a bowl of the stew. For a while, they ate in silence, sitting side by side with the blanket draped around their shoulders. The night air was chill, and Jemeryl shivered as she put aside her empty bowl.

"Are you all right?" Tevi asked, concerned.

"I will be. I simply got overtired." Jemeryl rested her head on Tevi's shoulder. "I wouldn't turn down another bowlful. Why don't you tell me what's been happening to you? My mind's working, it's just my body hasn't woken up yet."

By the time Tevi finished the story of her capture and escape, the clouds had completed their advance and cloaked the moon. The firelight cavorted demonically now that it had no rival. The stew was finished, and the empty pot stood to one side. Tevi concluded with a brief description of her entranced arrival at the camp.

"I've wondered what it's like to be caught in a spell." Tevi's face held a bemused frown. "It was odd. I knew something was up, but I couldn't be bothered to work out what."

"I'm sorry. I really am. I didn't want to ensnare you, but I didn't know how else to get you here. I was terrified you'd walk into the hornets' nest I've stirred up in Horzt."

"Hornets? What did you do?"

"At first, I sat and waited. By midmorning, I was convinced you'd been caught by Levannue. So I dropped the old crone disguise and went looking. It set off the mayor's wards, and some people started acting very silly. No one would tell me anything. In the end, I'm afraid I lost my temper." Jemeryl stared into the dancing flames. "In the Protectorate, you lose sight of what you can do if you want. Of how vulnerable the ungifted are."

"Did you hurt anyone?"

"Not seriously. The only real casualty was the mayor's dignity. I suspended him upside-down over a cesspit and threatened to drop him. He blabbed everything, but by then, you were too far away." Jemeryl shrugged. "So I dropped him anyway. Then I thought it would be tactful to leave town. I didn't want a confrontation with the militia."

"I doubt they'd have fought you. Most are guild mercenaries, so they're sworn to obey Coven sorcerers, and I'll bet even the non-guild militia appreciated what you did to the mayor."

"It's true that nobody risked their neck coming to his aid, but I couldn't count on it lasting. With rumours of a renegade sorcerer going about, it only needed someone to take the initiative and things could have got nasty."

"Could they have hurt you?"

"Unlikely, but they might have forced me to hurt them. Oaths go both ways. I'm sworn to defend Protectorate citizens. So I came up here. I guessed they wouldn't chase me once I left town, but I was worried about you."

"It could have been unpleasant if the mayor got his hands on me. I suspect he's the sort of person who holds grudges."

"Which is why I haven't dared sleep. I didn't know when you'd escape or whether you'd arrive by day or night."

"You knew I'd escape?"

"I had faith in you." Jemeryl caught one of Tevi's hands. "And no matter how faint the chance you'd return, I couldn't take the risk of your getting caught."

"So Levannue's plan worked. She managed to pin us down and get away."

Jemeryl hesitated before saying, "I don't think Levannue had anything to do with your arrest."

"She must have. Who else is going to send a false warrant?"

"I'm not sure it was false. Your captors had been warned of your strength. Levannue wouldn't know about that." Jemeryl pursed her lips. "After we left Ekranos, there weren't enough sorcerers to send a message by magic, so Neame needed to find a ship bound for Lyremouth, which would take a month to arrive. A few more days for the Guardian to make a decision and the pigeon to get to Gossenfeld. If you add the dates up, it ties in with when the warrant arrived."

"But why?"

"Levannue fell for the lure of this spell. With me absconding from Ekranos, people might be worried that I've found out what the spell does and have given in to temptation as well. I might be about to swipe the chalice from Levannue and set off on my own. Perhaps the Guardian wanted to find out what was going on and whether it's one or two traitors they have to deal with."

"But taking me prisoner stopped you from catching Levannue. Either way, they'd have been better leaving you alone. If you were loyal, it was insane to distract you. And even if you weren't, after you and Levannue had fought for the chalice, they'd be back to just one traitor again."

"I don't think they'd have done the sums that way, and for the very same reason that Levannue wouldn't have used you as a decoy." Jemeryl raised her hand and guided Tevi's face so that their eyes met. "It would never have occurred to either the Guardian or Levannue that I'd stop doing something important for the sake of one ungifted mercenary. I'm afraid, my love, they wouldn't believe that I'd think so much of you."

"The Guardian knew we were lovers."

"And I'll bet she's certain I've tired of you by now. Brief affairs are rare enough between sorcerers and the ungifted; long relationships are unheard of. The Guardian would reckon that if I'd turned traitor, I'd be using you, so arresting you deprived me of a servant, and if I was still loyal, she'd be doing me a favour by taking you off my hands." Jemeryl's hands slipped around Tevi and held her tight. "Very few sorcerers have any real regard for the ungifted. Our oaths to protect them are just the glue that holds the Coven together. This time last year, I felt the same. I saw the ungifted as pawns a sorcerer uses when playing for status." Jemeryl's words were murmured into Tevi's shoulder. "Between Neame and you, I've learnt an awful lot."

A series of emotions chased through Tevi's head. Her eyes caught sight of the tattoos on her hands. "Does this mean we'll be in trouble when we get back to Lyremouth?"

"They can't blame you. You acted in good faith. If we return with the chalice and Levannue as prisoner, they'll forgive us everything."

"That's a big 'if.' She could be anywhere."

"We can still catch her. Don't overestimate her abilities. Magic removes some physical restrictions, but she's still an old woman. Even sorcerers don't find flying a practical mode of transport. I think she'll stick to caravans."

"She may have swapped route. According to the traders in Horzt, there's a campsite at the other side of the pass where people can change caravans."

"Then we need to pick up her trail there." Jemeryl looked thoughtful and then sighed. "Of course, she might be stopped just north of the pass, using Lorimal's spell to create an army of hideous monsters ready to sweep down on the Protectorate."

"In which case she won't be hard to locate."

Jemeryl laughed and snuggled back against Tevi. "I guess there would be that advantage."

Tevi was silent and then said, "I wonder what the spell does, because..." She paused. "Has it struck you that right from the beginning, the Coven leaders were far more concerned with keeping the spell secret than with catching the traitor?"

Jemeryl chewed her lip. "You've got a point."

❖

By the time they were ten miles north of Horzt, the landscape was noticeably drier. Dusty hollows pitted the crumbling soil. Even in sheltered valleys, the covering of trees was thinning out, giving way to matted gorse and bracken. The air was thinner too, and colder. On all sides, the mountains rose to new heights. Bare fists of rock punched the sky.

The late-morning sun was on their backs as Tevi and Jemeryl followed a trail across open moorland. Ahead of them was a saddleback ridge slung between two peaks. They paused at the crest. On the other side, the terrain plunged in a series of vertical steps, which sprouted around buttress-like folds on the mountainside. The Danor glittered white at the bottom of the gorge, twinned with the darker line of the wagon road.

Until this point, the route had been clearly defined. Faced with the precipitous descent, the path broke into a web of goat tracks, as if the trail makers had been unable to agree on how to proceed.

Tevi followed each track with her eyes until it dropped out of sight. She turned to Jemeryl. "There probably isn't a best way down, but do you have any idea which might be the least worst?"

"Would it be unduly smug of me to point out that those of us who can fly are all right?" Klara was perched on Jemeryl's saddle.

"Yes, it would," Jemeryl said firmly.

Tevi looked at the magpie. "Could you use Klara to check out the route?"

"I'll give it a try, but paths that look fine from the air are sometimes impassable on foot." Jemeryl's voice held little optimism, but she scooped Klara onto her wrist.

Tevi watched, intrigued. Jemeryl's eyes closed. Her expression froze and then faded. It was as if the air thickened and stilled with the weight of the spell-casting.

Without warning, the silence was broken by a shout. The sound ricocheted around the gorge. Jemeryl jerked out of her trance. Her eyes chased the echoes.

Tevi had already located the source and was urging her back from the ridge, out of sight of the horsemen who had appeared below. The riders were more than a hundred yards away on their ascent of the cliff path, but closing in rapidly. They were clearly a militia patrol. Helmets glinted in the sun, and the distinctive cloaks flapped. The leader stood in the stirrups and called again—an assertive cry demanding attention, but not yet hostile.

"Jem, we've got to get away. If Russ has returned to Horzt, they may have my description. The guild members won't let me go. Not with the guild's integrity at stake."

"No. There's no need. I can take care of it. Come on. Get out of their way so they don't ride into us."

Jemeryl led the way towards a small knoll twenty yards from the path. Her horse stepped high over the coarse vegetation. Tevi followed, towing the spare horse and looking around in despair. There was no cover on the open heath. The knoll was barely high enough to hide a cat, and Jemeryl made no attempt to get behind it. She stopped to one side and faced the road. Her fingers started to trace elaborate patterns.

Tevi brought her horse to a halt beside Jemeryl's and waited. Her mouth was dry, and her eyes jumped between her sword hilt and the point on the skyline where the riders would appear. She tried to convince herself of her faith in Jemeryl's abilities but felt hopelessly exposed and vulnerable.

In a fury of pounding hooves and the clash of metal, a score of militiamen exploded over the ridge and thundered down the trail. Almost immediately, their impetus started to fizzle out. One by one, they pulled back so that within seconds of their appearance, the charge collapsed in a melee. The lead rider reined in her horse. The plateau provided no hiding place, yet her confused gaze passed by Tevi and Jemeryl. From the body of the patrol came anxious queries.

"Where've they gone?"

"They were here, clear as anything."

"There's nowhere for them to be." Panic tinged the voices.

In sudden comprehension, Tevi looked at Jemeryl's calm face. The sorcerer's hands were now motionless. Her eyes were glazed, focused on a world beyond the open heath. Tevi took a breath and forced her hands to unclench. She looked around, savouring the dreamlike quality of the blue sky and the rough vegetation. It felt so very strange to stand on a hillside in broad daylight and know herself to be invisible.

"Meric. Come here. Examine the track, and see what you can spot." The sergeant barked the order. It made little impression on the wiry scout who sat leaning forward in his saddle.

"I don't need to look for footprints. I can see the same thing as you. The work of a sorcerer."

Despite his words, the scout dropped lightly from his horse and walked along the track. He knelt and traced over the soil before raising his head. For a moment, his eyes fixed directly on the knoll.

He stood, faced his sergeant and shrugged. "There were three horses, two with riders, but there ain't now. They might have taken wing and flown, for all I can tell, or they might be standing by my elbow, invisible."

His words did nothing to calm his colleagues. Several shuffled nervously in their saddles.

Smiling at their discomfiture, the scout added, "I wouldn't worry. If the sorcerer wanted us dead, we wouldn't be standing here now."

The sergeant was clearly unhappy with the scout's assessment. She chewed her lip while making her decision. "Tadge. Elamis. Go back to the main road. Catch up with the lieutenant and report what we've seen. Tell him the rest of us will carry on." She snapped out the order and raised an arm to wave the rest of the patrol forward.

Tevi grinned, recognising the style of an officer who does not worry whether a command achieves anything worthwhile, as long as it is given and obeyed. From the expressions of the militiamen at the rear, she was not alone in her opinion.

The horsemen rode two abreast along the path. The sound of hooves and harness faded as they shrunk into the distance. Behind them, the detailed militiamen waited until the others were out of earshot.

"What good is telling the lieutenant? What can he do about a sorcerer?" the younger one asked, using a show of anger to hide her nervousness.

"I know what I'd like to do," the other said calmly.

"What?"

"If it's the same sorcerer as what dunked the mayor, I'd like to offer to buy her a drink."

A yelp of laughter met his words. "You and the rest of the militia."

"It doesn't pay to make enemies you can't beat." The older militiaman urged his horse around. "And it's good news for those three mercenaries who arrived back in Horzt last night."

"In what way?"

"I know one of them. Russ. From what he said, they've had a prisoner abscond, and I'll bet it was this sorcerer's companion. Once we tell Russ that his prisoner is under the protection of a sorcerer, the three of them can stop wasting time on the search and report back to their captain. There's no way they'll recapture the prisoner now, and no one will blame them for the escape. Like you said, there's nothing an ordinary person can do about a sorcerer. If anything, I reckon Russ is due a commendation for not getting anyone killed. Or he will be, if he tells the story right."

"Stupid to send them after a sorcerer's servant to start with. The entire Horzt militia couldn't stand up to her."

"Was that your excuse for not rushing to rescue the mayor?" The militiaman laughed. "I guess both Russ and the mayor were lucky that this sorcerer doesn't seem too aggressive. Like just now, hiding rather than blasting us to ash."

"You say the most comforting things." The young soldier shuddered. "Let's go."

After a last jittery glance over the heath, the militiamen wheeled their horses around and trotted back over the ridge. Jemeryl's head followed them, though her eyes remained unfocused.

"Can you keep this up if we follow? They probably know the best route down," Tevi said quietly.

"As long as we don't get too close." Jemeryl's voice sounded oddly flat.

With the help of their unwitting guides, the steep descent proved reasonably easy. The route twisted down the hillside. Several times, it seemed certain that a sheer drop would block their way, only for a side path to branch off at the last moment. As the gorge rose above them, the sound of the Danor grew, an unceasing roar of white water. The last few yards were a steep gravel slide onto the road. The militiamen turned south. With high shouts, they spurred their mounts into a gallop, raising a plume of dust behind them.

Tevi and Jemeryl also made it to level ground. They watched the militiamen disappear around a towering column of rock. The last echo faded, and the two women turned their own horses north. The valley bottom was noticeably warmer than the heath, though a chill breeze gusted down the gorge and stirred the dust in smokelike wisps that chased over the road.

Jemeryl was subdued. She rode with downcast eyes.

"What's wrong?" Tevi asked after a while of travelling in silence.

"The tattoos...some of that patrol were guild members."

"So?"

"Which means they're Protectorate citizens. I tampered with their perceptions. By Coven rules, I'm not supposed to do that without their consent."

"But they weren't hurt."

"It still counts as an abuse of power."

"Don't some sorcerers do things like that just to impress people?"

"Oh, all the time."

"So why are you upset? It's not as if you had any choice."

"I know. "Jemeryl sighed. "I'm just not happy about it."

Klara looked up from her perch on Jemeryl's saddle. "It's your own fault. I always warned you that if you started noticing the ungifted, you'd go and develop a conscience."

⁂

A field of stars hung in the black sky. Their brilliance pierced the night with cold purity now that the moon had set. Jemeryl stood, arms folded, looking north. The terrain before her flowed away in ever-fading ripples. It became a flat plain on the horizon. The northern grasslands.

The mountain chain was not wide above Horzt, no more than twenty miles as the eagle flew, although closer to fifty on the twisting wagon route. Dusk had been falling when she and Tevi reached the ruined city at the northern end of the pass. The last of the daylight had shown shattered, fire-blasted walls. Only one-twentieth of the site was occupied. People lived in hovels patched into the broken shells of buildings.

With suspicious eyes, the surly inhabitants had watched the two women arrive. The folk traded with the caravans, but only from necessity. Their distrust was unsurprising; they had been noticed once by the outside world and now wanted only to be ignored.

Jemeryl sighed as she wandered back to the fireside. Their camp was well away from the inhabited section. The remains of buildings in this area were too fragmentary to guess at their original function. Jemeryl threw herself down and stared into the campfire.

The ruins looked tranquil in the starlight, but Jemeryl had seen the walls torn apart by raw magic. They were a testament to a city that had died in the power games of sorcerers. She could sense the imprint of magic soaked into the stones, deeper than the blood that rain and time had washed away.

Her brooding was disturbed by approaching footsteps. Tevi wove her way through the shattered masonry. Doglike at her heels was a local man who scurried along with anxious glances in all directions. Jemeryl waited until both were seated, Tevi a little to one side and the local directly opposite. His face was turned down so that he watched her through a fringe of straw-coloured hair.

"You want to know things." The local spoke with a stilted monotone.

"Yes, as my friend will have told you. A caravan passed through here three or four days ago, heading to Uzhenek. I am interested in one of the passengers."

"I remember it."

"I'm afraid you might only..." Jemeryl hesitated. She had been about to explain her intentions, but watching him rub his hands on his knees, she realised that the man was terrified. A word about magic would send him into flight. "Tell me everything you remember about the caravan."

Jemeryl let her gaze drop to her hands clasped in her lap. She listened to his halting description, but her attention was fixed on the seething mass of his thoughts. Even as a sorcerer, Jemeryl could not read minds. The human intellect was too transient and bound in convoluted contradictions to pick out a single thread, but spotting if memories had been altered or removed was not hard.

Eventually, the local's mumbling stuttered to a halt.

"What can you tell me of the road to Uzhenek?" Jemeryl asked.

The man twitched and swallowed before forcing out his answer. "There's no road over the grasslands...except that the river Rzetoka can only be forded in three places."

"Which ford would the caravan use?"

He shrugged.

"Do you know which ford is the most common one?"

The sharp shake of his head might have been a nervous shiver or an expression of denial. Either way, Jemeryl sensed that she would get no further information. He almost bolted when Tevi leaned over to offer the promised coins. He snatched the money, then leapt to his feet and rushed off into the shadows.

"Levannue stayed on the caravan to Uzhenek?" Tevi asked.

"Yes. I'm certain of it."

"There doesn't seem much chance of finding her in the grasslands."

"We'll go to Uzhenek and wait for her. I'm sure she won't be expecting that. Though it does mean gambling with the weather. I don't want to be trapped north of the Barrodens by winter." Jemeryl frowned. "It's frustrating we got delayed. Between them, Russ and the Guardian really did Levannue a favour. I'd intended to ambush her here. The ruins hold so much residual energy, it's like fog in the sixth dimension. It would have been the perfect spot for a trap, and by now, we'd have been safely on our way back to Lyremouth with her and the chalice."

"It was bad timing. If Russ had arrived a day later, we'd have left Horzt." Tevi slid around the fire to sit closer to Jemeryl. For a while, she sat staring at the crumbling walls. "You said about energy in the ruins. Did magic destroy this city?"

"Yes."

"I noticed that the inhabitants are terrified of sorcerers. It was difficult finding anyone willing to talk to you. "

"If you told people that's what I am, I'm surprised you found anyone. It's why I asked you to go alone."

"Do you know what happened here?"

"Yes." Jemeryl indicated the broken walls. "Two hundred years ago, this was a thriving city, built solely by the ungifted. It's unique. The people here wouldn't tolerate anyone who could work magic. As soon as any child showed signs of being gifted they were killed. It made for a stable society. It grew slowly, not like a sorcerer's empire, and it lasted nearly one hundred and fifty years. In the end, it grew big enough to attract attention. A third-rate sorcerer who'd been displaced by the Protectorate heard of it. She walked in and took control. Nobody could stop her. They'd killed the only ones who could have made a stand."

"As you said about the men on my islands, it sounds like poetic justice."

"Maybe not what happened after. Taking over the city gave the sorcerer delusions about her own ability. She tried to expand her territory, which annoyed a more powerful sorcerer off to the west. By the time the dust settled, virtually everyone was dead, and the city was destroyed." Jemeryl stared at the ground. "I used to think the people got what they deserved. If I'd been born here, I'd have been killed. But..." She raised her head. "Tevi, how do the citizens of the Protectorate really feel about sorcerers?"

"From what I can tell, they feel varying levels of unease and resentment, coupled with varying levels of gratitude and respect."

"You must have heard more specific views expressed."

"Oh, yes, but I couldn't take them seriously. It's ridiculous to lump all sorcerers together. Some are all right and some aren't, much like any other group."

"But there's more to it. Being a sorcerer is so—"

Tevi caught hold of her hand. "Supposing I were to ask you what women really think about men. Women on my islands would have no trouble answering on behalf of 'all women.' Though as soon as you put it to the test, you'd realise that they hadn't even got the answer right for themselves. But if I asked the question in the Protectorate, I'd only get blank stares. It's a meaningless question. And it's like asking me about sorcerers. I don't have any strong emotional feelings about sorcerers in general; I only know how I feel about you." Tevi gently cupped Jemeryl's face. "I love you."

Chapter Thirteen—The Empress Bykoda

The grasslands were a green sea that rippled in the wind. Huge herds of deer and wild horses dotted the plain. The sky hung overhead like an upturned bowl of flawless blue. No landmark broke the horizon once the Barrodens sank from view. The uniformity of the scenery gave the impression of not moving, although the miles rolled by beneath the horse's hooves. Swapping mounts allowed them to rest one horse at a time and increase their speed. The only signs of other travellers were the spreading fans of wheel ruts on either side of the Rzetoka ford.

In late afternoon, nine days after leaving the ruins, Tevi and Jemeryl stood at the top of an escarpment overlooking a broad river valley. Tevi shaded her eyes against the sinking sun. To the east, a dark smudge stained the green.

"I think that's Uzhenek."

It took a while for Jemeryl to pick out the distant city. She grinned. "I did a good job with your eyes. Do you think we'll make it by nightfall?"

"Easily."

Once down the incline, they urged the horses into a brisk canter. A pair of parallel furrows through the grass grew thicker and deeper as more tracks converged, becoming a road. After an hour's riding, the city was close, although the sun in their eyes reduced the buildings to washed outlines ringing a gentle hill.

They entered the outskirts of Uzhenek. On either side, the road was packed with an untidy line of round huts made from rotting straw. Farther from the highway, the structures became ever more primitive until the shanties gave way to tents and horse pens. Decaying rubbish filled the spaces between the shelters. The place seemed more like a temporary encampment than a city.

Sprawled outside the miserable dwellings were large numbers of fair-haired men and women gossiping or calling to neighbours. Their clothes were brightly coloured but filthy, bearing signs of much wear and repair. Many looked the worse for drink. Children ran shouting through the dust, half-naked and unkempt. Nobody paid any attention to the women riding past.

The whole town held an air of lethargy. Only by the horse pens was there any activity. Groups hung around the rope barriers, voices raised in bartering and betting. The horses alone looked clean and cared for. Several races were in progress on the plain. Some onlookers even had the spirit to cheer their favourites.

Jemeryl was pleased. "We did very well. We must be days ahead of Levannue."

Tevi nodded, though her thoughts were on the scene around her. "Uzhenek isn't quite what I was expecting. Traders in Horzt spoke like the town was worth visiting. From what I can see, it comes a poor second to the rougher parts of Torhafn. And that's saying something."

"The traders would have been referring to the citadel." Jemeryl grimaced at the surroundings. "I'll agree this bit isn't too good."

"Why do the people stay here? There's plenty of game to hunt. If I were them, I'd be out in the open country."

"It's safe and easy. The Empress Bykoda has ruled these parts for nearly fifty years. Before her, these people were nomadic tribesmen. Nomadic mainly because they were always fleeing one danger or another. Bykoda has given the region stability. She's got a reputation for being a despot, but no worse than others of her ilk. And the folk will be worse off when she dies, which won't be much longer. She's getting old."

"What will happen to her empire?"

"On past experience, there'll be a futile struggle among several junior sorcerers before the whole place gets overwhelmed by something nasty from outside. It will be an awkward time. Bykoda has been a good neighbour to the Protectorate."

The ground was rising as they approached the citadel, enthroned on its lonely hill. Tevi felt her mouth go dry at the sight of battlements and high towers looming above the shantytown. By now, the road was paved with dressed stone, clean and weed free. The wretched press of huts ended abruptly, and the two women emerged into the open twenty yards from the citadel gates.

Black walls rose without the trace of a join, as if carved from a single rock. A gatehouse stood foursquare and imposing. The teeth of the portcullis lined its open mouth.

Tevi flinched at the sight. "It's a bit overwhelming." Her voice betrayed her in a squeak.

"Mainly because of the glamour spell Bykoda is projecting. I can lift it from you, if you want."

Tevi shook her head. "Maybe later. At the moment, I think it adds to the effect."

A dry moat spanned by a bridge separated the citadel from the straw huts. The road to it was lined on both sides with tall wooden stakes—a dozen or so, each mounted with a small round object. As she neared the first post, Tevi took her eyes from the battlements, intending only a quick glance. The shock was like a kick to the stomach. Each pole bore a severed human head. Old blood, dried brown, stained the wood beneath the trophies. Tattered skin drooped in shreds from the necks. Slack jaws hung open.

After a long silence, Tevi said quietly, "On the islands, we give fair burial even to enemies and criminals. You said Bykoda was a good neighbour. What are the rest like?"

"Worse."

"She knows how to make an impression. Let's get inside the citadel. Or is there likely to be more of the same?" Tevi coaxed her horse down the grotesque aisle.

The eyes of the first head snapped open. "I was a traitor. Do not do as I did. Be loyal to the Empress Bykoda."

The head on the other side joined in. "I was a murderer. Do not follow my example. Obey the laws of the Empress Bykoda."

At the sound of the first voice, Tevi stared around wildly until her eyes fixed on the talking head. She pressed her lips hard together, fighting down nausea.

However, Jemeryl's face held a look of wonder. "That's amazing." She slipped from her saddle and stepped up to the nearest head. "I would never have thought of doing that."

"Of course you wouldn't. It's foul." Tevi was appalled.

"No. I mean the technique. It would never have occurred to me to use the upspin currents of the sixth dimension like that."

"Jem!"

Jemeryl was too intent on the impaled head to respond. She raised a forefinger to the chanting lips. As if the strings of a puppet had been cut, the confession stopped mid-word and the semblance of life vanished. The features sagged, so flaccid as to lose the bearing of humanity. An alarm sounded from beyond the gate.

Tevi leapt from her horse and grabbed Jemeryl's elbow. Noises from the gatehouse alerted them to the guards spilling onto the bridge. Tevi's hand moved to her sword hilt.

Jemeryl stopped her. "They won't attack if we don't do anything else to alarm them."

"We?"

"I'm sorry. I got carried away."

"I thought we didn't want to attract attention."

"I know. I'm sorry."

The guards marched forward to make a cordon around the two women. Their movements were precisely synchronised without audible command. The footsteps fell as one. When they finally snapped to attention, the soldiers' faces were frozen, inhumanly devoid of emotion. Even to Tevi's ungifted eyes, it was obvious that they were enslaved.

"What do we do now?" she whispered to Jemeryl.

"We wait."

"Until?"

Jemeryl shrugged. "Someone with a brain to call their own gets here."

❖

It seemed like hours before an official dressed in black and silver appeared at the gates. He studied the scene for a few seconds before walking sedately towards them. With precise, mechanical movements, the line of guards parted at his approach. The official gave Jemeryl a curt, formal bow. Tevi was ignored.

"Greetings, sorcerer. I am town steward for the Empress Bykoda. Her imperial majesty wishes to speak with you."

"Please, lead the way." Jemeryl answered as if nothing unusual had occurred.

No further words were offered. The steward returned across the bridge at an unhurried but purposeful pace, clearly taking it for granted that Tevi and Jemeryl would follow and not cause trouble. The horses were left by the gatehouse, but no attempt was made to remove their weapons. None of the guards escorted them.

Inside the walls, the reasons for Uzhenek's reputation became obvious. The road was paved with slabs of soft blue light. Buildings rose in delicate tiers, too ethereal to support their own weight. It was architecture that could be created only by magic.

The citadel was beautiful, but Tevi was too appalled by the scene outside the gates to take any pleasure from it. Above all else, it was Jemeryl's reaction to the undead heads that tore at her. In the past, she had been bewildered by her lover's abilities but never alienated. If asked beforehand, she would have staked her life that Jemeryl's disgust would have matched her own.

At first, Jemeryl was absorbed in the sights. When she did notice Tevi's withdrawn manner, she clearly misunderstood. "Don't worry. We're not in danger. Bykoda won't want unnecessary conflict with the Coven, even if I did break one of her toys," Jemeryl whispered.

Tevi could not help flinching at the word *toys*. From Jemeryl's tone, it might have been a row of daffodils outside the gates.

Jemeryl carried on, oblivious. "I'm surprised if she's actually here. Her capital is Tirakhalod to the north, and she hasn't left it for years."

"What will she want?" Tevi forced herself to speak.

"Probably just to know why I'm here. It will be all right if I tell the truth. A renegade Coven sorcerer is the last thing she'll want running around. Bykoda will be very happy with my offer to remove Levannue from her lands."

"As long as Bykoda's not in league with her."

"Unlikely. She'd have to trust Levannue not to usurp her empire, and Bykoda hasn't survived this long by trusting anyone."

The steward led the way through another set of gates. The top of the hill was a field of rock, devoid of grass. Crouched at the summit was an immense round building, obviously styled on the straw huts but dwarfing them in scale. It was carved from the same black rock as the city walls. Flying buttresses ringed the hall like articulated legs. It gave the impression of a huge black spider, brooding and waiting. Stairs swept up to the entrance in a domed extension of the main building. It looked like a head and added to the spider effect.

The interior of the anteroom was lit from an unseen source that cast more shadow than light over walls and floor of polished black marble. Tall guards stood on duty. Straight ahead were huge double doors of embossed silver, which swung open of their own accord. Jemeryl strode forward, clearly unworried. Tevi hesitated at the thought of what might await, but despite her confusion and distress, she would not let Jemeryl face it alone.

The scale of the main hall was breathtaking. The perimeter circle of pillars faded into the gloom on the far side. Interspersed alternately were black-clad guards and silver tripods holding burners. Plumes of incense billowed in shafts of milky daylight. The centre of the hall was empty except for a dais where the silver statue of an elderly woman sat on a simple throne.

The steward halted by the pillars and indicated that Jemeryl should carry on alone. When Tevi began to follow, the steward reached out to stop her. She threw off the restraining hand but was then swamped by uncertainty and settled for merely taking another three steps. She watched uneasily as Jemeryl walked on alone.

A dozen paces before the dais, Jemeryl stopped and looked around. She appeared intrigued rather than impressed. A faint sound, like a sigh, came from the statue's lips. Slowly, joint by joint, a tremor of articulation rippled through the silver figure.

With the most deliberate of movements, the statue raised its head. "Greetings, sorcerer. I am a projection of the Empress Bykoda, ruler of these lands from the Barroden Mountains to the Gulf of Czeskow. Might I be privileged as to know your name?"

"I am Jemeryl, oath-bound sorcerer of the Coven of Lyremouth." She gave a formal bow.

"From Lyremouth?" The statue's voice held the suggestion of a question. "I hold the Coven and its Guardian in high regard, and trust we may always maintain the convivial relationship between our two lands. Do you come from Lyremouth as an envoy?"

"No. In fact, when I left Lyremouth, it was not envisaged that I would come here. Yet I know the Guardian would want me to express her appreciation of you and your courteous dealings with the Coven, that has been to our mutual benefit."

The words of both sorcerers, while not exactly insincere, reminded

Tevi of the initial exploratory parries of fencers.

Bykoda's next question was more direct. "May I enquire about the reasons that have brought you to my lands?"

"One of our sorcerers has turned traitor. I think she may have fled here."

"How disconcerting for you. What do you intend to do once you find her?"

"Capture her and return with her to Lyremouth."

"If you wanted to take her by surprise, you made a rather conspicuous entrance to the citadel."

For the first time, Jemeryl looked off-balance. "It's unlikely she will have reached here yet, but I admit my behaviour was unwise."

"Upsetting me was certainly not a good first move."

"Please accept my apologies." Jemeryl paused but then her enthusiasm broke through in a blatantly genuine outburst. "I'm afraid I forgot myself when I saw your warders. It was an inspired use of the upspin currents. I've never seen anything like it. The idea was elegantly simple, yet very effective. I was impressed, really deeply impressed."

The statue's laughter echoed around the hall. Tevi could tell that the atmosphere had changed, as if a decision had been made or a truce called. Jemeryl stood more easily.

"Spoken like a true Coven sorcerer. Too busy playing with magic to keep sight of your goal."

"I fear you're right on this occasion. I just had to know how you made it work."

"You think I could teach the Coven a few tricks?" The statue's voice was lightly ironic.

"I think you could teach the Coven a lot, if you were willing."

"And what could the Coven give in return?"

"What does the Coven have that you want?"

"Nothing."

"Then we have no basis for a trade."

The statue was silent for a while. "When I was younger, I thought the Coven sorcerers were fools or cowards, serving the ungifted. Now that I'm getting older, it doesn't seem so clear-cut. Not that I'd change a thing if I had to do it all over again. 'Empire' is a wonderful game. You live and die by your own strength and skill. No rules and no boundaries."

"We all make our own choices."

"Or maybe not everyone enjoys playing the same game. And some people expend so much effort going round in circles, I suspect they are not bothered about winning." The statue tilted its head and studied Jemeryl thoughtfully. "I would have said you wanted to win. I wonder what game you're playing in the Protectorate."

"Such as?" The initial fencing returned to Jemeryl's voice.

"You may be motivated by concern for your fellow human beings. Or you may get satisfaction from working for something that will exist long after you're dead." The statue's tone became more pointed. "Or maybe you dream of becoming Guardian one day and having hundreds of powerful sorcerers under your rule, rather than merely ungifted masses."

"Maybe." Jemeryl made the word sound more like agreement than equivocation.

"It's an interesting prize to play for."

"But not one that tempted you?"

"It's too restricted a game for my tastes. I never could stomach playing by other people's rules. I'd have ended up like this poor fool you're chasing who hasn't toed the line and is about to be dragged back to Lyremouth like a naughty child. She has my sympathy. But don't worry; I'm not going to stop you. I'd be a fool to let her stay, and I've never let pity cloud my better judgement. I'll even offer you assistance. My steward will give you a talisman. Show it to anyone in the city, and they will let you pass without hindrance. Although I will be watching you."

"Thank you." Jemeryl hesitated. "I suppose you wouldn't want me to examine the heads again. I really am fascinated to know how you do it."

The statue laughed. "Capture your traitor and remove her from my lands. Then, if you want, come to me at Tirakhalod, and I will instruct you."

The laughter drifted away, muted and hollow. The life drained out of the statue, leaving a frozen silver shell sitting on the throne in the empty hall. The audience was ended.

❖

Tevi and Jemeryl were escorted to a hostelry in the south of the citadel. The rooms were large and well furnished, to the point of being a gratuitous display of wealth. Even the doorstop had inlays of gold. Stony-faced servants brought their belongings. The same servants prepared the room with clean bedding, water for washing, and wine to drink. Then, without having spoken a word, they bowed and left.

Once they were alone, Jemeryl opened the window and admired the view. Light flowed over the shimmering turrets and delicate archways with a rainbow sheen. Tevi dropped onto a cushioned bench and stared at the walls.

"What do you think of Uzhenek now?" Jemeryl asked over her shoulder. When there was no answer, she turned around. "Are you all right?"

Tevi shrugged.

"Tevi, what's wrong?" Jemeryl left the window. She slid onto the bench and put her arm around Tevi's shoulder.

"I'm reconsidering my views about sorcerers." Tevi spoke without turning her head.

"Why? Was there something about Bykoda that upset you?"

"And you."

"Me?" Jemeryl sounded shocked. "Tevi?"

"I've been thinking about the wealth inside the citadel and then what's outside. Not just the heads. The stinking poverty and the guards with their minds gone. It's worse than slavery. For the first time, I see the gulf between sorcerers and the rest of us. And you and Bykoda seemed so much a pair."

"Nearly all of the citadel is illusion. A play with coloured lights. There's no real wealth here. If you could see this room without the overlay of magic, it's rather plain and shabby. And I don't agree with the way Bykoda rules her lands, but telling her so wouldn't have done any good, and I had to get her support."

"You were full of admiration for the way she keeps the heads alive. You didn't see them as people, just an interesting use of magic. It's evil and callous. I don't understand you, Jem."

Jemeryl pulled Tevi's face around so their eyes met. "They weren't real heads. They were fashioned from resin. Not that I think Bykoda would have hesitated to use real ones if it was the only way to achieve her aim, but the resin would prevent problems with decay.

Bykoda was using a very original way to animate the shapes. That was what surprised me. Nobody was hurt. Wanton cruelty is usually a sign of madness or insecurity, and Bykoda doesn't suffer from either."

"You wanted to learn how to copy her. Why?" Tears filled Tevi's eyes. "To frighten people into obeying you?"

"Partly because it's so inventive, and partly because I wondered if it might be possible to make artificial limbs. It could be useful to your colleagues in the guild. They're so good at losing the ones they're born with." Jemeryl spoke softly. "Please, Tevi. I know it must be hard sometimes, but trust me."

Tevi's distress gave way to confusion. "Why didn't you say before?"

"I'm sorry. I didn't realise you were upset, and I guess I forgot that you...." Jemeryl's words faded awkwardly.

Tevi shifted around and rested her head on Jemeryl's shoulder. There was comfort in the contact, although some nasty questions still pricked the edges of her mind. One in particular slivered to the front.

"Was it also true what Bykoda said? You're only in the Coven so you can become Guardian one day?" Tevi mumbled the question. "And the only reason you want to be Guardian is so you get to order other sorcerers around, because the ungifted don't count?"

"It was once...to some extent. And I do still want to be Guardian. Bykoda is very astute. But it isn't the only thing that motivates me, and there are some prices I wouldn't pay to achieve it."

"Do ungifted people, the Protectorate citizens, really matter to you?"

"I can't pretend to care passionately for millions of people I've never met, and I don't believe you do, either. However, I can honestly say that I wish them well and will always try to do my best for them."

"I guess that's the best we ungifted can hope for from our sorcerers."

"I could give you another, more specific thought about me, empires, and one particular ungifted person."

"What?"

Jemeryl pulled Tevi into an embrace. "How about that I'd happily swap all Bykoda's empire for one night in your arms?"

❖

Tevi rested her elbows on the parapet and considered the view. Just below the balcony, a fountain shot brilliant plumes of coloured spray into the air. The water was luminous in the encroaching dusk. Musical chimes sounded as the breeze stirred trees with leaves of gold and silver.

"Could you create a city like this?" The question had crossed Tevi's mind several times during the previous six days, while waiting for Levannue.

"I could, but it would be a lot of work for something I've no use for. Even Bykoda has it only for show. It keeps the tribes awestruck and submissive. It couldn't support a population like a city in the Protectorate. No more than a hundred people actually live in the citadel, and they're here purely for visitors. Only five or six buildings really exist."

"It's still very pretty."

"I find it disconcerting. I keep seeing through the illusions. Even where the basic structure is real, the work is crudely functional. Bykoda just overlays a glamour of luxury, and she doesn't do it very thoroughly. In the Protectorate, we're used to working with other sorcerers, so we carry the illusion through and tidy up the edges. Bykoda doesn't bother. Most of her work looks appallingly slipshod, but then, other bits are breathtakingly imaginative."

"Like her audience hall?"

Jemeryl gave a yelp of laugher. "Maybe not that."

"What was wrong with it?"

"Oh, the illusion matches the quality of the rest of Uzhenek, but it was a child's fantasy of a necromancer's castle. I'm only surprised she didn't have a pet griffin by her feet."

"Well, speaking on behalf of the ungifted, it was overpowering," Tevi said, grinning. "Is there anything else here that is real?"

Jemeryl moved to an adjacent balcony with a view of the land beyond the outer wall. Farmland and orchards stretched down to the river.

"That is. Bykoda organises the tribesmen to do most of the work; then she uses magic to inhibit weeds, destroy pests, and ensure a bumper crop each year. That's why there's an encampment outside. Here, the tribes find safety, food, and water...and they also provide an army, should Bykoda need it."

Tevi shaded her eyes to study the fields, but any further questions were curtailed when Klara swooped onto her shoulder.

"A wagon train has just reached the encampment. Unless you want to hang around and shake Levannue's hand, perhaps you should get out of sight."

The two women hurried back to their room. Jemeryl threw herself onto a couch. "Wait here. I'm going to mind-ride Klara. I want to be sure Levannue is on the caravan."

"Can't Klara go on her own?"

"She could, but I'll feel happier if I'm there myself."

Bird and sorcerer locked eyes. Between one breath and the next, Jemeryl became motionless, dropping into a state beyond mere sleep. Klara's head twitched, as if she were trying to dislodge an itch from her neck, then she extended her wings and flew to the open window.

She perched on the ledge and looked back. "Wish me luck."

"Take care, Jem."

"I will."

The magpie departed in a streak of black and white. In the quiet that followed, Tevi paced the room, pausing repeatedly to look at the comatose sorcerer. The shadows slowly thickened. From the distance came voices, the creek of wheels and the clop of hooves. Cautiously, Tevi peered from behind the shutter. Wagons were stopped at the end of the street. Levannue's nervous gait was not evident among the people who were unharnessing horses and dragging loads from tailboards.

Tevi walked back and sat beside Jemeryl's motionless body. It was impossible to relax. With each passing minute, the knots in her stomach tightened. Her heart leapt up her throat at the sound of something rushing into the room. Tevi spun about. Klara was at the window.

On the couch, Jemeryl opened her eyes. "She's here."

❖

"I wish to see the innkeeper."

It took only a glimpse of the talisman to send the night porter scuttling off across the dimly lit lobby, alarm transforming his bland, youthful face. The patter of his footsteps faded and was replaced by tense silence.

Tevi watched him disappear. "The talisman certainly gets a response. I wonder what its significance is?"

"We're probably happier not knowing."

"You sound on edge."

"Of course I am."

"You'll be all right with Levannue, won't you?" Tevi wanted the reassurance, but Jemeryl only shrugged.

"She's far more experienced than me, and I can't see her surrendering quietly. Plus I feel duty-bound to try to capture her alive, while I'm sure she won't feel the same restraint with me."

"But you'll have surprise on your side."

"Hopefully."

"You said she's returned to her true form. That must mean she isn't expecting us."

"Or maybe she now has good reason to be confident."

Tevi did not want to think about the possibility. She set off on a circuit of the lobby. After pausing to peer suspiciously down several passages, she stopped at the main doorway.

Night was well advanced. The Uzhenek display of sculptured light had softened to a fluorescent glow. The streets were deserted, but above the rooftops, sentries paced the battlements. Tevi wondered whether the bodies and masonry were real or illusory.

Whispers and footsteps announced the return of the night porter, trailing in the wake of an older man—surely his father, judging by the likeness. Both were thickset, with round faces and fair hair pulled back in braids. The main difference was that the son's muscle had turned to flab on the father. Red, bleary eyes further impaired the older man's appearance. He was still in the process of tying a long robe over his bulging waist. He wobbled to a halt, eyeing Jemeryl and the talisman nervously.

"Can I help you, ma'am?"

"You are the innkeeper?"

"Yes, ma'am."

"An elderly woman arrived this evening. Thin, about my height, with short grey hair. You may have noticed an amulet like this." Jemeryl held up her arm. "Although she was probably keeping her wrist covered."

"Yes, ma'am, I know who you mean." The innkeeper's anxiety increased visibly. He would have dealt with enough travellers from the Protectorate to know what the amulet meant.

"I want you to lead us to her room." Jemeryl fixed the man with a grim stare. "But very quietly. It would be best if she didn't hear us coming. Do you understand?"

"Yes, ma'am."

The innkeeper looked as if he understood only too well. His shoulders were twitching as he led the way along a wide corridor. Light from the lantern he held lurched wildly, magnifying the shaking of his hands. Hanging tapestries gleamed with rich colour where the light fell, but shadows in the folds dissected the pictures, leaving a montage of heads, arms, and half-animals.

The innkeeper stopped outside a door. He pointed to it with an overdramatic gesture and then nearly tripped in his haste to back away. His clumsy retreat drew fierce glares.

Jemeryl stood in front of the door and studied it intently. The fingertips of one hand traced the frame without making contact with the wood, while her other hand held her iron-tipped staff level with her eyes. As her examination progressed, her frown deepened. At last, she drew back and indicated with a jerk of her head that Tevi and she should return to the lobby.

"What's wrong?" Tevi asked once they were there.

"The door is barred on the inside. That wouldn't be a problem, except Levannue has placed alarms across the higher dimensions. I can't open the door by magic without alerting her."

"Are you going to break the door down?" The innkeeper hovered nervously. Both women ignored him.

"I suppose she's locked the windows as well."

"We could go outside and check, but I'm sure she will have."

"And there wouldn't be a wide chimney or anything like that?" Tevi looked at the innkeeper.

"No, we don't have fires. Bykoda heats the inn directly by her magic arts. She—"

Jemeryl let the innkeeper go no further. "Impossible! Do you think I wouldn't know if Bykoda was shunting that sort of load through the sixth dimension, all the way from Tirakhalod? Don't be stupid. They'd sense it in Lyremouth."

The remnants of the innkeeper's composure dissolved. "It's not proper magic, but it...I-I-I'm not supposed to tell visitors."

"What?"

The innkeeper's eyes darted to the talisman "The floor is raised on pillars. We've got a fire in the stoke room, and hot air is drawn through. The whole inn gets heated without any fireplaces. We like visitors to think it's magic. In winter, the fire burns continually, but at this time of year, we let it go out at night. Otherwise, if you touched the floor, you'd feel the warmth."

Tevi knelt and rested her fingers on the ground, as if testing his words. She picked at the join between two flagstones. "Would you have a crowbar?"

"You're thinking we could get in that way?" Jemeryl asked while the innkeeper still stared blankly.

"I could. Once I'm in Levannue's room, would it upset the alarms if I then opened the door for you?"

"No. Only magic will trip them."

"The floor stones are too heavy for you to lift." The innkeeper's words seemed to escape his mouth against his will.

"That will be my problem."

"But—"

"We would like a crowbar." Jemeryl's tone left no room for argument.

The innkeeper's son was dispatched. He reappeared shortly, bearing a metal bar, curved and flattened at one end. The innkeeper fluttered around fearfully. There was no mistaking his relief when he was told to stay in the lobby.

The flagstones outside Levannue's door were a yard square. To Tevi, they looked like close-fitting marble, the work of a skilled craftsman. However, Jemeryl had no trouble inserting the wedged end of the crowbar between two.

"You did that by magic?" Tevi whispered, looking anxiously at the doorway.

"No. As I said before, the workmanship isn't good. I can see around Bykoda's attempt to hide the cracks."

Tevi took over with the crowbar. The flagstone rose to the rasping of grit. Once it was high enough to get her fingers under, Tevi lifted the slab and rested it against the wall behind.

Warm air rushed out, carrying the smell of wood smoke. Beneath the flagstones, a forest of stone pillars stretched off in all directions into the black void. Between ground and floor was a gap of nearly two feet. Tevi studied the crooked avenues of pillars, then slid her legs into the opening.

Jemeryl squeezed her shoulder. "Take care."

Tevi smiled stoically in reply.

The ground and pillars were hot to the touch—uncomfortable, although not enough to burn her. The smoky air stung Tevi's eyes. Space was tight. The pillars were barely wide enough apart to let her shoulders through. The ground was too rough to slide over. She fought for progress inch by inch, wriggling on her back. The light vanished as she moved away from the entrance. In the dark underworld, she lost all sense of distance.

Tevi marked her progress by feeling for joins on the underside of the floor, but it was as if the flagstones had grown. Her sweat-drenched clothes clung to her. The air rasped her throat. She tried to focus on her task, but a bubbling hysteria threatened to erupt. In the back of her mind, a voice screamed that she was buried alive. Tevi fought to ignore it.

At last, she reached the fifth flagstone. Four hard-won yards, far enough to be clear of any furniture around the edge of Levannue's room. Tevi pushed against the paving above. The stone did not budge. Suddenly, Tevi was desperate to escape the claustrophobic prison. She pushed again, borrowing strength from the wave of panic. This time, the flagstone shifted.

A second, strenuous effort let in a rush of cold air to play over the sweat on Tevi's face. A thin line of moonlight, dazzling after the darkness, broke along the crack. No sound came from the room above, but Tevi's imagination pictured Levannue, silently watching the moving flagstone.

Tevi ignored her fear. There was no going back. She braced her knees against the pillars on either side and raised her shoulders off the ground, her arms locked rigid. Every muscle in her legs and stomach strained. To her ears, the scratching of stone on stone was deafening, even louder than her pounding heart.

Tevi found herself inside a large room. Moonlight flowed in through tall windows, throwing the ornate furniture into silver relief and shimmering off the drapes around a four-poster bed. Just as Tevi started to relax, a sound from behind the curtains ruptured the silence—a raw sound, swelling to a feral growl. Tevi jumped, but then her lips pulled into a mirthless grin, mocking her own nervousness. The sound was merely heavy snoring. A nearby fur rug made a silent cushion for the flagstone—once she managed to loosen her fingers from their deathlike grip.

The bolts gave only the faintest metallic squeak as Tevi eased them back. The door hinges made a similar sound. From Jemeryl's expression, it was clear that the long wait in the corridor had held its own strains. Jemeryl clasped Tevi's hand before passing over an iron collar.

The rasping snores did not falter. Jemeryl's eyes met Tevi's in a last supportive exchange. She moved towards the bed, gesturing for Tevi to take up position on the other side. Cautiously, they pulled back the curtains. In the centre of the bed, Levannue lay encased in folds of blankets. Her head was completely hidden between the pillows. Locating her neck would not be easy. It was hard even to be certain which way up she was. Briefly Tevi was struck by a simpler solution involving the use of a sword, but killing in cold blood did not fit well with her conscience.

On the other side of the bed, Jemeryl held her staff above the sleeping woman and looked over, waiting for Tevi's signal. Instead, Tevi mimed the words, "Where's her neck?"

Their plans depended on catching Levannue by surprise, preferably without waking her. They certainly could not waste time scrabbling about in the bedclothes.

Jemeryl frowned, but then reached out and shook Levannue's shoulder gently. "Excuse me disturbing you, ma'am, but Bramell wants to see you right away." She spoke with a servant's deference.

"What..."

Lost between dreams and reality, Levannue pushed herself up. Her eyes searched about wildly until they fixed with disbelief on Jemeryl. Suddenly, Levannue's body seized, freezing as if time had missed a step.

"Now, Tevi!" Jemeryl called, her voice straining with the effort.

Tevi sprung forward, diving across the jumbled bedding with the open jaws of the iron collar held ready. The air felt viscous, heavy with the weight of Jemeryl's spell clamping down on her opponent.

Tevi did not need a sorcerer's senses to feel Levannue fighting back, tearing through the ether at the bonds holding her. The air changed to static. The hair on Tevi's arms stood upright, and ozone filled her nose. Levannue's hand shot out, wrapped in blue fire, and Jemeryl stumbled back, dropping her staff. The magical bonds were unravelling—but too late for Levannue. Before the dropped staff had hit the floor, Tevi snapped the two halves of the collar shut around her neck.

CHAPTER FOURTEEN—THE RUINS OF GRAKA

Stars still shone undimmed, but the black sky was yielding to the first shades of blue. The stables were set in a small courtyard behind the inn. The warm smell of hay and animals countered the predawn chill. Jemeryl and Tevi escorted Levannue to the tethered horses. The porter and innkeeper trailed behind, bearing Levannue's belongings. Tevi held the stirrup while the prisoner mounted and then she tied Levannue's hands to the saddle.

Jemeryl knelt to rifle through the baggage. "I just want to be sure there's—" She broke off.

"What is it?"

"Do you recognise this?"

Tevi took the chalice from Jemeryl's hands. Her fingers traced the remembered pattern of small dents. "Yes. This is it."

"So you may get to complete your quest after all."

A succession of emotions chased through Tevi's mind. "It might be best if I don't."

Jemeryl continued rooting through the bag and pulled out her next find. "Lorimal's manuscript. That will please Moragar. We knew Levannue had taken it, so it couldn't be used to track the chalice again, but he was worried that she'd simply destroyed it."

"Why didn't she?"

"Sentimental reasons?" Jemeryl looked up at the prisoner as if hoping for confirmation, but Levannue's face was turned away.

The innkeeper's relief at their departure was unmistakable. He dithered outside his inn, his need to be certain that they were gone clearly battling his urge to run and hide. The women passed through empty streets. They saw no one until the southern gatehouse loomed before them. Even at that early hour, a full compliment of vacant-eyed sentries stood watch. At the sight of Bykoda's talisman, the guards unbarred the gate. Tevi grimaced with abhorrence. The soldier's mechanical movements were as devoid of true life as the walls.

The southern approach to Uzhenek was less populated than the east, where they had entered. Only a scattering of shoddy huts were squeezed between the cultivated fields and the road leading down to the river. They crossed the dark, sluggish water on a solid and very real-looking bridge. The road divided on the far bank.

Jemeryl circled her horse around and looked back. Thin bands of golden cloud lined the horizon. The pink flush in the eastern sky was reflected in the citadel walls. Graceful spires and turrets caught the dawn light in ripples of colour.

"Isn't that an amazing way to deconstruct transient cross-flow?"

Tevi laughed at Jemeryl's tone of wonder. "I'm afraid I haven't a clue what you mean, and I doubt you'll get any show of enthusiasm from Levannue."

No word came from the prisoner. Levannue had hardly spoken since her capture. The collar was clearly troubling her. She rode with her eyes fixed on the distance and an expression of strained disbelief on her face.

"I guess you're right," Jemeryl conceded. "I'll save my praise until I meet Bykoda in person. I want to learn whatever she's willing to teach. That's the road to Tirakhalod." She indicated the wider fork, heading north, then she turned and urged her horse onto the smaller western track. "But first, it's back to Lyremouth. This will link with the Old West Road, which goes over the pass above Denbury. Once there, we can catch a barge down the river Lyre."

Jemeryl set off across the open plain with the sun creeping into the sky behind her. Levannue's horse trotted forward to go two abreast.

Tevi fell in behind. Several times, she glanced back at the road to Tirakhalod. For her, it was a relief to be out of Uzhenek and heading to the Protectorate with Levannue as prisoner. She had seen enough of Bykoda's empire. Jemeryl had not discussed her plans for the future, and Tevi had chosen not to ask, unsure of what part she would be allowed, or wanted, to play. Yet there were decisions to be made, and they were not going to be simple. Tevi's eyes fixed on Jemeryl, full of doubt, but then they shifted to Levannue, and her face hardened. When Levannue was safely delivered to Lyremouth, there would be time to consider her options.

❖

That evening, they camped on the plains under a translucent new moon. A sharp wind from the north hissed through the long grass and snapped at the campfire made from dried dung. The horses grazed nearby. Out on the plain, an immense herd of shaggy, cowlike animals shuffled through the dusk. Apart from the track, there was no sign of human life. Uzhenek lay many miles behind. A fair day's journey, but one planned not to push the horses too hard. It was a long ride to Denbury, with no chance to swap mounts.

Jemeryl and Tevi talked of routine matters, their speech inhibited by Levannue's sullen presence. She listened but made no attempt to join in. Her expression had settled into one of resentful scorn.

As true dark fell, Tevi shook out the blankets. She looked at the prisoner. "What about keeping watch? Should we take turns?"

"No need. The horses are mind-locked, so they won't wander and won't let Levannue within twenty yards without one of us present. And Klara's slept on my saddle all day. She can stand sentry. She'll wake me if Levannue sends so much as a filthy look in our direction."

"If Klara does that, on today's evidence, you won't get much sleep."

"True. I don't think Levannue is our friend at the moment."

This finally provoked an outburst. "You're so pleased with yourself. Does it feel good, getting revenge for what happened in Ekranos?"

"Revenge doesn't come into it. I'm just obeying the Guardian's orders," Jemeryl replied without bothering to turn her head.

"'Obeying the Guardian's orders.' You make it sound so virtuous." Levannue sneered.

"If you remember, it's something you once swore to do as well."

"Look at you, the Guardian's trusted follower! I'll bet she hasn't even told you what the spell is all about."

"No. And we don't want to know, either," Tevi cut in.

"I wasn't addressing you. You shouldn't interrupt when your betters are speaking."

"You can drop that attitude," Jemeryl exploded, stung more by Levannue's arrogant rebuke of Tevi than the venomous tones directed at herself. "You're a traitor who's broken her oath of allegiance. You've got a nerve to claim superiority to Tevi."

"I don't have to claim it. If you took this collar off, I could demonstrate it."

"No. All you could demonstrate is that you're more powerful than her. Every honest citizen of the Protectorate counts as a better person than you. You once swore to support the Coven, but you've been trying to destroy it."

Levannue's anger faded into amused contempt. "Is that the lie the Guardian told you? The spell will destroy the Coven? You're wrong. Lorimal's spell won't hurt anyone. Quite the opposite. All Lorimal's spell does is give eternal youth. Immortality. Nothing more, nothing less."

"You're lying. If that was all, the Coven wouldn't ban it," Tevi said quickly.

"How dare you accuse me of lying?"

"Why not? I think it goes quite well with theft and murder."

While Levannue floundered for a reply, Jemeryl answered. "Levannue might be telling the truth, as far as immortality goes, but it's not that simple. The Coven bans work on immortality because all attempts have done more harm than good. At best, they've raised false hopes. At worst, they've been..." Jemeryl considered her words. "Evil. Sacrificing the lives of others in an attempt to prolong one's own."

Levannue made a sweeping gesture, as if knocking the argument aside. "No. Lorimal's spell is different. For one thing, it works. Look at me! And the spell is only beginning to show its effect."

Jemeryl opened her mouth but then froze. Now that her attention was drawn, it was obvious that Levannue was more youthful than the woman who had left Ekranos. The lines on her face had softened; skin and muscle were firmer.

Jemeryl's expression hardened. "I concede that it's done something, for now. But do you really think it will work forever? And who pays the cost of your youth?"

"No one."

"I don't believe you."

"Don't you—" Levannue bit back her words. She glared into the fire while she mastered her anger. "I'll tell you how the spell works."

"I don't want to know."

"If you're going to accuse me of lying, you might have the decency to let me defend myself." Without waiting for agreement, Levannue continued. "What Lorimal worked out is this: Our bodies grow from conception to adulthood, following a plan held within our cells. But then the plan fails. It builds a healthy body but can't maintain what it created."

"I know the theory," Jemeryl cut in. "The plan becomes corrupted with time."

"Not completely. Else what do we pass to our children? If the plan had worn out, then babies would be born as old as their parents."

"There's more to it than that."

"True, there is. But it's the starting point of Lorimal's work. The other attempts at immortality went wrong when they saw death as an enemy to defeat. Messing about with zombies and life forces was childish idiocy. Lorimal's great achievement was realising that death is merely the failure to remain living. She worked out how to make the plan repair itself. Soon, I'll be back at my prime. I'll still be vulnerable to sickness or injury, but I'll never get old."

"If that was all, why would the Coven ban it?"

"A good question. You tell me." Levannue's voice was quietly triumphant.

The two sorcerers stared at each other. For the first time, Jemeryl looked unsure.

Tevi broke the silence. "Perhaps they thought the Protectorate couldn't sustain the rise in population. How could the farmers feed us if nobody died?"

Levannue replied condescendingly. "You couldn't give the drug to everyone. It would be limited to certain people."

"Oh, of course. People like sorcerers." Scorn dripped from Tevi's voice.

"Of course."

"Anyone else you'd include in your elite band of deserving cases?"

"You can't be expected to understand the issues, but you should know when it's your place to keep silent." Levannue spoke as if addressing a naughty child.

"I think I understand you very well."

Levannue turned away. "You see, Jemeryl, what happens when you favour the ungifted? They get inflated ideas of their own importance."

"At least I keep my word."

"I'm sure that's a very desirable trait for someone of your calling."

The patronising tone no longer drew a response from Jemeryl. Tevi's eyes darted angrily between the two sorcerers before she jumped up and marched into the darkness. When Jemeryl caught up with her, she was standing by the horses and staring out across the darkening plain.

"Tevi?"

"Wouldn't you rather talk to a fellow sorcerer?"

"Tevi!"

"I'm sorry." Tevi was instantly contrite. She clasped her hands behind her neck. "What do you see in me?" she asked at last.

"I love you."

"You're a Coven sorcerer, and I'm just a junior mercenary. Levannue is being spiteful but honest. I'm not in your class."

"No. You're a far rarer thing than me." Jemeryl pulled Tevi around so their eyes met. "There are too many who think like Levannue, including most of the ungifted. You don't know what it's like being a sorcerer. Most people could accept me more easily if I were green and had three heads. It's hard making real friends, let alone anything deeper. Even other sorcerers have their own ideas they expect me to match." Jemeryl's voice dropped. "But not you, because you don't see sorcerers as different to anyone else. Forget Levannue winding you up just now. You've got no expectations of me as a sorcerer. You don't see me as a sorcerer; you see me as me. I need that. I need you."

"I can't see that I'm so rare."

"There can't be more than a couple dozen like you in the entire Protectorate, and I probably wouldn't get on with most of them if we met. I like you. If nothing else, I'd want to be your friend." Jemeryl's arms slipped around Tevi's waist. "On top of that, even after knowing you nine months, you can still smile at me and turn my knees to water. Don't let Levannue bother you."

Tevi let herself be drawn back to the fire, but she knew, no matter what Jemeryl might say, that as far as the rest of the world was concerned, Jemeryl's name and hers did not fit together in the same breath.

❖

By the following afternoon, Levannue's mood had softened to dejected resignation. She even made an effort to be pleasant to Jemeryl, although she ignored Tevi. When they stopped to rest the horses, she deliberately sat close by Jemeryl. Tevi stood to one side, arms folded, certain that the elderly sorcerer was planning something.

Levannue addressed Jemeryl with a studied nonchalance. "Have you thought about what I said last night?"

"Of course."

"And?"

"If you think I'm going to say the Coven is wrong and let you go, I'm afraid you're in for a disappointment."

From the way Levannue's face fell, Tevi guessed that had indeed been her hope.

"What purpose does banning the spell serve? Who benefits?"

"I'm not sure if 'benefit' is the right word, but I think this spell could destroy everything good about the Protectorate."

"That's ridiculous."

"Not if you think it through."

"I have!" Levannue's composure was unravelling.

"So what about Tevi's point that the Protectorate couldn't support an unceasing rise in population?"

"I agreed. Which means Lorimal's potion must be strictly limited."

"How would those who didn't get the potion react?"

"They'd be no worse off than before."

"Would they see it like that?"

"Exceptions could be made, if you're worried about your mercenary, sweetheart, though I doubt your affection for her will last all eternity." Levannue's smile did nothing to remove the barb from her words.

Jemeryl was undeterred. "It's not the particular cases that are the problem. It's the effect on all citizens."

"I don't see your point."

"That's because you don't put yourself in their shoes." Jemeryl ran her hand through her hair. "It's hard to think of anything that could cause more resentment. In most people's eyes, there's a very thin line between allowing someone to die and murdering them, particularly when it's their own life in question. Try to imagine being an ordinary citizen, getting old and watching the people you loved die. Imagine there were immortal sorcerers selfishly denying you the potion. How would you feel?"

"What could they do about it?"

"Get angry and resentful. At the moment, most ordinary folk see the Coven as a necessary evil. They don't like sorcerers, but we provide stability and protection. The Protectorate exists in this balance. Lorimal's potion would shift everything."

"Bykoda on her own holds the north in thrall. I'm sure the Coven could contain the disquiet."

"Yes, and that's the problem. At the moment, the Coven governs by consent when it bothers to govern at all. Mostly, we let the guilds sort out their own business. If we withheld the potion, we'd lose people's trust, and in turn, we'd be unable to trust them. The Coven would have to govern by decree. No matter how well intentioned we might start out, in time, we'd become corrupt. When you run other people's lives for them, you begin by treating them as children and end up treating them as slaves. The Protectorate would become a tyranny, run solely for the benefit of the Coven."

"You'd see sorcerers die just to keep the ungifted happy?"

"Yes. And that's exactly what you swore to do. To give your life, if need be, to protect the citizens of the Protectorate."

"I don't see the oath as referring to something like this."

"Neither did I at the time. I was thinking more about something like fighting a horde of dragons. Agreeing to submit to old age is no different, just less heroic sounding. You don't end up any deader."

Levannue got to her feet and said vehemently, "One sorcerer is worth ten thousand ungifted."

"Why?" Tevi entered the debate for the first time. Levannue ignored her, so she asked again, "Can a sorcerer be happier or suffer more than a potter?"

"No, but they can achieve greater things." Levannue condescended to snap an answer.

"What do their achievements count for? You obviously don't value people in general, or what they think, so how do you measure worth? All you've got is your personal opinion. And I'm sure a potter is as pleased with a well-thrown pot as you are with a spell."

"Some things are more important."

"I'd say a useful pot is better than a useless spell."

"And we're taking about a spell that could inflict misery on millions." Jemeryl added her weight.

"I see your mind's made up." Levannue got to her feet angrily.

"Don't go far."

"I'm hardly likely to run away on foot, and I see you have the horses tightly mind-locked," Levannue threw over her shoulder as she marched away.

"So you've tried?" Tevi asked, amused, although Levannue was no longer close enough to hear.

Jemeryl stood by Tevi's shoulder. "Am I being brave or stupid?"

"In doing what?"

"Refusing Levannue's offer to share the spell. That's what this discussion was about, you realise."

"You sounded totally against using the potion," Tevi said, surprised.

"I was arguing generally. It's harder when it gets to specifics, like you and me. Will I remember this day when I'm on my deathbed and curse myself as a fool? No wonder the Coven leaders were desperate to keep Lorimal's work secret. Levannue setting herself up as an immortal empress is less of a threat than the truth becoming common knowledge. It presents an utterly appalling temptation." Jemeryl's face twisted in a grimace. "Say something helpful. What do you think?"

"I think I'd take a very simple view."

"Which is?"

"I'm oath-bound to the guild. I've never broken my word in my life."

"If I broke my own oath to the Coven, would you follow me?"

"I..." Tevi's voice died in confusion. She realised that she did not know the answer. "Maybe. But if it helps, I'll still love you when you're old and wrinkly." Of that much, she was quite sure.

❖

On the following day, their path joined another road running straight across the open plains—unnaturally so. It travelled from one horizon to the other, unbending, as if drawn by a giant craftsman with a ruler. Paving slabs were revealed where the wheel ruts dug deep or weather had scoured the topsoil away. At one spot, a meandering stream had undercut the road. Crumbling slabs of stone jutted from the sides of the gully. Tevi dismounted to examine the ancient workmanship.

"Who made this?"

"I'd guess slave labour did the actual stone-laying. A sorcerer must have commanded it. Don't ask me their name. They were long gone before the Coven was founded," Jemeryl answered.

"Where does it lead?"

"Ahead, it goes over the pass at Denbury and down to the sea. There's still a port where it ends. Behind us, it probably goes to the ruins of a city, out beyond Uzhenek. Whoever the sorcerer was, nothing remains of their empire except this road. The trade route has followed its path for centuries. It's known as the Old West Road."

Tevi hopped back into her saddle and looked up and down the road. No one else was in sight. "It doesn't seem very well used."

"Too late in the year. We'll be all right as long as we don't hang about, but this isn't the season that most people choose to set out."

The truth of Jemeryl's words was self-evident. Autumn was well advanced, with shortening days. They woke most mornings to glistening frost on the long grass, making it crunch underfoot. Probably little more than a month of safe travel remained before the harsh northern winter swept over the plains.

❖

Over the following days, they met only one caravan hastening back to Tirakhalod after its summer trade cycle. They overtook no one going in the same direction as themselves. The few villages they passed were merely huddles of temporary shelters for the nomadic plainsmen.

The interaction of the three women improved. Levannue seemed resigned to accepting her capture with as much grace as possible, although she sometimes gave way to bitterness and was best left alone, fidgeting irritably with the collar. Her relationship with Tevi could never be called warm, but with Jemeryl, mutual regard lightened at times into camaraderie. Lorimal's spell continued to work, and Levannue became gradually but unmistakably more youthful. Tevi guessed that by the time they reached Lyremouth, they would all look about the same age.

The landscape changed. The plains gave way to undulating slopes. To the south, the high Barrodens marched into view. Vegetation became more profuse: first stubby bushes, followed by isolated trees and then clumps of thicket. By the twelfth day from Uzhenek, they were riding through what might pass as woodland. Still the road continued its remorseless advance over the folded ridges and off into the distance, although now trees encroached, narrowing the highway. Roots ploughed through old paving, littering the ground with rubble.

The unbending road held a hypnotic quality, so Tevi received a jolt when she saw the road ahead turn sharply aside. She reined in her horse at the bend. Despite a thick covering of bramble, it was possible to pick out the original line of the road on its old, unwavering course. The new route curved over the hillside, its camber lurching up and down with the contours.

"Do we leave the old road? I thought you said it went all the way to Denbury."

"It's just a detour. We'll join up with the road again soon," Jemeryl answered.

"Why? You're not going to tell me this is a shortcut."

"No. There's an obstruction in the way."

"Can't it be moved?"

"No one's found the courage to try. It's the town of Graka, or by now the ruins of it." Jemeryl guided her horse onto the new track. "Ghouls have taken it. Lots of them, which is unusual. Normally you don't get more than one or two. Graka is notorious. It's the result of a sorcerer's experiment that went very seriously wrong."

"What are ghouls?"

"No one knows for sure. It's hard to get close enough to study them." Jemeryl paused. "Actually, that's not quite true. It's easy to get close. It's getting away afterwards that's the problem."

"They're dangerous?"

"Oh, highly." Despite her words, Jemeryl sounded unconcerned. "They scare people to death. Literally. There's no physical violence, but if they touch people, the lucky ones get heart attacks from sheer terror. The unlucky ones go through stages of madness before hitting catatonic shock. But ghouls have no effect on animals. Most nonhumans can't even see them."

"It's assumed that they directly stimulate the compound fields of the human aura and need to interact with complex reasoning. Even their appearance is purely a mental projection," Levannue added.

Tevi nodded to be polite, although she had only a vague idea what Levannue meant. She stared over the treetops, trying to spot the cursed town. At first, there was only the forest. Then her eyes picked out the crumbling finger of a ruined tower, maybe half a mile distant. Slightly closer, a broken wall peeked between the trees. To one side was a roof with half its tiles missing.

Tevi inched closer to Jemeryl. "You don't sound worried. You're sure you can handle them?"

"I'd have no problems with one. The whole town would be a different matter, but ghouls are tied to one place. People used to think it was their graves, but ghouls aren't human or the remains of anything that used to be human. They merely base their shape on people, although they have a poor grasp of biology and appalling taste in colours."

"We're outside their range?" Tevi guessed, hoping.

"A bit close to be absolutely safe, but they only come out at night. We'll be miles away by sunset. The new road has been cut because the traders get nervous, but as long as it's daylight, you could walk through the centre of town. Do you want to see?"

Tevi realised that she was being teased. Just as she relaxed, a trio of crows erupted from their nests. Tevi's heartbeat leapt. However, there was no sign of danger. The crows flapped in untidy excitement and then, equally abruptly, sank back to their roost. The midday sun bathed the scene, defying any threat. Still, Tevi felt a cold shiver run through her. She fixed her eyes on the road.

By evening, they had rejoined the Old West Road and put several miles between themselves and Graka. They camped under the spreading arms of an ancient oak. Klara took a sentry post high in the branches among clumps of acorns. The ferns of summer had died back, leaving the ground clear of undergrowth. To the south, a swath of grass provided grazing for the horses and a view of the high Barrodens.

While they ate, Jemeryl chatted with Tevi and watched the sunset fade behind the mountains. Levannue kept to one side, eating in silence. Her mood was withdrawn, as it had been since the ghoul town. At last, she put down her bowl and shifted closer.

"Is there nothing I can say to make you reconsider your views on Lorimal's spell?"

It was not the first time Levannue had returned to the subject. Jemeryl was finding it tedious. "No. We've been over it enough."

"You think the Protectorate depends on keeping this spell secret?"

"Yes."

"Because of some vague idea of how the ungifted would react?"

"There's more to it."

"Such as?"

"The Coven. At the moment, we toe the line largely in the hope of advancement. Take Alendy. He's been deputy for a few years. He must have his eye on becoming Guardian. And he won't if Gilliart never dies. Not that he wishes her harm, but how many centuries would he be content playing second fiddle? If we were immortal, it couldn't be long before the Coven fell apart."

"You don't think knowledge and the freedom to learn count for anything?"

"I wouldn't say that, but I'm suspicious of disembodied ideals. The ideals themselves are fine, but when they're needed to excuse actions, they're usually a blanket to hide a feeble justification. If there's a genuine problem, people point it out. They only resort to words like 'freedom' when they need a smokescreen."

Levannue leant forward, impatient. "You want a genuine problem? How about dying? It's easy for you. You're young, and death must seem a long way off. It's getting much closer for me. Each year passes quicker than the last. Surely you understand that I don't want to die if it isn't necessary."

"It depends how you define what's necessary. I think the Coven is worth dying for."

"Because you value the freedom of the ungifted."

"No, their happiness. The Coven allows millions to live out their mundane little lives with adequate food and shelter for today and the reasonable hope of the same for tomorrow. It may be uninspiring to say we should be willing to die so that lots of people can have a tolerably nice time, but that's what it comes down to." Jemeryl gave an ironic smile. "I just hope they appreciate it."

"Surely you cannot value sorcerers' lives so cheaply."

"Like you did when you tried to murder Jemeryl?" Tevi cut in.

Levannue flinched. "I had no desire to harm her."

"I'd hate to see what you'd do to someone you really had it in for. And how about Druse and Aris?"

"Aris was an accident. I knew she was unstable, but I didn't think she'd kill herself. I had her treatment planned for when she came back. I didn't mean for her to die." Levannue stared unseeing into the fire. "That's when it became serious. Until then, finding the chalice had been a game. Piecing together scrambled clues from Orrago, hunting through the library. It was such an absurd rule, there seemed no harm in breaking it. Then Aris killed herself. She was under a loose link to me, but I couldn't pull her back. I felt her die, and I knew it wasn't a game anymore. It was only a couple of hours later that Druse asked me about the book I'd taken from the library. I was still shocked. I panicked and swapped his drugs. He didn't notice. He was too ill...and too trusting. Next morning, when I woke, I rushed back to stop him, but it was too late. Druse was a friend. Do you know how much I've regretted his death?"

Would you have regretted Jemeryl's? The words were on Tevi's lips. Jemeryl could see them as clearly as if they were spoken.

The silence was broken only by the crackle of the campfire and the rush of wind. Jemeryl watched the column of sparks rise up into the darkening sky and drift away. A whinny and stomp of hooves came from a short distance off.

Tevi got to her feet. "I'm going to check on the horses before it gets too dark."

Jemeryl nodded. Levannue did not stir as Tevi left the fireside. The elderly sorcerer's eyes were fixed on the flames. By the pained set of her lips, she was viewing other scenes, other times. Jemeryl sat quietly, ready for Levannue to speak or keep silent, as she wished.

"Did you talk with Bramell after I left Ekranos?" Levannue's voice was stretched. It was the first time she had mentioned her partner's name.

"No. Tevi spoke to him a few times, but he'd left for Lyremouth by the time I was well enough to talk."

"Do you know how he took my...departure?"

"I've heard that he was upset, but he was coping."

"He would." Levannue managed the ghost of a smile. "Was there talk of him resigning?"

"Some."

"Do you think he knows that I still love—" Levannue's voice broke off. Her head dropped. Jemeryl reached out to touch her shoulder. She was interrupted by Tevi's excited shout.

"Look at that!"

Levannue tensed and drew away.

"What?" Jemeryl's attention was torn.

"Do you get fireflies here? I saw some before, in the desert."

"No. We're too far north."

Jemeryl scrambled to her feet. She halted, unwilling to abandon Levannue in her distress. However, the older sorcerer had withdrawn into herself. Her face was averted, and both hands gripped the opposing elbow, barrierlike, in front of her. It was clearly an end to the conversation.

After one last pitying look, Jemeryl turned away.

Tevi waited on the other side of the road for Jemeryl. "Look there, by that beech tree."

"What is it?"

"I'm sure I saw lights."

Jemeryl's face scrunched as she peered into the dimness. Suddenly, her expression changed to horror. She spun back to where Klara sat sentry, oblivious to any danger.

"Oh, gods, no!" There was panic rather than denial in Jemeryl's voice. "Klara can't see them."

"What is it?" Even as she asked, Tevi felt a cold fist clamp her stomach. "Ghouls?"

Jemeryl did not bother to give confirmation. She held her hands out as if to ward off an attack and slowly turned around.

"How many?" The news had brought Levannue to her feet.

"The whole foul town. We're surrounded."

"You said they didn't travel," Tevi protested.

"These ones have." Jemeryl looked to Levannue by the fire. "What do you recommend?"

"Rissom's web?"

Jemeryl gave a sharp nod. "Tevi, quickly, get the collar off her."

The urgency in Jemeryl's voice goaded Tevi to retrieve the key from the cord about her neck, but as she reached for the collar, she hesitated. "Can we trust her?"

"We've got no choice. I can't hold them off on my own, and right now, she's in as much danger as us." The words were thrown over Jemeryl's shoulder while she dug frantically through the baggage.

The collar fell from Levannue's neck. The elderly sorcerer gave a convulsive shudder and took a deep breath, sucked through flared nostrils. Jemeryl stood up, wrenching two staffs free. She tossed one to Levannue and then spoke to Tevi.

"Stand between us. We're going to create a barrier to keep them out. Stay inside, and try not to panic. It won't be easy, but the barrier will dampen their projections." Jemeryl's voice dropped. "Keep your sword unsheathed and to hand. If you see the net fail before sunrise, use it on yourself. I'll be doing the magical equivalent... if I can."

The two sorcerers faced each other a dozen feet apart. Levannue clasped her staff in both hands and raised it above her head. Jemeryl was only an instant behind her. They began to chant in unison, a driving rhythm that rose and fell in power—strange words, yet disquietingly familiar to Tevi's ears.

She stared around, wondering what to expect. The chant stopped as abruptly as if a knife had severed the string of arcane syllables. Lines of white light leapt between the tips of the staffs and collided in midair. New rays shot from the points of impact, criss-crossing, colliding, and bouncing to the ground. More lines flared from the staffs. Within seconds, a complete dome had been formed over the three women. The web of light glowed luminously in the gloom under the trees.

All action stopped. Minutes passed, and nothing happened. The silence was unnerving. Both sorcerers were rooted to the ground, their sights fixed on other dimensions. Tevi drew her sword, mainly for comfort, and scanned the woods for florescent lights.

Jemeryl's final sentence echoed in her head. Too late now to wish that they had exchanged more personal words, if they were to be their last. Tevi rubbed her face, feeling the chill of her skin. It was also too late to wish they had positioned the barrier with the campfire inside.

Tevi stared ruefully at the warming blaze. With no one to tend them, the flames would soon die.

An unearthly scream rent the air behind her. Tevi spun about as a green, glowing figure hurled itself against the net, shrieking in manic fury. Behind it a second form, pale as a corpse and blotched with vivid purple, crawled across the ground. It shuffled through the leaves until it nosed close to the net, then it plucked at the lines with stubs of fingers sprouting from a wasted arm. Its movements were confused, clawing swipes, and all the while, the ghoul whined and sobbed. More figures emerged, clothed in yellow and green fluorescence. They spun about the web, tearing the silence of the night with screams and howls. Eyes set in molten faces leered in.

The sword slipped from Tevi's hand, and she dropped to her knees. Her whole body shook, fighting back the nausea that churned her stomach and the terror that set the pulse jumping at her throat.

Across the road, the horses grazed calmly as if nothing more dangerous than gnats were abroad. The ghouls seemed equally unaware of them. The focus of their onslaught was the net of light and the three women it sheltered. The deformed shapes writhed around the dome, flowing in a depraved dance. Whispers came from lipless mouths. Towering shapes crashed down upon the net, and senseless, silly, smiling faces chewed on its strands. Unbelievably, the web held firm.

Slowly, as if she feared that a rash movement might provoke a greater frenzy, Tevi grasped the handle of her sword and then edged back to Jemeryl's feet. She averted her eyes from the horror surging outside the net and picked a point near the apex of the dome where the lines of light showed crisp against the night sky. All Tevi could do then was sit, wait, and pray for morning.

Above the mountains, the stars stepped slowly across the heavens while hell ran brawling through the forest. Tevi marked the night's progress by watching the turning sky slide stars from line to line across the web. In desperation, she kept her eyes locked on the stars, battling the urge to cheat herself by moving her head.

Hours crawled by. A dozen times, Tevi's hopes betrayed her when she thought she saw the first hints of morning to the east. In the end, she felt something like surprise when she realised the sky beyond the mountains was truly beginning to pale. She rubbed her eyes and took several deep breaths, then looked again. There was no doubt.

Even as relief flooded over her, it seemed that the intensity of the ghouls' attack was decreasing. For a last time, she lowered her eyes and looked at the monstrosities besieging the web. They were weakening, drawing off. Abruptly, the sounds of chaos stopped. The last pale figures faded away as predawn peace settled beneath the trees. In the distance, a bird sang. Still the net held, as clean and true as it had been all night.

The muscles in Tevi's legs were cramped and frozen. The cold had gnawed into her bones. It took minutes of painful exercise before she could stagger to her feet. She wondered whether it was safe to step through the net and light the fire. In the absence of advice, she thought it best not to try. Instead, she concentrated on stamping feeling back into her limbs.

To the east, the light was growing behind the mountains. The stars above were twinkling out when, with an audible snap, the net vanished. Tevi spun about at Jemeryl's gasp and caught her as she fell forward. Jemeryl's skin was as cold as ice, and her body was trembling violently.

"Are you all right?" Tevi asked.

"I will be. I just want to sit down."

Tevi supported Jemeryl's weight and lowered her gently when, in her inner ear, came Blaze's sardonic voice, drilling out the lessons of the islands. Never, never, never turn your back on your enemy.

Still holding Jemeryl, Tevi twisted just in time to see Levannue complete a throwing motion. Tevi had only an instant to realise that nothing as ordinary as a knife was aimed at them. The invisible projectile hit, and red light exploded. She had the distinct sensation of being turned inside out. Up became down as darkness overwhelmed her.

Chapter Fifteen—In Pursuit

"Wake up, Tevi. Wake up."

Tevi opened her eyes. She was lying where she had fallen. Her body ached, and the pulse throbbed at her temples. Light filtering through the trees was a painful glare. A purposeful rustle came from beside her left ear. Slowly, she rolled her head sideways and found herself staring into two beady eyes three inches from her nose. The effort of focusing at such short range made Tevi groan and close her eyes again. Klara gave a disappointed croak. Then memory of the previous night's events rushed back, and the pain was forgotten. Tevi shoved herself into a sitting position and looked around.

The sun had climbed above the horizon. Clean, bright beams fell dappled between trees alive with liquid birdsong. Two horses were grazing at the roadside. By the sun's position, Tevi estimated that well over an hour had passed since she and Jemeryl had been blasted senseless. There was no sign of any threat, or of Levannue.

Jemeryl lay sprawled a few feet away. Tevi scrambled to her side. Jemeryl's hands felt clammy, and her face held a bloodless pallor, but a strong pulse beat at her wrist. A raw graze on her cheek was the only apparent injury.

"Jem, are you all right?" Tevi shook her shoulder.

Jemeryl's face tightened into a frown, and her hands moved slightly.

"Jem?"

"I'm cold." Jemeryl mouthed rather than spoke the words.

Only blackened ashes marked where the campfire had been, but two blankets were among the scattered baggage. Tevi helped Jemeryl into a patch of sunshine, wrapped her in the blankets and then set about rekindling the fire. By the time that flames were leaping over the logs, Jemeryl was looking more alert. A bowl of porridge further improved her condition.

"I take it Levannue has fled?"

"Either that or she's popped off to pick blackberries for our supper."

"And she knocked us out cold so not to spoil the surprise on her return?" Jemeryl had recovered enough to indulge in humour.

"She might be up to something just as strange. Else why didn't she kill us while we were unconscious?"

"Perhaps she lacked the strength after she'd removed the mind-lock from the horse and saddled it. Holding the net was hard work. If she feels like me, she wouldn't be in a fit state to get serious with a knife."

"She could have stabbed us first and then escaped at her leisure."

"Perhaps she's too tired to think straight. I know I am." Jemeryl rubbed her face. "Most likely she couldn't face killing in cold blood. I really don't think she's that callous."

"I guess there's not much point debating Levannue's motives. We can ask her when we catch her." Tevi looked at Jemeryl with concern. "How do you feel? Can you travel? We daren't stay here another night."

"I'll be fine. The blast was a bit much after holding the net all night. What I need is a good sleep. But Levannue must be in the same state. Once she lies down, the end of the world won't wake her. If you can keep going, we'll overtake her, and I can guarantee she'll be too tired to fight off a geriatric dormouse."

Tevi nodded and looked at the sun. By the time they were ready to move, Levannue would have a three-hour lead. The hunt would begin again, and this time, Levannue would be expecting them. Jemeryl seemed confident that they would have no problems, but Tevi felt doubts twist in her gut. There was trouble ahead.

❖

The ground was dry and hard. Even so, Tevi was able to pick out Levannue's trail, heading west. "She went this way."

"Are you sure?" Jemeryl's eyes were dark hollows in an ashen face. Tevi judged that she clung to the reins more to stop herself falling than to prevent the animal's straying.

"I'm sure. I'm not up to the level of a guild scout. But I grew up hunting wild boar through forests like these."

"Good. I don't think I'm up to helping you magically."

"Do you think Levannue will keep to the road?"

"I should think so. As I've said, sorcerers don't find flying a practical mode of transport at the best of times. Right now, Levannue will be doing well just to keep sitting on her horse."

Tevi thought that Jemeryl also looked worryingly insecure once she had been helped to mount, although she made no complaint.

As they left, Tevi gave one last look back at the campsite under the trees. She was relieved beyond measure that Levannue was heading away from Graka. The surroundings looked peaceful. A shudder ran through Tevi. She would never forget the night she had spent there, but she wished so desperately that she could.

They rode in silence, Jemeryl with shoulders hunched and head sagging and Tevi scouring the ground for hoofprints. The forest stretched away over the hills. The only things disturbing the peace were the rustling of small animals through the leaf litter and the occasional distant bellow of a deer. The air was rich with the musty smell of autumn.

The sun had just passed midday when a path left the Old West Road, heading south. A few yards farther on, a trickle of water oozed across the side trail. A solitary line of hoofprints was imprinted in the mud.

Tevi examined the marks. "This is Levannue's horse. She's left the main road."

"I wonder if she knows where she's going. Because I certainly don't."

"You don't have any idea?"

"None." Jemeryl scrunched her face as she battled with tiredness. "A group of minor sorcerers established a centre for studying something obscure up in the mountains around here about forty years ago. I can't remember what, but the group fell to infighting after a few years. And it was more a hermit's retreat than a city. They certainly didn't go in for building roads."

"This path is much less than forty years old." Tevi examined the sawn stump of a sapling. "I'd say this was cut back during the spring."

"And if Levannue doesn't know who's maintaining the road, it may turn out to be a big surprise for all of us," Jemeryl said with a trace of a smile.

The new path was too narrow and uneven for carts. It wound up into the foothills, rolling from ridge to ridge, climbing ever higher. As the afternoon progressed, the trees thinned out. Oaks gave way to birch, interspersed, to Jemeryl's disgust, with patches of rowan. In late afternoon, the trail crossed a shallow ford. The water rippled over a bed of smooth, round pebbles. To the west, the sun hovered low. Its last misty rays played warmly over a hillside of brown and orange.

Tevi knelt to examine the marks in a patch of wet sand. "A guild scout could be more accurate, but we're definitely gaining on her. She can't be more than an hour ahead of us." She got no answer. Jemeryl was swaying in the saddle, her face colourless and drawn. "Jem, are you all right?"

"Do I look it? Don't panic. I'm just very tired."

Clearly Jemeryl was in no fit state to ride. Tevi walked to her side and slipped her foot free from its stirrup. Before Jemeryl could object, Tevi swung up behind her and reached around to take control of the reins.

"Lean against me. Sleep if you can. We can swap horses when this one gets tired."

"I'm fine."

"No, you're not."

The most worrying thing for Tevi was that Jemeryl was too tired to argue. She closed her eyes and sank back into Tevi's arms.

"If we're lucky, Levannue will be passed out around the next corner, but it's my guess that we won't catch up with her until after nightfall. Can you hold out that long?" Tevi asked.

"Only if the ghouls don't get us first."

"You don't think—" Fear sharpened Tevi's voice.

"No. It was a bad joke. We must be outside their range."

"You said that last night."

"True. It was a fluke. The phase of the moon or something. We can ask Levannue when we catch her. That sort of thing is her speciality." Jemeryl's voice was a soft mumble.

"Perhaps that's why she didn't kill us. She knew the ghouls would come again tonight and do her job for her."

"There's nothing to worry about. Ghouls are quite predictable."

"They weren't last night. Perhaps these are a different sort of ghoul."

"There's only one sort, and they don't travel. To get them here, Levannue would have to..." Jemeryl's voice died. Suddenly, her eyes snapped open, all tiredness swept away. "Quick, check the bags."

"What for?"

"A charm. Levannue's speciality. She could call a ghoul halfway across the Protectorate if she wanted to."

"You said the collar would stop her working magic."

"No, it only handicaps her, like working blindfolded. She wouldn't perceive the aura of the charm, but she wouldn't need to. The exact combination is probably etched in her memory." Jemeryl pulled a bag onto her lap and tugged open the drawstring.

Tevi jumped down and pulled open the pack on the other horse. "What would the charm look like? How do I—" Tevi's words stopped abruptly. Lying in her palm was a small bundle of leaves, bones and feathers. "Like this?"

From Jemeryl's expression, no other answer was needed. Tevi looked to the west. Framed at the end of a long valley, the sun was kissing the skyline. Barely half an hour remained before dark.

"What do we do? Search the other bags?"

"There isn't time. And the stuff will be contaminated. We must leave the charm here as a decoy and get as far away as we can. And wash your hands, check your clothes, and..." Jemeryl pinched the bridge of her nose. "We passed a stand of rowan a couple of miles back. We need to sort ourselves out and go there. If we can make it before sunset."

"You hate rowan."

"So do ghouls, and it should disguise any residual traces of the charm."

They left everything except the clothes they wore, the saddles, and one blanket in a heap by the ford and then spurred the horses into a race against the failing light. Dusk had set in by the time they got level with the rowan grove. Between them and the trees was fifty yards of matted scrub. Tevi tore her eyes from the darkness flooding into the valley, dreading the sight of dancing florescent lights.

Jemeryl's endurance had gone. Her knees buckled as she dismounted. Tevi drew her sword and hacked her way through to the rowan, carrying Jemeryl. Desperation added strength, speeding her progress. The horses followed obligingly.

Tevi deposited Jemeryl beneath the trees, unsaddled the horses, and then settled down to keep guard. Klara perched in the branches. Wrapped in the blanket, Jemeryl did no more than mumble "Gods, I hate rowan" before giving in to exhaustion. Tevi was determined to face whatever the darkness might bring, but she also had not slept the night before. Her face contorted as she tried to keep her eyelids open. Eventually, she gave up the struggle and curled under the blanket beside Jemeryl.

After all, she thought, surrendering to fate, *there's nothing I can do anyway. If they come.*

Tevi awoke at dawn. She lay on her back, looking up at wisps of blue sky through a swaying lacework of rowan branches, heavy with bright red berries, and soaked in the relief of greeting a new morning. It was a morning that Levannue had planned she should not see. No doubt existed about the traitor's intentions. Tevi's jaw clenched. The image of the ghouls arriving again was all too easy to conjure up. She breathed out hard and watched the cloud of her breath trail away white.

Jemeryl's arm lay flopped across her. Tevi studied her sleeping lover. The night's rest had softened the dark bruises under Jemeryl's eyes, and her face was peaceful and unguarded. The sunlight heightened the warm flush of her skin. Gently, Tevi disentangled herself from the encircling arm and stood up, brushing dead leaves from her clothes. The movement woke Jemeryl, though she did no more than pull the blanket up about her neck.

"We're still here, then?" Jemeryl asked without opening her eyes.

"So it would seem."

"Then is breakfast a possibility?"

"I don't know. We left everything at the ford. It depends on what the ghouls have left." Tevi hoisted a saddle onto the nearest horse.

"They won't have eaten much. As ethereal spirits, they have remarkably light appetites, although it still doesn't pay to invite them to dinner."

"Their table manners are pretty poor," Klara elaborated.

Jemeryl looked up at the waving rowan branches and winced. "I realise I should regard these particular trees with gratitude, but I'd rather do it from a distance."

"Get up, then." Tevi yanked the blanket away, unmoved by Jemeryl's yelp of complaint.

It did not take long to ready the horses and start back. Strands of mist drifted around the horses' legs. In low-lying spots, treetops floated above a sea of cloud, though the rising sun was burning through.

"How long do you think Levannue was planning this?" Tevi asked as they rode.

"Probably ever since we left Uzhenek. She couldn't have collected all the bits she needed for the charm on the spur of the moment, certainly not with us watching her."

"Would she have known the road led by Graka?"

"Yes. The town is notorious. And once she'd called the ghouls, we had no option but to remove her collar. I couldn't have held them all off on my own. "

"I wonder what she'd have done if I hadn't spotted the ghouls when I did."

"No doubt she had something planned. She'd been very careful up to then." Jemeryl shook her head at her own folly. "I shouldn't have let myself feel sympathy for her."

"It wouldn't have made any difference."

"Oh, it would. Towards morning, I felt her end of the net weaken. I thought, 'She's old,' so I let her push more of the burden onto me. Of course, she was just gathering her strength, ready to cast the aural bolt. I should have made her carry her share. It might have stopped her escape."

"And her plans didn't end there."

"I know. I wish I could believe she left the charm by oversight."

"Why?"

"I don't like to think I'm so gullible. The version of events that she gave by the campfire—I felt sorry for her. I thought she was just an old woman who was frightened of dying and hadn't meant any harm. I was taken in by a lying, murderous traitor."

"If it makes you feel happier, I'd guess the truth lies somewhere in the middle, with a strong pinch of self-delusion on her part thrown in."

"She meant to kill us."

"True. It wasn't as sure as stabbing us while we were unconscious, but it's definitely her style—like leaving poison to be taken when she's absent. Perhaps if she doesn't witness her victim's fate, she can tell herself it wasn't her fault."

The ford appeared around the next bend. Everything looked unchanged. The bags were piled where they had been left. Jemeryl stared at the scene with her lips tightly compressed.

"They were here last night?" Tevi asked.

"Oh, yes."

While Tevi prepared breakfast, Jemeryl went through their belongings, removing all traces of the charm.

"You know, it must have added impetus to Levannue's flight—the fear that we'd overtake her before nightfall," Tevi said after a while.

"Undoubtedly."

"Maybe she'll slow down now if she feels safe."

Jemeryl paused in her work. "Maybe. But I don't think Levannue will rely on the ghouls. She's too cautious. We must be on the lookout for further traps."

"We can't go too slowly. I reckon Levannue will have nearly half a day's lead on us."

"At least now that I've slept, I can help track her. It shouldn't be too hard. There hasn't been anyone else along this path for months, so there are no distracting auras."

"Apart from this bit reeking of ghouls," Klara added.

"You still can't tell who made this path?"

"No."

"Call me a pessimist, but I can't see it being the work of a sweet little old man who's going to welcome us into his home like long-lost relatives."

"You're a pessimist," Jemeryl said. "And almost certainly right."

❖

It soon became obvious that Levannue wasn't relying on the ghouls. She pressed ahead at a rate that was savage on the horses. In mid-afternoon, Tevi and Jemeryl stopped for a pitifully inadequate break. Lush grass lined the banks of a stream, yet the horses were too tired to eat. Tevi rubbed their drenched coats with fistfuls of leaves, more to ease her conscience than for any aid it might give. She could feel the animals trembling.

"We can't push the horses this hard. It's cruel."

Jemeryl lay on her back a few feet away with her arms crossed over her eyes. "I know, but we must catch Levannue."

"Is there nothing you can do?"

"I can try." Jemeryl sat and hugged her knees while flexing her neck. Tevi was concerned to see signs of exhaustion returning to her lover's face.

Jemeryl stood in front of one horse. Deftly, she placed her palms over its eyes. Her fingers splayed out towards its ears. The startled horse tried to back away, but almost immediately it calmed. Only its ears flicked, as if trying to dislodge a fly. Gradually, a change came over the animal. The trembling went. Vigour returned to the set of its legs and arch of its neck. When Jemeryl stepped away, the horse tossed back its head, fidgeting like a skittish colt, radiating strength.

Tevi was impressed. "Could you do the same for me?"

"Yes, but I wouldn't want to. It's not safe." Jemeryl moved to the other horse.

"Does it harm the horses?"

"Not if it only lasts a day or two, but much longer, and it will kill them. It's like burning a candle at both ends."

After the short rest, they continued until nightfall. They resumed the chase at first light. The trail no longer climbed so relentlessly, though the landscape was more rugged. Sheer cliffs of limestone broke from the bleak mountainsides. Snow covered the tops and glinted in the depths of crevasses. The streams were icy. Winter was close, and both women were glad of their hooded, fur-lined cloaks—presents from Bykoda. At the end of the morning, a squall of sleet pounded them for an hour and turned the ground to slush.

The afternoon was well advanced when they descended into a wooded valley. A piercing wind hissed through the trees, carrying bursts of freezing rain that stung like needles. At the bottom of the slope, their trail met another, wider path. It was well worn and clearly well used. Jemeryl frowned as she looked both ways along the path. Her head leaned to one side as if listening.

"Of course. The dwarves. Several clans live in these mountains."

"Dwarves? I saw some in Lyremouth. "

"Those you meet in the Protectorate are a bit unusual. Most won't have anything to do with humans, but they travel a lot among themselves. They're very keen on keeping in touch with all their relatives."

"What you mean is, this lot won't be friendly," Tevi said bluntly.

Jemeryl's nose wrinkled. "It might depend what side of bed they got out of this morning, but they shouldn't give us trouble. They've learned to treat human sorcerers with respect. They don't have any of their own, although they all possess extra senses to humans. Their eyes can see in the dark, for example, and they're immune to illusion."

"I thought they were just like us...except a bit shorter."

"That's deceptive. They're really quite strange. They have their own laws and culture, totally centred around family, wealth, and revenge."

"Doesn't sound so different to some people I've met."

"The dwarves are an awful lot more excessive about it." Jemeryl pursed her lips. "Do you have any idea which direction Levannue went? Up until now, there's been nothing to distract from her aura, but the dwarves confuse things around here."

Tevi dropped to the ground and paced a few yards in either direction. Where the road led east, she crouched and brushed aside the wind-blown leaves. "This way."

The new trail kept to the valley floor, driving deep into a mountain range. The peaks rose on either side, while the walls of the valley became closer and steeper until they were passing along a flat-bottomed gorge. Bare faces of limestone gleamed ghostly white as the light faded. They camped in the shelter of a knot of stunted trees, enveloped in matted undergrowth.

The cold wind blustered throughout the night, rustling the leaves. Towards dawn, it strengthened with a damp heaviness that carried the promise of rain. In the overcast light, Tevi and Jemeryl continued their pursuit. They had been travelling for less than an hour when they came across the doused remains of a campfire in a narrow clearing. Tevi poked the embers. Smoke wafted from the charred logs.

"How long?" Jemeryl whispered.

"Half an hour, maybe a little more."

Jemeryl was about to return to the path, but Tevi spotted a nearby opening in the bushes. A track wove through the tress. It was probably the work of deer, but something much larger, the size of a horse, had recently passed along.

"She went this way."

For the sake of quietness, they left their own horses behind and crept along the track. Klara went ahead. Suddenly, the hefty snort of a horse broke the silence. The sound came from less than fifty yards away. Tevi froze. The dense undergrowth concealed whatever was ahead. She glanced over her shoulder. Jemeryl had her eyes closed. As the minutes passed, her expression became more confused.

"Klara can't find her," Jemeryl whispered.

Slowly, inching from bush to bush, the women advanced until they reached the end of the trees. Before them, broken rock lined the foot of a towering cliff face. Levannue's horse wandered nearby, alone and packless. There was no sign of Levannue. Jemeryl edged into the open and looked at the weathered wall of limestone. Deep cracks gashed the surface, and caves punched black chasms into the rock.

"She's entered the dwarf mines."

"Do we wait for her to come out?"

Jemeryl shook her head. "I don't think she's coming out. Otherwise, she'd have taken better care of her horse and not let it stray."

"I'm not sure if I fancy following her in there."

"Nor do I. It would be impossible to track her. We'd be more likely to run afoul of the dwarves first."

"Won't they object to Levannue?"

"They will if they find her. It might depend on what her plan is."

"Might she be in league with them?"

"Unlikely, else she'd do the same thing we're going to."

"Which is?"

"Go in by the front door."

❖

They collected Levannue's horse and returned to the main path. The threatened rain held off while they rode deeper into the mountains. On either side, the gorge closed in until the tops of the cliffs hung over them. The dull light was reduced still further. Trees were replaced first by straggling shrubs and ivy, and then by cushions of moss. In the barren landscape of rock, echoes were snatched away by the cold wind.

The path climbed in high steps, with the rock hacked back where necessary to allow passage. A small river cascaded down the gorge in a series of waterfalls. Spray was whipped up by the wind. The gorge had narrowed to fifty feet when they rose over one final step and saw a fortified wall spanning the valley floor. The battlements stood three times Tevi's height. Heavy wooden doors were firmly shut. The river poured out through a barred culvert at the side.

Shouts and the sounds of activity erupted behind the wall. Heads moved behind the parapet and then were still. When they were within twenty yards of the gates, Jemeryl dismounted and gestured for Tevi to do the same. They walked a few steps clear of the horses. The only noises were the rush of water and hooves shuffling on bare rock, but the glint of helmets and arrowheads revealed the presence of the dwarves.

"I don't suppose you speak common dwarvish?" Jemeryl whispered to Tevi.

"No. Don't you?"

"Only a few standard phrases. I'm not up to holding conversations. If I'd known we were coming here, I'd have brought a translating device."

"If I'd known we were coming here, I'd have slit Levannue's throat back in Uzhenek."

Jemeryl raised her voice. *"Llig duhli kurtorct. Tivil duhli Torgan ut."* She smiled wryly. "I'm hoping that was 'We come in peace. Take us to your leader'."

A cry came back. *"Zkath drogn ritu."*

"What did that mean?"

"I think it was a question."

"How about *Why don't you go away*?" Klara suggested a translation.

The shout was not repeated. For a long time, nothing happened; then the gate opened a crack, and a small bowlegged figure emerged, hefting a large axe and glaring belligerently. The dwarf was of stocky build. Although his head came no higher than a human's waist, Tevi estimated that the fists clenched around the axe shaft were as broad as her own. His clothing was brilliant blue but was almost completely covered in chain mail and bands of armour. A long red beard spilled over his chest.

The dwarf advanced slowly and walked around them. Once the circuit was complete, he stood in front of the two women, staring intensely. Seen close to, his eyes were dark, devoid of whites. Tevi smiled in what she hoped was considered a friendly fashion.

"Trogn duh." The dwarf spat out the words, but as he turned to go,

he gestured for Jemeryl and Tevi to follow. Three other dwarves slipped out to claim the horses.

Inside the wall was an enclosed courtyard lined by low stone buildings that could have been either stables or barracks. Ahead was a cliff face, breached by the mouth of a cave from which the river gushed, bubbling over rocks. Strands of vegetation adorned its edges.

The road continued unchecked, plunging into the cave beside the leaping water and disappearing into darkness. A score of dwarves were assembled in the open. More lined the wall, while others peered from windows. The harsh shouts of the captain spurred eight armed warriors to form a guard around Tevi and Jemeryl. Further gestures indicated that the two women, with their escort, should proceed into the cave.

By the time they had gone sixty yards, the light had faded to a sheen on wet rock. A turn in the road left them in darkness so thick it made no difference whether Tevi opened or closed her eyes. Only the ground beneath her feet relieved her of the sensation that she was adrift in a black void. The dwarves marched on. One pushed Tevi's back.

"Jem, can you see anything?"

"It's all right; I'm creating a light globe."

"Won't the dwarves mind?"

"Maybe, but it might be good for them to know that I can."

A glow blossomed in the darkness, growing into a steady ball of light. It illuminated the tunnel in a stark contrast of pale limestone and shadows, and glinted off grotesque stalactite formations that rolled down the rough rock walls in molten globules. The chain links of the guards' armour threw back the light.

Although they may have had no need for it, the dwarves were certainly aware of the light. Its creation was greeted by a burst of guttural muttering. There was no direct appeal to Jemeryl, but thereafter, the dwarves marched with crisper discipline and clearly viewed their guests with more respect.

The road continued through echoing vaults and narrow galleries. For a long time, it climbed gently before descending by a spiral stairway cut into the rock. The river disappeared and returned repeatedly, thundering along eroded basins. It was finally lost, and its roar faded. Frequent passages led off from the main route. The dark shafts and fissures swallowed the beams from Jemeryl's light globe as they passed.

They had gone about two miles when Tevi noticed the nature of the cave change. The floor had always been as level as the streets of Lyremouth, but now the walls were also smooth. Increasingly, they met with other dwarves, who viewed the humans with suspicious scowls. Doors started to appear on the walls. From beyond the circle of light came the sound of voices, growing ever more numerous. Soon, they walked in busy streets where shouts from the guards were needed to clear the way. The crowds, surging around at waist height, made Tevi feel out of scale.

They entered a wide thoroughfare. Columns were carved from the rock on either side. Stone faces glared sternly from friezes. This was clearly the heart of the city. The doorways were grander than any they had yet seen. The largest of all were huge double doors at the far end. A dozen dwarf warriors stood guard outside. They stepped back to allow the women and their escort to enter.

Another corridor ended in a large hall with a raised dais at one end. The floor was polished to a mirror shine. The walls were covered with banners and racks displaying axes, bows, and spears. Embossed patterns ran across the ceiling. The armed escort melted into the shadows, and two officials took their place. These dwarves were also dressed in a military fashion, although their armour looked more ceremonial than warlike.

"The royal audience hall," Jemeryl said as she and Tevi were directed to a spot several yards from the dais.

News of their arrival had obviously preceded them. The hall was a bustle of activity. Dwarves rushed back and forth before finding places around the edge. Everyone seemed to be shouting, but the sounds faded to muttering and then silence as an elderly dwarf was escorted into the hall. He stood proudly in the centre of the dais and glared down at his visitors. His armour gleamed golden. Precious stones glinted in the dragon motif that coiled around his breastplate. His stubby hands were heavy with rings.

"The king?" Tevi whispered.

Jemeryl nodded. "Hopefully he has an interpreter in his retinue. One way to find out." She raised her voice. "Our greetings to your majesty. May your wealth be as great as your wisdom."

The guess proved correct; one dwarf stepped forward and loudly translated her words. The king nodded sternly in acknowledgement.

Jemeryl continued, "We have come to offer help. A source of great danger has just entered your kingdom."

This time, the king replied in a harsh, guttural voice. *"Zkorn kaligwi ritu ut drogn duhli. Zkorn throgal ritu lan duhli."*

"Why think you we need warnings? Why offer you to help us?" the interpreter provided.

"We come from the Protectorate of Lyremouth in search of a traitor who has hidden in your kingdom. It is true we want her for crimes against the Protectorate, but while she is here, she is a danger to you and your subjects."

"You have lose her. Us you want find her. You can go. If we find her in our land, we deal with her. We need not your help," came the translated answer.

"I think you might. The traitor is a Protectorate sorcerer, like myself."

When these words were translated, the king frowned and examined the two women, as if taking them seriously for the first time.

"What help offer you?" The interpreter's tone also reflected a different mood.

"We can tell you where she entered your kingdom. If you find her and lead us to her, I will attempt to capture or kill her. She is a great sorcerer. It may be beyond my power to defeat her, but you lose nothing by my trying."

"Perhaps she is the good sorcerer. Perhaps you is the danger. What proof have you?"

"None, except the evidence of my good faith in that I came to you. It is my enemy who has stolen into your kingdom like a thief." Jemeryl paused while that was translated and then added, "And at the worst case, if you take my offer, you will have only one sorcerer to deal with, rather than two."

"We think about it."

The king gave one last, hard glare and then left the hall. All about, the assembly broke into a collection of confused melees.

"I may not know the language, but from the king's posture, I think the answer is yes," Tevi whispered as they were led from the hall.

"Of course. Stupid kings don't last long among the dwarves. He can't afford to have Levannue on his land any more than Bykoda could."

They were taken through a series of corridors. Tevi and Jemeryl were repeatedly obliged to duck under low openings. At last, they reached a full-height door and were ushered through. The room was obviously intended to be their quarters in the dwarf city. The saddlebags from the horses were already piled in the centre.

The room was a comfortable size, although the decoration was grossly overdone to human eyes. Everything was covered in intricate designs and flamboyant colours. Gold and silver were abundant. The furniture was a haphazard collection, but at least some had been made with humans in mind. There were even gilt candleholders fastened on the walls.

Once their hosts had gone, Tevi walked to a chair and sat down. It was somewhat lower than she would have liked, forcing her to sit with her legs out straight.

"Do you think we'll be here long?" she asked.

"I hope not. I'd guess that search parties are being dispatched at this very moment."

"I hope they find her quickly. I'm not keen on living underground."

"And I don't think the dwarves are keen on having us here. In fact, everyone will be happier once we're away. I'm not sure how long I can put up with the decoration." Jemeryl grimaced.

"Oh, well, look on the bright side; it's nice to be with men who look the part."

"What do you mean?"

"The bright colours and beards. I've never got used to men on the mainland shaving. It doesn't seem quite right."

"They're not men."

"All right, they're dwarves. But at least you can be sure they're male."

"Actually, you can't. Dwarves are hermaphrodites."

"But—"

"I'll admit most people get confused by the beards. But technically, all dwarves should be referred to as it, rather than he."

Tevi stared at Jemeryl and then slid down in the chair. With a sound halfway between a laugh and a groan of despair, she buried her face in her hands.

Chapter Sixteen—The Cairn and the Remembrance

For all the opulence of their room, Tevi and Jemeryl were virtual prisoners. A guard was always outside their door. Servants attended to them regularly, and occasionally, the interpreter came with questions, but they were never allowed out. The time dragged. For diversion, they requested chalk and a slate, and Jemeryl gave Tevi her first writing lessons.

By Tevi's estimation, it was their fifth day in the dwarf city when news finally came. Tevi was practising her letters, sitting cross-legged on the floor, while Jemeryl was stretched out on the bed, feeding breakfast remains to Klara. The door opened, and the interpreter returned in the company of two other dwarves. Tevi scrambled to her feet, expecting further questions.

The interpreter was a small yet extremely rotund figure, stout even by dwarven standards. Unlike the others, he wore practically no armour—only a light chain surcoat with the securing buckles left undone, so the mail flapped over his bulging stomach. Tevi studied his girth with interest. She had frequently wondered whether he was pregnant or simply overweight.

"We found the one you hunt. You get ready to go now."

Jemeryl swivelled into a sitting position on the side of the bed. "Does she know that she's been found?"

"How we tell what a sorcerer know?" The interpreter talked briefly with another dwarf. "We think not. We careful were."

"Is she far away?" Tevi asked her own question.

"Four, five hours. No more. We give food. We take you there. What more you need now?"

"I don't—"

Jemeryl interrupted. "Could you get my friend a lantern? I can make my own light, but she might need something...in case we become separated."

"We see. You pack now. The guide soon be here." After rigid bows, the three dwarves left.

"What did you mean about becoming separated?" Tevi demanded.

"Levannue is an experienced sorcerer. She may defeat me," Jemeryl replied while shoving items into the saddlebags. She stopped and faced Tevi. "Is there any point in me asking you to stay here?"

"None at all."

"It would be wisest. Or you could go to the entrance and wait for me. If I didn't show up within a day, you could get news to the Guardian."

"I'm not leaving you."

"I'd be happier knowing you were safe."

"But how would I feel, knowing you were in danger? Anyway, it's irrelevant; you're going to beat Levannue." Tevi picked up a bag and started to help pack. "Or I'll never forgive you."

Their guides arrived as Tevi and Jemeryl were tightening the final drawstring. The ten dwarf warriors formed a silent, surly line outside the room. One presented a small brass lantern to Tevi. She attached it to the side of a bag after a meaningful look at Jemeryl.

The captain of the dwarf band spoke. "We go now." His accent was so guttural that the words were almost unintelligible, but it was a relief that he knew some of their language.

The departure added little to their knowledge of the dwarf city. Tevi suspected that the route was chosen to avoid things the dwarves did not want them to see. Their hosts had shown an intrinsic love of secrecy. Apart from Jemeryl's conjured globe, the only light was on an altarlike structure, which they glimpsed in passing, but their escort would not let Jemeryl stop to examine it.

Soon, they left the inhabited region behind. For a time, they travelled on level paths hewn into the rock. The journey then continued into natural caverns with slick, sloping floors. The party scrambled, climbed, and slid their way for several hours until the dwarves stopped in a large cavern.

The captain pointed to a narrow slit halfway up the wall. "In there. The bad woman. She sleep."

With no attempt at stealth, he scrambled up the rock, heedless of the noise from dislodged stones bouncing to the floor.

"Won't she hear?" Tevi asked, confused.

"No. She sleep."

"What does he mean?" Tevi turned her questions to Jemeryl.

"I'm not sure, but we might as well go and look."

"And rethink the plans for a surprise attack," Klara added.

They dropped their packs and followed the dwarf captain. The cracked surface presented an easy climb. When they reached the cleft, they saw that it was the entrance to a sloping shaft, so narrow that Tevi and Jemeryl were forced to squeeze through sideways. Eventually, they edged into the chamber beyond, where the dwarf captain was leaning against the wall, waiting for them impatiently.

The space was fifty feet across. The floor was hollowed out like a dish; lines of stalactites ran across the ceiling. In the centre was a shimmering green sphere encasing Levannue, lying motionless on a limestone block.

"Oh, of course," Jemeryl exclaimed.

"Is she alive?"

"Yes. She's created a force field and gone into a trance. There's no need to whisper. We won't wake her. The roof collapsing wouldn't do that."

"How long can she stay like this?"

"Indefinitely. Entranced sleep is easy. You can set when you want to wake. The drawback is that you still grow old, but that's no longer a problem for Levannue. She could stay here a hundred years and not come out until everyone who knows what she'd done is dead."

Tevi studied the sleeping sorcerer thoughtfully. "Do you think this has been her intention all along? The reason why she came north?"

"Maybe. These caves are a good place to hide. The dwarves might have found her, but they couldn't get to her, and they wouldn't have rushed out to tell anyone. And even if rumours did get back to Lyremouth, what would they have been? Simply a tale of a mysterious woman asleep in a northern cave."

"So can we leave her here and go for help?"

Jemeryl thought it over. "We don't know how long she means to stay put. She might be merely sleeping out winter and be gone by the time we return."

"Is that likely?"

"She can't be certain the ghouls got us. Even if she intends to spend decades in a trance, she doesn't have to do it here. The safest thing, from her point of view, is moving to a new location come spring, before we can return with reinforcements. And we can't risk losing her again."

"So what now? Can you break down the barrier?"

"Yes."

"What can I do?"

"Stay safely out of the way."

"There must be something."

"There's nothing you could do except be a target for Levannue to attack." Jemeryl squeezed Tevi's shoulder. "I'm afraid I'm in this on my own. Come on, let's go back. I might as well eat something first."

They returned to the outer cavern and found some provisions; however, neither woman had much appetite. The thought of the coming battle left Tevi's mouth dry. Food stuck in her throat and was impossible to swallow.

Jemeryl also made little attempt to eat. "I would be so much happier if you were a long way away."

"There's no point. Levannue must realise that I'm the only one, apart from you, who knows she's here. If she kills you, she'll chase me all the way back to the Protectorate to keep her whereabouts a secret."

"Maybe."

In unspoken agreement, they stopped the pretence of a meal and packed away the unwanted food. Jemeryl lit the lantern for Tevi.

"Whichever way the battle goes, it won't take long. If I don't come out after it goes quiet, you should sneak back in. Even if I don't kill Levannue, I might injure her. If she's weak or unconscious it will be your best chance to finish her." Jemeryl squared her shoulders. "Wish me luck."

Tevi wrapped her arms about Jemeryl. "Take care. I love you."

"I know, and I love you."

Tevi closed her eyes and kissed Jemeryl's lips very slowly and deliberately. She did not want to even consider the idea that this might be the last time, but she could not stop herself from making mental notes, as if trying to impress on her memory how it felt to hold Jemeryl and feel their mouths joining together.

Jemeryl was the one who broke away. She stared into Tevi's eyes. "I'll always love you. Please, never forget that."

There was nothing else to be said and no other excuse for delay. Jemeryl, with Klara on her shoulder, climbed to the opening and disappeared from view.

❖

Nothing had changed inside the chamber. Levannue still lay in her enchanted sleep. Jemeryl viewed her foe uneasily. Surprise was on her side, but Levannue had years more experience. The crucial difference might be Klara. Using her familiar meant that Levannue could be attacked from two directions simultaneously. It might make all the difference.

Jemeryl stroked the magpie and then sent her to a perch on the far side of the chamber. She grasped her sorcerer's staff firmly. The force field was a knot in the sixth dimension, unbreakable by those who could not see it for what it was but simple for Jemeryl to unweave.

The bonds stripped back. The force field ruptured in a storm of light and sound. Jemeryl was prepared for a booby trap, but even so, she was knocked to the ground. A bruising rain of broken stalactites fell. The blast left her blinded and deafened. She struggled back to her feet, rubbing her eyes clear of dust. Levannue was also recovering from her violent awakening. The two sorcerers studied each other coldly. Only dripping water broke the silence.

"Will you surrender?" Jemeryl asked.

Her answer was a slashing kick of raw power ripping through the ether, but the attack was miscued and easily parried.

The fight was brief. Three times, Levannue sent balls of white lightning hurtling towards Jemeryl. A desperate effort was needed to dissipate the bolts before they struck, and Jemeryl was forced backwards. Then she made her own assault, opening a drain under Levannue and attempting to suck all heat into the rock below. The older sorcerer dammed the outflow, responding far more quickly than Jemeryl expected. The speed of the riposte loosened Jemeryl's hold on the lines of power. Immediately, Levannue caught the rippling forces, ready to subvert the flow for her own use. However, she had committed herself to a path of attack and shifted her guard.

Jemeryl seized the chance. From a mesh with Klara, she sent a hail of ion darts towards her enemy's back. Levannue raised a shield, reacting frantically, yet she was only just in time, and her defence was unwieldy. Her aura was off-balance, and her grip on power weakened. Before she could recover, Jemeryl struck out, aiming at the ether rather than her shielded opponent. The shock waves shattered Levannue's persona in the sixth dimension. Again, Jemeryl ripped open the drain, and this time, there was no countering the freezing onslaught. Ice washed over Levannue's feet, flowing up her legs in a surging tide.

Levannue's expression changed to horror. "No!"

A pleading hand shot out towards Jemeryl. Levannue's scream faded. She flung back her head and raised both arms. Thunderbolts shot from her fingertips. As the encircling ribbons of ice reached Levannue's heart, the roof came crashing down about their heads.

❖

The sound of Jemeryl scrabbling down the shaft faded, and the last beams from her light globe disappeared. Tevi shuffled back against the opposite wall with her eyes locked, unwavering, on the black shadow in the rock face.

Long minutes dragged by. Staring into the darkness made Tevi's eyes sting, but the sense of helplessness was far worse. There was nothing she could do—no activity in which to lose either the tension shaking her hands or the dead weight of fear in her stomach. Her attention was caught momentarily by the dwarves standing several yards away, muttering among themselves in their guttural language. However, they provided only the flimsiest of distractions.

The first explosion had Tevi leaping to her feet, but after two indecisive steps, she halted. The last echoes rumbled away, and silence again claimed the dark underworld. Even the dwarves stopped talking.

For a time, nothing was heard. Tevi began to wonder if the battle was over already. Then three ear-splitting roars boomed from the inner cavern. For half a minute, the sounds of raging chaos rose and fell until the caves were rocked by the most violent explosion of all. The ground shook. A billowing jet of dust erupted from the fissure; while in the background, the pounding of falling rock went on and on. And then all was quiet.

It took a moment for Tevi to register the meaning of what she had just heard. She sprinted across the cave and vaulted onto a ledge running below the fissure. A slab of limestone a yard in length was wedged across the entrance. Farther beyond, other dams of rubble blocked the way, barely visible in the clouds of dust that eddied in the lamplight. Tevi rammed the lantern into a niche in the rock and wrapped her fingers around the first obstruction. She threw all her potion-enhanced strength into the struggle to pull it free, heedless of the abrasions torn into her hands.

The dwarf captain stood below her. "All am dead. We go now."

His shout was ignored.

"We go now."

Tevi had one knee braced against the wall. Every muscle strained in her effort to shift the block. Slowly, she worked it forward, leaving lines gouged in the sides of the fissure. When it finally shot free, the rock nearly took Tevi with it, crashing to the cave floor. The captain yelped, diving clear of the avalanche. The dwarves' muttering ceased abruptly. Tevi slid into the shaft until she met the next blockage. This consisted of smaller debris that she plucked free and tossed away.

The captain's head appeared cautiously in the opening, dodging the flying stones. "We helping. You go after," he suggested.

Tevi stopped and looked back. "You'll help me get through to her?"

"We think rock. We good. No more rock fall. We good."

Tevi nodded and edged out of the shaft. Within seconds, the captain's barked commands oversaw a relay of dwarves passing back broken stone. The stream of excavated rubble built in a mound in the outer cave while Tevi paced impatiently.

Twice, the dwarves met with stubborn obstacles, so that Tevi, with her greater strength, was called on. Once, a fresh fall of loose chippings caused a momentary panic, but in less than an hour, the shaft had been cleared. Tevi was the third to slip through. She turned up the wick on her lantern and looked around.

Huge fractured slabs reduced the cavern to half its original size. Piles of smaller rubble littered what was left of the space. Deep cracks radiated from the rockslide. Of the stalactites, only a few broken stubs still hung from the ceiling. Just to the left of the entrance, a mound of boulders hid Tevi's view of part of the chamber. When she stepped forward, she saw that the area behind had sustained less damage. Lying unconscious in a clear patch was Jemeryl.

Nothing else mattered as Tevi rushed to her lover's side, scrambling over smashed boulders and skidding on fragments of stalactite. Her panic eased only when she had her ear pressed to Jemeryl's chest and heard the heartbeat. Jemeryl's face was pale, and her pulse was erratic, but she was definitely alive. The surge of relief left Tevi light-headed. When she was again able to think clearly, she looked at the devastation around her. Obviously either Jemeryl had been very lucky or she had partially protected herself from the collapsing roof.

The sorcerer lay sprawled on her back, covered in dust and chips of rock. An arm was trapped between two stones. It bent sharply just below the elbow and was undoubtedly broken. Blood trickled from cuts on Jemeryl's face; more flowed from a gashed knee. Dark bruises marked her skin. Nothing appeared life-threatening, although Jemeryl lay deeply unconscious. A gentle shake got no response, and only the whites of her eyes showed when the lids were pulled back. Tevi sat on her heels and felt the niggling onset of returning fear.

By now, the whole band of dwarves was inside the cavern. What seemed to be an argument on the fracture forms of limestone had broken out. Tevi ignored the babble until a more excited outburst caught her attention. The dwarves had gathered around something hidden behind two large slabs in the centre of the chamber. The captain was posing arrogantly atop a nearby boulder. Tevi went to see, even as she guessed the probable cause.

Levannue lay on the ground. A large block had fallen across her left side, crushing her ribcage and arm. The white ends of broken bone poked through torn flesh, and the force of the impact had sent blood spurting from her ears, mouth and nose. Other stones had cracked her skull. From mid-thigh down, Levannue's legs were buried under rubble. Blood formed a red carpet on the stone beneath her.

There was no need to test her pulse to be sure she was dead. Tevi's brief doubt that this might be illusion was also rejected. Jemeryl had said the dwarves were immune to that sort of magic, and if Levannue were still able to cast spells, she would have no need of deception.

Tevi looked down at her lifeless enemy, aware of an array of emotions that she was too drained to distinguish. The Guardian's assignment was complete, yet Tevi felt no sense of victory. She started to turn away when she spotted a saddlebag half buried in the rubble. It came free after a few sharp tugs. Tevi slung it over her shoulder and returned to Jemeryl. Meanwhile, the dwarves had decided to complete the work of the rock fall by erecting a cairn over Levannue. Tevi left them to it.

A temporary splint soon had Jemeryl's broken arm strapped securely to her side. Tevi lifted the unconscious woman and carefully made her way across the rubble-strewn floor. The dwarves were occupied in moving rocks onto Levannue's body. They scurried about in preoccupied silence, but just as Tevi reached the exit, one gave a startled cry.

Tevi looked over. The dwarf had levered up a limestone slab. At first, in the wavering lamplight, it was hard to see what had caused the excitement. Then Tevi spotted the black and white feathers crushed on the ground—all that was left of something that had once been a magpie.

❖

The need to protect Jemeryl's broken arm made manoeuvring her inert body through the fissure all the more difficult. The final drop from the shaft entrance was particularly awkward. By the time Tevi reached the spot were their packs lay in the outer cavern, the dwarves had finished Levannue's cairn and were also returning. Tevi hoped that everyone would soon be ready to depart. There had to be some sort of healer in the dwarf city, and Jemeryl needed skilled medical attention as soon as possible.

It took a torturous amount of time for all the dwarves to reappear and collect their gear. Tevi cursed their indifference as they argued and fussed over nothing, although once they were ready to go, two of them helped by carrying the saddlebags. Another took the lamp, leaving Tevi free to concentrate on Jemeryl. Even so, the journey was a painful battle over the rough limestone. Tevi's main concern was to guard Jemeryl from further injury, so she let her own body absorb the knocks as she slid on glasslike floors and crawled over jagged stone.

After ten minutes, Tevi's knees, knuckles, and shoulders were bruised and cut. Her whole world was focused on searching for safe footholds, so she did not notice the blackness in the distance give way to grey. Only when the faint natural daylight fell across her path did she look up, surprised. It had been her unquestioned assumption that they were returning to the city. However, after another five minutes the whole group stood, blinking, in the open air.

Dusk was near. Low clouds shrouded the peaks, and an ice-cold wind snatched at Tevi's face. The scent of wet earth told of recent rain. They had emerged at the bottom of a cliff face. A broken slope of scree cascaded into the woods fifty yards below. Beyond that, mountains to the west, east and south ringed a small lake. To the north, a silver river flowed away through a marsh. This was not the spot were they had entered the mines or anywhere else Tevi recognised.

"Why are we here? Where—"

The captain pointed down the hill. "You go now."

Tevi was stunned. "You can't mean that. You said you'd help."

"We help. We go with you to the bad woman. We go with you here now."

"Jemeryl needs help, and we can't travel without our horses."

"No. All done. You go."

"At least give us our horses."

"Horses go. We eat. You go now."

"We can't."

The captain had been growing steadily more hostile. At a sign, two dwarves pulled their bows into sight, although not yet drawn. Others loosened axes from the straps across their backs. The threat was unmistakable. Torn between outrage and bewilderment, Tevi backed away. The captain picked up the saddlebags and hurled them down the slope, then stood scowling belligerently.

"Go."

Tevi held the captain's eyes for the space of a dozen heartbeats, but even if she were not carrying Jemeryl, the odds would be hopeless. She had no option except to turn her back on the dwarves and walk away, showing what disdain she could by refusing to hurry on the loose footing.

The bags had rolled down the slope and finished up entangled in undergrowth beneath the trees. With Jemeryl in her arms, getting them free and over her shoulder was not easy. Tevi looked back. The squat figures of the dwarves were concealed in the cave entrance. Watery daylight touched on the outlines of helmets and axe blades. Tevi's face twisted as she bit back the childish urge to shout threats. After a last bitter glare, she turned and plunged into the forest.

It was dark under the trees but sheltered from the cutting wind. Tevi forced her way through small branches, using her shoulders to shield Jemeryl, until she met a winding deer track heading downhill. The trail allowed her to make better progress through the woods, although with no idea where she was headed. Wind swept across the branches overhead, shaking dead leaves loose. Twigs cracked underfoot. The route twisted between lichen-covered trunks and tussocks of moss.

After half a mile, the track crossed a shallow river. The forest canopy was broken above the water, but the light falling through the gap in the branches was sullen and dim. Leaden, low-hanging clouds were darkening to black. White plumes of foam shone with a luminous quality in the gloom. Soon, it would be too dark to travel. Tevi halted and looked around.

Slightly upstream, a jutting limestone platform overhung a dry recess. The ground was further sheltered by a dense clump of thicket on the windward side. A drift of leaves was piled high. The site was as good for a camp as anywhere she was likely to find. Tevi spread a blanket and lay Jemeryl down gently. Plenty of dead wood was at hand, quick to burn. Soon, Tevi had flames racing over logs in a blazing campfire. The red glow washed over the rough rock wall and chased shadows through the matted bushes.

Tevi made a thorough examination of Jemeryl and tended her to the limits of their medical resources. Apart from the broken arm, Jemeryl's injuries were superficial. A careful search found no sign of a head wound. Tevi's shoulders slumped. It was the result she had feared. Jemeryl's coma was due to magic—either Levannue's attack or the loss of Klara. The condition was beyond her ability to understand or help. Tevi did not know what to do, how long the coma might last, or how dangerous it was.

Despair overwhelmed her. For a while she sat staring blankly into the darkness beyond the fire. The cries of animals in the forest depths rose and fell on the wind. Small things nearby burrowed through the leaf litter. Dangerous predators might come to drink at the river, but Tevi could not keep guard alone, and Klara was not there to watch over them.

Tears of pain and guilt rolled down Tevi's face. She had been forced to leave Klara's remains as the dwarves had found them. Jemeryl had come first. Yet the magpie had deserved the cairn and the remembrance far more than Levannue the traitor. Tevi could not go back to rectify the omission. All she could do was pray that she would not have cause to build another cairn—for Jemeryl.

Tevi busied herself with tasks about the camp. Anything to occupy her thoughts and put off trying to sleep. But at last, she banked the fire to keep it safe until morning and slipped under the blanket next to Jemeryl's unmoving form. For once, there was no reassurance in the shared body warmth. After a long, long time, Tevi drifted into an uneasy sleep.

❖

Tevi awoke in the dreary half-light of the next dawn with Jemeryl's arm pressed into her back. A wet mist rolled through the forest, condensing on every surface and dripping from branches. The damp air deadened the splashing of the river. It felt as if the cold had welled up from the ground and seeped into Tevi's bones.

No sound came from Jemeryl. Tevi shuffled around. The sorcerer had not stirred all night. Her lips were bloodless white; her features, flaccid. Tevi reached out in dread to touch Jemeryl's throat. The skin was cold, but the muscle still held firm and a butterfly-like pulse beat there. Faint breath from Jemeryl's lips misted on the air. Tevi felt her own face crumple in relief.

When she had recovered her composure, Tevi crawled from the blankets and removed the turf from the campfire. Embers still glowed deep inside the ash. Soon, they were fanned back to life. Tevi moved Jemeryl closer to the fire and tried to chafe warmth back into her. In Jemeryl's weakened state, the cold might be the finishing blow.

Food and drink were also an issue. Despite the sickness in her stomach, Tevi forced herself to take care of her own needs, but she could do nothing for Jemeryl. She poured a little water into Jemeryl's mouth but could not prompt her to swallow, and the liquid dribbled out from between slack lips.

Meanwhile, the light had grown into an overcast morning, and the mist had blown away. Tevi buried her head in her hands and wondered grew in power. After another mile, she had left the basin around the lake behind. The river rushed tumbling down a narrow valley cut into the mountains. Sheer cliff faces overhung the river, and both banks were lined with eroded platforms of rock. Sheets of green water swept over boulders on the riverbed.

Tevi made better progress than she had in the forest or the marsh, yet treacherous wet moss slicked the smooth rocks. With Jemeryl in her arms, travel was a fight for balance. Even with her potion-enhanced strength, Tevi was forced to stop for frequent rests.

At one such break, in late afternoon, Tevi saw signs of a path on the opposite bank. Half a mile downstream, a well-marked ford crossed the river. For a short way, the track kept low on the bank. Then it climbed the hillside and was lost from sight amidst the trees. The path was clearly much used. The few blades of grass on it were trampled flat, and imprinted in the mud were the marks of dwarf boots.

Tevi had no wish to encounter the dwarves again, but the path would be safer and quicker than the riverbank. There was also the likelihood that it would join the one leading to the dwarf mines. Once she reached somewhere she recognised, it would be straightforward to retrace the route to the Old West Road. On the other hand, although the river was still flowing north, there was no saying it would not loop back or that its banks might become impassable. A few nervous jitters unsettled her stomach, but Tevi turned her back on the river and took to the dwarf road.

❖

For the rest of the afternoon, Tevi followed the path out of the wooded valley and across the rugged uplands. Stubby trees were interspersed with gorse that rattled in the cold wind. As evening approached, the sinking sun finally broke from under the clouds, brightening the scene although adding nothing by way of heat. The oblique rays cast a stretched yellow light over the scene.

Dusk was falling as the path rolled over one more ridge. The terrain ahead dropped into a shallow valley that snaked away westward. The dwarven route bent east, climbing and disappearing over another hilltop. Bracken covered the upper valley slopes. A band of stunted trees filled the bottom. Directly opposite where Tevi stood, the ruins of a village clung to the hillside. Crumbling masonry rose above the straggly vegetation—the remains of at least thirty buildings with broken doors and gapping windows.

The wind stiffened at Tevi's back, stinging the exposed skin of her neck. She glanced over her shoulder. Clouds were piling up from the south, thick black thunderclouds that looked too heavy to hang in the sky. Tevi could smell the charged air carried on the gusting wind. A distant roll of thunder echoed over the mountains.

Memories of Graka urged Tevi to flee the ruins, but the coming storm made finding shelter a necessity. Jemeryl would not survive the night in the open. The ruined village was the best shelter they were likely to find. Tevi's heart pounded, but she left the path and scrambled down the hillside. The dangers of the ruins were hypothetical; the dangers of the coming storm were not. As she crossed the small stream at the bottom of the valley, the wind rose in earnest, snapping at her clothes. Rain began to fall, pierced with hail.

The nearest building was a dozen yards above the stream. The roots of a young birch ploughed through its walls. Other trees grew wild, but the ruins had not been deserted for long, forty years at most. The remains of wooden doors hung from rusty hinges. Tiles still covered many buildings. Tevi began to climb the hillside, searching anxiously among the ruins for signs of life. Or other activity.

The first two structures she passed were completely derelict and offered no shelter. The next was more substantial, a long, low building with a wide entrance at one end. Tevi peered in. A central hallway ran the length, lined with empty doorways on either side. It had possibly been a dormitory or a store. Now the far end was open to the sky, but the remaining two-thirds kept their roof. Tevi halted by the first inner doorway. The room was intact except for a few missing tiles in one corner. The hole let rain trickle down the wall and soak into the ground, but apart from this, the floor was dry. Blown leaves and rubble littered the ground. A fox appeared to have made a meal of a rabbit in one corner, but there was no other trace of recent occupation.

Tevi lay Jemeryl down and went in search of timber. The wind was growing in strength with every minute. Rain whipped across the hillside in savage belts. The thunderclouds reduced the evening to darkness. Getting lost would be easy if she went far, but the remains of a door hung aslant on rusty hinges at the entrance. The old timbers were half-rotten and easily splintered by a few well-aimed kicks.

Soon, Tevi had a fire blazing within a circle of bricks. Old nails protruded from the lintel above the doorway to the room. Tevi impaled a blanket on them so that it hung down, keeping in both heat and light. It was unlikely that anyone would be out on such a night, but she had no wish to advertise their presence.

Smoke from the fire coiled under the ceiling before slipping out through the hole in the corner. The blanket over the door snapped as wind gusted down the hallway. Overhead, the tiles creaked, and the pounding of rain rose and fell.

Jemeryl lay motionless beside the fire, wrapped in a second thick blanket. At no time during the day had she showed signs of waking. Now her breathing was growing weaker, and her pulse was less stable. A bluish tinge mottled her cheeks and temples.

While the storm roared over the mountains, Tevi sat watching her lover. Jemeryl was fading before her eyes. Dying. Tevi fought back tears. The fire taunted her with its cheery light, mocking the memories of hearth and home. In a fierce mood, Tevi snapped wood and fed it to the flames. She knew she should eat and sleep but could not bring herself to care enough to do either.

She could think of nothing to do—at least nothing helpful. But if Jemeryl died, she would return to the mines and see what havoc she could wreak. A suicide attack. Jemeryl had said the dwarves valued revenge. Tevi was sure they would understand.

Chapter Seventeen—The Top of the Pass

Storm-blown debris clattered down the corridor. Wrapped in her plans for revenge, Tevi barely noticed the noise. No outside threat could be worse than what she already confronted. Nothing else could frighten her. Then, amid the random thuds, came the unmistakable sound of human footsteps entering the hallway and halting outside the room.

Tevi moved in reflex. Her hand leapt to her discarded sword, but her training held firm. She slipped it from its scabbard and rose without a sound. Firelight rippled over the blanket across the doorway. Tevi watched a hand appear around the edge. With unnerving nonchalance, the blanket was drawn aside, and a figure stepped into the room..

The new arrival was an old man with skin like cracked leather. He was half naked and filthy. Rain plastered the scant white hair to his head and ran in clean lines through the dirt smeared across his sunken chest. Tattered rags flapped against the sinews of his legs. An incongruous garland of red leaves sagged wet about his neck.

"Who are you? What do you want?" Tevi kept her voice level.

"You're upsetting my storm."

"Who are you?"

"You're drowning out the thunder."

"What do you want?"

The old man showed no sign of hearing. His voice sunk to a mumble punctuated by "Whoosh, whoosh" in imitation of the wind. Tevi lowered her sword. He was clearly mad and probably harmless. Then, suddenly, he dropped to Jemeryl's side and grabbed her shoulder. Tevi leapt forward, but a blow from an invisible fist slammed into her. She crashed backwards into the wall behind, stunned. The sword fell from her hand.

It was several seconds before her head cleared. "You're a sorcerer?"

This time, he answered. "I'm me. I wanted to watch the storm, but you brought her here, and she's all wrong. I heard her from up on the rocks, thinking she's a dead magpie."

"Can you help her?" Tevi hardly dared hope.

"I don't help. I watch."

"She'll die if you don't."

He removed his skeletal hand from Jemeryl's shoulder. "She'll die if I do. We'll all die. If isn't in question, only when."

"True. But I don't want the *when* to be now."

"Of course it will be now. All time is now sometime. It makes no difference."

Tevi struggled with the viewpoint. "Maybe it makes no difference to you, but it does to me. Jemeryl is running out of time. She'll die very soon."

"Yes. Before tomorrow sunset, but not soon enough to stop her ruining my storm." With a scowl of disgust, the hermit clambered to his feet and turned to the doorway.

"You have to help us."

"No, I don't." The blanket swung closed behind him.

His abrupt departure caught Tevi by surprise, staring in disbelief at the swaying curtain. Her inaction lasted only an instant. She hurtled after him into the dark, deserted hallway. The man was clearly a sorcerer of the mad-hermit type. He was also Jemeryl's best hope.

The wind was blowing a stream of leaves down the corridor. Tevi took a moment to check the dark recesses of the building before stepping out onto the open hillside. Within seconds, she was soaked to the skin. The storm pounded the mountains. Trees whipped and twisted in the gale. Bushes were flattened beneath the blasts. The crescent moon lit the chaos through holes torn in the clouds. Of the hermit, there was no sign.

The ruined buildings were stable points amid the surging vegetation. Tevi struggled to the nearest and began searching, passing from one to another. Eventually, towards the top of the village, she found the hovel that was his home. A bed of bracken lined one wall. The floor held a cold central hearth and scattered rubbish, but the owner was not there.

Several paths led away through the undergrowth, although the storm had washed away any footprints. Tevi shielded her eyes from the

the hermit. She stopped. The light in the hallway was strong enough to reveal the paler lines of mortar. The first true shaft of daylight ghosted the upper wall. Dawn had broken.

Tevi fell back to her knees and stared at Jemeryl's face. Sickening, gut-wrenching pain raked her. In agony, Tevi flung back her head and screamed, "Jemeryl!"

A shudder washed over the unconscious woman, then a longer, slower movement as muscles tensed. Jemeryl's eyelids fluttered. Disbelief froze Tevi for a moment before she hauled her lover into a crushing embrace.

Jemeryl gasped and made a feeble effort to free herself. "Careful. My arm hurts."

❖

A nearby building yielded more wood to revive the fire. Jemeryl sat shivering in silence while Tevi related all that had happened since Levannue had brought down the cavern roof. The account was punctuated by frequent anxious looks. Jemeryl replied with weak smiles, but mostly, her eyes were fixed on the flames.

"I didn't realise when the hermit said 'call you,' he meant bawl my lungs out. But it worked, and you'll be fine now, won't you?"

Jemeryl gave no answer. Reaching over, Tevi gently stroked her ashen face. Jemeryl leaned into the caress and closed her eyes.

"Klara..."

"She's dead." Tevi spoke softly.

"I know."

"She can't have suffered. It must have been very quick."

"It was." Jemeryl's face contorted in grief. "When I realised what Levannue was doing, I put a field up to cover myself. I should have cut loose from Klara, but I couldn't bear to let her go. I tried to shield her, but I wasn't strong enough. The stone hit, and she...wasn't there. Just a hole. I fell in and...I'm lost. I can't tell where I am. I can't even see you, except with my eyes, and I could always see you so clearly." Jemeryl slumped forward.

"You can't see me? But you're not blind," Tevi said, puzzled. "Do you mean your extra senses?"

Jemeryl nodded.

"All of them?"

"I...it's..."

"You mean you're not a sorcerer anymore?" Tevi bit her tongue at her tactlessness.

"No." Jemeryl's shoulders shook.

Tevi held her close for a long time. Eventually, Jemeryl pulled free. Her expression became apologetic at the distress on Tevi's face.

"I'm sorry, my love. I didn't mean to upset you."

"You'll get better...won't you?"

"I don't know. I must get back to the Protectorate. Perhaps someone there can help, but right now, I won't qualify as a third-rate witch." Jemeryl's brave smile was blatantly forced. "It's awful. I don't know how you stand it."

"It's all I'm used to. Come on; you'll feel better after breakfast."

"I don't think I can face food."

"You didn't eat yesterday."

"I know. I feel like I've been through a mangle. My head aches and my arm's throbbing. I can tell you did a good job, but..." Jemeryl met Tevi's eyes. "I don't mean to sound pathetic. Just hold me for a while longer, please."

Tevi did so; however, they both felt a rising urgency. A long walk lay ahead, all the worse with Jemeryl's weakened state, and they dare not let winter catch them in the wildlands. After a few minutes of comfort in each other's arms, they ate and packed quickly. Soon, they were ready to leave.

It quickly became clear that Jemeryl was not exaggerating her frailty. She needed help across the stream and was stumbling before they were halfway up the hillside. When she slid to her knees for the second time, Tevi ignored her protests and carried her to the dwarf road. Once there, they stood looking back at the village, while Jemeryl caught her breath. There was no sign of the hermit.

"I guess it's the remains of the old retreat. He must be the last survivor," Jemeryl said between gulps of air. "I wish I could remember what they were studying. Did he give any clue?"

"Maybe some sort of dancing academy. Or do all sorcerers have that innate grace and rhythm?"

"I'm afraid not. As you'll discover from my abilities if we get to Lyremouth in time for the midwinter festival."

Tevi's smile became a yawn; she was tired from her sleepless night. She turned to squelch through the muddy puddles dotting the path, saying nothing, but she knew there was no hope of reaching Lyremouth by midwinter. They would be doing well just to get over the Barrodens and back into the Protectorate before bad weather made travel impossible.

❖

The dwarf road climbed to the head of the valley and down again through groves of spindly trees and boulder-covered slopes. The sky was clear, but the raw wind snapped at their faces. At the bottom of the next valley, the path swung southeast. In her exhaustion, Jemeryl's eyes were fixed on the ground. She did not notice when another rough track dropped down the hillside. However, Tevi stopped walking.

"We've gone in a circle."

"We've done what?"

Tevi pointed to the track. "When we were chasing Levannue, this is where we joined the road to the dwarf mines. I've been thinking for the last few minutes that the scenery was looking familiar. I didn't say, in case it was wishful thinking. But I'm sure this is the way back to the Old West Road."

"I think you're right." Jemeryl started wearily up the track but Tevi remained standing on the road. "Is there something else?"

"The mine entrance isn't far."

"And?"

"Do you think they've really eaten the horses? The journey would be so much easier if we had them."

"I couldn't say. Dwarves don't go in for riding, but horses are valuable. They might be kept to sell. However, we can't take on the entire clan, certainly not with me in this state."

Tevi scowled in the direction of the mines but then turned and followed Jemeryl on the steep track. Mud clung to their shoes. Before they were a third of the way up, Jemeryl was gasping. Yet she stubbornly continued putting one foot in front of the other.

"Don't be silly. I'll carry you," Tevi said at last.

Jemeryl was unwilling to accept her own weakness. "You can't carry me all the way to Lyremouth."

"I will if I have to."

"I might be all right if we take it slowly."

"We don't have the time."

The assertion was undeniable. Jemeryl made no further objections and tried to relax in Tevi's arms, but she knew tears were close. It was not so much the infirmity. That, she could have tolerated. But not to be a sorcerer, to be confined in the mundane world, was unbearable. Klara's death was the final bitter wound. Jemeryl closed her eyes and rested her head on Tevi's shoulder, trying to block out her pain with the comfort of Tevi's physical presence.

❖

In the following days, Tevi's arms were a source of comfort that often felt like the only thing keeping Jemeryl going. The rough terrain that had passed quickly under the horses' hooves was an arduous slog by foot. The effects of the coma faded and Jemeryl was able to travel farther each day unassisted, but her paranormal senses showed no sign of returning. Except sometimes, as she drifted into sleep, she felt the hint of the world beyond in taunting images that blended into dreams.

Five days after leaving the hermit's village, they reached the Old West Road. The climate had grown milder as they dropped in altitude, yet there was no mistaking the wind's icy bite. The sky was blue, with wisps of cloud, but the sunlight carried no warmth. Winter would soon be sweeping over the forests. With good luck, it might hold off for a month. With bad luck, the next day could see them snowbound.

"Uzhenek is east; the Protectorate is west. Which way do you want to go?" Jemeryl's tone left little doubt that she preferred the second option.

"Which is nearer?"

"Denbury. But—"

"We have to get over the Barrodens." Tevi finished the sentence for her.

"We won't go past Graka."

"You've talked me into it."

They set off west.

❖

Once again, they were following the Old West Road on its remorseless advance across the landscape, but a change had come. The forest was stark; only withered leaves still clung to branches. Birdsong was rare, and few small animals disturbed the leaf litter. The overnight frost turned puddles to ice. One brief flurry of snow fell but did not settle. To the south, the Barrodens dropped in height, although the snow-capped peaks still formed an unbroken barricade.

After fourteen days, the Old West Road finally deviated from its ruler-straight line. The road swung south and began to climb. The following night, they camped in a wide valley that drove into the heart of the Barrodens.

"Another three days to Denbury," Jemeryl estimated.

"Good job, too. We're nearly out of food."

"It's enough for a couple of meals."

"As long as they're not big ones. It's lucky we're not expecting company."

"I don't suppose it's worth trying to gather something before we tackle the pass?"

Tevi shook her head. "There isn't much around that's edible. It's been five nights since the snares caught anything, and I doubt I'd have any more luck hunting—even if we had the time."

"We've done well."

"We have. At least twenty-five miles a day."

"From the blisters, I'd have sworn it was twice that." Jemeryl raised one foot to illustrate.

"And it will be for nothing if winter closes the pass."

"We're going to make it."

"Is that prophecy or wishful thinking?"

Jemeryl smiled ruefully. "Even if my senses were restored, I probably couldn't answer that one."

They set off just before dawn the next day. The road climbed steadily along the bottom of the valley. Mountains rose above the pine trees on either side. Eventually, the valley ended in a steep escarpment. Here, the ascent began in earnest, zigzagging up the almost-vertical walls. The weather was bitterly cold, numbing their toes and fingers.

After four hours of hard climbing, they stood on the top of the escarpment. The road ahead ran across rolling moorland, surrounded by jagged peaks. Snow crept down from the heights, encroaching on the plain. Several miles distant, they could see the road rise over another ridge slung between two craggy peaks.

"With any luck that's the top of the pass," Tevi said.

"It's more likely just a good viewpoint to see the next part of the climb."

Tevi smiled and turned to look back over the valley they had just left. The panorama was breathtaking. Snow-covered mountains stretched off on either side above wooded slopes. The dazzling white contrasted with the green pines in heartbreaking beauty. However, what caught Tevi's attention were the heavy black clouds piling up on the horizon.

"How long do you think we have?" Jemeryl asked quietly.

"Not long enough. Do you think you can outrun a blizzard?"

"Do I have a choice?"

"We could find shelter."

"Unless you can see something I'm missing, there doesn't seem to be much on offer."

"Maybe over the ridge ahead there might be...something?" Tevi finished uncertainly.

"Such as?"

"Ideally, an inn with roaring fires and well-stocked kitchen, but I'd settle for a cave."

By the time they had crossed two-thirds of the moor, the storm clouds were blocking out the sun. The wind at their backs picked up sharply. The first of the snow rippled across the ground in rolling, snakelike bands that broke about their knees. A few larger flakes whipped past their faces, and then, as suddenly as if a door had opened, the snow became a hurtling onslaught carried vertically on a screaming wind.

Jemeryl's breath was laboured. She staggered under the repeated blasts and eventually slipped to her knees. For the first time in days, Tevi picked her up and carried her, but it would not be long before even Tevi's superhuman strength was overwhelmed. The road began to climb while the blizzard gained in force. The raging whiteness blotted out everything. The wind tore the air from Tevi's lungs and her feet sank past her ankles into banks of snow.

The road climbed higher. As an act of will, Tevi kept moving forward. Abruptly, a dark shape materialised out of the white chaos.

In the space of a dozen footsteps, the shadow became solid, acquiring detail. Tevi found herself standing outside a high wooded stockade. She set Jemeryl down, and the pair edged along the wall until they reached a large gateway.

Tevi hammered on the door with the pommel of her sword.

"There's no point!" Jemeryl screamed in her ear. "They won't hear us over the wind!"

A smaller doorway was set into the main gate. Tevi stepped back and then threw all her strength into a kick. The whole gateway rattled, but no shouts came from inside. A second, third and fourth kick followed, by which time the door was hanging off its hinges. Tevi delivered a final blow with her shoulder and the door flew in.

The two women stepped over the splintered wood into an enclosed courtyard. Low timber buildings lined all sides. It was more sheltered than the hillside, yet the wind still whipped around the yard and sent streamers of snow over the rooftops. Some of the buildings were clearly stables and sheds. The largest hall looked to be the domestic quarters. Tevi led the way forward and lifted the latch. To her relief, it was unbolted. Billowing snow chased them inside until Tevi shut the door. Suddenly, it was very quiet.

They were in a long room with a stone fireplace and one wall lined with bunks. An ancient table and two benches stood in the middle. The walls were split logs; the floor, beaten earth. The place had clearly been deserted for days, but in the circumstances, it was pure luxury.

"Do you know what this is?" Jemeryl asked

"I'd guess it's a mercenary patrol post. It probably doubles as a shelter for herdsmen and maybe an inn for travellers. Some of my colleagues in Horzt served in places like this."

"Where is everyone?"

"In winter, there are no animals on the high pastures, no wagon trains, and only very stupid bandits."

"It's run by the mercenaries?"

"If the local guild council is prepared to pay us."

"So it must mean we're at the top of the pass and back in the Protectorate."

Tevi smiled ironically. "Welcome home."

During a lull in the storm, Tevi checked the other buildings. She found firewood, neatly cut and stacked; clean straw for bedding; and oil lanterns, but little else. When the blizzard returned, the two women sat beside the blazing hearth, listening to the roaring outside. The immediate threat was over. They would not freeze, but Tevi wondered how long they would be pinned down. Their supply of food would not last another day.

❖

The blizzard abated late the following afternoon, although fitful gusts still made the roof creak. Tevi went to look out over the winter landscape. The patrol post was situated a hundred yards below the top of the ridge. Dark clouds hung overhead, bearing down oppressively. A thick coat of snow covered the moor, softened to grey in the hollows.

The road was hidden under the snow, but it was not hard to guess its line. Beyond the shelter of the stockade, the wind snapped at Tevi with renewed force, cold and biting. The snow was knee-deep, and the frozen crust broke underfoot. Heather snared her boots when she strayed from the path. Several times, she stumbled into windblown drifts.

In five minutes she reached the crest of the pass. The wind ripped over the ridge in unrestrained savagery. It roared in Tevi's ears and flung volleys of stinging ice particles in her face. Through the shield of her fingers, Tevi saw broken hills drop away before her, scored with valleys. On distant lowlands were the distinctive patterns of cultivated land.

When Tevi returned Jemeryl was waiting by the fire, stirring a pan that's contents consisted mainly of water. "I'm afraid this is the last of the food. Did you find out anything promising?"

"We are at the top of the pass."

"Good."

"I could see farms. They're at least a day away, and it's getting dark, but if it's clear tomorrow, we have to set out."

"The snow will be back before sunrise." Jemeryl continued stirring but then stopped and stared at the pan.

"Are you all right?"

"I'm not guessing."

"What?"

"I can see it. I can feel the storm. I'm starting to—" Jemeryl broke off and raised her hands. They were shaking, but then, between her fingers, a blue ball of light shimmered, stuttered, and failed. But it was enough. While Tevi held her, Jemeryl sobbed with relief.

"Will you recover completely?"

"I don't know, but I'm starting to heal. There's a major ordinance of the Coven at Denbury. Perhaps someone there can help."

Hissing announced that the pan was boiling over, reclaiming their attention. Once the food was safely in bowls, they ate the meagre supper and talked of plans while it grew dark outside and then went to bed, still hungry.

❖

Jemeryl was awoken from deep sleep by a draft of freezing air. Once her eyes adjusted, she saw Tevi standing by the partly open door, sword in hand.

"What is it?"

"There's something moving outside."

In an instant, Jemeryl joined her at the doorway. A dark animal shape appeared on the far side of the courtyard. It was black against the white snow, as tall as Tevi's waist, lean and powerful. It paused, one paw raised, sniffing the air.

"Wolves. They've got in through the broken door," Tevi said

Jemeryl's face contorted in the effort as she probed with her damaged senses. "They're an ordinary pack. I'm sure of it. Not werewolves."

"Probably on the scent of the animals that were kept here."

"Shut and bar the door. We'll be safe."

Tevi had other ideas. "Stay here. I won't be long."

Before Jemeryl could respond, Tevi had slipped outside and pulled the door shut.

Jemeryl opened it again immediately. "Tevi. Come back."

"I know what I'm doing," Tevi whispered from a dark shadow.

Three more wolves appeared at the entrance to the stockade and padded into the open. Jemeryl stepped back and pulled the door to. Through a finger-wide gap, she watched the pack circle the courtyard.

Suddenly, the quiet was broken by a burst of snarling mixed with Tevi's shouts and then a high-pitched yelp. As abruptly as it had started, the noise stopped. Unable to stay back, Jemeryl tore open the door and stepped out in time to see the last wolf skidding in the snow in its panic to flee. From the other direction, Tevi was returning, dragging a limp form that left a dark trail in the snow.

The wolf seemed smaller and far less intimidating lying dead beside the hearth in the light of a lantern. It was no consolation to Jemeryl, who was furious at the scare she had received.

"That was stupid. There was no need to take risks."

"I was quite safe. I told you I knew what I was doing."

"But why?"

"I had good reasons."

"Such as?"

"Roast wolf, fried wolf, wolf stew."

The answer stopped Jemeryl in her tracks. It was several seconds before she said, stunned, "We can't eat it."

"Are your objections moral or culinary? Because the way my stomach feels, you'll have a hard job talking me out of it." Tevi grinned and pulled a knife from her pack. "One thing about a good barbarian upbringing. It helps you cope with life's little emergencies."

❖

The blizzard returned before dawn, an invasion of white that engulfed the mountains in bludgeoning chaos. On the fifth night, Tevi and Jemeryl lay snuggled in bed listening to the howling wind. A blazing fire lit the room. Tevi felt safe, warm, and comfy.

Jemeryl lay on her back, staring at the ceiling. "We should leave tomorrow," she announced unexpectedly.

Tevi raised herself on an elbow. "Are you sure?"

"I...yes." Jemeryl looked as if she had surprised herself. "It will be our best chance. The weather will hold for a few days."

"You're recovering, aren't you?"

"Slowly. Hopefully, I can be cured completely, so I'll—" Jemeryl broke off. "Does that bother—"

"What?"

"Would you prefer that I stay ungifted?" Jemeryl's voice was very quiet.

"No. Why should I?"

"It's just...at the moment, we're both the same. And I wondered if that might be easier for you."

Tevi stared at the fire while she sifted through her thoughts. "I admit, sometimes...I don't like how people react to you...and then how they react to me for being with you. It's not your being a sorcerer that's the problem; it's the rest of the world." Her eyes returned to meet Jemeryl's. "But at the moment, we're not the same, because I'm content with being ungifted, and you're not and never could be. I can ignore everyone else, but I could never ignore the fact that you're unhappy." Tevi dipped her head and kissed Jemeryl, slowly and very softly. "I love you."

"I love you, too."

Uncertainty still remained in Jemeryl's eyes. Tevi sensed that actions, rather than words, would most readily push away any doubts—both Jemeryl's and her own. Maybe it was not quite so easy to ignore the rest of the world as she had implied. Which made the times when the two of them were alone together all the more valuable.

Tevi stroked her hand over Jemeryl's shoulder and down her side. Jemeryl's body had become very familiar to her but was still a source of wonder. Starting at Jemeryl's hip, Tevi traced a soft line of circles along the junction between body and leg. Immediately, Jemeryl's breathing quickened, and her eyes half closed. Tevi's smile grew. By now, they knew each other's likes and dislikes, and although their lovemaking had become more predictable, it was no less rewarding.

❖

The women woke to silence, broken only by the whisper of shifting snow and the occasional creak from the roof. Jemeryl packed while Tevi called on all her strength to open the frozen door and dig a passage out. Before long, they stood at the entrance to the stockade. The sky was clear blue, and only a breeze stirred across the mountains.

Despite the fine weather, it was a slow fight through snowdrifts to the top of the pass. Thereafter, the journey was downhill. Pristine fields of white swept between rock precipices, in a series of giant steps. Guessing the line of the road was impossible, so they settled for heading in the direction of down. By midday, they were below the tree line. The temperature rose beneath the dark green pines, and the snow was heavier and wetter.

Night was falling when they reached a level plateau on the mountain side. They paused at the edge. Farms and hamlets were spread out in the valley below, but purple dusk was already swallowing the scene. Lights from fires and lanterns dotted the lowland.

"You're better at judging distance than me. Do you think we can make it down tonight?" Jemeryl asked.

"We might. But then we might step off a cliff in the dark and break our necks." Tevi pointed to a small round building. "We'd be safer stopping there until morning."

"Is it another of your guard posts?"

"I'd say it was a shepherd's hut."

"I don't see any sheep."

"You won't see any shepherds, either. This hillside would be summer pasture."

The hut had drystone walls and a straw thatch. There was a low door and no windows. No one answered their call, but a supply of split logs was piled outside and the door was unbarred. The single room held a mildew-covered straw pallet and an overpowering smell of sheep. The ground was wet where snow had blown under the loose-fitting door. A blackened circle of stones in the centre marked the hearth.

"It'll be better than sleeping outside."

Jemeryl looked as if she might have disputed the statement but said nothing.

A fire soon warmed the room and dried the pallet, although it did nothing for the smell. Smoke flowed under the rafters before seeping out into the night. The two women sat side by side, watching their supper cooking on skewers. A blanket was draped around their shoulders to ward off the draft from under the door.

Tevi looked at the backpack propped against the wall. In it was Lorimal's chalice. The quest was nearly over. She fought the urge to take the chalice out. For the first time in ages, memories of Storenseg stirred in her, a sharp longing mixed with a ragbag of other emotions.

"We should get to Denbury tomorrow." Jemeryl broke the silence.

"Maybe."

"I guess we won't reach Lyremouth until after the spring thaw."

Tevi did not reply.

"What are you thinking about?"

"Storenseg."

"You miss it?" Jemeryl asked softly.

"It's hard to explain. This hut...it's cold and squalid, but it's just like home. It ought to make me want to stay away, but..."

"Do you want to go back?"

"I don't know."

Jemeryl was silent for a while before launching into awkward, unstructured sentences. "I think I understand how you...want your home, but...you know I want to go to Tirakhalod. I should have asked... but if I clear it with the guild, that you're a bodyguard or something... though if you don't..." Jemeryl hesitated. "Would you come with me?"

Tevi met Jemeryl's eyes. When it came to it, the decision was really very easy.

Chapter Eighteen—Storenseg

The island hove into view above the bow of the small boat. Tevi ducked under the sail and looked at the familiar outline against the pale spring sky. The rush of homesickness surprised her. Just over two years had past since she left. Tevi watched the mountains grow and considered all that had happened and how much she had changed. She was not the same woman who had been exiled.

Her hands bore the visible reminder: two red and gold swords on each. The more recent tattoos stood out in darker hues, though they would soon fade to match the rest. A smile crept over Tevi's face. Other changes went far deeper, though they left no visible mark.

Tevi looked over her shoulder. In the stern, Jemeryl was trying to calm the juvenile magpie in her lap as it fidgeted and fluffed its plumage.

"We'll be at Storenseg soon."

Jemeryl greeted the announcement with a wry grin. "I'm not surprised you don't have any sorcerers. This whole area is a sink, magically speaking. I've got enough trouble hanging on to Klara II." Jemeryl wiggled her fingers experimentally, leaving a trail of green sparks. "I can raise a few visual effects. They'll have surprise value but no real use if things get nasty."

"Shouldn't be any need. Thanks to Lorimal, my people worship sorcerers. A few pretty lights, a herbal cure for a hangover, and they'll be singing your praises for generations." Tevi grinned. "We're not staying. Once my family learn that, they won't cause trouble. We'll just give them the chalice and go."

"What if people guess that we're lovers?"

"I'm sure my grandmother will work it out in an instant, and she'll want to ensure that nobody else gets the same idea. One thing Grandmother does extremely well is manage rumours, as long as we don't make her job too difficult."

"You mean I can't kiss you in the village square?"

"No." Tevi laughed. "And asking my mother's blessing for our relationship would also be a bad move."

Jemeryl settled back in the boat. "You know, I'll be sorry to hand the chalice over, after all we went through."

"I'll be pleased to see the end of it." Tevi paused while she tacked into the wind. "You're sure it's safe?"

"Absolutely. The Guardian herself scrubbed its memory clean. I think she wanted it as a trophy, but your guild master insisted that you complete your quest."

"Mercenaries always keep their word. Rule number one. Our livelihoods depend on it." Tevi shrugged. "I pointed out that I hadn't actually sworn to return the chalice, merely not to go back without it, but they said I was quibbling, and we're not supposed to do that either."

The crashing of waves against rock became a roar. In a plume of spray, the small boat rounded the Stormfast Cliffs. The calmer waters of the bay glittered as the boat skimmed over the waves. Straight ahead was the beach, with fishing boats hauled onto the sands. Not far inland, the long halls of Holric clustered beside the river. Tevi frowned; she had not expected to see the village again, and now her memories were juggling with her emotions.

Jemeryl shuffled forward. "What do you think they'll make of you bringing back the chalice and then going again?"

"If Grandmother has anything to do with it, it will become a heroic tale with very little resemblance to the truth."

The keel scraped on sand. Tevi jumped out and hauled the boat up the beach. She reached in and grabbed the bag containing the chalice, then swung it over her shoulder. "Come on. Let's get this over with."

With a laugh, Jemeryl joined her, and the pair walked up the beach towards the small group of armed women assembling on the dunes above.

❖

The sea breeze hissed through the tall grass on the hillside. Tevi nestled into the sheltered hollow. The Stormfast Cliffs rose on the other side of the bay. Beyond them, bands of foam chased across the open sea and two fishing boats were returning with their catch. Smoke rising from Holric spiralled away in the wind.

Preparations were in progress for another feast in her honour. Tevi did not know whether to laugh or be sick. When the absurdity had got too much to stomach, she had escaped to her hidden vantage point, but she could not spend all night on the hillside. Somehow, she would have to get herself through the charade.

If only she could have simply tossed the chalice to her grandmother and then got straight back in the boat and left. However, questions were asked; Jemeryl had answered; and before Tevi had time to react, there were emotional speeches, and all sorts of folk were taking turns to hug her. It felt as if everyone was playing a game, but nobody would tell her the rules.

It was far worse than the return to Lyremouth, which had been nerve-racking enough. There, they had been questioned until everyone was happy that she and Jemeryl were innocent of any wrongdoing. Then had followed congratulations and rewards, but all done very discreetly. The story was not going to become common knowledge. Tevi had been promoted to vouchsafed guild member, and Jemeryl had been given permission to study with Bykoda. As a final mark of favour, Tevi was to go with her. Many clearly disapproved of their relationship, but the Guardian was not putting obstacles in their way.

Tevi had learned that Russ and the others had not been blamed for failing to deliver her to Lyremouth as prisoner. Not when they had been contending with a sorcerer. Tevi was relieved, and if Russ's report did not exactly match her memories, she was not about to contradict it. She hoped that someday, they would meet up again and could joke about the affair.

The sound of someone approaching put an end to Tevi's musing. Laff appeared at the edge of the hollow. The two sisters studied each other awkwardly.

"Um." Laff cleared her throat. "People are wondering where you are. I've come to look for you. I saw you slip off, and I knew you used to like sitting here."

"Er, yes. It's just...I'm finding it strange being back after so long away. I wanted some time alone to think."

"If you like, I'll say I couldn't find you."

"Thanks."

Laff shifted from foot to foot a few times before sitting down, facing Tevi across the hollow. "Tomorrow, you're really going to leave for good...and not come back?"

"Yes."

Laff's eyes fixed on the ground between them. "You know, for a moment this morning, when I saw you on the beach, with the chalice, I thought...." She swallowed. "I've missed you."

"You can still make jokes about me while I'm not here." Tevi covered her surprise with irony.

"I'm sorry about all that. I never really meant it."

"You had me fooled."

"No, it was..." Laff took a deep breath. "I think I was hoping that if I pushed you hard enough, one day you'd snap and come back at me. Even when we were fighting, part of me wanted you to kick the snot out of me and put me in my place. I knew it wasn't going to happen, but..."

Tevi stared in astonishment, searching for something to say. "Well, if it will make you happy, we can try now. Jem has fixed my eyesight. It's made a big difference."

"Do you think you'd win?"

"Do you want to try?"

"No." Laff raised her head, but rather than meet Tevi's eyes, she looked across the bay. "You've changed."

"I know. My eyes are now grey, and everyone's been telling me I talk funny. I think Jemeryl's accent is rubbing off on me."

"It's not that. You're more like yourself."

"Who did I used to be like?"

"You know what I mean. It was like you were hiding yourself before."

"There were bits of me I had to hide...as you know."

Laff winced and bit her lip while she framed her next sentence. "This sorcerer you're leaving with. You're going to be travelling on together?"

"Yes."

"You're good friends?"

"Very."

"Um...you and her...do er, are you—"

Tevi interrupted. "Before you ask that question, you ought to be sure you want to hear the answer."

For a while, the only sound was the wind. Eventually, Laff said quietly, "I guess that means yes."

Tevi shrugged an agreement.

"When they told me what Grandmother was planning...with Brec in the hay barn...I didn't believe it, despite what I'd said. I was sure you'd tell Brec to go jump in the sea...and afterwards, when you'd gone...I didn't know what to think. I still don't."

"That's because life on the islands doesn't give you much practice at thinking."

Laff frowned in confusion. "So what would happen on the mainland if people found out?"

"Nothing. Lots already know."

"Don't they object?"

"Some mutter things like 'How can you let yourself get involved with a sorcerer?' But that's it."

"Why does it matter that Jemeryl's a sorcerer?"

Tevi choked back her laughter. "I don't know where to start answering that. It's all very different."

"So here's where you've run off to!" Jemeryl's voice made them jump. They had not heard her footsteps through the grass.

Laff sprung up. Her eyes darted between the two lovers, finishing nervously on Tevi. "I'll see you later, but, um.. I hope you...I hope everything goes all right. And if ever you want to come home..." Laff covered her embarrassment with a weak smile. "Look after yourself." She backed away and then all but fled the hollow.

Jemeryl turned apologetically to Tevi. "I didn't mean to interrupt anything."

"It's all right. I think the conversation was starting to run aground."

Jemeryl sat down, noticeably closer to Tevi than Laff had been. A second later, Klara II swooped down.

"Did the two of you come up here for a private chat?"

"No. I was hiding, and Laff found me."

"Why hiding?"

"It's all so—" Tevi waved her arm. "Everyone's acting like they'd always thought I was a hero and their best friend. I'm left wondering whether it's my memory that's cracking up."

"Your mother hasn't exactly clasped you to her bosom, and she's been sending some very filthy looks at me."

"Which is reassuring. I know just where I stand with her. Everything else is on its head. The only one who used to talk to me was Brec, and she's avoiding me, which I admit I'm pleased about, but for the rest..." Tevi threw up her hands. "And Holric. It used to be impressive, the biggest village on the island, with the royal hall. Now it looks small and shabby, and it stinks of rotten fish. And worse."

"Your grandmother is quite impressive."

"You've been talking to her?"

"Yes. I think I should suggest that every sorcerer in the Coven comes out here for a chat."

"Why?"

"It's brought home to me the way ungifted people on the mainland are so deferential. Making it clear that they'd never presume to see themselves as my equal." She snuggled closer to Tevi. "Except for you."

"It's the thing you love about me?"

"It's the thing that allows me to love all the other things about you. However, your grandmother was perfectly polite but made it quite clear that she saw herself as innately superior to me. I've never had an ungifted person do that before."

"Of course. She's the queen."

"Anyway, she's impressed me with her command of rumours. She's got everyone believing that you're going with me tomorrow because I need your help with something that is so mysterious and important that we can't talk about it. The clever thing is that she started the rumour by not saying it, and the more she doesn't say it, the more people believe it."

"I guess my grandmother hasn't changed much either."

"Despite what you said, if we kissed in the village square, I'll bet your grandmother could persuade people that it wasn't what they thought."

"Since we're outnumbered four hundred to two, I don't think we should put it to the test."

Jemeryl caught hold of Tevi's hand. "You know, I was worried coming here."

"I told you there wouldn't be any trouble."

"Not that. I was frightened that when you saw your old home, you'd want to stay."

Tevi laughed. "No chance. There's nothing here that I want. Maybe part of me thinks I should try to change things so that men get treated like adults and the women don't spend so much time killing one another. But they won't accept the message from me. I reckon it will take people here ten days at most to remember that they used to think I was a joke." Tevi pulled Jemeryl around and stared into her eyes. "But even if I could fit in here, I wouldn't want to. While you were in the coma, I was forced to consider what life would be like without you, and I'm not interested in it. As long as you want me, I'm staying with you."

"That might be quite some time."

Tevi planted one quick kiss on Jemeryl's lips. "Good."

Appendix

The Legend of Princess Tevirik

As told by the women of the Western Isles

Once upon a time, a daughter was born to the royal house of Storenseg. Her birth name was Strikes-like-lightning, but even as a small child, she was so warlike that her greatest delight was her armour and weapons, so the people called her Tevirik, after the goddess of blacksmiths. She grew to be tall and brave and was her mother's pride. All her people longed for the day when she would become queen and lead the war-band to victory.

Now, as is told elsewhere, Storenseg was where Abrak first made the magic potion that gives warriors their strength. The most precious of Abrak's relics was her chalice, but one day, when Tevirik was scarcely grown to womanhood, an evil sorcerer sent an enchanted raven to steal it. The women of Storenseg were angry and dismayed at their loss, but no one knew what to do about it.

Soon, the tale of the theft spread among all the Western Isles. The queen of Rathshorn especially found it amusing and joked that the women of Storenseg were so weak that even a bird could pillage their halls.

When Tevirik learnt of this insult, she turned white with anger. She went to her grandmother, the queen, and swore that she would go in search of the chalice and not return without it. At this, the hearts of the people sank, for there seemed no hope that she could achieve this quest. But Tevirik would not go back on her oath. The whole island turned out to see her depart. There were tears in many eyes, for none expected to see her again.

Tevirik sailed east for many days until she reached land. She left her boat on the beach and went from place to place, searching for news of the chalice, but nothing could she find.

One night, she was awakened by the sound of fighting. Nearby, she saw an old man cruelly attacked by robbers. Not hesitating, Tevirik drew her sword and set about the gang, so that within seconds, they were fleeing for their lives.

The old man turned to her with thanks. "My gratitude is yours forever. Yet I can see you are a stranger in these lands. Why are you here?" he said.

"I am searching for my people's sacred chalice, which was stolen by an enchanted raven. Do you know where it might be?" Tevirik replied.

"No," said the old man. "But the sorcerer Bakoda may know, for she is one of the wisest women in the world."

"Where may I find her?"

"She lives in her citadel, far to the north. To reach her, you must cross a sea of grass, and that will not be easy."

"I have crossed the true sea of water in the west. Surely a sea of grass shall prove no great obstacle," Tevirik said.

In the morning, Tevirik awoke and set out for the north. For many days, she walked until she reached a plain of grass that stretched to the horizon. The wind roared, causing the grass to ripple like the waves breaking on the shore. It blew so fiercely that for every three steps Tevirik took forward, she was blown back one, but at last, she arrived at a mighty citadel. Inside this citadel, the sorcerer Bakoda sat on a silver throne.

Tevirik stood before her and said, "I am searching for my people's sacred chalice, which has been stolen by an enchanted raven. Do you know where it might be?"

Bakoda sat and thought, and then she said, "Several months ago, I saw the bird fly out to sea, and I sensed the magic of the one who sent it, but who that was, I cannot say. Perhaps my sister, Kradira, may know, for she is wiser than I."

"Where may I find her?" Tevirik asked.

"She lives in her palace far to the south. To reach her, you must cross a sea of sand, and that will not be easy."

"I have crossed the true sea of water in the west and a sea of grass in the north. Surely a sea of sand shall prove no great obstacle."

The sorcerer made her welcome, and Tevirik rested from crossing the grasslands and prepared for the journey ahead. After three days, she set out for the south.

She walked for many days until the land became hot and dry, and only barren sand stretched out before her. The wind whipped the sand, building it high like waves on the open sea. The sun was like noon on the hottest summer's day. Tevirik filled her goatskin bags with water and then set off across the desert.

The sand was so hot, it burnt the soles of her feet. After four days, her water bags were empty, and thirst tormented her, but at last, she arrived at a great palace. Inside this palace, the sorcerer Kradira sat on a golden throne.

Tevirik stood before her and said, "I am searching for my people's sacred chalice, which has been stolen by an enchanted raven. Do you know where it might be?"

Kradira sat and thought, and then she said, "Several months ago, I saw the bird return from the sea and sensed the magic of the one who sent it, but who that was, I cannot say. Perhaps my sister, Jemera, may know, for she is the wisest of us all."

"Where may I find her?" Tevirik said.

"She lives in her castle far to the east. To reach her, you must cross a sea of snow, and that will not be easy."

"I have crossed the true sea of water in the west, a sea of grass in the north, and a sea of sand in the south. Surely a sea of snow shall prove no great obstacle."

The sorcerer made her welcome, and Tevirik rested from crossing the desert and prepared for the journey ahead. After three days, she set off into the distant east.

For many days, she travelled until a line of mountains appeared. Her road led ever upward. An icy wind soon became a torrent of snow. The blizzard was like a storm at sea when the tempest blots out the world and there is neither up nor down. Yet Tevirik was not deterred. She fought her way forward, though the cold was so bitter that her hair froze to her head.

At last, she saw a castle atop a rocky peak. "Surely here I will learn how I may achieve my quest," she told herself.

The climb was hard, but Tevirik eventually reached her goal. As she was about to enter the castle, she heard furious roaring, and a hideous monster charged towards her. Its claws were so sharp that they dug holes in the rock, and its teeth were as long as an arm. With scarcely time to think, Tevirik drew her sword and, in a single mighty stroke, cut off the monster's head.

Tevirik knelt to clean the blood from her sword. When she stood again, there was a woman standing before her. In an instant, Tevirik's eyes were blinded, so that she could not tell whether it was night or day.

"Who are you? And what have you done to me?" Tevirik cried out.

"I am the sorcerer Jemera. You have killed my beast, so I have taken your sight in payment," the sorcerer said.

"I am sorry for the loss of your beast, but I only defended myself."

"Be that as it may, it was my beast, and I must take payment for its death."

"If you will help me with my quest, I will gladly make what recompense I can," Tevirik said.

"Will you swear to meet whatever terms I say?"

"My people are not rich in gold or silver, but if it is within my power, I will do so."

"Then let us go inside and talk further."

As the sorcerer spoke, the blindness was lifted from Tevirik, and she could see again, though in marking of this change, her eyes had changed from brown to grey. The two of them went into the castle and Jemera sat on a stone throne. Then Tevirik stood before her and said, "I am searching for my people's sacred chalice, which has been stolen by an enchanted raven. Do you know where it might be?"

Jemera sat and thought, and then she said, "Several months ago, I saw the bird fly out to sea and return from the sea. I sensed the magic of the one who sent it, and I know her well. It was the evil sorcerer Levanno, a long-time enemy of mine."

"Where does she live, and how do I find her?" Tevirik said.

"She lives under the mountains at the bottom of the earth. Finding her will not help you, for she will turn you to stone as soon as she sees you."

"Nevertheless, I have sworn to recover the chalice, and I will not abandon my quest."

"Then I will come with you. Yet there is still the question of payment for my beast," Jemera said.

"What are your terms?"

"You must swear that if I help you achieve your quest, then you will follow me and serve me for five years."

"That I will gladly do."

For three days, they rested in the castle, and then they set out. They walked all day and that night they made camp. As they prepared for sleep, Jemera said, "The entrance to Levanno's realm is nearby, and this area is guarded by many deadly foes. It would be wise if we kept watch."

"I will take the first watch and wake you at midnight," replied Tevirik.

For the first half of the night, she kept a good watch, and it was as well that she did so. An hour before midnight, she heard howling, and a pack of wolves appeared. Tevirik drew her sword and set about them, so that soon a dozen wolves lay dead and the rest were fleeing to save their lives. At midnight, she woke the sorcerer and took her turn to sleep.

Jemera then kept a good watch, and it was as well that she did so. An hour before dawn, she heard the rattling of bones and saw a horde of ghouls with rotten flesh hanging from their skeletons. Jemera cast huge fireballs at the ghouls, and they were burned to ash.

With daylight, Jemera awoke Tevirik, and the two women continued on their way until they reached the entrance to a cave. Then Jemera spoke. "Now, listen to what I will say. Levanno is a mighty sorcerer, and any warrior, no matter how brave or strong, has no chance against her. I have a plan so that this may work to our advantage. When Levanno sees us, she will know I am a sorcerer, but she will not fear you, so her attack will be directed at me. I will give you an enchanted magpie. Keep it hidden under your cloak, and when the two of us are locked in battle, release it. Around Levanno's neck is an iron amulet that holds the root of her power. The magpie will fly to Levanno and take the amulet. Without it Levanno will be powerless."

Tevirik agreed to the plan, and the two women entered the cave. Once inside, they were surrounded by a crowd of tiny people who were so small that they barely reached to Tevirik's waist. Tevirik would have drawn her sword, but Jemera restrained her and said, "These are good folk who have been enslaved by Levanno. To gain their freedom, they will lead us to where she is."

They followed the small folk deep into the caves and at last reached a huge cavern. Standing in the middle was Levanno. The two sorcerers glared at each other, and then Jemera said, "Levanno, many times have you tried to kill me. Now I will have my revenge."

"Fool. All you will get is your death, for I am mightier than you," Levanno replied.

And so they began to fight with balls of fire and lightning bolts and magic arrows of ice. The small folk fled the cavern, but Tevirik knew no fear. She got as close to Levanno as she could without being burned or frozen by the magical weapons that the two sorcerers hurled at each other. Then she opened her cloak, and the magpie flew out. The bird circled the cavern once; then it dived down and plucked the amulet from Levanno's neck. The evil sorcerer screamed as she felt her power ebb. Jemera hurled one last fireball, greater than any yet cast, and cracked open the roof above Levanno's head. The rocks crashed down and ended Levanno's wicked life.

Tevirik and Jemera then searched the cavern and found the chalice stored with piles of gold, silver, and precious gems. "Do you want to take your share of the hoard?" Jemera asked.

"No. All I want is the chalice."

"That is wise," said Jemera. "For the treasure is cursed, and if you took even the smallest coin, you would not live to see another sunrise."

The two women left the cave and travelled west for many days until they reached Tevirik's boat on the seashore, and so they sailed back to Storenseg.

Great was the rejoicing at Tevirik's return, but her mother's tears of joy soon turned to tears of sorrow when she learned her daughter was oath-bound to leave again and serve the sorcerer for five years.

For many days, there was feasting on Storenseg, but the time for Tevirik to depart grew close. On the last night, Tevirik's younger sister, who was called Laughs-at-danger, came to speak with her.

"You have achieved great things. It is now my turn. May I not go in your place and serve this sorcerer?" Tevirik's sister said.

Tevirik replied, "Alas, that may not be. It was my oath, and I must discharge it. Yet it is heavy in my heart that this sorcerer will lead me to my death. In five years, I may return; otherwise, wait for three more years. If I have not returned by then, you will know that I no longer walk among the living. In that case, I entrust to you the care of our homeland and our people. Guard them wisely and well."

Laughs-at-danger wept as she heard these words and swore she would do as her sister asked. The next day, the whole island gathered on the shore and watched as Tevirik and the sorcerer Jemera sailed away.

Everyone waited for Tevirik's return, but after three years, her mother could bear no more and died of a broken heart, wishing only for the return of her brave and noble daughter. The next winter, the old queen also died, and there was no one to rule the island.

Then the matriarchs of the families came to Laughs-at-danger and said, "Your mother and grandmother are dead, and Tevirik is not here. Therefore, will you become our queen?"

"No," said Laughs-at-danger. "For my sister is due to return soon. I will not usurp her place. However, if you wish, I will rule as regent."

For four years, Laughs-at-danger was regent of Storenseg. Each morning, she walked onto the cliffs and looked out to sea, hoping for sight of her sister's boat. Yet her vigil was in vain.

At last, the matriarchs came to her again. "The time for your sister's return has passed, beyond all hope that she will come home. The uncertainty of a regency harms Storenseg. Therefore, we beg you to become our queen."

Laughs-at-danger bowed her head and wept, but she could no longer hope to see her brave sister again this side of death. So she built a pyre on the beach and held the funeral feast for Tevirik. Then she took the queen's throne and ruled Storenseg for many years, wisely and well, and her daughter and granddaughter after her. For Princess Tevirik never returned to the island of her birth, nor did any word come back of what fate befell her.

About the Author

Jane Fletcher is a GCLS award winning writer and has also been short-listed for the Gaylactic Spectrum and Lambda awards. She is author of two fantasy/romance series: the Lyremouth Chronicles—***The Exile and The Sorcerer***, ***The Traitor and The Chalice***, and ***The Empress and The Acolyte*** (due Nov 2006) and the Celaeno series—***The Walls of Westernfort***, ***Rangers at Roadsend,*** and ***The Temple at Landfall***. In her next writing project she will be returning to the Celaeno Series with ***Dynasty of Rogues***.

Her love of fantasy began at the age of seven when she encountered Greek Mythology. This was compounded by a childhood spent clambering over every example of ancient masonry she could find (medieval castles, megalithic monuments, Roman villas). Her resolute ambition was to become an archaeologist when she grew up, so it was something of a surprise when she became a software engineer instead.

Born in Greenwich, London in 1956, she now lives in south-west England where she keeps herself busy writing both computer software and fiction, although generally not at the same time.

Visit Jane's website at www.janefletcher.co.uk

Books Available From Bold Strokes Books

The Traitor and the Chalice by Jane Fletcher. Without allies to help them, Tevi and Jemeryl will have to risk all in the race to uncover the traitor and retrieve the chalice. The Lyremouth Chronicles Book Two. (1-933110-43-0)

Promising Hearts by Radclyffe. Dr. Vance Phelps lost everything in the War Between the States and arrives in New Hope, Montana with no hope of happiness and no desire for anything except forgetting—until she meets Mae, a frontier madam. (1-933110-44-9)

Carly's Sound by Ali Vali. Poppy Valente and Julia Johnson form a bond of friendship that lays the foundation for something more, until Poppy's past comes back to haunt her—literally. A poignant romance about love and renewal. (1-933110-45-7)

Unexpected Sparks by Gina L. Dartt. Falling in love is complicated enough without adding murder to the mix. Kate Shannon's growing feelings for much younger Nikki Harris are challenging enough without the mystery of a fatal fire that Kate can't ignore. (1-933110-46-5)

Whitewater Rendezvous by Kim Baldwin. Two women on a wilderness kayak adventure—Chaz Herrick, a laid-back outdoorswoman, and Megan Maxwell, a workaholic news executive—discover that true love may be nothing at all like they imagined. (1-933110-38-4)

Erotic Interludes 3: Lessons in Love ed. by Radclyffe and Stacia Seaman. Sign on for a class in love…the best lesbian erotica writers take us to "school." (1-933110-39-2)

Punk Like Me by JD Glass. Twenty-one year old Nina writes lyrics and plays guitar in the rock band, Adam's Rib, and she doesn't always play by the rules. And, oh yeah—she has a way with the girls. (1-933110-40-6)

Coffee Sonata by Gun Brooke. Four women whose lives unexpectedly intersect in a small town by the sea share one thing in common—they all have secrets. (1-933110-41-4)

The Clinic: Tristaine Book One by Cate Culpepper. Brenna, a prison medic, finds herself deeply conflicted by her growing feelings for her patient, Jesstin, a wild and rebellious warrior reputed to be descended from ancient Amazons. (1-933110-42-2)

Forever Found by JLee Meyer. Can time, tragedy, and shattered trust destroy a love that seemed destined? When chance reunites two childhood friends separated by tragedy, the past resurfaces to determine the shape of their future. (1-933110-37-6)

Sword of the Guardian by Merry Shannon. Princess Shasta's bold new bodyguard has a secret that could change both of their lives. He is actually a *she*. A passionate romance filled with courtly intrigue, chivalry, and devotion. (1-933110-36-8)

Wild Abandon by Ronica Black. From their first tumultuous meeting, Dr. Chandler Brogan and Officer Sarah Monroe are drawn together by their common obsessions—sex, speed, and danger. (1-933110-35-X)

Turn Back Time by Radclyffe. Pearce Rifkin and Wynter Thompson have nothing in common but a shared passion for surgery. They clash at every opportunity, especially when matters of the heart are suddenly at stake. (1-933110-34-1)

Chance by Grace Lennox. At twenty-six, Chance Delaney decides her life isn't working so she swaps it for a different one. What follows is the sexy, funny, touching story of two women who, in finding themselves, also find one another. (1-933110-31-7)

The Exile and the Sorcerer by Jane Fletcher. First in the Lyremouth Chronicles. Tevi, wounded and adrift, arrives in the courtyard of a shy young sorcerer. Together they face monsters, magic, and the challenge of loving despite their differences. (1-933110-32-5)

A Matter of Trust by Radclyffe. JT Sloan is a cybersleuth who doesn't like attachments. Michael Lassiter is leaving her husband, and she needs Sloan's expertise to safeguard her company. It should just be business—but it turns into much more. (1-933110-33-3)

Sweet Creek by Lee Lynch. A celebration of the enduring nature of love, friendship, and community in the quirky, heart-warming lesbian community of Waterfall Falls. (1-933110-29-5)

The Devil Inside by Ali Vali. Derby Cain Casey, head of a New Orleans crime organization, runs the family business with guts and grit, and no one crosses her. No one, that is, until Emma Verde claims her heart and turns her world upside down. (1-933110-30-9)

Grave Silence by Rose Beecham. Detective Jude Devine's investigation of a series of ritual murders is complicated by her torrid affair with the golden girl of Southwestern forensic pathology, Dr. Mercy Westmoreland. (1-933110-25-2)

Honor Reclaimed by Radclyffe. In the aftermath of 9/11, Secret Service Agent Cameron Roberts and Blair Powell close ranks with a trusted few to find the would-be assassins who nearly claimed Blair's life. (1-933110-18-X)

Honor Bound by Radclyffe. Secret Service Agent Cameron Roberts and Blair Powell face political intrigue, a clandestine threat to Blair's safety, and the seemingly irreconcilable personal differences that force them ever farther apart. (1-933110-20-1)

Protector of the Realm: Supreme Constellations Book One by Gun Brooke. A space adventure filled with suspense and a daring intergalactic romance featuring Commodore Rae Jacelon and a stunning, but decidedly lethal, Kellen O'Dal. (1-933110-26-0)

Innocent Hearts by Radclyffe. In a wild and unforgiving land, two women learn about love, passion, and the wonders of the heart. (1-933110-21-X)

The Temple at Landfall by Jane Fletcher. An imprinter, one of Celaeno's most revered servants of the Goddess, is also a prisoner to the faith—until a Ranger frees her by claiming her heart. The Celaeno series. (1-933110-27-9)

Force of Nature by Kim Baldwin. From tornados to forest fires, the forces of nature conspire to bring Gable McCoy and Erin Richards close to danger, and closer to each other. (1-933110-23-6)

In Too Deep by Ronica Black. Undercover homicide cop Erin McKenzie tracks a femme fatale who just might be a real killer…with love and danger hot on her heels. (1-933110-17-1)

Course of Action by Gun Brooke. Actress Carolyn Black desperately wants the starring role in an upcoming film produced by Annelie Peterson. Just how far will she go for the dream part of a lifetime? (1-933110-22-8)

Rangers at Roadsend by Jane Fletcher. Sergeant Chip Coppelli has learned to spot trouble coming, and that is exactly what she sees in her new recruit, Katryn Nagata. The Celaeno series. (1-933110-28-7)

Justice Served by Radclyffe. Lieutenant Rebecca Frye and her lover, Dr. Catherine Rawlings, embark on a deadly game of hide-and-seek with an underworld kingpin who traffics in human souls. (1-933110-15-5)

Distant Shores, Silent Thunder by Radclyffe. Doctor Tory King—and the women who love her—is forced to examine the boundaries of love, friendship, and the ties that transcend time. (1-933110-08-2)

Hunter's Pursuit by Kim Baldwin. A raging blizzard, a mountain hideaway, and a killer-for-hire set a scene for disaster—or desire—when Katarzyna Demetrious rescues a beautiful stranger. (1-933110-09-0)

The Walls of Westernfort by Jane Fletcher. All Temple Guard Natasha Ionadis wants is to serve the Goddess—until she falls in love with one of the rebels she is sworn to destroy. The Celaeno series. (1-933110-24-4)

Change Of Pace: *Erotic Interludes* by Radclyffe. Twenty-five hot-wired encounters guaranteed to spark more than just your imagination. Erotica as you've always dreamed of it. (1-933110-07-4)

Honor Guards by Radclyffe. In a wild flight for their lives, the president's daughter and those who are sworn to protect her wage a desperate struggle for survival. (1-933110-01-5)

Fated Love by Radclyffe. Amidst the chaos and drama of a busy emergency room, two women must contend not only with the fragile nature of life, but also with the irresistible forces of fate. (1-933110-05-8)

Justice in the Shadows by Radclyffe. In a shadow world of secrets and lies, Detective Sergeant Rebecca Frye and her lover, Dr. Catherine Rawlings, join forces in the elusive search for justice. (1-933110-03-1)

shadowland by Radclyffe. In a world on the far edge of desire, two women are drawn together by power, passion, and dark pleasures. An erotic romance. (1-933110-11-2)

Love's Masquerade by Radclyffe. Plunged into the indistinguishable realms of fiction, fantasy, and hidden desires, Auden Frost is forced to question all she believes about the nature of love. (1-933110-14-7)

Love & Honor by Radclyffe. The president's daughter and her lover are faced with difficult choices as they battle a tangled web of Washington intrigue for...love and honor. (1-933110-10-4)

Beyond the Breakwater by Radclyffe. One Provincetown summer three women learn the true meaning of love, friendship, and family. (1-933110-06-6)

Tomorrow's Promise by Radclyffe. One timeless summer, two very different women discover the power of passion to heal and the promise of hope that only love can bestow. (1-933110-12-0)

Love's Tender Warriors by Radclyffe. Two women who have accepted loneliness as a way of life learn that love is worth fighting for and a battle they cannot afford to lose. (1-933110-02-3)

Love's Melody Lost by Radclyffe. A secretive artist with a haunted past and a young woman escaping a life that has proved to be a lie find their destinies entwined. (1-933110-00-7)

Safe Harbor by Radclyffe. A mysterious newcomer, a reclusive doctor, and a troubled gay teenager learn about love, friendship, and trust during one tumultuous summer in Provincetown. (1-933110-13-9)

Above All, Honor by Radclyffe. Secret Service Agent Cameron Roberts fights her desire for the one woman she can't have—Blair Powell, the daughter of the president of the United States. (1-933110-04-X)